Isabella Macdonald Alden

Pansy's Sunday Book

Isabella Macdonald Alden

Pansy's Sunday Book

ISBN/EAN: 9783744746250

Printed in Europe, USA, Canada, Australia, Japan

Cover: Foto ©Andreas Hilbeck / pixelio.de

More available books at **www.hansebooks.com**

BY

FAMOUS AMERICAN WRITERS

FULLY ILLUSTRATED

BOSTON
LOTHROP PUBLISHING COMPANY

IN LATE NOVEMBER.

A STORY TO REMEMBER, IN NOVEMBER.

IF you'll sit on my knee
  As still as a stone,
And listen to me
  While we're all alone —
While the wind whistles cold,
  And the snow falls so fast,
While the young and the old
  Feel the chill of the blast —
I will tell you about
  A poor little lad
Who now, without doubt,
  Is smiling and glad.

(*His picture.*)
Brown and curly his head,
  Bright blue was his eye,
His feet bare and red,
  His look rather shy;
His face, somewhat soiled,
  Unfamiliar with soap,

Was thin, while there curled
  In his neck, like a rope,

Certain locks which had grown,
  Unhindered by shears
That he never had known,
  You would think, all his years;
His shirt was a sight,
  You may think, to behold,
Through which shone the light
  Unblushingly bold.

His trousers, in shreds,
  His legs dangled round,
Long needing the threads
  Which they never had found;
While his cap — what was left
  Of the original pattern —
Of all shape was bereft,
  And looked like a slattern.

Such, such was the creature
  Who stood in the door;
In dress, form and feature —
  Nothing less, nothing more.
May you love this, my lad
  From the slums of the city;
Not think him all bad,
  But regard him with pity.

(*The name.*)

Though nameless he stood
  Clad in rags in that door,
Whether evil or good,
  He is nameless no more.
We'll call him hereafter,
  If you make no objection,
In tears — or in laughter,
  On further reflection —
Thomas Tinker, all told,
  But "Tommy" for short,
Until he grows old —
  Perhaps then, when in sport.

But I'll tell you I think, sir,
  Before saying more,
This is not the "Tom Tinker"
  You've heard of before,
But another, whose fame
  Is as worthy of mention
As the first of his name
  Who claimed your attention.

(*The story.*)

We will trace him as we may, on his way
From that floorstep, where at play on that day;
  We will see just how he earned
  That for which his young heart yearned,
How from good he firmly turned not astray.

Selling papers he began, little man,
Then on errands often ran, like a "van";
  Then his matches he would sell,
  Blacking boots the while, as well;
And with cheerful voice would tell all his plan.

Tried his courage was, I'm told; nor condoled
By humanity, which rolled, with its gold,
  On its laughing, rushing way,
  Like a crowd of boys at play,
Or a flock of sheep astray from the fold.

But his heart was brave and true, and he knew
That to flinch would never do; so say you?
  Thus he bravely bore his part
  With a true and loyal heart,
Never doubting from the start; "tried and true."

The days seemed often long; but his song
Rang brave and strong; just the song
  Of the wares he had to sell;
  Of the news they had to tell —
Good and bad alike as well, for the throng.

And he worked, and worked away, every day,
With his heart as light and gay, as the May;
  And he did his level best, late and early;
  Never grumbling, never sad, and never surly;
With a smile 'neath his golden head and curly,
    as at play.

So he fought the fiends of hunger and of cold,
  true as gold;
Like a veteran tried and bold, I am told,
  Was this soldier in life's battle
  'Mid the daily hum and rattle;
Driven forth like sheep or cattle, to be sold.

Many brave fall by the way, every day;
Some survive, their country's stay; well they
    may;
  But of all the rank and file
  Grandly marching up the aisle
Of stern duty, all the while, who can say

Which the most deserve the name, writ in fame?
Those who fell 'mid shot and flame, on land or
    main,
  Or those who in obscurer strife
  Have given heart, and soul, and life
For husband ill, for child, or wife, in duty
    "tame"?

Well, Tommy stood, sturdy and grave — no
    slave —
His soul had what we well might crave; no
    knave
  Was he; but faithful in the daily fight,
  Cheerful, happy, eager, bright —
A nineteenth century valiant knight, youthful,
    brave.

Perhaps you'd like to know his foes, who arose
To strike him down with deadly blows. Who
    knows

But such as he? Who else can tell
The horrid shapes, the cruel spell
These demons from the pit of hell disclose?

"Hunger," you say, "sickness and cold; no
    fold;
No home that such as he might hold, to mould
    And make them good, and true, and wise?"
Ah, yes! and on the streets before his eyes
Were Satan's minions in disguise; so bold!

These dens of ill, they grow, you know;
We find them everywhere as we go, ready to
    throw
    Their snares with fiendish skill.
Almost 'twould seem, to suit their will,
They'd gorge earth's prisons to their fill below.

God looked on Tommy in the fight for right,
Saw darkness struggling with the light, so
    bright —
    That light which shone on Eastern plain
Where shepherds heard angelic strain
Such as will surely come again some night

God knew about the thrall, the small,
Weak hands which yet might fall, the call
    Which all too loud might prove to be
    For one so young, so little helped as he,
So tempted oft, and yet withal so free to fall.

And so, one cold Thanksgiving Day, so gay
With jingling bells, and sleigh and play,
    The father sent a messenger in love,
    To take poor Tommy to his home above,
Where, clad in garments whiter than the dove,
    he'll stay.

And now no more he'll walk that street, where
    sleet
And slush so cruel hurt his feet; repeat
    No more his song of paper vending,
    Shiver no more while restless horse attending,
But join in song triumphant, never ending and
    sweet.

But on this day of this November, remember
Tommies there are, with feet as cold and tender,
    remember,
    As his once were, who now on golden strand
Meet rich and poor, of this and every land.
These need your store, your love, your helping
    hand, remember!   R.

ROBERT TRUESDALE'S LOGIC.

 THEY were great friends, Robert Truesdale and Claire Waterman. During the long, bright summer at the seashore they spent as much time together as possible, and discussed all sorts of questions. They had opinions concerning everything under the sun, and agreed so well, generally, that to find a subject upon which they totally differed only added interest to the summer.

One of these subjects was found one morning when they sat together on the beach. It began —that is, the discussion did — by Robert's making the astonishing statement that he never went to circuses.

Claire stopped playing with the sand which she was letting run idly through her fingers, and turned so that she could see his face. "How very queer!" she said; "I thought all boys went to circuses. Did you never go?"

"I went once," said Robert, low-voiced, "when I was quite a little fellow, and that was once too often. I never cared to try it again."

"I cannot imagine why. I think circuses are splendid. We never go in the city, of course. Why, they don't have circuses in cities, do they? But I go to my Auntie's every summer for two months — I always have until this summer — and Uncle West takes us children to the circus just as regularly. That is the reason I like the country so much better than the city. you can go to such queer out-of-door things. And I think the little circus ponies are too cunning for anything; I have always wanted one for my own. Mamma laughs, and says she doesn't know but I will be a circus rider when I grow up — and then the clown is so funny. Why don't you want to go, Robert? What happened when you went once? Was there an accident?"

"No," said Robert slowly, "I suppose not; I am afraid it was an every-day affair. It is a long story, Claire, and begins away back of that day. I have been brought up differently from you. you know. My father was a minister, and he and my mother did not approve of shows of that kind, and I was never taken to them when I was a small boy. I never heard nor thought much about them; we lived in a large town, but not too large for the traveling circus; but I got the idea, somehow, that only low people attended such places, and never coaxed to go."

Claire exclaimed over this, "Why, Robert, where my Auntie lives everybody goes, only the minister and a few old dried-up people."

"Yes, I know," said Robert gravely; "some people in the country have different views from those which my father and mother had; but I did not know it when I was a little chap; I thought that all respectable people thought

the boys, the more I became convinced that it was because my father was a minister that I had been held away from such places. 'Of course ministers ought not to go,' I told myself, 'because'—and there I would have to stop; I knew no reason why they should not go where other people did, and could not reason about it any better than some grown people can nowadays; still I called it a settled point, and began to coax my grandmother to let me go to the circus. 'Just this once,' I said to her; 'I want to see for myself.'

"I have never understood how she came to let me have my way, unless it was because she

"HOW VERY QUEER!"

alike. The first time I changed my ideas any was when I had gone to spend the year with my Grandmother in the country — that was the summer after mother died, and my father had died the winter before. I found that a great many country people went to circuses. All the boys and girls who went to school with me in the little old schoolhouse were looking forward to going as a matter of course; and I heard more talk about the circus that summer than I had ever heard in my life before. I began to want to go very much. The more I talked with

was a very indulgent grandmother, and pitied the orphan boy, and could not bear to say 'No.' Any way, I received permission, and the necessary quarter of a dollar, and started off in great glee.

"I ought to tell you," he continued, after a slight hesitation — and the flush on his brown cheek deepened a little — "that although I was only a little fellow ten years old, I was a member of the church, and was trying to live my religion. There was a ragged little boy not much older than myself, very ignorant and neglected, but a leader in all sorts of mischief, whom I had had ambitions to help. I had been kind to him, instead of making sport of his rags, as the other boys did, until I had a certain sort of influence over him, and he had partly promised me to try to be a better boy.

"Well, I went to the circus, and saw the ponies, and heard the jokes, and was delighted; but as I stood around outside afterwards, open-mouthed and open-eyed, I saw two of the men whom I had most admired in the ring, fighting. They had been drinking just enough to make them quarrelsome, and such horrid oaths as they were using I had never even imagined possible before. I stood still with fright and horror and watched the blows, and listened to the vile language, until somebody touched my elbow, and there was little Pete, the ragged boy. He was grinning wickedly. 'My eyes!' he said, 'was you in there?' nodding toward the tent. 'I was struck all of a heap when I see you come out. I didn't think this kind was for you. I thought you belonged to the "goody-goodies," you know. Miss Wheeler, she said when she was talking to us fellows about it, "O, no! Robert Truesdale won't go to the circus, I am sure; he is his father's own boy, and is walking the same road he did." I guess you got off the road this time, didn't you?'

"I do not believe I shall ever forget the wicked leer in the little fellow's face as he said those words; and I am sure I shall never forget the feeling of shame which I had as I looked at those two dreadful men with the blood streaming down their faces, and the vile words streaming from their mouths, and realized that I had spent my afternoon in laughing at their speeches, and had been found out of the road in which my father had walked — so far out that this street boy had noticed it! I turned and ran away as fast and as far as I could, and I do not think I shall ever attend another circus."

"How very strange!" said Claire; "but then, after all, Robert, bad men will swear and drink and fight. You did not make them any worse by going to see them ride."

"I can't be sure of that, Claire. What if my twenty-five cents helped to encourage them to live the life which kept them in the midst of such temptations? That is what good men who have studied and thought about these things say of the circus. Besides," and here the boy's face took on a little touch of lofty scorn, "I want to grow up to be such a character that the jokes and jumpings of evil men cannot amuse me; I want to learn to be above them. Then you see what the ragged little street boy thought?"

"Yes," said Claire gravely; "I never thought much about it; I just went, of course, because the others did, but I shouldn't like to be counted on that side, exactly. Robert, maybe I won't go any more. I must think about it."

MYRA SPAFFORD.

HOW THE DEER KNEW.

MY neighbor's little boy one evening saw his teacher coming up the lane and called her in to take a look at his pet fawn.

"Well, if he didn't get half a foot taller since I saw him last," said the teacher; "if he keeps on like that, Tommy, he will be a big deer the first thing you know."

"Yes, he's growing," said Tommy; "but I wanted to see you about something else. He seems to be sick, and we do not know what to do about it."

"Why, he looks all right now; what seemed to be the matter with him?"

"He doesn't eat," said Tommy, "and he upset his water dish when I tried to make him drink. I went up on the hill to get him the best grass I could find, but it's no use; he must be sick."

"Let me see that grass," said the teacher. "I thought so," she laughed, when Tommy took her to the fawn's fodder corner; "you got a lot of wormwood leaves mixed up with the grass, and one of the leaves got in that water dish."

Tommy stared. "Oh! maybe that's the reason he upset his water," he burst out; "but I had no idea that would make any difference. What makes him so very particular about a few leaves, I wonder?"

"You will know if you taste them," said the teacher; "and maybe your fawn wanted to get even with you for teaching him to jump through a hoop."

"Why, he seems to like that," laughed Tommy.

"That's just what I mean," said the teacher; "he felt so much obliged to you and wanted to pay you back — by teaching you a good lesson. An animal, you see, won't touch any bad-tasting food if it is in good health, and if you give it the wrong kind of drink it doesn't mind its thirst, but waits till it gets something better. And that's an answer to the question you asked me a few weeks ago, when you wanted to know how people could help getting fond of drinks that make them drunk and sick. They should let such stuff alone altogether, if they find out it does not taste right at first. You found out something about that yourself, didn't you?"

"About what — the ugly taste of bad drinks, you mean?"

"Yes; don't you remember what you told me about that hotel where you got thirsty, and tried a glass of something you thought was lemonade, and found it was beer?"

"O, yes! I remember," laughed Tommy; "I never tasted anything worse in my life. I don't see how in the world people can get fond of such stuff."

"That's just it," said the teacher; "they should do as your little deer did this afternoon, and never meddle with a drink that tastes very bad the first time they try it, unless they should be sick and need a bitter medicine for particular purposes. If a healthy person should try to drink big glasses full of ugly medicine just for fun every day he would soon be sick, and few medicines taste as bad as some of the drinks so many people get drunk on."

"Cod-liver oil doesn't, nor herb tea," said Tommy. "I tried them, and know they are not half as ugly as beer. And they say beer isn't the worst yet," he added; "there are drinks that taste like burning fire, if you get a drop on your tongue. I don't see how in the world anybody can get fond of such stuff."

"Let me tell you," said the teacher. "The first time they try it they cannot help disliking it, and they should take the hint to let it alone altogether. But if they keep drinking it in spite of their horror, it will lead to a very strange result. Their nature gradually gets changed, till a time comes when they cannot do without a drink that made them shudder when they tasted it first. It is that way with beer and brandy, and even with a drink made of that very wormwood that would have made your deer sick if it had eaten it. Just rub one of those leaves between your fingers, and then put the tip of your finger to your tongue. That is just exactly the taste of a stuff called absinthe, and brandy and strong beer are almost as bad."

"You say people get fond of it if they drink it again and again," mused Tommy, "but what makes them do that, I wonder? What makes them try it at all?"

"They see other people do it," said the teacher, "and so they try it themselves, and keep on trying, because they think Mr. So-and-so ought to know better than nature. Their own nature warns them against it, but they do not mind that warning, and keep on till it is too late to turn back. Now you might ask me to tell you who first took it in his head to make himself sick with such a foolish habit. That seems a puzzle, indeed, but it has been explained in this way. Before people drank wine they drank the fresh juice of grapes — "must," as they call it — and probably tried to keep some of it in bottles and jars. Now in warm weather sweet juices of that sort are very apt to spoil — they ferment, as it is called, and their pleasant taste becomes sharp and disagreeable. Some stingy housekeeper in old times may have forced his servants to drink that spoiled stuff rather than throw it away, and after a while they got fond of it, and the foolish habit spread all over the country. Now wine is nothing but fermented or spoiled must. Beer is fermented barley water. They let barley get soaked in water, and then mix it and stir till it gets that sharp taste that made you sick when you tried it by mistake in that summer hotel last year."

"Yes; and on that same trip I once got in the wrong railway car," said Tommy, "and that car was full of tobacco smoke enough to

SHE'S SUCH A DARLING!

make my little brother cry, and I thought it would choke me before the train stopped and we got back in the right ear. I know a boy who got so sick he had to go to bed when he first tried to smoke; but I am sure I shall never try it at all."

"That's right, Tommy; let such things alone altogether," said the teacher. "It's very easy never to begin, but if you should get fond of such bad habits you might find it hard to get rid of them."

"I have a book about travels," said Tommy, "and I read that the American Indians first taught white men to smoke. One of my cousins has been in Mexico, and when I asked him what made the Indians so fond of tobacco smoke, he said they first used it to drive mosquitoes out of their cabins. They burn tobacco leaves on a hot pan, and the gnats all fly out of the window."

"I should not wonder," laughed the teacher; "and that would show that mosquitoes have more sense than those Indians."

FELIX L. OSWALD.

SOMETHING FOR MAMMA.

 I GET the idea and most of the details from Harper's Bazar. The article from which they are taken says the contrivance is for an invalid, but let me assure you that mamma will like it very much, or, for the matter of that, papa also, though they have not thought of being invalids.

First, contrive to get a nice pine board about twenty-five inches long and twenty-one wide (if you are making it for me I should like the board a little narrower, but perhaps mamma might not); cover it with felt of any color you please — perhaps it would be well to have in mind the furniture in the room where it is chiefly to live, and secure a color which will harmonize, or at least not "fight," with the prevailing color there.

Perhaps, however, you will be in the condition in which I have sometimes found myself; namely, with a piece of felt of a certain color which obstinately refuses to turn into another, no matter how much I might desire it; in that case, if I were you I would go right ahead with my present; I feel sure mamma will find it useful, even though it is not just the shade which you and she like best. The same remarks will apply to material. I have used cretonne, or even calico, where I would have preferred felt if I could have got it. Well, we will pretend to cover this pine board with felt; we will have the felt so long and wide that it will reach say for six inches or so below the board at both ends, and on the front side. Then make neat little pockets for these ends and side, with a flap to button down over them when desired. These are to hold letters, envelopes, bits of poetry, scraps of prose, recipes, in fact anything which mamma desires to have convenient when she sits down to write. If mamma uses a fountain pen I think she will like exceedingly a little narrow pocket, just wide enough for her pen to slip in easily, and just deep enough for it to stand upright and put its head out for her to get hold of. If she does not, a "traveler's inkstand," leather covered, may be glued at the right end of the board; it has a "spring" cover, you will remember, and takes faithful care of the ink when closed. A stamp box of wood or paper may be glued at the other end.

'What a delightful present that will be when you get it done! I am sure "mamma" will appreciate and enjoy it. The Bazar says a row of brass-headed nails should be driven all around the edges of the board, I suppose to hold the felt firmly in place; but a little girl who had no brass nails could very easily sew her felt or cretonne or calico around the under side of the board, and make her pockets separately, sewing them firmly to their places, if she wished.

In fact, there is room in this device for many changes and improvements. I can imagine an ingenious girl or boy — or perhaps it would be better to say girl and boy — putting their heads together, and making many variations which would be a comfort to the fortunate owner. Try it, and let me know the result.

PANSY.

SHE STRUGGLED WITH THE SLEEVES.

NANNIE'S THANKSGIVING.

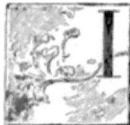IT was very early in the morning; earlier, in fact, than Nannie was in the habit of being up; but on account of Thanksgiving Day, and the fact that they were all going to Aunt Cornelia's to dinner, Nannie thought she ought to be on hand early. She was waiting for mamma to give her her bath, and sat down to pet Rosamond Catherine Lorinda in the meantime. The middle name, Catherine, was in honor of Grandma Patterson, but Nannie did not like it very well, and felt obliged to place it between two names which she called "delicious," in order to tolerate it. A bright thought occurred to her; she might dress the child for the Thanksgiving dinner while she waited. It was while she struggled with the sleeve which did not want to go on that the thought came which caused all her trouble.

"This sleeve is too small," she said; "I b'lieve my child's arm must have grown a great deal since she wore this dress before; she ought to have had a new dress for Thanksgiving; she would look sweet in a white embroidered one trimmed with lace." Just then the baby in the willow cradle at her side nestled in his sleep, and Nannie turned and looked at him.

"If Rosamond Catherine Lorinda only had one dress like what Teddy has so many of, I should be too perfectly happy," she said. "Just think, I b'lieve he has as many as 'leven or eight! Mamma might borrow me one just for to-day; it would be too long, but I could cut it off at the bottom; it would be just as easy to sew it on again when Teddy needed it; and the sleeves I could loop up with pink ribbons, and she would look too perfectly sweet!"

The more she thought about it, the more the longing grew; at last it began to seem a positive injustice that Teddy should have so many clothes and not be willing to lend any to Rosamond Catherine Lorinda. "I know he would, if he understood," said Nannie, looking approvingly upon the sleeping baby; "he loves my Rosamond, and kisses her just as cunning! And he has such a perfectly lovely lot of dresses! I just mean to look in the bureau drawer and count them." Saying which, she tiptoed toward the bureau behind the cradle, and opened the second drawer. To be sure she was barefooted, and could not have made much noise; besides, if she was doing right why should she care if her footsteps were heard? Nevertheless, she instinctively tiptoed along, and opened the drawer as softly as she could; and it was not for fear of waking Teddy, either.

There lay the dresses in a fluffy white heap; on the top was the one which Nannie most coveted.

"Teddy hardly ever wears it," she said reassuringly, as she drew it out; "I guess mamma doesn't like it very much or she would put it on him oftener; and Rosamond Catherine will look too perfectly sweet for anything in it. I am most sure mamma would not care. I could cut it off right through all those little embroidery holes, then Grandma could sew them together again just as easy."

I grieve to tell you that she did exactly that dreadful thing. Not immediately; she resolved to try the dress on first, and see if it would do; and despite the fact that the waist was many times too large, and the limp arms were altogether lost in the sleeves, the waxen-haired beauty looked so enchanting to her mother's eyes, under those billows of white, that in a very short space of time the shining shears were making a long, crooked line through the costly embroidery with which Teddy's best dress was trimmed.

O, me! the troubles which in this way were stored up for naughty, foolish Nannie. They began almost immediately; for despite the fact that Nannie had coaxed herself into the fancy that there was no harm in what she did, she found she was not willing to have her mother know about it, and crumpled the elegant dress into a small bundle and thrust it under the great rug at her feet when she heard her mother's footsteps. All through the breakfast hour, and even at family worship, she was engaged in planning how she should get Rosamond Catherine Lorinda dressed and wrapped in her traveling cloak without any one having seen her; for fond as she was of exhibiting the beauty, she found that to-day she would rather her charms were hidden from all eyes.

She was still planning ways and means when the discovery came. She was not prepared for it, because when Teddy had so many dresses, how could she suppose that when her mother opened the drawer to select one she would exclaim, "Why, what has become of his dress? I laid it on top so as to get it without disturbing the others."

A good deal of talk followed. Papa suggested that she had laid it in some other drawer, and Aunt Laura said perhaps Grandma had taken it to set a stitch in; and Grandma affirmed that she had not, and asked what Nannie was longing to: "Why don't you take one of the others, daughter, and get the little fellow ready while he is good-natured?"

"Well, but where can it be?" asked the puzzled mother, closing the drawer. "I am sure I laid it here, on the top. I wanted Adelaide to see him in that dress, because she sent me the embroidery for it, you know, and it is more expensive than any I should have bought."

Nannie caught her breath nervously over this; she had not supposed the embroidery was so choice; she might just as well have taken one of the other dresses if she had only known.

Just at that moment Susan, who was bustling about, packing Teddy's traveling bag, stooped down and pulled at something white under the rug, as she said, "Shall I put in some playthings, Mrs. Walters? Why, what's this?"

What was it, sure enough, but the lost dress cut in two, in a fearful zigzag manner, directly through the costly embroidery! Can you imagine what followed? I am sure you will not be surprised to learn that poor, naughty little Nannie had a whipping then and there. Her mother did not even wait for Susan to leave the room, as she generally did before punishing any of her children. It is true the whipping was not very severe, for Mrs. Walters was never severe; but the disgrace of it was terrible, for Nannie was very rarely whipped.

However, this was by no means the worst of her troubles; behold, mamma declared that she could not go to the Thanksgiving dinner, but must stay at home with Susan and the cat.

Now when you reflect that they were to ride four miles in a beautiful sleigh drawn by two prancing horses, and meet a baker's dozen of little cousins, some of whom Nannie had never seen, to say nothing of the delights of the Thanksgiving dinner, and the little pies with their names on, done in sugar plums, which were to be ready for each cousin, I am sure you will feel with Nannie that her punishment was greater than she could bear. In truth, the others thought so. Papa said, "My dear, couldn't you reconsider, somehow?" Aunt Laura said, "Jennie, I think you are horrid!" And even Susan ventured to say, "I don't think she knew it was his best dress, ma'am; and she says Grandma can sew it together, poor little heart." But Mrs. Walters was very firm. She did not deign to answer Laura or Susan, but said to her husband, "Richard, I don't know how I can change, now. I said she couldn't, and you know I ought to keep my word. Besides, the child needs a serious lesson; it is quite as hard for me, I think, as for her," and the mother's lip quivered a little. Then the father said soothingly, that of course he knew she was doing it for Nannie's best good, and he could trust her judgment where he couldn't his own. But Aunt Laura remained indignant, and the whole household was in trouble. "Our Thanksgiving is spoiled," said Aunt Laura; "I've a good mind not to go."

Meantime, Grandma said not a word. It was nearly an hour afterwards, and the preparations for starting, which had gone on much more silently, were almost completed, when Grandma opened the door of Mrs. Walters' room, dressed in her best black silk, with her beautiful white satin hair peeping out from under the soft laces of her best cap, and holding by the hand a little girl with very red eyes, and a red nose, who kept up a suspicious little sniffing, as though it was only by great effort she refrained from bursting into fresh tears. Grandma walked straight toward her daughter, and said, "Mamma, we have come to ask you if you will not forgive poor little Nannie, who is very sorry, and let her go to-day, for Grandma's sake — not for hers at all, but for Grandma's."

And the handsome mother, with a sudden

glad light flashing in her gray eyes, stooped and kissed the cheek of her sweet old mother, and then of her own little daughter, as she said, "Dear mother, you know what you ask for your own sake I could certainly never refuse."

The years have rolled on since then, enough of them to make little Nannie twenty-six, and the mother of our Rosamond, who has golden hair like the dollie, her namesake, but who is mischievous, as Rosamond of old never was. And I heard the sweet mother say, last Thanksgiving morning, after having told this story of her past for the benefit of some young mothers, "I am thankful for two things: that I had a mother who taught me that wrong-doing must bring unhappiness, not only to myself, but to others; and that I had a dear Grandmother who taught me what it was to have a powerful friend to come between me and Justice, and say, "For my sake."   PANSY.

PAPA'S CHOICE.

HERE stands my baby,
    On two little feet;
With her bushy brown head,
    And her dimples so sweet.

Her arms are all ready
    To give me a hug;
So give me my baby,
    And you keep your pug.
                            R.

NOVEMBER.

WHAT is thy mission, November,
        Thou link 'twixt the living and dead?
What message would'st have us remember,
    Writ on thy dried leaves, to be read
        As lessons to youth and to age,
        To the simple, the student, the sage?

Stern duty, thy scepter of power,
    The husbandman readily sees;
And takes up the tasks of the hour
    As the limbs bear the buds on the trees;
        For he sows not, ploughs not, nor reaps;
        He laughs not, he frowns not, nor weeps.

The frosts, without cost, starch the ground;
    Spread a mirror o'er river and lakes;
While nuts scattered thickly around,
    More treasured than apples and cakes,
        The children may gather with ease,
        With the squirrels which hide in the trees.

The apples are now in the bins,
    The pumpkins upon the barn floor,
Save those which, bereft of their skins,
    Hang to dry on the biggest barn door;
        The banking's high piled 'gainst the house,
        To keep it as snug as a mouse.

Thou wast wisely ordained for man,
    For time was much needed, we see,
In which for cold winter to plan,
    And prepare for the storms which must be;
        So, while few may sing of thy praise,
        We will welcome and treasure thy days.

Not all the best things of this grand old earth,
    Not all the hours of the year around,
Are welcomed here with the songs of mirth,
    Nor in fields of pleasure are ever found,
        For cloudy are the days of welcome rain,
        And sharp the sickle for the golden grain.
                            G. R. A.

THE soul that perpetually overflows with kindness and sympathy will always be cheerful.

NOVEMBER.

BABY'S CORNER.

WHAT MADE BABY LAUGH?

ABY DALE'S mamma had a great many pictures of her little boy, but they were not pretty.

The trouble was, he would not sit still even for one little minute. He was always jumping or clapping his fat hands, or saying "Baa, baa!"

One of his pictures had three eyes, and one had no nose.

One funny one had his mouth wide open like a big O, for he was crying.

And there was one where he had his mouth shut, but he looked very cross. He had a frown between his eyes. Mamma said she would not know it was her sunny boy.

But by and by a man came who could take pictures whether babies kept still or not.

One day little Dale was in his high chair by the window. Outdoors it was snowing.

Baby thought the snowflakes were pretty white feathers coming down from the sky. Mamma and he played with a feather once that came out of his pillow. It was nice.

Such a lot of feathers! They made pretty white caps on the fence posts. And there were great heaps of them on the ground!

"Some day," thought Baby, "I will go out that door, and I will creep right down the steps, and I will go to that big pile of feathers, and I will get my hand full, and I will throw them away up, up, back into the sky!"

Then baby laughed, and the man who had come to take his picture touched a button on a queer little box he had, and there was Baby just as you see him.

That is how Baby Dale came to have a picture that mamma loved.

All the aunties, when they saw it, said, "Oh! how sweet."

Mamma sent a picture to the grandma down in Flor-i-da, and one to the grandma up in Maine. One went over the ocean to Uncle

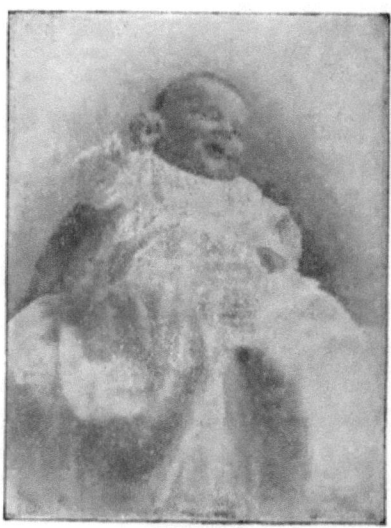

"I WILL GET MY HAND FULL."

John who loves Baby Dale very dearly. One went out West to Auntie Lou, and one went to Boston, to be printed for you.

MRS. C. M. LIVINGSTON.

SOMETIMES in the early springtime,
The sunbeams floating 'round
Are caught out in the showers,
And are washed into the ground.

But, ere the summer's over,
They take root in the sod,
And grow up with fresh brightness
In the form of Golden Rod.
— *Selected.*

LORA'S SERMON.

IT was Sunday morning, and all the family except Lora and her mother had gone to church. As a rule they, or at least Lora, were the first to be tucked into the sleigh; but on this particular morning Mrs. Wheeler had said she was not going; that she had a little cold, she believed, and was "all tuckered out" with the week's work, and just in condition to get more cold very easily; and Lora's coat did look too ridiculous to wear to church, so she had better stay at home with her.

"By next Sunday you will have your new coat," she said, to console the child, "and be all in order for church for the rest of the winter."

Lora looked sober for a few minutes; she was very fond of riding to church tucked in among the great soft robes, and she did not mind the service so very much, though the sermon was pretty long. However, she was naturally a sunny little girl, and her face soon cleared as she buttoned her somewhat shabby coat, and went out to watch the snowbirds, who were gathering in great numbers near the barn doors.

Lora and the snowbirds were friends; indeed she made friends with all sorts of dumb animals, and had queer little ideas about them.

"You will fall," she said gravely, addressing a fat bird who swung on a tiny branch almost at her side; "you have picked out a very slimsy branch; it looks as though it was almost broked off; maybe it will break while you are swinging on it — I most know it will — then you will fall down in the snow and hurt yourself. I falled off of a limb once, and it hurted."

The bird paid not the slightest attention to this friendly warning, but Lora continued to stand still, looking at the swaying bush, her face full of earnest thought. She had already turned from the bird, and was thinking about the verse sister Nannie had taught her that morning. It was a long verse for a little girl, with some hard words in it; but Lora had mastered them, and said them over in her mind, revolving, meanwhile, the explanation which Nannie had made of them. "If a man abide

not in me he is cast forth as a branch, and is withered." "Branches do wivver as soon as they are broked off," said Lora. "I've seen them; and papa and Moses burn them up — that is what it said.

"This stick is broked off," she continued, carefully examining the one which she grasped with both chubby hands; "it used to grow, but it won't ever any more. All the leaves have wivvered off it, and some day it will get burned up, I s'pose; it isn't good for much."

Words stopped just here, but that little Lora's brain went on with the great thoughts which she could not express, was evident from the look on her face. The Bible verse and Nannie's careful explanation of it had taken deep root in her heart. She went into the house presently; the thoughts had grown so large that she felt as though she must ask some more questions.

As a usual thing, Sunday quiet reigned in Mrs. Wheeler's kitchen at this hour of the day. But this day was an exception. Mrs. Wheeler, bustling about doing up the last things connected with the morning work, had come across a bowl of mince meat and a lump of dough evidently left from pie crust. "I declare for it!" she exclaimed, "I thought Kate made up all the pies yesterday. What a careless thing, to leave this bowl of mince meat here over Sunday! It would make two good pies, and if all the folks come for Thanksgiving we may fall short; they set such store by my pies. I wonder what Kate was about? It must have got dark before she finished. These must be made up the first thing to-morrow — but there is pretty near everything to do to-morrow, too; it makes a great deal of work getting ready for such a house full; and pie crust is none the better for standing, either; I declare, I've a mind to slap this on to a couple of tins and set them in the oven; there is fire enough to bake them nicely, and it won't take five minutes, hardly, and there are so many ways to turn to-morrow."

There were more thoughts about it not put into words, but it ended in the moulding board being spread out on the table, and the flour jar and rolling-pin and pastry knife being laid beside it. I wonder they did not all blush for shame, for such a thing had never happened to them before on a Sabbath. Mrs. Wheeler's cheeks were rather red, and she felt what she would have called "kind of queer"; but she flew about very fast, and meant to be soon seated in the best room in her Sunday dress.

It was just at that moment that Lora pushed open the kitchen door and entered, her eyes large with the thoughts about which she wanted to question. They grew larger as she took in the situation. Her mother rolling out pie crust! And it was Sunday! Such a thing had never happened in Lora's experience. Nobody knows why the queer little brain put together the thoughts which had come to her outside, and the pie crust in the kitchen; but it did, and there came, presently, this question: "Did you get broked off, muvver?"

"Did I what?" said Mrs. Wheeler, her cheeks very red. There was something in Lora's look and tone which made them redder.

"Get broked off. That is what Nannie said. She said folks that got broked off did things that Jesus did not want done, and kept doing them. Does he want you to make pies to-day, muvver?"

"If I ever saw such a child!" said Mrs. Wheeler, making the rolling-pin revolve over the board at railroad speed. "What does Nannie mean putting such notions into your head? Go into the other room, child, and take off your coat; I'll be there in a few minutes. I'm not going to make pies; I shall wad up this dough and keep it until to-morrow."

And she did.

MYRA SPAFFORD.

THAT RAINY DAY.

 THE Stautenbergers were not rich, neither were they poor. Their house was not large, neither was it very little; but there was none too much room in it.

Mrs. Stautenberger was dead; had "fallen asleep," as the father called it, that very autumn; so when he went to the shop for his day's work, Pauline, the eldest, had to be both sister and mother to her three sisters, and one little brother.

The teacher of the school in their district was very kind, and after her first call at the "home without a mother," she said to Pauline, "Do not stay at home to care for baby sister; bring her with you, and we will manage in some way. I think she will be a good little girl."

Then Pauline felt sure she should love the teacher very much. When her father came home she told him what Miss Gilbert had said, and as he wiped a tear away, he, too, thought she would be a nice teacher, and must have a good heart to be so willing to help his motherless ones.

There are a great many things I would like to tell you about this little family and their splendid teacher, but all I will have time for now, is the story of one rainy day, and what they did about it.

The storm was so hard they could none of them venture out; certainly little Gretchen must not be taken out, so there seemed a prospect for a dull, dreary, lonesome day.

The few dishes were soon put away, and all were hungry for school.

"I know what to do," said Pauline; "let's play school. We can read and spell and make numbers, and maybe we can study geography a little; then when we go to school to-morrow teacher will be so s'prised to see how much we have learned; and then she'll smile, and maybe she will kiss us, every one! Won't that be fun?"

She didn't try to rhyme, but in her eagerness it came of itself.

So they had school, and Metza played teacher, and Pauline sat by little Gretchen, and Fritz and Mary sat with them on the long lounge, and they had such a nice time they forgot that it was storming outside, and were much astonished when at noon papa came home to lunch, and so sorry they had forgotten to heat the water for his coffee.

But when they told him what a nice time they had had, he smiled, and said, "My Pauline has been a good mother to-day." And she thought, "I have the best papa in the world."

G. R. A.

"THIS STICK IS BROKED OFF," SAID LORA.

PERFUMED GLOVES.

PERFUMED gloves were brought from Italy by Edward Vere, Earl of Oxford, after his exile, and his present to Queen Elizabeth of a pair with embroidered roses is mentioned in history. But the refinement of perfumed gloves had been known for three centuries in France before the days of the Virgin Queen, and in Spain the gloves were famous for the scent imparted to them long before her day. The luxurious court of Charles the Second used perfumed gloves, and those "trimmed and laced as fine as Nell's," you have no doubt read about. Louis the Fourteenth also issued letter patents of his "*marchands maîtres gantiers parfumeurs.*" In Venice, where the love of dress was conspicuous, perfumed gloves were introduced by a dogess as early as 1075. — *Selected.*

> THAT day is best wherein we give
>   A thought of others' sorrows;
> Forgetting self, we learn to live,
>   And blessings born of kindly deeds
> Make golden our to-morrows.

A SABBATH IN A BOARDING-SCHOOL IN TURKEY.

I.

IT was the dawn of a winter morning. Ding-dong-ding clanged the chapel bell. I sprang up and began to dress, while Marta went to the mission-house for a cup of coffee. As I fastened the last button, there was a rap at the door. "Come," I called, and in walked

QUEEN ELIZABETH WHEN A PUPIL.

the dear little maid with a cup of coffee carefully covered to keep in the steam, and a roll done up in a napkin, which the cook had insisted upon her bringing.

Ding-dong began the bell again. "Tell the girls not to wait for me," I said; and soon the clatter of many feet on the stairs indicated their departure. The coffee must be swallowed, and the little roll must not be wholly neglected; then putting on bonnet and ulster, I started to follow. Fido, our little spaniel, was standing disconsolate in the hall below. Her eyes were full of entreaty, and wagging her tail persuasively, she accompanied me to the door.

"Go back, Fido. Can't take little dogs to church!" I exclaimed. She knew it was no use to tease, and stood watching me as I opened the heavy door with difficulty, and slammed it after me — it would not latch unless slammed. As I reached the church door, I heard the organ — that meant the service had begun, and I was late! something I never meant to be, but this was so early to go to church! The Armenians are all accustomed in the Gregorian Church to a service even earlier, and when they become Protestant, or Evangelical, they still cling to the old way of making worship the first thing in the morning, and giving breakfast the second place.

Instead, then, of going up the men's aisle, and sitting at the further end where we missionaries usually do, I went on to the door at the left — the women's — and slipped into a back seat. A little girl just in front of me passed me her hymn book, so that I could join with the congregation in singing "*Garode yem, voh garode yem*" — "I need Thee, O, I need Thee." Just as the hymn closed, the sun's rays struck the eastern window and streamed in; then the preacher arose and read the epistle to Philemon, and also 1 Cor. vii. 22. . . .

The benediction was pronounced, and the congregation slowly streamed out. The walk from the chapel to the street is narrow, and as it is not proper for women to crowd in among the men, we waited till they had mostly passed on. While standing outside, Shushan, one of our day pupils, came along with her mother; both were completely enveloped in the white crapy wrap which is worn by the Armenian women in this section. Shushan's bright-colored dress showed through, and at the same time set off the figure in the wrap.

"*Par-ee loo-is*, Shushan; are you of the same mind as yesterday about going to Kozloo?"

She returned my good-morning, and said she was; yes, indeed!

"Why should we change our minds?" said her mother. "Are we not also Christ's servants?" referring to the sermon we had just heard.

You see, Shushan's brother was bitterly opposed to her going away to teach, and I thought it quite possible that he had influenced her to give it up. It was years after girls' schools were opened before people were willing to send their children to a woman teacher — I mean a native — still worse if she was "only a girl." They would far rather send them to a man, however ignorant and incapable. That long struggle has ended at last in victory, and we have no more trouble in finding work for our girls; but we have another difficulty now. Well-to-do parents and brothers consider it a disgrace — at least many of them do — to have their daughters and sisters work as though they were obliged to earn their support.

"Haven't you food and clothes?" they ask indignantly, when a girl, filled with a desire to do something for her people, intimates a purpose to teach. Perhaps I may as well complete this little tale here and now, although it does not belong to the incident of the Sabbath I have been describing.

A few days later the (native) pastor came to me and asked anxiously, "Can't you persuade Shushan, for the sake of peace, to give up going to Kozloo? Her brother is very violent, and talks terribly, declaring that even if she were mounted, and going through the most public street, he would drag her off the horse; if she should by any chance succeed in carrying out her plan, she should never come home again — he would never again acknowledge her as his sister." The pastor went on to say that he thought the brother had offered to send her away to school if she would give up "this crazy scheme," as he called it.

I sent for Shushan, and finding that her brother had made the offer referred to, advised her to accept it. The sacrifice of her will for the sake of avoiding scandal would, I was sure, be as acceptable to the Master as the service she had intended. In less than a week thereafter, she was on her way to a distant school.

We passed out through the arched gateway, and then parted with a mutual "*yer-tak par-roo*" — "good-by." How the sun sparkled on the snowy street, on the mountains which seemed to stand across it, so near they looked, and reared their dazzling summits into the brilliant blue of the winter sky.

The girls with their shawls modestly over their heads, crossed the street in a straggling little procession. Fido appeared in the window which she had pried open with her little black nose — windows are hung like doors — gave an eager and joyful bark or two, and rushed down to welcome them home. Then they sat down to their breakfast of tea and bread. The former was seasoned with white lump sugar (brown sugar is unknown), but there was no butter for the bread.

I doubt whether my readers would have recognized the thin, whity-brown sheets, or the rags placed before one of the girls who had elected to take the pieces, as bread, but so it was. They have many kinds in Turkey, and this thin kind, a little thicker than blotting-paper, is very popular here. In the autumn it is a very common thing for a girl to come and say, "Teacher, mother says will you please excuse me from school to-day?" And she explains that they are baking bread, and need her help.

"But why doesn't your mother get some woman to help her?"

Then I find that it is a regular "bee" — a bread bee! The neighbors are already there, and they will work all night — it is no small job to roll it out so thin. There will be no more baking till the worst of the winter is over. It is stacked away in a dry place, and when wanted the requisite number of sheets (about two feet long by one wide) is taken, sprinkled as you would clothes for ironing, and after a few moments, folded once lengthwise and laid around the edge of the table. If, instead of being sprinkled, the bread is held over the fire a moment, it becomes crisp and really nice; but this is seldom done.

After the housework was done we had prayers, and then the girls were dismissed with a charge not to hang about the halls or stairways, as the boys were coming over again to sing, and to keep their doors closed. "Not ajar as last Sunday, to my mortification and your disgrace; most likely the boys thought you left them open on purpose so that they could look in." Somehow the boys and girls are wonderfully interesting to each other all the world over.

Soon the young fellows filed in, looking half-pleased, half-shy — big, six-foot Isaac, and clever little Bo-ghos; Sumpad, with his bright, frank smile; poor, awkward Deekran, the best writer in school, and his brother Arsen. We practiced "Hold the Fort"; there were two bad mistakes with which we struggled for a while. Then we sang "What a Friend we have in Jesus," "Sweet By and by," "Almost Persuaded," "Go Bury thy Sorrow," "The Ninety and Nine," and others — all in Armenian, of course.

Then I said just a word to Deekran about money I entrusted to him — merely a caution to be careful to return any money that might be left over. It was hardly the thing for the Sabbath, but I was not likely to see him for some days, and I wanted to prevent any carelessness — it is so important for boys that they learn to be careful and business-like.

HARRIET G. POWERS, *in the Evangelist.*

THE HARD TEXT.

(Matt. xii. 31, 32.)

MANY have been troubled over this text. Some have been in despair of being saved because they thought they had committed this unpardonable sin.

Probably many are mistaken. Any one that truly feels sorrow for his sins, and really longs for forgiveness and hungers for holiness, shows some of the best signs that he has not committed this. God will not cast out such a person, if he comes in Jesus' name.

But there is a sin against the Holy Ghost so great that it cannot be forgiven, and probably when one has committed it he is so desperately wicked, so hard in heart, that he never asks to be forgiven.

You will wish to know what this awful sin is, so that you may never commit it. The thought of being doomed never to see heaven and Christian friends after death fills you with horror.

But then, why should you not tremble at

A SELFISH KID.

committing any sin? One little sin leads to another, and so on, until the sin of sins is the end of it all. Take care!

But how is it — or was it — worse to sin against the Holy Ghost than against the Son of Man?

Well, the first might be done in ignorance. The Roman soldiers did not know what a dreadful thing they were doing when they nailed the dear Lord to the tree. They might be forgiven that. But the Holy Ghost comes to show one the truth; then that one has no excuse, you see. His sin is against light. It is most deliberate, willful, determined. It is much more. But remember it is sinning against light, great light.   L.

AN AMUSING ANECDOTE.

SOME time ago an amusing little anecdote was related about the German Crown Prince whilst having a lesson in grammar from his tutor. One is now being told about the second son of the imperial couple, Prince Eitel Fritz. The Emperor is exceedingly strict about his son's behavior at table. Not long since little Prince Eitel Fritz, using his fingers instead of his knife and fork, was corrected by his father several times to no purpose. At last the Emperor's patience was exhausted, and he said :

"Children who eat with their fingers are like little dogs that hold their food with their paws. If you use your fingers again you must go under the table, the proper place for little dogs." The little Prince did his utmost not to forget this time, and used his knife and fork like a man ; but all at once he forgot again and began using his fingers. "March under the table," said his father. Prince Eitel Fritz crept under as bidden. After a little while the Emperor, thinking the Prince very quiet, lifted up the tablecloth and peeped underneath. There sat little Prince Eitel Fritz undressed. His father asked him what he meant by undressing himself. The child answered, "Little dogs don't wear clothes; they only have skin." — *Selected.*

A STRANGE GENERAL.

YEARS and years ago there was a busy housekeeper thrown into a fever of anxiety because she heard a certain famous general was coming, and that she would be expected to entertain him. She flew about in the greatest haste, pressing all the people around her into service to help make ready for the distinguished guest.

Among others was a man who, by his dress and general appearance, she took to be a neighbor's servant. "Take hold and help us here a minute," she said, and set him at some work in the kitchen. That being done the man volunteered to split some wood to a certain size, as it was greatly needed. While he was thus employed the lady's husband, who had been absent, reached home, and was informed of the honor in store for him. He, too, set about helping with the preparations, and presently went to the kitchen, where the strange servant was just laying down an armful of the wood he had split.

Imagine the man's stare of astonishment, mingled with dismay, when he recognized in the stranger the famous general in whose honor all this bustle of preparation was going forward.

In stammering confusion he approached the supposed servant, who, by the way, was slightly deformed, and asked for the meaning of such an extraordinary state of things.

"Why," said the helper, with a broad smile on his face, "I am paying the fine for my deformity."

I leave the Pansies to learn who this great man was, and who was the woman who in her haste to honor him mistook him for a house servant, and also what happened in consequence of this.   PANSY.

CRICKETS are bought and sold in various parts of Africa. People capture them, feed them, and sell them. The natives are very fond of their music, thinking that it induces sleep. Superstitions regarding the cricket's chirp are varied. Some believe it is ominous of sorrow and evil, others consider it a harbinger of joy.

CASTLE QUEER.

BABY'S CORNER.

A HAPPY CHRISTMAS.

"CHRISTMAS is coming! Christmas is coming!"

That is what little Lucy sang as she went through the hall with a hop, skip and jump, clapping her hands for joy.

"And what is little daughter going to do to

ONE OF THOSE LOVELY ROSES.

make somebody happy on Christmas day?"

Papa asked this as he came out into the hall. Then he kissed Lucy good-by, took down his

hat from the rack, and went out of the front door before she had time to tell him.

Lucy stopped running, and looked out of the window and thought about it.

Then she went upstairs to mamma and said:

"Mamma, what am I going to do to make somebody happy to-morrow? What can little girls do?"

"You can be just as sweet as a rose all day, and obey mamma as soon as she speaks. That will make me very happy," said mamma.

"But I want to give something to somebody to s'prise 'em and make 'em glad," Lucy said.

"Who is there that you would like to surprise?" her mamma asked.

Lucy thought a minute, then she said:

"Mrs. Bly."

Mrs. Bly lived in the "Home for Aged Women." She was a nice old lady, and Lucy often went with her mother to call upon her.

"Very well, dear," said mamma; "there is your gold dollar; if you want to give it you may."

"May I buy 'zactly what I please, mamma?"

"Yes, dear."

"O, how nice!" said Lucy. "Can't we go now, right off, to buy it?"

Mamma said "Yes" again, and Lucy ran off to get her hood and cloak and mittens. In a few minutes she was out on the street with mamma, gazing into all the shop windows. "What shall I buy? What shall I buy?" she kept asking.

Mamma said a little shawl for Mrs. Bly's shoulders would be nice, or a pair of warm stockings or some handkerchiefs. But Lucy shook her head.

"Wouldn't she like a bu'ful dollie or a sweet little kitty better?" she asked.

Mamma had to laugh at that.

Just then Lucy cried out, "There it is! I see it! That is what I want."

Guess what it was.

off one of those lovely roses and put it in a vase. She carried it to a poor old lady across the hall who was ill in bed, and it made her glad.

So you see little Lucy made three people happy that Christmas day — the sick old lady, Mrs. Bly and herself.

Mrs. C. M. Livingston.

WHAT THEY NEED.

It was a beautiful large rosebush in a pretty pot. There were two roses on it and plenty of buds.

So they went in and bought it. The man said he would send it up right away.

Old Mrs. Bly was sitting in her rocking-chair knitting. There came a knock at the door. She opened it, and who should be there but Lucy and her mamma, and a boy with a rose-bush!

How surprised Mrs. Bly was, and how pleased, when she knew that little Lucy bought the plant with her own money.

"You dear little lamb," she said; "it will make me very happy. It is like the roses in my old home."

When Christmas morning came Mrs. Bly cut

FROM THE HEART.

O N the eve of Christmas,
    Ready each for bed,
And with heart most anxious,
    Bends each little head,
While the prayer was whispered
    Close to Grandma's chair.
Were the angels bending
    O'er a sight so fair?

" Dear Jesus, please to listen,
    For Christmas comes to-morrow,
And we so much need some dollies,
    So we needn't have to borrow!
Please have them made of wax,
    Wiv blue eyes, and pretty curls;
And we'll love you more than ever!
    We're your own dear little dirls."

k.

A LONG CHRISTMAS.

THERE had been the usual Christmas-tree, which the cousins from three homes had gathered to enjoy. There had not been a Christmas since the oldest of them could remember—and he was sixteen—that the cousins had not been together in one of the homes, and had a frolic around the Christmas-tree. It was always hung with bright-colored balls, and strings of popcorn, and all the bright and pretty and useless things which people from year to year have contrived for such trees. It always had clustered about it the various sorts of fruits which refused, because of their weight, to be hung upon the branches—dolls, and kites, and wagons, and swords, and books and baskets. Every year the fruit grew stranger in some respects, with a dreary sameness in others, which was actually beginning to weary the hearts of the cousins.

The first excitement was over. The fathers and mothers and maiden aunts, together with three grandmothers and two grandfathers, had retired to quieter parts of the house, and the young people were left to their enjoyment. It was not very noisy in the room, nor were most of the cousins absorbed in their gifts; in fact their faces were already sobering. Little Nell was still happy over her new building-blocks, and Dell, her other self, was trying to advise her concerning them, while Harold tried his new paints and brushes on the chair he occupied, his guardian sister leaning over the back of the chair, so absorbed the while in her own grave thoughts that she did not even notice the mischief he was doing.

"It is all over once more," said Holly. He was the sixteen-year-old cousin, and he thrust his hands in his pockets, and said it with a yawn.

"Some of it is a good deal of a bore," answered Tom, the cousin next in age, echoing the yawn. "I didn't get the first thing I expected or wanted."

"Neither did I; but then I don't know what I wanted, I am sure, unless it was a bicycle,

and you can't put that on a Christmas-tree very well."

"Why not, as well as the trumpery which is put on?" asked Tom contemptuously. "I tell you the whole thing is getting to be a bore. Even the small fry don't care for it half so much as they think they do; there's Nannie sulking this minute because her dollie, which she has deserted, is not so nice according to her notion as Lily's is. And Ted has turned his back on the whole of it because he didn't get a drum. This crowd needs something new."

"I don't know what it would be; we have had everything imaginable, and if the simple truth were told need presents less than any young folks in the kingdom, I do suppose. My father says there is nothing new to get for pampered young people like us; and I don't know but he is about right."

"There's a whole lot of money spent about it every year, though." This was from Hortense, the oldest of the girl cousins, and a sort of adviser of the two older boys.

"I know it," said Holly; "and a good deal of it is wasted. Nannie, for instance, did not need another doll any more than the cat needs two tails, and as for me I have seven jack-knives now."

At that moment Helen turned away from the paint brush which she had not noticed, and joined in the conversation.

"Isn't it funny? I have five new balls, and I don't care for any of them. They keep giving us the same things over and over."

"They forget," said Holly; "and there is nothing new for them to get us, anyhow."

"I know something that would be new." It was Hortense again, speaking with grave thoughtfulness. The boys turned and looked at her inquiringly. "Don't you know what Mr. Briggs told about the children out in the Colorado mountains, who never had a Christmas present in their lives, and didn't know anything about such times as we have? I was thinking what if we could make up a box and put into it all the dollies, and balls, and jack-knives, and things that we don't want, and some books, and perhaps a little candy, and send it out there, wouldn't it be nice?"

THEIR FACES WERE ALREADY SOBERING.

"Too late for this year," said Tom promptly.

"Why, no, it isn't; if we hadn't had any Christmas at all, ever, we would be willing to have one come to us in January."

The boys laughed, and Holly said heartily, "That's so." And Hortense began to tell a story that she had heard Mr. Briggs tell to her uncle, and the younger ones gathered about her, leaving dolls and paints, and the interest grew.

It was the very next day that Hortense and Tom and Holly went to Dr. Parsons' house to see Mr. Briggs.

"Why, yes," he said, looking perfectly delighted with them, when Holly explained; "let me tell you about a brave little chap out there, only eleven years old; his father was guide to the tourists who wanted to climb the dangerous and difficult mountains, and lost his life from exposure, hunting a party of men who had strayed away. Little Teddy is as brave as a soldier. He is a guide himself, though so young, and getting to be one of the surest and safest to be found in that region, only he is so young and small yet, that strangers are afraid to trust him. A dreary life Teddy leads; he and his mother live all alone in a little house at the foot of a mountain. The boy has only the clothes which his father left, made over for him the best way his mother can. He never had anything that fitted him; and he never had any playthings in his life, only what he picked up; as for knives, or balls, or any of the things which boys like him enjoy, I don't know what he would think if one should happen to come to him. You needn't suppose that he hasn't heard all about Christmas; his mother used to live in a farmhouse in New York State, and the stories she has told have almost driven him wild. A few rods away from their cottage lives a family with five children — three little girls, and a four-year-old boy and a baby. I happen to know that Teddy set his heart this year on having some sort of a Christmas present for every one of those children — and failed! I did not mean that he should, but I was sick at just the wrong time after I reached home, and my plans did not work. I heard from there only last night, and poor Teddy's plans did not work, either."

Holly had his note book and pencil in hand. "Will you give us his full name and address?" he said.

Such a time as the cousins had packing that box! Every baby of them contributed, not only the toys which they did not want, but a few that they loved, and parted from with sighs. The same may be said of the elder cousins, especially when it came to books; Holly was a miser where these were concerned, and Hortense knew how to sympathize with him. It took these two several hours to be willing to pack in that box some of their handsomely bound volumes, written by favorite authors.

But they had to go; for Mr. Briggs, among other things, had said, "I never saw a boy so hungry for reading in my life as Teddy; and he has only scraps of old newspapers, which he has picked up from time to time among the tourists."

And more than books and toys went into that box.

"It is a shame for a fellow to have no clothes that fit him!" declared Tom. "I've been there myself, and I know how it feels. I had to wear my brother Dick's overcoat once, and it was too large for me. Mr. Briggs says he is about the size of Roger" — he meant Teddy, and not Mr. Briggs. "We must ask mother about that."

They asked her to such purpose, and Aunt Cornelia as well, that two neat suits of Roger's and Cousin Harry's second best clothes went into the box.

The day in which it was finally packed was a jubilee. The cousins were all invited to Aunt Cornelia's to supper, and packed the box in the large dining-room after supper, with a little of Aunt Cornelia's and Uncle Roger's help.

"I don't know as I ever had so much fun in my life," said Holly, looking up from the driving of the last nail to make the remark. "It is better than Christmas a dozen times; in fact it is a Christmas extension."

"And won't it be fun to hear from Teddy?" said Hortense.

But as for us, we cannot expect to hear from Teddy until January.

PANSY.

VOICES OF THE BELLS.

IN yonder tower high hangs the brazen
    bell,
    Tolling, tolling;
Upon the frosty air its echoes heave and
    swell,
    Tolling, tolling:
The bell has a tongue that is easily heard;
When it is swung many hearts may be stirred,
Though its tale it tells with
    never a word —
    Tolling, tolling.

THE BELLS SWING AND RING.

It swings and dings in the morning air,
    Ringing, ringing!
Tells of the birth of a baby fair,
    Ringing, ringing!
Tells the glad news so that all may know;
Those in the village asleep below,
Those on the streets moving to and fro —
    Ringing, ringing!

Aloft it swings in the schoolhouse
    tower,
    Dinging, dinging;
With brazen tongue it proclaims the
    hour,
    Dinging, dinging:
Calls to the work of storing the mind
With useful knowledge of every kind,
Urging the laggards left far behind,
    Dinging, dinging.

Gently it swings in the steeple high,
    Pealing, pealing;
The steeple that points to the upper sky,
    Pealing, pealing:
Calling to worship on hallowed day,
Calling the faithful to come and pray,
Even to those who are far away —
    Pealing, pealing.

Again it calls in a joyful tone,
    Ringing, ringing!

Hinting that man should not walk alone,
    Ringing, ringing!
And so they throng with the bridal pair,
And the glad bells sound on the clear sweet air,
For the bells all ring for the belle so fair —
    Ringing, ringing!

Ah, me! but that tongue will swing again,
    Tolling, tolling;
Swing again with a solemn strain,
    Tolling, tolling:

EASTER LILIES.

A STALK of tall white lilies
    Bloomed out in a garden fair;
Their breath, so sweet and fragrant,
    Scented the ambient air.

As Easter day came on apace,
    It seemed as if they tried
To grow still sweeter, for the morn
    When rose the Crucified.

THE BELL HAS A TONGUE THAT IS EASILY HEARD.

It will tell how some one beloved has died,
How the cold dark earth has claimed his bride;
And 'twill seem in its strains as though it
    sighed —
    Tolling, tolling.

But the bells above may swing and ring,
    Swinging, ringing,
In the temple towers of the Lord the King,
    Swinging, ringing;
And the bells below, with the bells up there,
May sound their joys for this Child and Heir,
Who is called to heaven its joys to share —
    Swinging, ringing.   G. R. A.

When dawned the holy Easter tide,
    And they were full in bloom,
A sad-eyed woman gathered them
    And laid them on a tomb.

And as she knelt in deepest woe
    Beside the flower-decked mound,
And felt that all her hope was dead,
    The lilies' fragrance stole around.

It stole into her wounded breast;
    The sacred odors seemed to be
A message for her bleeding heart —
    "The Crucified pities thee."
    CAROLINE STRATTON VALENTINE.

The "Chebec"

from our heads

THE BELL HANGS IN THE TOWER.

CHARACTER STUDIES.

I.

EDWARD STEADMAN was at home for the Christmas holidays. Everybody was glad to see him, of course, particularly his mother; because in the first place mothers always are a little bit more glad over the home-coming of their boys than anybody else in the world can be, and secondly because she needed some help very much, and knew that he could give it. She explained matters to him that morning: "I want to get Grandma's room all in order, Edward, and her new carpet down, and every thing, before Christmas, you know; and we shall have to work like bees. I'm so glad you came home this week, instead of stopping at your uncle's first. To-day we can hang all her pictures, and put up the curtains and the wall-pockets, and do things of that kind; they will not make a speck of dust in putting down the carpet — it is new, you know. I want to get all those things done to-day, they are so puttering — take a great deal of time and judgment. I'm so glad to have you to depend upon; you are such a tall boy that you can reach where mother can't; and Dick is so clumsy I hate to have him stumping about Grandma's room. Your father was going to help me, though he did not know how to spare the time; he was as pleased as could be when I told him that you could do it all. 'Sure enough!' he said; 'we have got a boy to depend upon once more; how good it seems!'"

The sentence closed with a fond smile, and such a look in the mother's eyes as ought to have made a boy happy. Edward was happy; he whistled as he went down the stairs, and thought to himself that there were not many fellows who had such a mother as his, and that he would show her just how tall, and how handy and how wise he was.

She called after him as she heard the street door open.

"Where are you going, Edward? We ought to get right to work; it will be an all-day job,

do the best we can, and the light is good in Grandma's room now for hanging the pictures. Must you go to the post-office first? O, well! that is but a short distance; run along, and get back as soon as you can."

"Halloo!" said Mr. Arkwright, the post-master, who had known Edward ever since he was a little fellow in kilts and curls, "back again, are you? How you do shoot up, to be sure! I believe you are about a foot taller than you were in the fall. Here's your mail; nothing but papers this time, but enough of them to snow you under!" And he pitched them through the little window so fast that they fell to the right and left.

"Catalogues, some of them," said Edward, smiling; "I asked them to send me a number of the new ones; and the reports of our commencement and society exercises are in these papers."

"Like enough," said Mr. Arkwright; "had a grand time, I suppose? You carried off a first prize, I hear? Glad of it. I always knew it was in you. Do you happen to be going directly home? If you are, would you mind taking this letter and handing it in at Westlake's as you pass? I see it is marked 'Important,' and it may save him some trouble to get it right away. He's all alone in the office to-day; his boy is sick."

"Certainly, sir," said Edward, reaching for the letter, and dropping it into his jacket pocket. Then he walked away, looking steadily at one of the papers, which he had already opened.

"I do not see what in the world can have detained Edward!" said Mrs. Steadman, speaking as well as she could with her mouth full of tacks. She was mounted on a box which in its turn was mounted on a chair, and was trying to reach to fasten the curtain in Grandma's room.

"I should think you would wait for him," said her daughter Fannie anxiously. "You ought not to climb up like that, mother; father would not like it at all, and I'm afraid you will fall. You are not high enough yet to get it right."

"I know it; and I can't drive a nail away up here, either. I cannot understand why Edward doesn't come; it seems as though something must have happened to him. I explained to him particularly what a hurry we were in, and how much there was in which he could help me."

"What has happened to him is that he has found something to read, I suppose, and has seated himself somewhere to enjoy it." Fannie spoke a little irritably; she was worried about

"CERTAINLY, SIR," SAID EDWARD.

her mother, and they had been waiting for Edward for more than two hours. The short December day was hurrying toward its noon, and nothing had been done of the many things in which he was to have been a central figure. Fannie was very fond of her brother, but she realized his besetments better than the others did, or at least she said more about them.

"O, no!" said the mother decidedly, taking a tack out of her mouth to enable her to speak plainly; "Edward wouldn't do that, after all I said to him this morning. He knew how anxious we were to have everything ready for Grandma by Christmas. Something unusual has happened, I feel sure. I don't know but Tommy would better run out and see if he can find him, only it seems rather absurd to be sending out in search of a big boy like Edward."

"I should think so!" Fannie said, and they waited another half-hour. Then a sharp ring at the door-bell startled Mrs. Steadman so that she nearly lost her balance. Fannie screamed a little, and ran toward her.

"I didn't fall," she said, leaning against the window-easing for support; "but I think I shall have to get down. I don't see what makes me so nervous. It seems all the time as though something was going to happen; I suppose it is because Edward doesn't come. Did Jane go to the door?"

Yes, Jane had; and now they listened and heard Mr. Westlake's, their neighbor's, voice.

"Is Edward here?"

No, Jane said, somewhat shortly, he was not; and as to where he was, that was more than they knew. Jane had been called from her work three times that morning to help with something which Edward could have done, and she did not feel sweet-natured.

"Well, I wish you would ask your folks if they have any idea where I might find him," Mr. Westlake said anxiously; "I have just come from the office — it was the first chance I had for going this morning — and Arkwright says he sent a letter to me marked 'Important' — sent it by Edward nearly three hours ago, he should think. I have some business matters that are very important, and I thought this might be a summons to me to go away on the express, and there is but a half-hour or less before it goes."

Before this long sentence was finished Mrs. Steadman was at the door; but she had no information to give, and could only tell the annoyed man that she was sorry, and that she could not imagine what had detained Edward.

"I can," muttered Jane, as he turned hurriedly away; "his own sweet notion is detaining him; he's enjoying himself somewhere, readin' a book or paper, and letting others get along the best way they can." But Jane was only talking to herself.

The Steadman dinner bell was sounding through the house when Edward, flushed and embarrassed, came bounding up the stairs two steps at a time, to assure his mother how sorry he was.

"I hadn't the least idea how time was going," he explained; "never was so astonished in my life as I was to hear the bell ring for noon! Why, you see," in answer to her anxious questions, "I got a lot of papers at the office — all about our closing days, you know; of course I was anxious to see what they said about the examinations, and essays, and things, so I stepped into Dr. Mason's office just to glance them over. The doctor was out, and I sat and read first one thing and then another, and talked a little with folks who kept coming in search of the doctor, until, to my utter astonishment, as I tell you, I heard the bell."

"Then nothing detained you, Edward?"

"Why, no, ma'am; nothing but the papers, as I tell you. I had not the faintest idea" —

She interrupted him. "Have you seen Mr. Westlake?"

"Yes'm," and now Edward's face crimsoned; "I met him on the street and gave him his letter. I'm dreadfully sorry about that; almost as sorry as I am about keeping you waiting, mother."

"He said it might want him to take the train; do you know if it did?"

"Yes'm, it did."

"And he missed it?"

"Why, of course, mother dear; the train goes at eleven, you know. I'm awfully sorry. It is perfectly unaccountable what has become of this forenoon!"

Mrs. Steadman made no comment; she did not want to trust herself to do so just then. She turned away with a sigh so deep that it would have cut Edward's heart, had he heard it.

And Jane nodded her gray head and muttered, "I told you so!"

MYRA SPAFFORD.

A TEN-DOLLAR CHRISTMAS.

ADELE CHESTER had never spent a Christmas in the country before; neither had she ever felt quite so desolate. Mother and father were in Europe, in search of health for the father, and Adele, who had been left in charge of Aunt Martha, had herself decreed that she would go nowhere for Christmas.

"I can't be happy and frolic when papa is sick," she said; "and as for the country, if Aunt Martha can live there all her life, I think I can endure one Christmas." So she had staid; but it must be confessed that the world looked dreary to her that wintry morning, with nothing but snow to be seen from her window. She almost thought she would have been wiser to have joined the Philadelphia cousins. "At least there would have been a chance to spend my Christmas money," she murmured gloomily, as she tapped on the frosty window pane with restless fingers. "I'm sure I don't know what I can buy in this little tucked-up place."

The "tucked-up place" was really a nice town with about five thousand people living in it, but to Adele, whose home was in New York City, it seemed absurd to call it a town. Aunt Martha's farmhouse was only half a mile from some very good stores, where Adele had found a few things to suit her during the three months she had spent there, and on the whole she had managed to be quite happy. But she did not feel like being suited with anything this morning. Such a queer Christmas for her! She had had her presents, as usual — a new fur cap from Aunt Martha, a writing-desk well furnished from Uncle Peter, a lovely ring with a real diamond in it from mamma, and a new chain for her pretty watch from papa. What more could a reasonable girl want? Truth to tell, she wanted nothing but the dear home, and mamma's kisses, and papa's arms around her. The ring and chain were beautiful, but they did not seem like presents from them, when she knew they crossed the ocean weeks ago, and had been lying in Aunt Martha's bureau drawer waiting for this morning. She valued the letter more which had arrived only the night before, and she drew it from her pocket and kissed it, letting a tear or two fall on the words, "My Darling Child," as she read them once more. "Papa and I are so sorry to be away from you to-day," the letter read; "we have tried to find something suitable to send on so long a journey, and planned to reach you on the very day, but have failed; papa has not been well enough to look about much for a few weeks, and I could not go alone. At last we decided to send you a fifty-dollar bank note and bid you go and spend it in the way which would make you happiest."

"The idea!" said Adele, smiling through her tears, as she refolded the letter, "just as though I could find anything here to buy to make me happy! Mamma must have forgotten for the moment where I was. Yet I want a few things, some Christmas bonbons, at least, if they know the meaning of the word in this little place, and above all, I want a brisk walk in the snow. I shall take ten dollars of my fifty, and go out and spend it; I won't waste another cent on this old town. I wonder what I can do with ten dollars to make me happy?" She laughed half scornfully. Ten dollars seemed so very little to this girl, who had always spent money as freely as water, and done as little thinking about it as the birds do over the spring cherries.

In a very few minutes she was wrapped in furs and out upon the snowy road. Aunt Martha offered her the sleigh and the driver, and her "leggings" and woollen mittens, but she would have none of them. She was a good walker, and had been used to miles in the city. She hid her nose in her muff, because the wind over this wide stretch of snow was very keen, and sped along "like a snowbird," Aunt Martha said, watching her from the window. And then she sighed, this dear old auntie whom the country satisfied. She saw the shade on the face of her darling this morning, and was sorry for her, and wished so much that she could do something to brighten her Christmas day.

The little town was reached in due time, and the streets were gay with Christmas finery; the stores were open quite generally, to catch the belated Christmas buyers. In an hour or two they would close for the day; but the custom in this thriving manufacturing town was to give the tardy ones a Christmas morning chance. Adele went from one store to another, dissatisfied, disconsolate. Nothing suited her. The truth is, when a girl does not need an earthly thing, and is yet determined to spend some money, she is sometimes rather difficult to suit. She halted at last before a show window and looked at the bright fineries displayed there. So did little Janey Hooper, who had come out with ten cents to buy a soup bone for the day's dinner. Adele, turning from the window, jostled against her, and looked down upon the mite. She seemed not more than eight, yet there was a wise, grown-up look in her eyes which held the homesick girl's attention.

"Are you trying to make Christmas too? What do you see in the window you like?"

"Everything," said the little girl simply.

"Do you? you are fortunate. Are you going to buy them all?"

"O, no! not a single one. I couldn't."

Adele, looking closely at her, was seized with a sudden impulse. "Suppose you could buy one thing, what would it be?" she asked.

The little girl's eyes flashed. "Oh! I would buy that shawl — that soft gray one with pussy fringe — it looks just like mother."

It was a dingy little shoulder shawl, of the kind which can be bought for two dollars. "Does your mother need a shawl?" asked Adele.

"O, yes'm! she needs it badly enough; but we are not going to get one, not this year; we can't."

There was decision and composure in the tone, like a woman who had settled the whole question, and put it beyond the range of argument. Her manner amused Adele.

"That was for your mother," she said; "what would you choose for yourself?"

"Me?" said the child, surprised. "Oh! I don't know. I might take that brown coat, maybe, or some mittens, or — I don't know which I would take. What's the use?"

She was turning away; but Adele's gloved hand detained her. The little sack she wore was much too thin for so cold a morning.

"Wait a minute," she said gently. "Tell me what your name is, won't you, and where you live, and what you came out for this cold morning with so thin a sack?"

"I'm Janey Hooper; we live down there on Factory Lane. It wasn't far to go, and my sack is worn out, that is why it is so thin; but it will do very well for this winter. I came out to buy the Christmas dinner."

"Did you, indeed! Aren't you very young to go to market?"

"O, no, ma'am! I'm turned nine, and the oldest of four, and father's dead. Of course I have to do all I can. I know how to choose a lovely soup bone."

"Do you? Are you going to have soup to-day?"

"Yes'm, a big kettle full; I've got ten cents to buy a bone with. I generally get a five-cent one; but we thought for Christmas we would have it fine. My brother is to be home to dinner; he is most twelve, and likes soup."

There was a mist before Adele's eyes that the frosty air did not make. She brushed it away and settled her plans.

"Come in here with me a minute," she said; "I want your help about something." The child followed her wonderingly, with eyes that grew every moment larger, as the thick brown coat which hung on a wire figure was taken down and deliberately tried by the smiling shop girl on her quaint little self.

"It fits to a T," said the girl; "Janey has a pretty figure, and that just suits her."

"It is warm, at least," said Adele. "Did you say it was two and a half? What an absurd price! Keep it on, child; it is for you. This is Christmas, you know, and Santa Claus sent it to you. Now that shoulder shawl."

A moment more, and it was in Janey's astonished arms. Her eyes sparkled, but she made an earnest protest: "Oh! if you please, I don't think I can; I am afraid mother would not"—

"Your mother cannot help herself," interrupted Adele. "Don't you know I told you it was Santa Claus? He does what he likes always. Come along, I'm going to market with you; I want to see you pick out a soup bone. Is it to go in that basket?"

She picked it out with grave care and with skill, Adele and the market man watching her

the while. "Isn't it a nice one, Bobby?" said the child, to a stout boy who had also stopped. Adele turned as the freckled boy nodded.

"Who is this? Is he a friend of yours? Well, Bobby, Santa Claus wants you to do an errand for him, will you? He will give you four of those red-cheeked apples if you will."

The boy laughed good-naturedly, and said he didn't know much about Santa Claus, but he would do whatever she wanted done.

"Very well," said Adele merrily; "I want that market basket which hangs up there. Can you lend it to this boy for a little while?" The market man declared his entire willingness to do so, and kept Janey Hooper waiting for her bone while he filled that basket with everything which Adele's eyes could discover, which might add to a Christmas dinner. There was a plump chicken, a roast of beef, a string of sausage, some potatoes, apples, onions, turnips, a great bunch of celery, and, in short, whatever the market man suggested, after the girl's skill was exhausted.

"Is that too heavy for you?" said Adele.

"O, no, ma'am!" Bobby assured her.

"Very well; I want you to take it to this little girl's mother's house, and tell her Santa Claus sent it to go with the soup, and that it has given him a happy Christmas to do so. Will you remember?"

He nodded brightly, stuffing rosy-cheeked apples into his pocket the while, and they trudged away, Janey trying to murmur her bewildered protests, while Adele paid her bill.

"I've spent every cent of my ten dollars," she told Aunt Martha an hour later. "I hadn't even enough to buy you any Christmas bonbons; but I have obeyed mamma's directions; I was to buy something to make me happy, and I haven't felt so happy in weeks as I do this minute. When I get my things put away I'll come down and tell you all about it."

Aunt Martha watched her bound up the stairs, a glow on her cheeks and a sparkle in her eyes which they had lacked when she went out; and whatever the purchase had been, she was grateful.

As for Janey Hooper and her mother, to say nothing of Bobby, who took dinner with them, you must imagine how they felt.   PANSY.

MAKING THE SHEEP CLEAN.

MISS PARKER'S GIRLS.

THERE were thirteen of them, all told. An "unlucky number," one of them said, and laughed; they were girls who did not believe in "luck." They laughed a great deal during these days, and were very happy. They had as lovely a secret on their minds as thirteen girls, all of them between the ages of eleven and thirteen, ever had. They were also very busy, and held many committee meetings, and discussed plans, and went in companies of twos and threes to transact business. "We were never so busy before at this time of year, were we?" they said to one another. "And we never had so much fun in our lives!" some one would be sure to say. To this sentiment they all agreed.

"This time of year" was a few days before Christmas. The preparations for Christmas, so far as these girls are concerned, began two weeks before. It started on Sunday afternoon in the Bible class. Miss Parker had been even more interesting than usual that day. She succeeded in so filling their hearts with the lesson, especially with one thought in it, that Cora Henderson said, half enviously:

"O, dear! I can't help wishing that we had lived in those times. Of course it was dreadful; but then, after all, it gave one such splendid opportunities! Think of John having a chance to take Jesus' mother home and do for her. And to know that Jesus wanted him to, and was pleased with it! I think it would have been just lovely; there are no such chances nowadays," and Cora, aged thirteen, sighed.

Miss Parker smiled on her brightly. "Are you sure of that, my dear girl? Remember we are talking about a history which is different from any other in the world, because Jesus is "the same yesterday, to-day and forever."

"O, yes'm!" Cora said civilly; "I know it; but then, of course, things are different. His mother is not here on earth for us to take care of; I should love to do it, I know I should," and Cora's fair face glowed, and her eyes had a sweet and tender light in them.

Miss Parker looked at her fondly. "My dear child," she said, "I think you would; but do you forget how He said, 'Whosoever shall do the will of my Father which is in heaven, the same is my brother and sister and mother'?"

Cora looked a little bewildered, and Miss Parker explained.

"I think we all forget that according to that verse Jesus has many 'mothers' on earth, in the persons of his dear old saints, who are poor, and weak, and tired, and are only waiting to be called home. There are so many things we could do for their comfort, if we only remembered that they were the same to Jesus as his own dear mother."

The girls looked at one another wonderingly. This was a new way of putting it. Cora did more than look. "What a lovely thought!" she said; "I should never have thought it out for myself, but it must be so, because what would that verse mean if it were not? O, Miss Parker! couldn't we girls do it? Do you know of any old lady whom we could help a little — make a pretty Christmas for, perhaps? Girls, wouldn't you all like to do it?"

So that was the beginning. Yes, Miss Parker knew an old lady; had had her in mind all the week; had wondered how she could set to work to interest her dear girls in her. She needed a great deal of help, and Miss Parker had very little of this world's goods. She knew that some of her girls came from homes where there was plenty. "But I do not like to be always begging," she told her mother. Then she had asked the Lord Jesus to show her some way of interesting the girls in poor Grandmother Blakslee. And here they were asking for the name of an old lady whom they could help! What a lovely answer it was to her prayer.

Grandmother Blakslee's story was a sad one, though only too common. Her two daughters and her one son had died long years before, leaving a little granddaughter, who had grown to girlhood and married a worthless drunkard, who deserted her, and at last she died, leaving to Grandmother Blakslee the care of her poor little baby boy. In many ways life had gone hard with Grandmother Blakslee; and now in her old age, when she was too feeble to work, the thing which she had dreaded most in the world, next to sin, had come to her door. She could no longer pay the rent for her one little bare room, and must send her little boy to the orphan asylum. and go herself to the poorhouse. It seemed a very pitiful thing to Grandmother Johnnie was to go with her for that one day, and the next morning he was to be taken in the market wagon to the asylum. Poor Grandmother Blakslee! her heart was very sad and sore, but she tried to keep her face quiet and peaceful for Johnnie's sake. She had not been

"NOW LET US ASK A BLESSING."

Blakslee that she should have had to plan to leave the bare little room on Christmas morning, but that happened to be the day when it was convenient for the man who had promised to take her and her old arm-chair. Poor little able to make the little fellow understand that he was to be separated from her; the most he realized was that they were to take a ride together and spend the day in a big house, and he was happy. On the little three-cornered table was set a dish with baked potatoes and warm rolls, and the teapot stood near it; a neighbor only a little less poor than themselves had remembered them. Grandmother tried to have only thankfulness in her heart; but could she forget that she had lived in that town more than sixty years, and been a member of the church all that time? Occasionally she could not help feeling it was strange that there could have been no other way but to go to the poorhouse. "It won't be long now for me," she told herself, "and I should like to have kept Johnnie while I staid, poor little boy! But it was not to be." Then she smothered a sigh and said, "Come, Johnnie, let us ask a blessing, then we will have our last breakfast alone together."

It was while Johnnie stood with clasped hands, saying after Grandmother the words of blessing, that a knock was heard at the little door. "Come in," said Grandmother Blakslee the moment the words of prayer were spoken, and a strange head was thrust in at the door.

"I can wait, ma'am," said the owner of it respectfully. "I'm to take you in my rig, and my orders were to wait until you were ready."

"Did Mr. Patterson send you?" asked Grandma, her voice all in a tremble. "I thought he meant to come himself, and I thought he said about ten o'clock; but we'll hurry, Johnnie and me; we won't keep you long. Can you take the chair, too?"

"Yes'm; them's my orders; and no hurry in life, ma'am, take your time," and he closed the door.

Johnnie stuffed in the buns and potatoes, and pronounced them good; but poor Grandmother Blakslee only swallowed a few mouthfuls of tea which almost choked her. Life was very hard.

She was soon ready; it would not do to keep Mr. Patterson's team waiting. But she stared at it when she came out. It was not the market wagon; instead it was a handsome two-horse sleigh, with gay robes on the seats, and gay bells on the handsome horses. "You needn't be at all afraid, ma'am," said the strange man, "these horses is gentle as kittens, if they do love to go," and he lifted her in as though she had been a kitten, tucked Johnnie under the robes beside her, and before

she could get her breath to speak they were off. Just a gay dash around the corner, down one familiar street, up another, and they halted before a tiny white house set back among tall trees which staid green even in winter.

"There is some mistake," faltered Grandma Blakslee, more breathless than ever. "I wasn't to be brought here; I was to go to the asylum out on the Corning Road, near two miles; I don't know the folks that live here; I didn't know it was rented."

The strange man chuckled. "I guess there's no mistake," he said, "and you'll like to make their acquaintance; anyhow, I must do my duty and leave you here; I'm under orders."

Trembling and bewildered, poor Grandma, because she did not know what else to do, let herself be set down in front of the door, which the man opened hospitably, saying as he did so, "Step right in; the folks that live here will be glad to see you." Then he shut the door and went away. They were left, Grandmother and Johnnie, in a little hall opening into a pretty room at the right. The door was wide open, and a bright fire burned in a shining stove. There was a bright carpet on the floor; there was a rose in blossom in one window, and some geraniums in the other. There was a large easy chair in front of the stove, with a table beside it on which was set out a lovely breakfast for two. On the stove the tea-kettle sang, and some genuine tea in a little brown teapot on the right-hand corner back, sent out its delicious aroma. In an alcove, behind some pretty curtains which were partly drawn, waited a plump white bed; and Grandma Blakslee stood in the midst of all this luxury and stared.

"Grandma," said Johnnie, "have we got there? Is this the big house? Where are all the folks? Where is this, and whose breakfast is that? Are we to eat it, Grandma? It is nicer than ours. Why don't you sit down in that pretty chair? Here is a little one for me, with red cushions. Can't we stay here every day, Grandma?"

Grandma, feeling unable to stand another minute, tottered forward and dropped into the softness of the easy chair, and spied, tucked under the edge of a plate, a sheet of folded paper. Then she fumbled for what Johnnie called the "speticles that could wead," and read:

Welcome home, dear Grandma Blakslee. Merry Christmas to you and Johnnie.

FROM MISS PARKER'S GIRLS.

No, they hadn't "done it every bit themselves." There had been several fathers and mothers who were glad to help, as soon as they thought about it. Cora Henderson's father had said, "Why, Grandma Blakslee might live in the little empty cottage this winter and welcome; he wondered they had not thought of it before." Anna Smith's mother said she would be glad to get rid of that carpet rolled up in the attic; she had no use for it, and it was a pattern she had never liked. Ella Stuart's mother said the old arm-chair and the old lounge would do nicely if they were re-covered, and she was sure she did not want them. And so the plan grew and grew, and the girls were O, so busy and happy! It was the best Christmas of their lives, they all declared, especially after they made their call on Grandma, and found her almost too happy.

"It is almost pitiful," said Anna Smith, "to see a poor woman cry for joy over one little room and a few old duds!"

And Cora Henderson, with her eyes shining like stars, said, "Isn't it lovely? I'm so glad that verse is in the Bible, and Miss Parker thought it all out!"   PANSY.

A SABBATH IN A BOARDING-SCHOOL IN TURKEY.

II.

 I MUST explain that some time before this I had learned that the boys in the boarding-school who had no pocket money, could not go to the bath as often as I thought they ought. While I was considering this problem, an Armenian gentleman gave me something over two dollars to use as I saw fit. Thinking "cleanliness next to godliness," though the Bible does not say it in just those words, I used to give Deekran a quarter or so now and then to use for himself and the other poor boys.

When they rose to go, I asked Sumpad if he could stop a moment, I wanted to have a little talk with him. How glad I was to find that he had a hope in Christ, and was trying to live for him. It was a great privilege to speak a few words of sympathy and encouragement.

How can I believe the terrible news that has just come to me here in free America? How can I think of him in his young, Christian manhood as dead in a horrible Turkish dungeon! Why, what had he done? He had written a few lines of boyish admiration for the heroes of his own race, the Armenians. And so he must die alone of typhus fever after a four months' imprisonment, utterly cut off from all his friends. Poor young martyr! No one could get access to him; yes, there was one Friend whose entrance neither bolts nor bars could prevent — the King of heaven and earth; what need of any other? Death has now unlocked the prison door, and opened the gate of heaven; no more tears should be shed for him — happy young martyr.

But I have wandered far, both as to place and time, far from that peaceful, happy Sabbath. It was now lunch time; then came Sabbath-school. The men and boys met in the chapel, but as it was not large enough to accommodate more, the women's, girls' and the infant class met elsewhere. Isgoohe, a member of the senior class in the high school, took charge of the second of these. After going over the lesson, she began to ask personal questions:

"Now, girls, what have you done for Jesus this week?"

A hand was raised.

"What is it, Marta?"

"I let Funduk have my comb for Jesus' sake. It was such a nice one, I did not like to have her use it; but Miss Goulding told me I ought to be kind to Funduk."

Then Armenoohe said that going home from school one day, a girl she did not know very well called out, "Armenoohe, run and get me another clog; mine's broken." (The clog is a wooden sole with a heel at each end, as it were, and a leather strap to slip the foot into. These heels are from one to three or four inches in height, and raise the foot well out of the mud or snow.) "At first," said she, "I thought that it was no affair of mine, and that the girl was rather impudent to ask such a thing. Then I remembered what you told us, Isgoohe, about not pleasing ourselves; so I asked her which was her house, and got the clog and brought it to her, and she never even thanked me!" (It was not so very long since Armenoohe herself had learned to say "thank you.")

Two or three others told their little efforts at denying self; then the bell rang for the afternoon service.

In the evening I invited any who wished to talk with me to come to my room. Soon afterward Rakel came. She was rather a pretty girl, with bright red hair; she was full of fun, and a dreadful tease. She dropped on to the hassock at my side in a bashful sort of a way.

"Was there something you wanted to say, Rakel?"

"Yes," came the whispered answer; "I want to love my companions."

I enlarged a little upon the duty and privilege of loving others, and then waited for her to speak; but she was silent so long, that I finally asked if there was anything else she wished to say.

"Yes; how can I love those who make me angry?"

Well, that was a problem, to be sure! But then, the dear Saviour can help us solve every problem, so we knelt and prayed, both of us, for his help in this particular matter.

She had been gone but a minute, when her cousin Sarra came, Bible in hand, to ask the meaning of the verse, "Whether therefore ye eat, or drink, or whatsoever ye do, do all to the glory of God." There were several other verses she wanted explained, and then by a little gentle questioning, I learned some more of the trouble between her and Rakel, who she said was always teasing her, using her books, and leaving them about carelessly. Then she hung her head and confessed that when she found her Bible on the divan, and Fido tearing out a leaf, she had at once blamed Rakel, and retaliated by getting her Bible and banging it on to the floor.

"Was that right, Sarra? Do you think that was one way to glorify God?"

"No," she replied honestly, but her voice was low and husky. Then we talked of the way Christ bore with men and their cruelty and sins, and we asked him to make us gentle and patient, kind to others, even when they were unkind to us.

The retiring bell tinkled through the hall, and so ended the beautiful, blessed day.

HARRIET G. POWERS, *in the Evangelist.*

GOOD FUN!

THE BATTLE IS ON.

HE WAS COMING FROM THE OLD WELL.

"WHAT IF I HAD!"

EW YEAR'S morning and the snow lying deep over all the paths, drifted even to the tops of the fences! Plenty of work for Stephen Watson; he frowned a little as he looked out of his attic window in the cold gray of the early morning and saw his nicely-made paths all carefully covered. But almost before the frown had cleared away he laughed, and broke at last into a cheery whistle. " No great loss without some gain." He stopped to make this wise remark aloud, then went on with his whistling. What he longed for just now was a holiday—a chance to take a run across lots to Dick Wheeler's home and see the new book which his uncle sent him for Christmas. A beautifully bound book with "oceans of pictures," and telling all about a journey to Europe. " Not a stupid history," Dick reported, " but a regular story, telling all about how some folks went and had jolly times, and saw no end of things, and described them." Stephen's brain was fairly whirling with a desire to examine this book. It may as well be owned that a book of almost any sort had wonderful attractions for this boy; and books and papers, and indeed reading matter of any kind, were painfully scarce in the country farmhouse where Stephen was chore boy. Mrs. Griggs, the mistress, did not more than half believe in them; she eyed even Stephen's Geography with suspicion, and occasionally asked her husband " What sense there was in that boy's learning where all the rivers and mountains in creation with outlandish names were to be found. What good would

it do him? He would never find them outside of a book."

Well, Stephen had smiled and whistled, because he saw that this heavy fall of snow was likely to further his plans for a holiday. If it had only drifted enough to make the roads to the ledge farm impassable then Mr. and Mrs. Griggs would stay at home and take care of the house, and when his chores were done, he might possibly be allowed to go over to Dick's.

Everything seemed to be shaping according to his plans. Mr. Griggs remarked at the breakfast table that there "wouldn't be no sense in trying to get to Mary Ann's that day; the ledge road always drifted if it could get a chance, and the wind was still blowing in that direction." Mrs. Griggs had sighed, it is true, and said that "Mary Ann would be dreadfully disappointed," but she, too, had said that she supposed there was no use in trying to go.

Stephen went about his chores with a will, a trifle sorry for Mrs. Griggs, and a little curious over the idea that anybody in the world could be much disappointed over not receiving a visit from her and Mr. Griggs. "But then I suppose it is because they are her father and mother, and that makes a difference," said this orphan boy, with a sigh. But he could not help being glad that they were not to go. What if he got the chores all done so early that there were several hours before dinner, and Mr. Griggs would let him go in the forenoon? Wouldn't that be a lark worthy of the day! Dick Wheeler's mother was always good-natured, and twice she had asked him to stay to supper with Dick; there was everything to be hoped for in that direction. He was coming from the old well with two brimming pails of water, when Mr. Griggs, out by the ash barrel, with his hands in his pockets to keep them warm, dashed the boy's hopes to the ground. "Got about through, Stephen? Then I guess you may hitch up, after all. The wind has gone down, and Mis' Griggs is disappointed, and she thinks we better try it. You may get things ready as fast as you can; we ought to be off if we are going; then you'll have a long warm day in the kitchen. Don't on no account leave the place; that wouldn't do, of course."

Not a word said Stephen, though he would like to have thrown the pails of water over Mr. Griggs, and kicked the empty pails into a snow-drift. He had never been so disappointed in his life! "A long warm day in the kitchen!" If there was any day which he utterly hated it was such an one; not even a new almanac to read — Farmer Griggs had been waiting for one to be sent to him from somewhere, and it had not come. Of course there was nothing to do but obey; but Stephen felt that he hated New Year's dinners, and wished that "Mary Ann" lived fifty miles away, and hoped that Farmer Griggs would encounter a drift so deep that Mother Griggs would be rolled over in the snow! Oh! he was fierce enough to wish almost anything.

It was because of all this that a very glum-faced boy looked out of the small-paned kitchen window about two hours afterwards, and watched a single horse and cutter skim gaily along. Only one person in the sleigh, and he muffled in furs, and looking as though life was one long holiday. Stephen believed that everybody but himself was having a holiday. Suddenly the sleigh drew up in front of their gate. "Halloo!" said the man in furs, and Stephen ran out and down the snowy path. "Good-morning! Happy New Year," said a pleasant voice. "Can you tell me whether this is the right road to Mr. Bennett's farm?"

"Yes, sir, it is."

"How far from here to Mr. Bennett's?"

"Five miles, sir; but there are none of them at home."

"They are not? How do you know that?"

"I know the boy who drives their horses, and he went by awhile ago; he was on his way back from Dr. Freeman's, where he had been to take Miss Carrie — Mr. Bennett's daughter — and the boy said her folks were all away for the day, and he was going to his grandmother's to dinner."

Stephen could not help adding that last, because it had been a very bitter drop in his cup of trouble. Mr. Bennett's house could stay alone, it seemed, while the boy went to his grandmother's to dinner, whereas this old farm-house had to be watched as though there was danger of its running away.

"That is the state of things, is it?" said the stranger. "Thank you; I do not care to take a five-mile drive through these drifts to find a shut-up house. Can you tell me where Dr. Freeman lives?"

"He lives about a mile from here; but Miss Carrie Bennett isn't there now, sir; she has gone with Miss Freeman to bring a Miss Banks, who lives two miles west, to eat dinner with them at the doctor's." Stephen told this story with an amused twinkle in his eye; it struck him as a queer thing that he should be so well posted concerning matters which evidently interested this handsome stranger. The stranger turned on him a keen, questioning glance. "You seem to understand your neighbors' affairs very well indeed, my boy. How does it happen?"

Stephen laughed. "Why, Pete just happened to tell me about it, sir; he said he was in luck, and did not have to drive them there himself, because the doctor's team drove up in just the nick of time and took them. Everybody is in luck except me."

"Is that so?" asked the stranger, his face breaking into a genial smile. "I am certainly, since I have found a quick-witted boy who has saved me ten miles of useless driving. Can you do me another favor now, and let me come in and visit with you for awhile, until in your judgment the doctor's team has had time to find Miss Banks and bring her back? I do not happen to be acquainted with any of the party save Miss Bennett, and would prefer waiting until she is there before I make my call."

Mr. Griggs never refused travelers a chance to warm, and of course Stephen invited this one into the house and did the honors of the kitchen as well as he could. Somehow — he never quite understood how it was — he found himself telling the story of his bitter disappointment to this stranger — all about the wonderful book full of pictures and stories of travel. He was astonished afterwards to think how much he talked; but then, the stranger listened so kindly, and his eyes were so bright, and his smile so pleasant, and he asked so many questions, it seemed impossible not to confide in him.

"So you like books," he said, as at last he arose; "and books of travel? Well, I do my-self; and it happens curiously enough that I have a package of books in my sleigh at this moment, two of which I think you would enjoy. I was taking them to a nephew of mine, and missed seeing him; probably because it was intended that you should have them instead. I owe you a debt of gratitude; and I'll exchange the information you gave me for whatever information you can find in the books, which are yours to keep, you understand. And now don't you think Miss Banks may have arrived at the doctor's by this time?"

Stephen helped him off in good style, but in such a flutter of excitement that he could hardly respond to the cheery "good-by," for in his hands were two very large, very handsomely bound books, sparkling with pictures, and with the most inviting-looking reading. They must certainly be larger than Dick Wheeler's one, for that had been minutely described to him. Besides, there were two of these; and besides, oh! besides, they were his very own, to keep!

As he turned the leaves, like one in fairyland, he said aloud, "What if I had got a chance to go to Dick Wheeler's this morning and missed this? O, my! what if I had!"   PANSY.

LOOK OUT! WE'RE COMING.

BABY'S CORNER.

WHAT HAPPENED TO BUNNY.

BUNNY is the name of a squirrel with a very long tail.

When nuts were ripe Bunny worked hard to pick them and store them up for his family to live on through the cold winter.

His house was in a big hollow tree. The door to it was a little round hole. He had a nice large pantry.

All day long, in the pleasant Oc-to-ber weather, when children were playing, Bunny was picking nuts and scampering down the trees to put them safe in his pantry.

He had a good many kinds of nuts. There were butternuts and wal-nuts and chestnuts, and tiny beechnuts for the teeny weeny squirrels. At last Bunny's pantry was full, and he was all ready for December with its cold winds and snow-flakes.

One morning something happened! Just as Bunny started out he found a wire cage in front of his door. He thought it was a pretty little house, so he walked in.

Snap! went the door of this pretty little house, and shut itself tight.

Bunny tried on every side to get out, but he could not. He was in a prison.

While he wondered what he should do a big boy came and looked at him.

"Hurrah!" he said.

Then big boy took up the cage and carried it off home.

He gave Bunny to his little sister Susie.

Susie was kind to Bunny. She put him in a basket with a soft bed and gave him cake and candy.

But Bunny was not happy. He was too warm in the house with his fur coat on, and he wanted to get back to his dear children. He would not play; he sat still and looked sad.

"Poor Bunny!" said Susie's mamma; "he is used to being outdoors, and frisking about. He wants to see his little children and eat the nuts he laid up."

"Then he shall go," Susie said.

"THEN HE SHALL GO."

So she told him good-by, and carried the cage out in the garden and opened its door.

Away went Bunny! He scampered over the fence and whisked up a tall tree as quick as wink.

How happy he was to get to his hollow tree once more.

Was not Susie a nice little girl?

MRS. C. M. LIVINGSTON.

A LONG CHRISTMAS.

PART II.

IT was a January night, very cold. The snow which was always on the mountains looked down on the snow which sometimes melted from the valleys, and seemed to smile at it in a hard, cold way, for supposing itself to be of any importance at all. · The white cross made by the peculiar shape of the mountains, and the action of the sun on the snow, gleamed in the moonlight more beautiful than usual to Teddy Simpson, as he pushed back the overcoat several times too large for him, thrust his hands into his pockets, and leaned against the snow-covered hill to think. Hundreds of stars twinkled down upon him, brighter and more filled with jewels than they ever are in any other sky, I think; but Teddy's thoughts were not of them.

He was waiting for the teamster whose route lay along this mountain side, and who always brought the mail from the distant settlement, as well as any supplies or packages which the miners might need. Not that Teddy expected any mail! Bless your heart, he had never received a letter in his life, nor even a paper through the mails. To have done so even once would have almost taken his breath away. Yet he was deeply interested in the teamster's wagon; as he stood still in the moonlight to think, there was an eager look in his eyes, and he listened for the sound of the cracking whip with such an air of expectancy as his face did not often wear. The fact is, Teddy Simpson had planned a wonderful surprise for his mother which his friend the teamster was helping him to carry out. Very poor they were, he and his mother; she cooked for the miners, and washed for them, and mended their clothes, but the miners, too, were poor, and could pay but little. The truth is, the people who lived and worked in this beautiful, desolate region were all poor together. Teddy had had plans, beautiful plans, for the Christmas three weeks behind him, and had failed in them. He and his

mother knew all about Christmas; had not she hung up her stocking every year of her life until she was a great girl fifteen years old? Teddy never had, because Santa Claus seemed never to get so far West as where he lived; but while the father was alive Teddy always had at least one Christmas present, if it was nothing but a picture cut from some of the illustrated papers of the tourists, and framed by his mother with some bits of bright paper laid away for such purposes. Teddy had been a man grown now for two years — at least he felt like one — with no time for such trifles; but he had longed to make a bright Christmas for the miner's family with five little children, their nearest neighbors. If his mother had not had a sick day when he was obliged to do her work as well as he could, and in doing it wasted some of the material and lost a good deal of time, he thought he should have accomplished it. As it was, he could not get the Christmas treat ready for them, but promised himself that another year he would be on hand. Then he had turned his thoughts to a surprise for his mother. That, too, had been a Christmas plan, but failing then, he resolved that he would not wait for the next season. The surprise was nothing more nor less than a half-pound of the best tea which the silver half-dollar he had sent by the teamster could supply. The poor little overworked mother was very fond of tea; he had often heard her say that a good cup of it after a hard day's work seemed to rest her as nothing else would; but since the father died, she had bravely put it aside as one of the luxuries which they could not now afford.

If there were time to tell you how long and hard Teddy had worked for that extra half-dollar, never taking a cent for it from the regular wages of the day which he earned as his share of the family support, you would not wonder that he had grown almost feverish in his anxiety as the weeks went on, lest he should fail in having the right amount. He had accomplished it, and the day had come for the teamster to go on his fortnightly trip, and the day and evening had arrived for his return, and here at a bend in the road Teddy waited for him.

Away in the distance on the still frosty air broke at la t the sound of a cheery whistle, and Teddy held himself still and listened. Jim Coon, the teamster, was a friend of his, and Teddy did not believe he would whistle if anything so cruel had happened as that the supply grocer had been out of tea.

"Halloo!" said Jim, as he came with a flourish around the bend in the snowy road, "waitin', be you? I thought it was a ghost froze stiff to the rocks. Climb up here, and we'll be home in a jiffy. Beats all what a hurry this team has been in this afternoon—all owing to you, I s'pose. O, yes! I got it, safe and sound; the very best kind of tea ever brought to these parts, Joe Derrick says, and he put in a good big half-pound of it, I'm witness to that."

Then Teddy drew a long breath, and immediately the longing which he had kept in the background came to the front; also the problem over which he had been studying for weeks. Wouldn't it on the whole have been better to have gotten a quarter of a pound of tea and spent the rest of the money in sugar? mother did so like a little sugar with her tea. But then, a quarter of a pound seemed such a very little bit, and the winter was long in this mountain region, and there was no telling when he would have a chance to get any more. But he wished, O, so much! that he knew how to get just a little sugar; that would make the present complete.

"I got somethin' else," said Jim, with a curious note of suppressed excitement in his tones; "somethin' for you."

"For me?" echoed Teddy, amazed.

"Yes, sir, for you; Teddy Simpson is the name on the box, as large as life."

"On the box!" In his astonishment and excitement all that Teddy could do was to echo Jim's words.

"Yes, sir, on the box; a good-sized box, and as heavy as though it had been stuffed with lead. Come by freight; got there yesterday just about an hour before I drove into town; come all the way from New York State, too."

After that, the quarter of a mile between Teddy Simpson and home seemed endless. A box by freight for him! What would mother

think, and the neighbors! Above all, what could be in the box?

Before it was half-unpacked the question became what was not in it? Two suits of clothes for Teddy, two new dresses for his mother—or dresses quite as good as new—a warm, bright shawl, and a fur hood. Shoes, and stockings, and socks, and mittens, and oh! books, and papers, and pictures, and more books. Was ever anything so wonderful? Then there were toys—dolls, and balls, and tops, and wooden dogs, and wax cats, and cloth elephants—and some little bits of dresses and sacks which could fit only the children further down the mountain. Teddy felt this, even before he discovered that these were all labeled, "For Teddy to give to his friends, the little Perkinses." Moreover, there was a little leather bag in the very bottom of the box, drawn together by a bright cord and securely tied, which when opened was found to contain seventeen bright silver dollars, the gifts of the cousins and aunts and uncles for Teddy to use as he thought best. Do you want to know what he thought of first? A whole pound of sugar to go with that half-pound of tea which was still lying snugly in his overcoat pocket, where Teddy meant to leave it until the next morning. Such a box as that, and a half pound of tea in the bargain, he considered altogether too much for his mother's nerves in one evening.

Such a wonderful morning as it was—such a wonderful day, indeed! The Perkinses were hopelessly wild all day, and their poor little half-discouraged mother was not much better.

The next time teamster Jim went over the snow road between the mountains he carried a fat little letter written in Teddy's best round hand—and he was by no means a bad writer; his mother had taught him. In this letter he described to the cousins just how he stood by the rocks and waited for Jim Coon's team, just how surprised he was, just how the box was opened, just what he and his mother exclaimed as long as they had any breath for exclaiming, just how the Perkinses acted the next day—at least as well as language would do it—and altogether wrote so surprising a letter that Hortense said, drawing a long sigh of delight:

"Isn't it lovely? Hasn't this been a long Christmas? It is better than the Christmas-tree a great deal, isn't it?"

"It is the jolliest Christmas I ever had," said Holly.

"And it has taught us how to have some more jolly ones," said Tom.

As for Tom's father, he said: "That boy Teddy is a smart fellow; he ought to have an education. There ought to be a good school out there. Why wouldn't that be a good place for us to send Richard Winston? He would be a grand fellow to work among just such people."

So the "long Christmas" is in a fair way to grow longer, you see, for every cousin in the three homes is interested in Tom's father's idea, and so is Richard Winston.

PANSY.

"HE STOOD STILL IN THE MOONLIGHT TO THINK."

SOMETHING FOR MAMMA.

YOU want it for Christmas, of course; and you are a little girl who has very few pennies of your own to spend; and mamma, like other mammas, thinks that something which her daughter has made with her own hands is of far more value than an article, however fine, bought at a store. You have been disconsolate for several days because there are so few "things" which you know how to make, and because you have so little money with which to buy material. Take heart, my dear, there are happy surprises in store for mamma.

How much money have you for this particular gift? "Twenty-five cents," and you blush and are troubled, and say in your heart, "Just as though anything worth having could be made for twenty-five cents!" Why, my dear, that is enough and to spare. Did you notice the table mats yesterday at dinner? They are made of bits of oiled wood ingeniously put together, and in their prime were pretty, and rather expensive; but they are sadly worn now — so much so, indeed, that Hannah declared only yesterday that she did not know what to do with the things; they were so much worn that she could not wash them any more. She knew what she would like to do with them; if she had her way she would "chuck" them into the fire.

What I propose is, that you plan your Christmas present so that Hannah can have the pleasure of doing just that thing.

What you want is a ball of macremé cord, of a delicate creamy tint, price fifteen cents, and a ball of candle wicking for three cents, or possibly five, though it ought not to be if your merchants are up with city prices. Positively that is all. O, yes! a crochet needle, large size; but that of course you have; or if not, I am almost certain that mamma, or better still grandma, will make you a present of one, because of the many useful things you can make with it; still, if you wish to be entirely independent, why, buy one, for five cents surely (a large price), and you are ready.

Hold the end of candle wicking over your left forefinger and crochet the macremé cord over it with what is known as the long stitch; it is very rapid work after you have once mastered the stitch, and before you realize it, you will have a long, long rope of creamy cord. Do not pull hard on the crochet cord, but let the work lie up loose and fluffy. When you think you have enough done to experiment with, get your neat little work box, thread a needle with strong cotton — number thirty being a very good size — curl the beginning of your cord into a graceful circle, and take firm stitches on the under side to hold it there; then another coil, and another, sewed neatly and firmly, and continue until you have a table mat large enough round to take the vegetable dishes, or the soup tureen, or whatever you wish to set on it. Then cut off the supply, fasten the end firmly, and finish the whole with a pretty crocheted scallop all around. Just compare that mat with the slippery, stained wood one with frayed edges! You admire it now, but what will it be when Hannah has washed and starched it until it holds its shape as firmly as the wooden one, and yet is flexible and graceful? More of them? Certainly, an entire set, varying in size to match the uses to which they are to be put.

Have I made a mistake? Are your vegetable dishes all oval? Well, my dear, your table water pitcher is not, I am sure. Just use this first one for it, and start your next sewing with an oval shape instead of a circle; it must be a very small oval for the beginning — not over three quarters of an inch in length — else your mat will grow too long for its width. Your best plan would be to experiment a little. Lay the work loosely, confined by a mere basting stitch, and see whether, when the mat has grown as long as your paper pattern, it will be of the proper width. You will not find the planning difficult; it merely needs the patience and carefulness which I feel sure you will bestow; and the result will be an entire nest of pretty and useful mats which will be a delightful surprise to mamma on Christmas morning, and a comfort to her as well as to Hannah throughout the year. Try it, and be sure to let me hear how you succeeded.　　　　　　　　PANSY.

CHRISTMAS EVENING.

ETHEL CARLISLE'S FACE.

(Character Studies.)

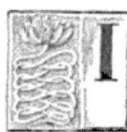I CAN see her now as she looked to me that winter morning wrapped in furs, ready all but her fur cap to brave the frosty air, when she held up in triumph a spray of brilliant bloom, and said: "Look, Aunt Myra, did you ever see anything prettier than that from a conservatory? And they blossomed in my window-seat!" I was not her auntie, but was so old and intimate a friend of the family that the children had adopted me.

"Hasn't Ethel a beautiful face?" I said to Miss Margaret, another friend of the family, who, with myself, was a guest at the Carlisles'. "It is so very bright. Did you notice what a peculiar brightness there is to her eyes when she smiles? And she has a lovely smile."

Miss Margaret looked grave, almost troubled. "It is a sweeter face than it will be in a few years, I am afraid," she said, shaking her head, which already had threads of silver in it. Miss Margaret was a wise sweet woman, not given to croaking, so I waited somewhat anxiously to hear her words. "Ethel is cultivating habits which will spoil her face," she said; "I have not been here before for two years, and I notice a very decided change in it since then. She was one of the sweetest little children I ever knew, but if you watch through only one day you will discover what I mean. Unless something occurs to change her habits, there will be another spoiled face in the world in a few years."

I had been in the house but a day, and had been absent from the country for more than two years, so I knew very little of the younger Carlisles. Ethel had always been my favorite, and it made me sad and a trifle annoyed to hear Miss Margaret's words. I felt sure she must have grown over particular.

Of course, with such a warning, it would have been impossible not to have watched. Long before night I knew what Miss Margaret meant.

"Where in the world is my French Grammar?" I heard Ethel's voice, with a very sharp note in it, rasping through the hall. "I left it on the dining-room table while I ran out to speak to Nellie, and somebody has taken it. I declare, I cannot lay down a thing for a second and find it again. I do wish Ann could be taught to let my books alone!"

"Indeed, Miss Ethel, I have not touched a book this morning; I have not dusted in the dining-room yet." This was Ann's voice; then Ethel's, by no means sweetened: "That is perfect nonsense, Ann; I left it here not two minutes ago, and now it is gone. What do you think could have become of it? It couldn't walk off without hands."

"Ethel!" from Mrs. Carlisle, in a reproving tone, "do not speak so to Ann, daughter; she has not been in the dining-room since breakfast."

"Well, but, mother, my French Grammar is gone that I just laid there, and the bell is ringing; I shall be late, and I think it is just too bad!" There was an ugly frown all over the fair forehead, and a sharp and at the same time whining tone to the voice which had been so sweet but a little while before.

"Ethel," called her older sister Nannie from the hall above, "here is your book; you left it on the hat rack a few minutes ago."

Away went Ethel without a word of explanation to mother or to Ann, and we heard her voice, still sharp, saying to Nannie, "Why couldn't you have told me before, and not kept me hunting half the morning?"

I heard the mother sigh, and was sorry for her, and glad that the alcove curtains shaded me from view, and that I had a book in my hand and could appear not to have heard.

Ethel came home at lunch time, and was out of sorts with the soup because it tasted of onions, and with the squash because it had been peppered. She said she wished anybody ever consulted her tastes, and she would just as soon think of puffing tobacco smoke in the face of people as of eating onions for them to smell afterwards. She scolded her brother Tom for forgetting the music he was to call for; and when he said he was very sorry, and it was because he had so many important errands for his father that he forgot it, she tossed her head and said sharply, "Oh! you needn't

ETHEL HELD UP A SPRAY OF BRILLIANT BLOOM.

explain; of course you would forget what I wanted; I'm of no consequence."

In short, with my eyes opened as they had been by Miss Margaret I could not help seeing that Ethel spoiled the sweetness of almost every room she entered that day, and complained of unkindness or of discomforts at every turn. Yet at family worship, when she played,

"Sun of my soul, thou Saviour dear,"

and led the singing with a very sweet voice, she looked like an angel. It broke my heart to hear her, not ten minutes afterwards, scolding Baby Frank for overturning her spool basket. "You are just a little nuisance!" she said, sharp-voiced again; "I think mamma ought to whip you. Well, mamma, I do," in response to a reproving look from her mother; "you are just spoiling him, I think."

"Is it possible that this is a fair specimen of that child's days?" I asked Miss Margaret.

"I am afraid it is," said Miss Margaret. "She is learning to frown and fret over the veriest trifles, and to answer even her mother rudely, as you noticed just now. How many years of such living will it take to utterly spoil the pretty face? Isn't it strange that a young girl who believes herself such an ardent admirer of beauty, should deliberately undertake to spoil the lovely work of art which God gave her to take care of?"   MYRA SPAFFORD.

ORIGIN OF A NEW ENGLAND INDUSTRY.

IN 1798 Betsey Metcalf, of Dedham, Mass., made a bonnet out of oat straw, fashioning it after an English bonnet then very fashionable. She flattened the straw with the blade of her scissors, split it with her thumb nail, braided it into the requisite number of strands and bleached it by holding it over the vapor of burning sulphur. She afterward taught the young ladies of her vicinity how to do it, and thus laid the foundation of the extensive business now carried on in straw hats in New England. — *Selected.*

MOTHER DUNLAP'S STORY.

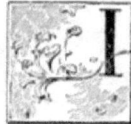

IF my father and mother had been at home it would never have happened, but they started in the morning as soon as they could see the road for my Aunt Margaret's, taking Emeline with them. I remember just how I felt when I saw them drive from our gate with Emeline sitting between them; it seemed so terrible, somehow, to think of her sitting in my place, because I was the one who always sat between father and mother. But Cousin Emeline was Aunt Margaret's little girl, and word had come that Aunt Margaret was very sick, and that Emeline must be brought home as fast as possible; so of course they started, though there was every sign of a storm, Uncle Peter said, and he hardly ever made a mistake in the weather. He was our "signal service" in those days. Cousin Edward was at our house, too; he was Uncle Edward's son, and always spent his short vacation with us, because his folks lived too far away for him to go home. He was thirteen years old, and thought he knew all there was to know in life. He was a smart fellow, and would have been real nice if he had not felt so sure of it himself. Father and mother had not been gone an hour when he began to plan to drive to town to the New Year festival which was to be held in one of the churches, and take me along. Kirke said everything in the world to hinder us from going; he thought it was going to storm.

"Who's afraid of a few snowflakes?" said Edward. "I want Nannie to have a cheery time for New Year's; it is dreadful dull for her with Auntie and Uncle both gone."

Kirke was a boy who did chores at our house for his board, and went to school; we lived two miles nearer the schoolhouse than his mother did, and they were pretty poor, and Kirke earning his board away from home helped them a good deal. We all loved Kirke; he was a good sensible boy, and stood at the head of his classes in school. But I did not approve of him that day; I wanted to go to town. I was a silly little thing in those days, not afraid of anything; I laughed at the storm just as Edward did.

"It will be more than a few flakes," Kirke said, shaking his head gravely; "I think we are going to have the worst storm of the season." Then Edward began to make fun of him — call him Uncle Peter, and ask what kind of a winter it was forty years ago; because Uncle Peter was always going back to old times and telling stories about the weather. Kirke kept good-natured, and laughed with me over Edward's speeches, but for all that he did not stop trying to keep us from going to town.

"Look here," he said, "I have a tip-top plan for this afternoon. Mrs. Baker gave me a jug of molasses and some splendid ears of pop-corn to take home; suppose you and Nannie walk out home with me, and we will pop some corn, and make candy with hickory nuts in? We've got a bushel of nuts stored away in the garret, and we'll have no end of fun. Nannie can stay all night — she has done it before, you know — and sleep with my sister Mary, and you and I will turn in with little Billy up in the attic; he likes company."

The picture looked quite inviting to me; I had often been out to Kirke's house, for my father and mother liked their family very much, and were always willing to have me play with their children.

But Edward was not to be persuaded. "No, you don't, old fellow," he said; "candy and nuts are first-rate things for any night in the year but New Year's; a fellow needs something extra then. I've set my heart on seeing the festival tables, and watching them give out the prizes, and I'm going; my uncle said three days ago that I could."

"But he did not know that it was going to snow," Kirke said, more and more anxious. "Really, Edward, I do not think Mr. and Mrs. Baker would like to have you take Nannie out when it looks so much like a storm." Then Edward got angry and told Kirke to mind his own business, that we were not left in his charge at least, and that he should do as he liked; and Kirke was to remember that Mr. and Mrs. Baker were his own uncle and aunt, and that he might be supposed to know as much

about what they would like as a stranger could. Kirke said no more, but he looked very much troubled. I was half-disposed to give up the plan, but Edward laughed at me. The good-natured housekeeper in whose care we were left never paid much attention to the weather, and made no objection to my going. I don't know but that it would have come out all right even then, if Edward's pride had not got the upper hand. He took a notion to drive to town by the old road.

"O, don't!" I urged; "you do not know that way at all, and Uncle Peter said this morning that the wind last night must have drifted the snow on the old road."

"Poh!" said Edward, "Uncle Peter is an old croaker; he's an old man, Nannie, and always makes mountains out of molehills. The wind will be at our backs part of the time on the old road, and I'm going that way. What if I have not driven it? The horse won't get lost, if you think I will."

Well, we started, and for the first ten minutes everything was right; then we began to come to drifts, and I was dreadfully scared. We almost turned over two or three times. I kept squealing out, and that provoked Edward. "Keep still," he would say; "I did not know you were such a little coward." To make matters worse, it began to snow harder than I ever saw it before, and grew so dark that we could hardly see our way. We had been riding a good while, and ought to have reached the town, but no sign of a town was to be seen.

After a while Edward made up his mind that he must have taken the wrong turn, and said he was going back a little way to see if he had. He tried to turn around, but the wind blew so that the snow blinded his eyes; and it was not a good place for turning around, any way. The first thing I knew over went the sleigh, and I was in a snowdrift! That was not the worst of it, either; the runner of the sleigh snapped as if it had been a pipe-stem. Good old Jim stood still, fortunately. But there we were with a driving storm, with a broken sleigh! I do not think I was ever so glad of anything in my life as I was to hear Kirke's voice above the roar of the wind.

"What in the world are you doing there?" he said, bounding along over drifts of snow. "Is Nannie hurt? If she is not all right never mind anything else. Oh! the sleigh is broken. How came you to be on this road? This is not the way to town; it is an old wood road that was used early in the winter, but it is all snowed up; you could not have got much farther; you ought to have turned to the right a mile below here; I thought you knew the way. Now I'll tell you what will have to be done. Nannie must go to our house — it is less than a quarter

nie to your house I'll get this rig home myself and take care of Jim; it is not fair that you should lose your New Year's fun to help me out. I'll foot it out to your house if it is not too late after I have been to see Mr. Ormstead about mending this sleigh; but I'm not going to let you go for me a single step."

No amount of coaxing could turn him from his purpose. So at last Kirke, after helping him to tie up the runner with some twine which they found in their pockets, tucked me under his arm, and we marched off to their little house.

"THERE WE WERE, WITH A BROKEN SLEIGH!"

of a mile from here — and I'll get a rope and tie up that sleigh somehow, enough to get it and Jim back to the stable; then I'll tell your folks that you are going to stay at our house all night — shall I?"

He seemed to have forgotten how disagreeably Edward had spoken to him, and was just as nice as could be. But Edward's cheeks were pretty red. "No, sir," he said firmly; "I started out to have my own way and ought to have the benefit of it. If you will take Nan-

Their kitchen was the cleanest, brightest, cheeriest place you ever saw, and the molasses taffy was splendid. I had a lovely time; but there was such a dreadful storm that Edward could not get back that night, and Jim had lamed himself somehow in stumbling through deep drifts; and it cost four dollars to mend the sleigh, which Edward had to pay, because my father said he did not believe in boys having their own way and not being willing to take the consequences. To be sure he gave the

THEY STARTED FOR AUNT MARGARET'S. ("Mother Dunlop's Story.")

money back again, and more too, when Edward's next birthday came. But I don't think Edward ever forgot the lesson. I ought to have been punished too, for I pretended to agree with Edward, even when I thought he was foolish; but some way I slipped through the trouble and had all the pleasure, just as girls often do, I think.

"Mother," said little Cathie Dunlap, "father's middle name is Kirke; did he have anything to do with the nice boy who took care of you?"

"Why, yes," said Mother Dunlap, laughing, "come to think of it, his full name was William Kirke Dunlap."

MYRA SPAFFORD.

HUNGER AND THIRST.

THERE is a story of a little boy who was very fond of angling, and who one day told his grandfather that he had caught a fish as large as a horse.

"Look here, Tom," said the old man, "don't you know it's wrong for a little boy like you to tell such a big untruth? You are not six years, are you?"

"No," said Tommy; "I am only five, and I'll not do it again. After this I'm going to tell only little bits of fish stories."

That boy often reminds one of people who talk about being "temperate" and "moderate" in the use of things which they ought to let alone altogether. A little glass of strong drink, a little cigar, are just as certainly wrong as a little untruth.

But how can we know what is good or bad for the body? The answer is, that our body itself will tell us. The body has a conscience as well as the soul. Put your hand into a potful of warm water, and your hand will at once let you know if the water is too hot. Go out sleigh-riding in a light straw hat on a cold winter morning, and your ears will soon ask for a warmer cover. After a laborer has been hard at work for eight or ten hours, his body will ask for rest. Make a child sit down in a chair without moving for six hours, and its body will ask for exercise. Our body soon lets us know if a coat or a shoe is too tight, or if a burden is too heavy. And it can just as certainly be relied upon to warn us against unwholesome food. It is true that we can silence that voice of our body's conscience. After a man has swallowed a good many glasses of bad drink or smoked a cigar every morning for a couple of weeks, he at last gets "used to it," as we call it; his nature gets changed, and at last he is unable to let such things alone. But at the first trial our sense of taste will plainly warn us against unwholesome food and drink. Before an apple is ripe it tastes sour. The taste of over-ripe or spoiled fruit gets more and more disagreeable.

An Italian naturalist, during his travels in Southern Africa, noticed that a little pet monkey of his never made a mistake in choosing its food, and could tell poisonous herbs and berries from good ones the moment he tasted them. The traveler made that little creature his kitchen master, as he called it, and always let it try a bit of every kind of food that was offered to him for sale. "If Jocko ate a spoonful of honey and stretched out his hand for more," he writes, "I was satisfied that it was worth buying; if the little chap grinned and flung the sample away, I felt sure that the bees must have gathered their honey from poisonous flowers. Jocko never made mistakes in such things, and that our own people blundered so often might be explained by the fact that we have blunted our sense of taste with strong drink and hot spices."

A boy who has been brought up on perfectly wholesome food can tell injurious things almost as quick as that little monkey. He will dislike the taste of sharp pepper sauces, of pickles, of strong cheese, of spoiled meat, and will not be apt to mistake a bitter swamp berry for a huckleberry.

Our stomach also lets us know when we should stop eating. In that case, too, it is not safe to disregard the warnings of our bodily conscience. If a boy keeps eating, just to while time away, after he feels that he has had enough, and after his stomach has asked him again and again to stop, his nature at last changes, and he wants to be stuffing himself all the time. I knew a little chap of ten years who seemed to think it a pity to lose a chance for gorging himself, and who had to be watched like a tricky cat to keep him from slipping into his mother's pantry and helping himself to all the good things in sight. On his way to school he would stop to buy a package of peanuts or pick up a pocketful of apples on the outside of an orchard, and when he came home for dinner he ate away as if nothing had happened. All his schoolmates called him "Glutton Joe."

Such gluttons are apt to think that they are getting more fun out of life than other people. The truth is, that they hardly ever know an hour of real happiness. They feel dull and weary; they become too sluggish to play; they take no interest in their studies, and drop a new book or new paper after a short look at the pictures; they would rather not know the end of a pretty story than go to the trouble of reading it through. They feel drowsy as soon as the weather gets a little warm, but when they go to sleep their rest is broken by ugly dreams. Glutton Joe had no friends; he was so cross and lazy that nobody wanted him for a playmate.

An old fisherman once told me that it was worth while going out sailing in bad, chilly weather, just for the fun of getting home again and taking a rest in a warm chimney-corner, and I have often thought that many people would find it worth while to fast once in a while, when they begin to complain that they cannot enjoy their meals. After a day's exercise in the woods and mountains the plainest food tastes well. A supper of bread, milk and huckleberries tastes better to the poor Tennessee mountain boy, who has been out herding cows all day, than a banquet of thirty dishes tastes to a rich merchant who has not yet digested his last meal. There is no danger in an occasional fast, though some people seem to think it a misfortune to miss one of their three daily meals. There was a time when rich and poor thought it enough to eat one good meal a day. The old Romans and Greeks ate a biscuit and perhaps half a handful of dried fruit in the morning, and then did not eat again till they had finished their day's work, when they took a bath, changed their dress, and then sat down to a good supper. An Indian hunter thinks nothing of going a day without any food at all. A few years ago an American physician thought it worth while to try how long a man could fast without hurting himself. People thought he was crazy, and told him he would kill himself in less than a week. He made no reply, and his friends changed their opinion when he had fasted forty days and nights. Few of those friends would have cared to try their own pluck in that manner, but they would certainly have been ashamed to complain of an accident that might lose them a dinner and oblige them to eat their principal meal in the evening.

But though there can be no harm in a day's fast, it is never safe to suffer for want of drinking water. The same doctor who passed nearly six weeks without a mouthful of food, took a sip of cold lemonade every few hours, and it is a curious fact that in warm weather a glass of water served with our dinner is by far the most important part of the meal. Hunger, or what we call a "good appetite," often stops after the mealtime has passed without a chance of getting a mouthful of food, but thirst cannot be put off in that way, and becomes at last so intolerable that a starved traveler, after a three days' journey in the desert, would give a wagon-load of food for a drink of cold water.

FELIX L. OSWALD, M. D.

WOULD AND SHOULD.

A PUPIL in a quiet boarding-school in —— displayed some time since no small degree of industry in collecting autographs of distinguished persons. The late James Russell Lowell was one of the number addressed. The address to him was in substance: "I would be very much obliged for your autograph." The response contained a lesson that many besides the ambitious pupil have not learned: "Pray do not say hereafter 'I would be obliged.' If you would be obliged, be obliged and be done with it. Say 'I should be obliged,' and oblige yours truly, JAMES RUSSELL LOWELL." — *Selected*.

WESTMINSTER ABBEY.

YOU see it is most beautiful to the eye, though you Pansies of the great cities may think some of your churches quite as handsome. But none of them has such a history. This church was founded — started, as some would say — more than a thousand years ago! Now where's your pretty "meeting-house" which was built only last year?

Old King Siebert, a Saxon, built Westmin-

For years and years the English kings and queens have been crowned here, and buried, too, nearly all. Here the great ones of the nation are buried — Shakespeare, Milton, Ben Jonson, Wordsworth, and many more, the poets in the "Poets' Corner."

Under the coronation (crowning) chair is the "Stone of Scone," which some actually say is the very one Jacob laid his head upon when he dreamed! However that be, many kings have sat upon it when they were crowned.

Of course you will search out the "Jerusalem Chamber" when you visit Westminster. The

A VIEW OF WESTMINSTER ABBEY.

ster Abbey, and many of the Saxons really believed that the Apostle Peter dedicated it, though Peter had died nearly one thousand years before!

However, this building is not the very same that King Siebert put up. That one stood several hundred years, when Edward, "the Confessor," as he was called, rebuilt it. Two hundred years later King Henry the Third enlarged it, making it look about as it now is.

Presbyterian Church began in this chamber. Here, too, the Bible was revised (re-translated from the Hebrew and Greek).

"Why do they call it the 'Jerusalem Chamber'?"

Probably because its windows came from that old city, and the Cedar of Lebanon forms the wainscoting.

So this wonderful building has served many purposes besides that of a church. For some hundred years the House of Commons (something like our House of Representatives) made laws here, especially laws to secure the liberties of the people.

So you see this building is something like Faneuil Hall of Boston and Independence Hall of Philadelphia.

What a book Westminster Abbey could make if it only could write. But somehow, like Nineveh and such places, it will rise up in the Judgment; then what will it say of the people who have had to do with it?   L.

A NEW YEAR'S TRIP:

 O Africa! Yes; here it is '92, January 1, early in the morning, and we are in the sleigh, and away we glide over the snow to Africa, to return to-night.

"Twenty thousand miles in twelve hours, pooh! and going to hot Africa in a sleigh!"

Suppose, then, we just think we are there, and we are there to all intents and purposes.

"Well, here goes; I think I'm in South Africa at the mouth of some diamond hole (tunnel), January 1, '92. Of course I'm there picking up diamonds to bring back for New Year's presents, eh?"

Indeed you—the best part of you, your soul, your thought—are. Just wake up your imagination, and it's about the same. Now you step down into the dark hole. Deeper you descend, as down a steep hill, to the very bottom—eight hundred feet or more—through fields full of diamonds.

See, just before you dim forms. They are naked natives digging. They fill up the small car of dirt, dotted with the precious stones, and away it goes up and out. It dumps its load and returns. It's a dirty, dreadful place. Every little while there's a roar; the ground shakes. There's dynamite blasting to loosen the earth.

Hurry out now; the tunnel may cave in, and you'll be choked, as were several hundred a few years ago.

Here we are outside. See, the ground is two feet deep with the earth carted out. They are harrowing it, or the rain is falling upon it. It is crumbling fine. Ah! see the shining treasures. But look out! Don't put one into your pocket without permission; you are watched.

Now back we come—in thought. There! have not we had one of the brightest New Year's?

Thus brighten up your imagination and you need not be bothering yourself forever with cars and steamboats and ships and seasickness and such things to see foreign lands. With a good book of travels or newspaper you can just trip over there—to Europe, Asia and Africa—in a moment, and see all you can carry back in a few more moments, and be home to tea the same day to show (tell) your treasures! L.

ON A VISIT TO GERMANY.

 ERE we are. It is midwinter—

"In Maine or New Hampshire or Canada, I guess."

Guess again, you mistaken Pansy.

"Norway, then."

Nor Norway, but just simply in Germany.

"Such snow-storms in Germany?"

Yes, and that miss with umbrella and fat face trudging on is—

"Fräulein, I dare say. Isn't that, or something like it, the name of all the German girls?"

Wouldn't that mix things in a family of six girls? Think of a mother calling each one Fräulein!

But that girl is no other than Bessie—

"Bessie a German girl? Never heard one called that in all my life."

Who said she was a German girl? Can't one be in Germany and not be a German? Do you expect to turn into one as soon as you get to—"Sweet Bingen on the Rhine," or Frankfort? Frankfort, once the home of the great poet, Goethe, some of whose sayings it may make your dear head ache to understand. Frankfort, once a free city, as free from any king or great ruler as—the United States is of Mexico; a queer, bright old city—

"Bessie! Bessie! what about Bessie? Won't she be lost in Frankfort? Who is she, any how?"

A Pansy, quite likely from Boston, by that name, on a visit to Germany. She will spend a few months in Frankfort, studying German and seeing the German sights, among them Luther's house.

"But you do not explain what Bessie is doing out in a Frankfort snow-storm."

Maybe she is after red checks; she left Boston looking pale enough. Her mamma thought a sea voyage and a few months in France and as many more in Germany would color her face again with rose tints as formerly. You see how she has improved. Now the Christmas festival of Frankfort begins, lasting three days. There will be trees and trees, and so much more that paper can hardly hold it or ink write it.

Bessie is on her way to the festival to see the German of it with Yankee eyes.   L.

STATUE OF SIR WALTER SCOTT, IN EDINBURGH.

HEN you go to Edinburgh, Scotland — as some day go you may — you must not fail to visit one of the finest structures there, the monument of Sir Walter Scott.

Before you go it would be well to read some of his charming books: Ivanhoe, Old Mortality, Tales of a Grandfather, etc.

The Scottish folks are justly proud of Sir Walter. Few nations have produced so delightful a writer. So no wonder this grand monument was built. It is a Gothic edifice, the top of the spire of which is two hundred feet from the ground. The lower part is open, and here is a fine marble statue of Sir Walter, his favorite dog by his side.

Seventy-five thousand dollars have been put into this edifice! Many of you would be satisfied with a house costing one thousand. Young Walter Scott did not expect to become so great a man when he first took up his pen.   L.

SIR WALTER SCOTT AND HIS BULL-TERRIER, "CAMP."
(From the painting by Raeburn.)

OUT IN A SNOW-STORM.

A HERO.

AT Fort Smith, Ark., is Mrs. Edith M. Degen. She knows a great deal about Mr. "In." If you will write her a letter saying you want to know something more about him, and if you will put in your letter a postal card addressed to yourself, it will soon get back to you with writing on the other side which you will like to read. Try it.

Now this man is really Mr. Lewis F. Hadley of Massachusetts. He has been many years among the Indians, studying their Sign Language.

You see the different tribes of Indians have different mouth or spoken languages, as do white people. To understand each other's speech they must have an interpreter to give its meaning; but they all seem to have about

MR. LEWIS F. HADLEY.

the same sign speech; by using this the different tribes can understand each other when they meet.

You know the deaf and dumb talk with their hands. So with the Indians of different tribes when they can't understand each other's speech. Here is a specimen of the sign language:

Country west I sit writing.
Morning come I give it Fire-
wagon; go fast; pretty soon you catch it.
Day you catch it you show it
man, woman, all Maybe so give it
money print book many. Printing
done, I show it Indian The same
see it, know it good. Done.
Lightning Afraid Not.

Well, Mr. Hadley has been mastering these signs, and now, after many years' hard study, you see he can write it.

"What for?"

To spread knowledge among the Indians. To give them the Gospel — the blessed good news about the Lord who came and died for them.

"But has not the Bible been put into Indian for them to read, and don't the missionaries preach to them in their own language?"

Yes, indeed; but don't you see that for each one of the many tribes it may be necessary to have just the Bible and missionary that each can understand? But if all the tribes now know this one Sign Talk, then all can read the Lord's Prayer, and any other part of the Bible, if put in this sign talk. And all the more so because every one can understand a thing better if he can see the language as well as hear it.

Now to do this good work Mr. H—— lived among the Indians. He is a missionary unlike any other. He has suffered much living as the Indians do to learn this language. Read what Mrs. Degen says: "Would you like to go out to dine where all the family kneel on an earth floor around the tin dish-pan in which the dinner has been cooked, and grab for 'a little white meat,' or 'a little dark meat,' or a 'little of both, if you please'? Would you like to see your fellow diners throw the bones they have picked back into the pan? Or would you like to have your food brought to you in a wash-basin?"

Now you can see something of what Mr. Hadley bears. He is a hero. You can help him. So write to Mrs. Degen.   L.

HIS GIFT.

A LITTLE boy in Russia lay dying. But a few months before he had heard of Jesus and his love, and given his heart to that wonderful friend. His greatest desire in life was to have other Russian children get acquainted with Jesus. He meant when he grew up to be a missionary among his people; but God wanted him in heaven. Just before he died he called his father, and told him how much he wanted to have the Bible sent to people who were not acquainted with Jesus. Said he: "I haven't much money, you know, father, but if you would take what is in my box and send it to the house where they print Bibles, I think there might be enough to dot the I's in the name of Christ. I feel sure there must be enough to do that in one Bible, and I would like it so much! Will you, father?"

You do not need to be told that the father carried out his boy's last directions, and the little purse of money is helping to-day to "dot the I's" in that blessed name.

Surely that little fellow ought to have had engraved upon his headstone, "He hath done what he could."

WORK ENOUGH.

SOME years ago —

"Some years ago!" Why, it was as long ago as five times the age of your grandpapa — he was eighty, I think — a brave man and a few sailors got into a small ship on the coast of Spain, spread its sails, and away westward they sped, over the ocean wide and rough with waves. They found America at last. Others came. Villages grew up. Still they came.

About this time, three thousand miles away, walked two —

"Lovers, I guess."

Indeed they did love each other, if that is what you mean. See them in the picture of the "Two Missionaries;" were there ever sweeter faces, purer and more pitiful? It is because the love of God is shed abroad in their hearts. Dress and feathers don't make beauty so much as a right heart, you must know.

These two hearts were walking near the dear old church, and as they walked they thought of the sermon the day before about bearing the tidings — the Gospel — to the needy. They had heard of America, and their hearts bled for the people here.

"And did they go to a seminary, and learn how to teach and preach, and get ordained, and get married, and come over here and have a Sunday-school and church?"

"They left all to follow Jesus — fathers, mothers, everybody, everything, "for Jesus' sake," for wild America.

"And how did most of the people in America look when they got here?"

How does this creature on the following page look? or that one?

"Now you don't mean that the Americans then were such objects?"

The very same. And our two sweet, beautiful missionaries came to them and learned their language and lived among them, and taught them of the true God, and Jesus Christ, the Saviour.

"Did they stay more than a year that way?"

They lived and died among them. Then their

children took up the work, and they have been carrying it on ever since!

"And what came of it all?"

ONE OF THE FIERCE SAVAGES.

Why, many of those fierce savages put off their war paint and wild ways, and settled down in good homes like nice Christian people, with churches and Sunday-schools and ministers of their own. Some of them now look almost as sweet as the two sweet faces of the Two Missionaries. That's the way it often works when God puts his grace into a rough heart. It really changes the face too into beauty. God can make everything beautiful.

"But what about the picture on the next page?"

You mean that queer-looking man going ahead with a child in his arms and a big boy by his side?

"It is a family on a journey somewhere."

The "somewhere" is America. They are peasants (the poor working folks) of — Denmark, maybe.

They have heard of America — what a goodly land it is for the poor and homeless, and where they can be free to worship God — so they have sold the cow and poultry and a few other things, and putting into bundles what they have over, and saying a sad good-by to the dear old hut where they have always lived, they are on their march to the sea. They will soon be aboard the ship, Safety; then, after two months —

"Two months! why, the Teutonic of the White Star Line has just crossed the Atlantic in five days, sixteen hours and a few seconds."

Yes, but this was long ago.

But the two months are gone; they have landed at Castle Garden, New York, and now those nine have become ninety thousand. You see, no sooner had they got nicely settled upon a little spot of land, and in a neat cottage, and two or three cows about them, and a patch of potatoes growing near by, when away went a letter back to Denmark to their cousins to pack up and come too.

Well, ever since the ships have grown larger and faster, bringing loads and loads of peasants, five hundred thousand some years, from almost every nation on the other side of the ocean.

ANOTHER TYPE OF SAVAGES.

"And those two sweet-faced missionaries, did they teach all these low people the good ways of God?"

DO YOU THINK THEY LIVE IN A PALACE? (*See "Work Enough."*)

Yes; they and their children. Don't you see, they stand for all good missionaries whom Jesus sends? They are all beautiful in his eyes. Where in the Bible does it say something like "How beautiful upon the mountains are the feet of him that bringeth good tidings; that publisheth peace, etc?" If beautiful feet, beautiful everything — so beautiful that all among whom they go with these tidings become beautiful too!

See those children in the opening picture, com-

DOLLIES TO THE FRONT.

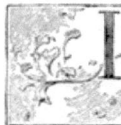 CAME across an old paper which told a pretty story that ought not to grow old. It was about a "doll's reception" which a certain Mission Band gave. The dollies were lent by the members and their friends, and the friends of their friends, until there was a great army of them. Then they were arrayed in

GOING ON A JOURNEY.

ing down the road with bundles under their arms? Look them over, and say if you think they live in a palace, and if they wear silks or furs.

No, no, poor things! a sorry dinner they've had. A bed of straw for them to-night. But in a few years some cousins in America will send them some money; then they will be here, and somehow they must be made beautiful as those two sweet-faced ones. Oh! so much work in this land for Jesus, to meet these heathen at Castle Garden with the good news and make them beautiful. Oh! for more home missionaries. What say you?   L.

choice robes and grouped with artistic skill. On the piano, under a lovely marriage bell of sweet-smelling flowers, were two bridal groups, dressed in satin and old lace regardless of expense. The friends of the bride and groom were numerous. Some of them were old, appearing in costumes of sixty years before; some were in Mother Hubbard dress, and one very large rag doll, with lips made of beet juice and eyes of black beads, came to the wedding in the little wooden cradle which had belonged to her mother's grandmother.

There was an "old ladies'" group arranged

on a round table, two of them dressed in Quaker attire, the others in the sweet old fashion of our great-grandmothers. Then there was a babies' group, and a group of children fresh from the schoolroom; there was a German table, a French table, and I do not know what all.

One hundred and thirty dolls were lent for the occasion. The description of each group was printed in rhyme made by the friends of the Band, and from time to time, as a crowd gathered near any of the tables, one member stepped forward and recited the descriptive poem. Ten cents admission was charged, and the hall was thronged on two afternoons. There was not a cent of expense in the entire affair, and there was nothing to sell. Over forty dollars were taken in at the door, and the Mission Band went home happy in the thought that they and their dollies had enriched a certain school in Japan by that amount.

WHAT HAVE I DONE?

I LAY my finger on time's wrist to score
The forward-surging moments as they roll;
Each pulse seems quicker than the one before;
And lo! my days pile up against my soul
As clouds pile up against the golden sun.
Alas! what have I done? What have I done?

I never steep the rosy hours in sleep,
Or hide my soul, as in a gloomy crypt;
No idle hands into my bosom creep;
And yet, as water-drops from house-eaves drip,
So, viewless, melt my days, and from me run;
Alas! what have I done? What have I done?

I have not missed the fragrance of the flowers,
Or scorned the music of the flowing rills,
Whose numerous liquid tongues sing to the hours;
Yet rise my days behind me, like the hills
Unstayed by light of mighty triumphs won;
Alas! what have I done? What have I done?

Be still, my soul, restrain thy lips from woe!
Cease thy lament! for life is but the flower,

The fruit comes after death; how can'st thou know
The roundness of its form, its depth of power?
Death is life's morning. When thy work's begun,
Then ask thyself — what yet is to be done?
LILLIAN BLANCHE FEARING,
In Home Mission Monthly.

WHEN ST. CHRYSOSTOM PRAYED.

'TWAS not enough to kneel in prayer,
And pur his very soul away
In fervid wrestlings, night and day,
For those who owned his shepherd care;
But faith and works went hand in hand,
As test of each petition made,
And saints were helped throughout the land
When St. Chrysostom prayed.

Within the closet where he knelt
A box of Bethlehem's olive wood —
"For Christ" engraved upon it — stood;
And ever as he daily felt
The pressure of the church's need,
Therein the daily gift was laid;
For word had instant proof of deed
When St. Chrysostom prayed.

Beneath his folded hands he placed
Whatever gold was his; and when
He travailed for the souls of men,
So long by pagan rites debased,
The more he agonized, the more
The burden on his spirit weighed;
And piece by piece went all his store
When St. Chrysostom prayed.

O, golden mother! let this thine alms
Rouse us to shame who daily bow
Within our sacred places now,
With outstretched yet with empty palms!
We supplicate indeed; but has
Our faith brought answering works to aid?
Have words by deeds been proven, as
When St. Chrysostom prayed?
MARGARET J. PRESTON, *in Missionary World.*

PUT TO SHAME.

THEY were sitting in the window-seat, Magdalene and Mabel, busy with their work, and talking. "The Mission Band meets this week, you know," said Mabel.

"I know it," Magdalene said, with a scowl on her face; "I've got to go, I suppose, but I don't want to a bit; I haven't any money to spare to give; I'm not going to give but a cent, anyhow, I just can't afford it. Isn't this blue silk sash lovely, Mabel? It just fits my dollie's eyes. It was horridly expensive; I had to give twenty cents just for this little piece."

"Nell is going to Mission Band," said that small woman from the carpet, where she played with her dollie. "Nell knows all about it; mamma told her. Nell doesn't want to be a selfish little girl and not give to the heathens; Nell is going to give her bestest thing."

Magdalene nudged her friend's elbow to call attention to what her darling little sister was saying, and the two listened.

"What are you going to give, Pet?" asked Magdalene at last, as the baby voice ceased its talking.

The little girl looked up with surprised eyes; she had not supposed anybody was paying attention to her.

"What are you going to give to the Mission Band for the heathens?"

"I'm going to give my bestest thing," said the baby, with sweet gravity; "I shall give my wubber dollie, that I love."

Mabel laughed, but Magdalene looked sober. Nobody understood better than she how the "wubber dollie" was loved, and she knew that Baby Nell meant what she said.

"I think I will give my twenty-five cents, after all," she said, after a moment's silence, "and let my doll go without a fur cape; there is a lovely fur cape for sale at the doll store for twenty-five cents, and I meant to have it: but I believe I won't."

"You want to match Nell's 'wubber dollie,'" said Mabel, with a good-natured laugh; "but I don't believe you can."

SOME summer day you may be in Saratoga, N. Y. Among other sights you may see Indian encampments. Thither they come to sell their curious manufactures — bows, arrows, bead bags and many other queer things.

The squaws (women) will be among them, dressed as Indian women have always dressed, but hardly so well as "Teweelema."

If you wish to see her you can now find her on her goodly farm near Lakeville, Mass., or traveling among the neighboring villages selling her wares — moccasins, necklaces of shells and beads, etc. She can chop a tree down or spade up the ground, and do almost any man's work.

TEWEELEMA.

She and her sister manage the farm. Her name is Wootonekanuske.

At Oneida, N. Y., you may always see a few Indian women on the cars or at the station, looking something like Teweelema.

But in a few more years there may not be any Indians left east of the Mississippi River. The Gospel is now among them, and maybe you will never again read of so fierce a warrior as Sitting-Bull or King Philip, Teweelema's great, great, greatest grandfather.   L.

EVERYTHING IS GAY AND HAPPY.

CARL HAMMOND'S LESSON.

FOR a boy who was usually happy, Carl Hammond certainly spent a very uncomfortable winter. It is true it was his first away from home, and some people thought he was young to be sent from home, but that was not the trouble. He was with Aunt Mary, which was almost the same as being with mother; and the schools where Aunt Mary lived were so much better than at Carl's own home, that his mother had made the sacrifice, and sent him away.

His unhappiness had to do with a certain September day which was as bright and beautiful as a sunny day in early autumn can be. Carl remembered every little thing about that afternoon — just how his father's desk looked, and what books were piled on the table at its left, and above all, just how Bunce looked when he bounded in at the window. He was writing to Aunt Mary then, he remembered, telling her on what train to expect him, and he had held the pen in hand and turned to laugh at Bunce because he was so ridiculously glad over having found him. He had leaned over and patted the dog's eager head, and had asked him how he was going to manage to get along without his playmate all winter; and Bunce had begun to run around his chair in that absurd fashion he had when especially pleased, and had bumped against the table just as Carl had shouted to him to "take care!" The shout came too late. Bunce succeeded in jostling the table, so that a ponderous book set too near the edge tumbled off, taking the great cut-glass inkstand with it, and the contents of that dreadful inkstand spread itself not only over the costly book, but the handsome carpet as well. If it had happened but the day before, Carl could not have remembered every little particular more vividly.

Especially what followed; there is no denying that Carl was very much frightened. It seems a strange thing to say, but the truth is, he was not very well acquainted with his father. Mr. Hammond was connected with a business firm which sent him every year, and sometimes two or three times a year, to Europe; and be-

tween times he had to go South and West, and Carl hardly knew where else, on business; so that he was not often at home for many days together, and when there, was so crowded with business as to have little leisure for his family. Carl had once complained that whenever his father was at home for an hour or two it was always after he had gone to bed. Perhaps on this account he was the more frightened; for his father had great respect for books, and was particularly careful of the large one that Bunce had ruined. Carl could seem to hear his quick firm voice giving directions:

"Remember, my son, you are on no account to allow Bunce in the study; he is a dangerous fellow in such a place; he can hardly move without doing injury. Be careful always to close the sash window when you go there, lest he might follow you." And Carl had been in the study on the day in question for a half hour, with the sash window wide open. Not that he had forgotten, but he believed Bunce to be a mile away taking a walk with his young mistress; and he said to himself: "It is very much pleasanter with the window open, and of course papa does not care when Bunce is away." As if Bunce could not return at any moment! which he presently did. Even then Carl might have ordered him instantly out and closed the sash, but the dear fellow was so absurdly glad to see him, and ran around in such a funny fashion to show his joy that it seemed too bad to dismiss him at once. Therefore the result which I have given you.

But this was not the end of the story. Carl arose in great alarm, and without even attempting to repair damages, which indeed would have been beyond his skill, made all haste from the room, taking Bunce with him and closing the sash window carefully. Then, an hour afterwards, when his father's stern voice questioned: "Carl, do you know anything about the accident in the study?" what did Carl do but ask: "What accident, sir?"

"The overturning and breaking of the large inkstand and the spoiling of a very valuable book. Did you have anything to do with it?"

"No, sir," said Carl; "I had not."

The poor fellow told his conscience that he

really did not have a thing to do with it, that the dog did all the mischief while he sat perfectly still, and that his father was the one who had left the book open on the table so dangerously near the edge. But his conscience had been better taught than that, and would have nothing to do with such flimsiness. It told him plainly before he slept that night, that the name of such talk, in plain English, was lying!

Nobody questioned Carl further; his friends were in the habit of believing his word, and his father had been almost immediately called away by a telegram, so that indeed there had been no time to investigate. Two days afterwards, Carl himself left home. Now you know why his winter had been uncomfortable. The simple truth was, that he was an honorable, truth-loving boy, who had been astonished and dismayed at himself for telling what was not true, and who could not help despising himself for it. Moreover, he knew that if there was one sin more than another which his father hated with all his earnest nature, it was the sin of lying.

It may be surprising to think that a boy like Carl should be half the winter making up his mind to tell the exact truth; nevertheless such was the case. The longer he put it off, the more impossible it seemed to him to write to his father and explain his share in the mischief. But at last, one snowy winter day, only two weeks before the holidays, he did it. He felt better as soon as the letter was mailed. He told himself that no matter what his father said in reply, he knew he had at last done right, and should be glad over it. Still he watched for the home letter more anxiously than ever before. It was from his mother, with a little note enclosed, for Carl's private reading, from his father.

"A fellow couldn't have a better letter," said Carl, wiping his eyes, and feeling a warm glow in his heart for the dear father who had been so kind and gentle, and yet honest and plain-spoken. Less than a week afterwards, Carl was on his way home. His mind was in a strange confusion as the train neared the home station. He could not help feeling just a little sorry that his father was at home. "Of course he will punish me," thought the poor fellow.

"I suppose he must; he always punishes disobedience. What if he should not let me see mother to-night! Or perhaps he will not let me go to Grandma's with the family to-morrow. I'd most rather he would whip me, and perhaps he will!"

Over this thought the twelve-year-old boy's heart almost stood still. His father had not often punished him in this way, but on the very rare occasions when it had to be done, it was managed in such a manner that Carl distinctly remembered it. By the time the train ran into the station he had succeeded in working himself up to such a pitch of excitement that he was almost tempted to run away, to avoid the disgrace of this home-coming. But his father was there, waiting.

"Here's my boy!" Carl heard him say, and in a minute more the father's arms were around him, and the father's kiss was on his cheeks. Mother was waiting in the carriage, and not a word during the quick ride home, nor at the joyous supper table afterwards, was said to him about his fault. They went to Grandma's the next day in great happiness, and the next day they went to Uncle Will's. "I am having a holiday," his father explained, "in honor of my boy's home-coming. I am taking a longer vacation from business than I have had before in two years." The days passed, and not a word was said to Carl about his disobedience and falseness. Nobody could be kinder or more thoughtful for his comfort and pleasure than his father, yet Carl could not help wondering when and how his punishment was to come. At last, one evening, when they were alone together for a few minutes, he resolved to discover. "Father," he said, and his voice trembled a little, "when are you going to punish me?"

His father turned astonished eyes upon him. "Punish you, my dear boy! For what?"

Carl's cheeks were very red. "Why, father, don't you know — surely you remember? I wrote about it."

"But surely, my boy, I wrote you about it! Did I not tell you I forgave you utterly?"

"O, yes, sir! but then I thought — that you would think" — Carl stopped in confusion.

"You thought I must remember the sin, and punish the sinner, even though I had forgiven him? Is that it?"

"Yes, sir," said Carl, low-voiced and troubled.

"No," said Mr. Hammond, and Carl noticed how tender his voice was; "I do not remember anything about it in the sense which you mean. Do you remember my telling you once that God meant fathers to be object lessons to their children, giving them some faint idea, at least, of what kind of a father God would be to those who trusted him?"

"Yes, sir," said Carl.

"Very well, then, here on this card, which I would like you to keep in your Bible, is my answer to your question."

The card was a lovely blue celluloid, and had printed on it in gold letters, the words, "I will forgive their iniquity, and I will remember their sin no more."

One evening, when Carl was twenty years old, he repeated that verse in a Christian Endeavor prayer meeting, and said that his father's commentary on it had made him understand it. Then he told, in brief, the story which I have given you.

MYRA SPAFFORD.

HE REMEMBERED JUST HOW BUNCE LOOKED.

THE STATE HOUSE AT BOSTON.

HOWARD'S WAY.

(Character Studies.)

THEY were all in the library after dinner, and were all talking at once, as the Edwards family were inclined to be. "I don't see why we always have so much more to say than other people seem to," Lora Edwards had once remarked, setting them all into shouts of laughter. Howard was not talking; his head was bent low over a Latin dictionary. They were waiting for some of the family, because they always gathered at this hour in the library for evening prayers; but Howard, while he waited, saved the minutes, remembering the hard lesson of the morning, and the liability to be interrupted in his study hour.

The back parlor door was pushed open and Uncle Edward's handsome form appeared. "Where is Ashman Square?" he inquired.

Several voices at once attempted to answer him. "It is just off of Second Street," said Lora. And Emma in the same breath said, "It is over by the river somewhere; near Park Street, isn't it?" Then Dickie, "Why, Lora, it can't be near Second Street, because Wyeth Avenue runs in there."

"No, it doesn't; Wyeth Avenue crosses at Third Street."

Then exclamations from at least four: "Why, Lora Edwards! Wyeth Avenue isn't near Third Street. I think Ashman Square is down by the Lincoln Statue; isn't it, papa?"

"I am sure I don't know," said papa, who just then entered the room. "The city changes so rapidly and adds so many fancy names that I cannot keep track of it. Who wants to know — Edward? There is a map about somewhere. I shouldn't wonder if Ashman Square was down near the old Ashman place, towards the river."

"There!" said Emma, "I was sure it was near the river."

"But the river is quite a stream, my dear niece," Uncle Edward said, smiling.

"Yes; but Ashman Square is not very far down; it is near the Westfield car line."

Then a perfect babel of voices ensued. "O, Emma, no!"

"Emma Edwards! it is a quarter of a mile from the Eastman line, I am certain."

"I don't think Ashman Square is on this side at all; I think you are all confused."

"Yes, it is; I pass it every day, but I don't remember on which side of the avenue it is. I go down one way and come up another, and so get things mixed."

"I don't think any of you know much about it," said Uncle Edward, and this time he laughed. Several voices began again in eager disclaimer, but Father Edwards silenced them: "See here, children, we must have prayers at once; I have an important engagement at seven. Afterwards, one of you can find a map and settle your discussion."

Lora struck the chord and the entire family joined in:

"While Thee I seek, protecting Power,
Be my vain wishes stilled."

In the momentary lull which there was as they rose from their knees, Howard spoke, for the first time that evening.

"Uncle Edward."

"Yes."

"About Ashman Square — do you know where the Station D post-office is?"

"Perfectly."

"Well, Ashman Square begins two blocks east of that."

"So it does!" declared Lora; "why in the world didn't some of us think of the post-office? that would have located it."

"I never noticed how near it was to the post-office," said Emma. "What I would like to know is, why Howard did not speak before, and save us all this talk."

"Sure enough!" said Dickie. "Did you find the answer to that conundrum in your Latin dictionary? Why didn't you look up, old fellow, and join the colloquy?"

"Couldn't get a chance," said Howard, with a good-natured smile; "you all had a great deal to say, and were bent on saying it, all at once; I thought I would keep still until the shower was over, and in the meantime a grain of fact might be evolved out of it; but there wasn't."

"Howard always waits until there is clear sailing," said Lora. "I've noticed that he is the only one in our family who isn't apparently burning to speak at the same moment when some one else is."

"And when he does speak it is to the point," said Uncle Edward. "Much obliged, my boy; you have saved me a bewildering tramp in the effort to follow the directions of these voluble young ladies." MYRA SPAFFORD.

ABOUT BOSTON.

BY THE PANSIES.

MAMMA told me why it was named Boston. There was once in old England a man so good and kind to sailors, and to people in distress on the water, that he was named St. Botolph, because the word "Botolph" is made from two words, which mean boat help. After a while the word "Boston" grew out of the name, and the place where this man had lived and died was called so. And Boston in New England was named for it. LUCY STEVENSON.

I SAW a picture of the first house that was ever built in Boston. It is very homely. There are only a few windows, and one door, I think; and it looks like some of the log cabins of the West. A man named William Blackstone lived in this house all alone. It was built on a hill, and the place where it stood is now part of a handsome street in Boston. But the town was not called Boston when William Blackstone lived there; it was Shawmut. WILLIAM BLAKE.

THEY used to have very strict laws in Boston about the Sabbath. From Saturday at midnight until six o'clock on Sunday evening no hired carriage could leave or enter the city, and during the hours of public service no wagon of any sort was allowed to move through the streets faster than a walk. Soon after the laws against using the bath-houses on Sunday were made, a person who thought himself witty had printed in the paper the following rhyme:

"In superstition's day, 'tis said,
Hens laid two eggs on Monday;
Because a hen would lose her head
Who laid an egg on Sunday.
Now our wise rulers and the law
Say none shall wash on Sunday,
So Boston folks must dirty go,
And wash them twice on Monday!"
REUBEN S. BENTON.

I READ about a town meeting which was held in Boston in 1789, in which they voted that there should be "One writing school at the south part of the town, one at the center, and one at the north part; and that in these schools the children of both sexes shall be taught writing, and also arithmetic in its various branches, including vulgar and decimal fractions."

Another law passed at the same meeting was, that there should be "A reading school in the north part of the town and one in the south part, and that the children of both sexes should be taught to spell, accent and read, both prose and verse." Girls were allowed to attend these schools only half the year — from April to October — but boys could go in winter. This latter rule was changed in 1828, and the girls were allowed to attend through the year until they were sixteen; boys could attend only until they were fourteen. The Bible was the only reader then in use. HELEN WESTOVER.

I WENT to Boston once to visit my grandfather, and he took me to lots of places, and showed me the picture of Ann Pollard; she lived to be a hundred and five years old, and she was the first to jump from the boat when the colonists came over from Charlestown; she was only ten years old then, and she gave a spring from the boat just as it was touching the shore, and landed. Grandfather showed her to me, and told me about her, because my name is Annie Pollard, and he said I had a little of the spunk of my old ancestor. ANNIE POLLARD.

WE have been studying in school about John Hancock and his times, and our teacher told us about his wife's breakfast party at the old Hancock House. It was in 1778, and a French fleet came into Boston harbor. Governor Hancock proposed that the officers be invited to breakfast; so his wife had her table set for thirty officers, and instead all the under officers of the fleet came also — a hundred and twenty more than were expected! Mrs. Hancock must have been in a panic for a few minutes, but she got out of her difficulties. First, she ordered all the cows on the Common milked, and the milk

WE have a picture in our library of the old Hancock House. It isn't much of a house as those things go nowadays, but when Governor Hancock lived there I suppose it looked fine. I like old John Hancock; it is great fun to read about him. Of course it was all nonsense for him to think that Washington ought to call on him first, that time when Washington went to Boston to visit in 1789, but for all that I think it was awfully cute, the way in which Hancock finally backed down. He had the gout, you know, so he did himself up in flannel and had his men carry him on their shoulders to call on

THE HANCOCK HOUSE.

brought to her; then she sent among her friends and borrowed cakes and other things to help out, and gave them all a very nice breakfast.

The French count who commanded the fleet was very much pleased, and invited the governor and his wife to visit his fleet and bring their friends. This was Mrs. Hancock's chance to be politely revenged upon him for bringing so many people to breakfast; she invited five hundred friends to go with her to the fleet! But they were politely received and entertained elegantly.   FANNIE BROOKS.

Washington. If he had got to make the first call he meant to do it in state, and he did.
       JOHN STUART WINTHROP.

WHEN I was just eight years old, my father spent a week in Boston with me, and showed me the Museum, the Navy Yard, the School for the Blind (I remember Laura Bridgman), the Idiot School, etc. He took me to the top of Bunker Hill Monument; I remember I counted the two hundred and ninety-seven steps. Not every father thinks that a child of eight could appreciate such things. Many and many a time since then, have I thanked my father for helping me to enjoy the remembrance of things which I never expect to see again. During that visit to Boston a boy ten years old took from my grandfather's library a copy of one of the "Jonas" books which he coveted. The book was never missed, but twenty years afterwards the boy returned it with compound interest and apologies; his heart had never been at rest about it. MRS. OLIVIA C. WARNE.

My father was in Boston when the statue of John Winthrop was unveiled; he walked in that great procession, and heard the speech made in the Old South Church. I have been to Boston myself, and walked around that very statue. It is in Scollay Square. Governor Winthrop is dressed just as they used to dress in his time; he has a Bible in one hand, and a copy of the king's charter in the other. There is a carved rope wound around a carved tree which stands for the ship that brought him over. I went to the beautiful State House, too. It is the one

THE STATUE OF WINTHROP.

which was begun in Governor Hancock's pasture! But it does not look much like a pasture where it stands now. HARRY WESTFIELD.

ONCE I went to the old North Church in Boston. I went up the tower to the steeple, where General Gage stood and watched Charlestown

THE OLD NORTH CHURCH.

burn. On the steeple is the date "1723." The chime of bells on this church are just lovely! I heard them play. One of them has on it these words: "We are the first ring of bells cast for the British Empire in North America." Another bell says: "Since generosity has opened our mouths, our tongues shall ring aloud its praise." Inside the church are some queer wooden angels. The pews are very old-fashioned. The Bible in the desk was the one that George the Second gave to the church. After making this visit I learned "Paul Revere" and recited it at school; you know the signal lights which warned him shone from the steeple of the Old North.

MARY WINTHROP SMITH.

[For want of space, we must bring this very interesting bit of history about old Boston to a close. It is certainly not for want of material that we do so, and our hearty thanks are due the Pansies and their friends for the letters full of interesting items which have come to us. It is noticeable that the young people of to-day are interested in Boston's past, which is a wise thing, for its history is full of suggestion for the future.

We earnestly hope that the city which we take up next, viz: Washington, D. C., may call out as many items of interest from the young people. — EDITORS THE PANSY.]

MAJOR'S AUTOBIOGRAPHY.

IF Bose and Fido and Sport and the rest will keep still long enough, I will tell you some things about myself which I should like you to remember.

I am growing old pretty fast, and if I had not the kindest master in the world I would stand a slim chance.

My smelling is good yet, and things taste nice enough, but my teeth are nearly gone. Bones which once would have been a luxury, now do me little good. The best I can do is to lap off a little of the meat and grease.

Yes, I can bark loud enough yet, but it vexes me terribly when I see the cattle in the field where they do not belong, or some wicked boys in the orchard stealing apples, to know that about all I can do is to bark.

I do not pretend that I have been a perfect dog, but I have had a great deal of experience in my day, and am not without the hope that you, my young friends, may profit by what I have seen and heard and felt myself, and known in the lives of others.

No, I shall not try to tell it all to-day; I have no wish to bore you with "long yarns," as the sailors say. Besides, there would not be time before Fido might be wanted to go with his mistress across the pasture when she takes that beef tea to Willie Jones. She never seems afraid with her pet along. Bose, too, will be wanted to drive home the cows; so I will tell you only a little to-day, and more another time.

Where I was born I really do not know, but I am inclined to think it was a great way from here, perhaps in another country; we will never know, I suppose, though it seems to me it must be nice to know where one came into the world, and what kind of father and mother he had. But, dear me, I have seen some dogs, and folks too, who would have been happier if they had never known their parents!

I can just remember seeing my mother once. I think she must have been beautiful. The man who took me away from her often said in my hearing that I had her hair and eyes.

I can remember how mother cried when they

carried me away. I had never seen her cry before, and though I was awfully frightened, yet I felt sorry for her.

I was petted enough, and had plenty to eat, but the journey was long, and shut up in that little box I was dreadfully lonesome.

But finally we reached home; then I had a warm bed, and a nice place; but some nights I was terribly scared there in the dark all alone. The boys had a pet donkey, and the first night I was there that fellow made his horrid bray. My! I thought I should die with fright. Well, when I had got a little used to the donkey, what should I hear in the tree over my head but a horrid "To hoo! to who?"

Yes, Sport, you may wag your tail and laugh; you know "who," for you are a full-grown dog, and know all about the great staring owl, but with me it was a different matter.

As I remarked before, I think, my master was kind, and so was mistress, and they had no very small children to torment a little pup. Their little girl was so sweet and kind, it was always a pleasure to kiss her soft cheek; I do not believe she ever had any nice thing to eat that she did not wish to share with me.

Her brother was a noble fellow, too. Not always so thoughtful as his sister, and sometimes pretty rough; but so long as he did not mean to be ugly and hurt me, I could bear it.

The worst, I remember, was when their cousins and some of the neighbors' children would come for the afternoon on a visit.

At first I was glad to see so many little children, but I soon found that all children had not such sweet dispositions as my master's, or else their parents had not taught them so carefully.

We all ran and romped, and for a time it was jolly enough; but when my young master and mistress were out of sight, one of those rough boys would do something to torment me. He pulled my ears and my tail; once he boxed my ears so hard that I cried right out.

Then they put me on that donkey's back, and while I was held there, the creature made one of those dreadful noises! Then I cried so loud my little mistress came and took me away.

Once I was so frightened by those rude children that I hid under the barn. I could hear them call my name and whistle for me, but I did not mean to come out till the children had gone.

It seemed a long time, but they finally went — I mean the visitors,— and then I was only too ready to get out, for it was growing pretty dark where I was.

We were all very much frightened, but when master came home he took a big iron bar and pried a stone out, and made a hole big enough for me to crawl through as easy as need be.

I cannot make myself believe that those children remembered with pleasure what they had done to me that day. They never looked sweet and happy like little Lucy and her brother.

I long ago came to the conclusion that if one would be happy he must try to make others so; and I do not believe it makes much difference whether he walks upon two legs or four.

Another thing, I believe one's usefulness depends very much upon whether he keeps his eyes open or not. Why, one does not need to be a full-grown dog to be able to make himself useful, and so thought a great deal of.

Take my case, for example: As I was saying, even when I was quite small the hired man used to take me when he went after the cows at night.

I suppose this was to give me the pleasure of a run in the pasture; they took old Sport along to do the work of driving. He, poor fellow, was getting pretty old, and could not run fast; but he was a good dog, and was well educated.

I did not at first understand how he could know so much — how he could tell the oxen from the cows, and the cows from the steers; and when there were other cattle mixed up with our master's, on the road or anywhere, how he could know which ones to drive in, and which to leave or drive away.

One day as we were waiting for the hired man to fix a little place in the fence, Sport said something that astonished me greatly.

I think I had been saying how I wished I knew as much as he, and could do what he did. Then he gave me this hint. Said he, "I think our good master is planning to have you take my place in a few months. Soon I shall not be able to do the work, and if you watch out you will be able to do all that I have done.

Even now," said he, "you are beginning to save me a great many steps by starting up the cattle which are lagging behind, or that get out of the way."

I shall never forget how pleased I was. I almost felt like another dog, and was so glad to think that I could do anything worth any one's notice. I feel sure it was a great help to me to have him speak like that, and cannot but think that a great many others might be encouraged in the same way.

Proud little puppy that I was, I almost split my throat barking at the cattle that afternoon, and was much pleased to see that I could help.

Well, it was not many weeks after that, when one day the hired man went off fishing, and the master was all alone at home. It was late in the afternoon, and he was resting upon the front steps, looking very tired, for he was not well. I remember I had been wishing for the time to come when I could do something,

OLD MAJOR.

and would be big enough to watch things. You see the fishing party had taken Sport with them to watch the wagon. I was thought too young to be taken off so far.

I had felt pretty sober all the morning, but the master had spoken very kindly to me several times, and while sitting there had called me to him and patted my head, and called me a nice little fellow. Finally he looked up from the paper he had been reading and said, "Well, Major, it is about time to go for the cows."

"Now is your chance," I said to myself, and off over the big stone wall I went. About the only thing I feared was that he would call me back, but he seemed too much surprised for that; so I ran away as fast as my four feet could carry me.

I did not know so well then where to look for the cows, but scampered around so fast that I soon caught sight of them and quickly had the whole lot on their way to the yard.

My only mistake was in doing my job too well, for I drove up the oxen and steers and yearlings as well as the cows.

When I had them all near the gate then I barked as hard as I could, and the master came and let down the bars, and drove in the cows and let the others go back.

Then I remembered how it was generally done, and felt much ashamed of my blunder. But master called me to him and petted me, and told me I had been a good fellow. Then late in the evening, when the others came home, he told them how I had surprised him by driving up the cows, and never said a word about my mistake in driving up the other cattle. I think that was so kind of him! I know a great many who would have been either so thoughtless or unkind as to have made fun of a youngster's little blunder when trying to do his best. But he was not that kind of a man. You may be sure I never made that mistake again.

Then old Sport came over to my kennel, and congratulated me heartily on driving up the cows. All I could do was to thank him, and tell him it was because of the way he had encouraged me, helping me to think I might do something.

There have been many changes in farming since I can remember, but the cows have to be got and milked just as ever, only there seem to be more of them, and so I must not keep you any longer this time.   R.

OUR GRANDPARENTS AT SCHOOL.

MAKING THE DUST FLY.

BABY'S CORNER.

A HAPPY LITTLE GIRL.

BESSIE has good times. She lives in the country where the hills are white with snow.

Every morning after breakfast she puts on her long cloak and her warm hood and mittens, and goes to school with her brothers. The schoolhouse is half a mile away, but she loves to go.

Sometimes she runs and draws her sled. It

BESSIE GIVES CARLO A RIDE.

is a new one, painted red, and is one of her Christmas presents.

Sometimes she sits on the sled, and her brothers give her a nice ride. They play they are ponies, and run very fast. Then Bessie shouts and laughs, and is happy.

Their home is in that little house beyond the hill. You can see the roof, and the smoke curling up from the chimney.

They are on their way home from school now.

Just as they got to the top of the hill Carlo came to meet them. He wagged his tail and licked Bessie's hand, he was so glad to see her, for Carlo gets lonely without playmates all day.

The boys saw a rabbit run through the fence, and they went up to watch for it.

"Carlo shall have a ride," said Bessie. So she took him in her arms and got upon the sled at the top of the hill.

She gave it a little push, and away they went, whiz! down the long hill so swiftly and smoothly. Oh! it was good fun.

Two more rides they took, then Charlie picked up the bag and said, "Come, Bess."

When they get home mamma will have a nice warm supper ready for them.

After that they will go out and ride down hill until dark.

MRS. C. M. LIVINGSTON.

THE SAND MAN.

EACH night a man goes round our town,
And into eyes of blue and brown,
He sprinkles, with a careful hand,
The finest, softest grains of sand.

Then as sweet blossoms close at night,
O'er shining eyes fall curtains white;
For all these precious grains of sand
Are gathered up in Slumber Land.

'Tis there the peaceful river gleams
Where children sail in happy dreams;
The Sand Man takes them in his boat,
So off my little pet must float.

MYRA GOODWIN PLANTZ.

TEDDY AND MARGARET CLIMBED INTO THE STRANGE WAGON.

"IF I ONLY HADN'T!"

OBODY could have started out with better intentions than did Teddy Brockway that bright spring morning. It is true it was only March, but Teddy lived so far South that the month of March meant spring; he was dressed in a neat spring suit, had his little sister Margaret by the hand, and Sally Amelia, her dollie, under his special care, and was started for a trip all by themselves to old Auntie Blaikslee's, almost a half-mile away!

"Aren't you afraid to let those two babies go off alone?" Grandmamma asked, looking up from her knitting with a somewhat troubled face.

Mrs. Brockway smiled as she answered: "O, no! what could harm them? Teddy knows every foot of the way as well as I do, and every neighbor along the road; and everybody knows him. Besides, he is seven years old, and I must begin to trust him." However, she went to the door and called after them: "Remember, Teddy, I trust Margaret to you. It isn't every little boy of your age who can be depended upon to take care of his sister. And, Teddy, remember you are not to ride with any strange person who may ask you."

"Course not!" said Teddy, with dignity; "not unless he is Uncle Ben or Deacon West. I can ride with Deacon West — can't we, muvver?"

"O, yes!" said Mrs. Brockway, smiling. "He is not much more likely to meet Deacon West on this road than he is to meet the man in the moon," she said laughingly to grandma, "but he has to provide for all the possibilities."

Two hours afterwards Teddy and Margaret, with Sally Amelia somewhat the worse for being handled by all the grandchildren of old Auntie Blaikslee, were trudging back in triumph. The errand entrusted to them had been carefully done, and Teddy had said over the message he was to give his mother until he knew it by heart, and had bravely resisted two invitations from good-natured teamsters to have a ride. He was almost within sight of the corner where they turned into their own grounds, and Margaret had been good and minded beautifully. Truth to tell, Teddy's heart was swelling with importance; he had never before been sent on so long a trip with only Margaret for company. He felt at least ten years old. At the top of the hill he came to a halt. There, just in front of them, jogging comfortably along, was Jake Winchell, Judge Aker's hired man. Everybody knew Jake and his old horse and cart, but nobody, or at least Teddy, had ever happened to meet him in that direction before; his road always lay the other way.

"Halloo!" he said, getting out to fix something about the harness, and spying the children as he did so, "here's luck; an almost empty cart and two nice passengers to have a ride in it down the hill. Don't you want to jump in?"

Teddy never wanted anything worse. For a small minute he hesitated. What was that "muvver" had said? "You are not to ride with any strange person who may ask you." "Course not!" said Teddy again, indignant with himself; "just as though Jake was a strange person." But even while his heart said the words, a voice away down deep contradicted it: "Teddy Brockway, don't you know she meant anybody you are not used to riding with? And you never had a ride with Jake."

"What of that?" said Teddy's other thought, still impatiently; "that's because he never comes the way we live; but I've talked with him, and muvver said she thought he was kind to boys, and patient with them, and everything. Just as if she would care for Margaret and me to ride down hill to the gate! We're most there; and it is a bad hard hill for Margaret; and she has had a long walk."

"Yes, sir, thank you," he said aloud to Jake, smiling and bowing like a gentleman. "I should like to ride ever so much, for Margaret's sake; she is tired."

"All right," said Jake, with a good-natured chuckle; "climb in and I'll tuck her in after you, and take you a few miles on your road as well as not."

Little Margaret, who paid small attention to

cautions, and who expected that everybody in the world was bound to be kind to her and help take care of her, took this ride as a matter of course, and was soon seated beside Teddy, with Sally Amelia tucked safely under her arm. Jake decided to walk down the hill. "It's a pretty steep pitch for this part of the world," he explained, "and the harness ain't none of the safest; I guess I better walk."

Teddy looked at the harness and trembled. What would his mother say if she could hear that? Even now it was not too late to ask Jake to set them back again on the dusty road, but how he would laugh and call him a coward! Teddy couldn't, and the down-hill ride began.

What made that poor old half-blind horse stumble on a hidden root that particular morning and pitch the crazy old cart forward with such a sudden lunge as to send Teddy rolling down the hill faster than the horse could have traveled? Above all, how did it happen that Margaret did not fall out, but lay flat in the bottom of the cart and screamed? Nobody knows how any of it happened. They only know that when the almost distracted Jake had succeeded in getting the horse on his feet, and lifting Margaret in his arms, and trying his best to hush her had stumbled with all speed to the spot where Teddy had stopped rolling, the poor little fellow had fainted, and had to be carried by Jake to the very door of his mother's house, Margaret trudging solemnly along by his side, occasionally asking pitifully why Teddy went to "s'eep," and why he didn't wake up.

Poor Teddy "waked up" almost too soon for his comfort. It had been a terrible pain, when he tried to pick himself up from the road, which had made him faint.

Days afterwards, as he lay in his white bed with his leg done in "splints," whatever they were, and watched the long, bright spring days full of Southern sunshine and sweet smells, and thought how long it would be before he could run about again, he would sigh out wearily, "O, muvver! if I only hadn't!" Of course his mother tried to comfort him. Once she said: "But, Teddy dear, you did not mean to do wrong. You supposed of course that because Jake was considered an honest, clean-souled man, mother would be willing to have you ride with him. It was what we call an error in judgment. If I were you I would be glad that you escaped with only a broken leg, and that dear little Margaret was not hurt at all, and then try to forget about it."

Teddy considered this for some minutes with a grave face, and in his eyes an earnest longing to take the comfort to his heart. But at last he spoke, in the slow, old-fashioned way he sometimes had: "No, muvver, it was an error in want-to! I knew 'not to ride with any strange person' meant with any person that you had not let me ride with before; and I knew I wasn't doing real heart right; so if Margaret had been hurt it would have been my fault. O, muvver! if I only hadn't!"

PANSY.

ABOUT WASHINGTON.

BY THE PANSIES.

 I READ a letter written by Mrs. President Adams in 1796. In it she complains that there are not nearly lamps enough to light the White House decently, and that the making of the daily fires in all the rooms, "to keep off the ague," occupies the entire time of one or two servants. She says there are no looking-glasses in the house but "dwarfs." I think Mrs. President Harrison must have found a very different state of things. It is just like women to complain about there not being looking-glasses!

JOHN WEST.

My great-grandfather used to be in Washington in Congress, when Daniel Webster was there. My father has told me all about it; they had great speeches. Grandfather heard Henry Clay when he made his wonderful speech. I'd like to have been with him! Father read to us last night about the speech, and in the book it said there were at that time two little boys, one eight years old and the other ten, whom nobody knew anything about until afterwards.

One of them went to a primary school in Boston and studied a primer, and the other didn't go to school at all, but had to work hard. The primer boy was named Summer, and the other boy was Abraham Lincoln. I guess if the people in Washington had known what those two boys were going to do a little later, they would have been astonished. LINCOLN STEVENSON.

The Washington Monument for fun

My father and mother lived in Washington in 1860. Father says it wasn't much like a city then; there were no street cars, and they did not light the streets, only Pennsylvania Avenue, and they got their water from pumps or springs. There were no sewers, and the streets were not paved, and the parks were all full of weeds. He told me about it one day last spring when we were in Washington, and sat under the trees

in beautiful Stanton Square. I could hardly believe that the lovely city ever looked as he described it. And to think that that was only a little over thirty years ago! Father says the changes seem like a dream to him.
LILIAN PRESCOTT.

In 1808 there were only about five thousand people in Washington, and lots of fun was made of the city. A great many people wanted the Capitol moved farther North, and the papers were filled with jokes about the "City in the mud," "City of streets without houses," "Capitol of huts," and all that sort of thing. I wish some of those simpletons who wrote that way could ride down Pennsylvania Avenue now! But they can't, because they are all dead.
ARTHUR BURKHARDT.

My mother used to be in Washington when the Northwest, where so many elegant houses are, was just a great swamp! When we were there a year ago she took me to walk on Connecticut Avenue, and showed me where she and Aunt Nannie used to play hide-and-seek. The elegant building belonging to the British Legation stands there now, and in every direction the houses and lawns are lovely! I asked mamma how they came to be allowed to play on such an elegant street, and she laughed, and said nobody in those days thought of such a thing as its ever being elegant around there. It seems queer to think what changes there must have been in a few years. My Auntie lives on Connecticut Avenue now, and I think it is one of the prettiest streets in Washington.
ALICE BARNES.

My brother Robert liked the great dome best, but I was very fond of the bronze door at the main entrance of the Capitol. I had just been studying all about Columbus when I went to Washington, and it was so interesting to see his history carved on the door. Then I staid in the rotunda a long time. I like round rooms when they are very large. The paintings are beautiful. There was one of Columbus landing, and one which showed the Pilgrims just starting, and one of Pocahontas being baptized.

I like to look at pictures of things that I know about. Of course I went up the round-and-round iron stairway which leads to the dome. I stood under the statue of Freedom and looked down at the city. It was beautiful.

CARRIE FOSTER.

WE went, last winter, to the Library of Congress. My uncle went almost every day, and I had to go with him, because I had nowhere else to go while he was there; but I had a nice book to read, and I liked it. The room is made of iron — I mean the shelves and rafters and all those things are — and the roof is of copper.

get books enough to last for a century, but hundreds of thousands of dollars have been spent for them since. I saw the new library building going up. It is to cost nearly five millions. When it is finished they will have room for four million books! It is to have a gallery three hundred and fifty feet long, for pictures and beautiful things.

My uncle says this letter is too long; but I do not know what to leave out, so I will send it.

MARGARET WINTERS.

I WENT to Congress two or three times last winter. They behave better in the Senate than

VIEW OF THE CAPITOL.

It is said to be the only library in the world that is entirely fire proof. There are more than six hundred thousand books, and thousands and thousands of pamphlets in this library. Every book which has been copyrighted has to send two copies to the library. It is about ninety years since books were first gathered there. It was in 1800 that Congress voted to use five thousand dollars toward buying books for a library. I suppose they thought that would

they do in the House. In fact, I don't think the people in the House were gentlemanly. They smoked, and they quarreled, and three or four tried to talk at once! ANNA BROOKS.

[This by no means exhausts the items of interest about Washington, but the article grows so long that we must omit the others, sorry as we are to do so. It is certainly a great pleasure to find our Pansies so wide awake, and so successful in selecting items which cannot fail to interest others. Remember the next city, and be in time for us to make careful selections. — EDITORS.]

MAJOR'S AUTOBIOGRAPHY.

II.

ALTHOUGH I am a dog myself I do wonder how some of my race can afford to waste so much love upon masters who have so little love for them, or, it would seem, for any one else.

Now, for instance, there is Mr. Billings who lives on the hill; just think how he ill-treats and almost starves his dog, cutting, scolding, licking him; and yet that poor fellow is just as glad to see him the next time as though he had been petted, and is ready to hunt, drive cows or sheep, or watch all night.

I have known that dog ever since he came into the neighborhood, and I knew old man Billings long before.

Being up that way I had a few words with friend Dash the day he arrived. I found him to be friendly — a dog that any man might love and be proud of. I was awfully sorry for him then, and have been ever since, for I did not think much of his master.

Sometimes, when I see the poor fellow coming, looking so lean and hungry, I run out into the road with the best bone I have on hand, for a bit of a lunch, and leave it where I know Dash will find it. My! it does me good to see him take it down.

I often think of him trotting for fifteen or twenty miles after that team, and as likely as not without a mouthful of breakfast before starting.

This is not mere surmise; he told me so one day — said he had been all day with nothing to eat but a scrap or two which he happened to find on the way; for he had not time to hunt for anything while in town, because he had to stay and watch the things in the wagon. It's too bad, too bad!

Just think what Dash has done for that man! You never heard about it?

Well, I will tell you. It was in the spring of last year — the time for washing sheep. When Mr. Billings went for his sheep, all his children who were big enough to help drive went along.

As he never pets anything that he has, so he never petted his sheep, therefore as soon as they heard him call they were much more afraid of him than they would have been of our master, I really believe, so away they went as fast as their legs could carry them.

If it had not been for Dash, Mr. Billings and all his boys could never have penned those creatures. But he seemed to know just what to do, and it was not long before they seemed to feel as though they had found a friend instead of an enemy in this dog; he worked like a good fellow, as he is.

After much skillful manoeuvering, hard running and gentle barking, the sheep were all finally gotten into the pen, where Billings and his boys could take them one by one and wash them with the water which fell over the dam.

After the father and older boys were gone, little Bennie Billings, who is only a few months more than three years old, crawled through the garden fence and started after the others.

His mother did not miss him, thinking he had gone with his brothers. As it was, Bennie came trotting along while the rest were absorbed in the work of washing sheep, and so was not noticed by any one of them.

But faithful Dash had his eye upon him all the while, and felt that it was more important that he should look after the boy than the lambs.

He tried hard to keep between Bennie and the water, but this he was not long able to do.

Sliding down the bank the boy crawled out upon a slippery rock, and from that fell into the water.

It was deep, and Dash had all he could do to drag the little fellow to the land. He could not pull him out; but holding on as well as he could, he growled very loud.

Dash was getting pretty tired, and the case was growing desperate, when a neighbor hearing the growl, came to the rescue.

Poor Bennie was almost gone; he would not have lived much longer; but if help had not come, Dash would have died with the little chap he was trying to save.

Think of that father kicking Dash after that, or ever forgetting to give him all he needed to eat! You would think the boy's mother would look after her child's rescuer; but it is said she has little to do with.

It would not seem so strange if the faithful fellow were not all the time doing things worthy of being remembered.

It was only last fall, when the corn was well grown, that this hard master came home one rainy night and forgot to fasten the gate after him. There were a great many cattle upon the road, and Dash told me he could hear the bell upon one old cow dingling away as plain as day all the time the master was unharnessing the horses. He said he ran out by the gate and barked as loud as he could when Mr. Billings was going into the house; but it did no good. So there was nothing for him to do but go and stay there all night in the hard rain.

Telling me about it he said: "I wouldn't have minded it, though it was so cold and wet, if master had noticed it; if he had just said, 'Good faithful fellow, you saved our garden and cornfield!' but he never noticed me except to scold me for getting in the way when I came into the kitchen to warm myself a little, though he knew there were more than twenty head of cattle which would have been in that garden and cornfield if I had not kept them out."

But for all that he would do the same things over again, or anything else that he can do for the comfort and help of his hard master.

I suspect Dash misses these little kindnesses more for the reason that he has not always been used to such treatment.

You see he once had a good master; but the man was taken ill and had to go away, and for some reason could not take Dash with him.

One day when we met down town near the post-office he told me this story.

By some mishap the house of his former master took fire. How it happened he did not seem to know. The mistress had gone into a neighbor's house for a few moments, and had left her baby asleep in the cradle, in charge of a little girl, while Dash watched at the front gate to see that no tramp came in.

Said he, "I smelt something, and looked around just in time to see that little girl as she ran out of the front door crying 'Fire!'"

"In a moment I thought of Baby, and saw that the girl had left it in the house; so I dashed through the door and into the thick smoke, and finding the cradle I caught the child by his frock, and pulling with all my might I got him out on the floor and dragged him to the door. Just as I got him to the first step, where we could breathe again, the mother arrived.

"But she came too late to have saved her baby if it had been in the cradle then, for that was already in full blaze. As it was, the poor thing was almost smothered with the smoke.

"How that mother hugged and kissed me! She made so much ado about it that I felt almost ashamed. Yet I must confess it was gratifying to know that the mother appreciated what I had done.

"Well, after that there was nothing in the house too good for me to eat, no place where I was not welcome, no kennel too nice for me to sleep in, nor was there any lack of petting."

Just imagine what a change from a home such as that, to the miserable one he now has to endure.

I do feel so sorry for him!

Sometimes I feel as though I should not be as faithful as Dash is if I were in his place; yet I must not forget that duty is duty, and that one must not do wrong because he has not been treated as he should be.

If this poor fellow's case were a solitary one, it would not seem so bad; but I am sorry to say that all over our land there are as faithful fellows as Dash treated no better than he.

Think of those dogs with drunken masters! Think how much they have to endure of hunger and cold and abuse, though they are as faithful as life. I can hardly keep from growling when I think of it!

But I must not talk in this way any longer to-day. I have spent the hour speaking of another, so we must wait till some other time before I can tell you anything more of my own experience.

Indeed I was not intending to talk all the time about myself; I would like to set before you a little of the lives of the best of our race, such as will afford you excellent examples for imitation, that your lives may be good and true.

R.

BENNIE'S FRIEND.

SILENT PARTNERS.

VESUVIUS.

NEARLY two thousand years ago there was a mountain, and its name was Vesuvius. From the foot of it to the very top it was almost like a garden.

At the bottom were two great cities, called Herculaneum and Pompeii. The mountain is there now, and near it is the city of Naples in Italy.

One day, when everything was going on in street, some took to the boats and rowed away as fast as possible, some screamed. Children clung to their mothers, hiding their faces in their dresses. Animals broke away and ran furiously, dashing themselves against the rocks or plunging into the sea; the very birds sighed as they swept through the sky.

The mountain — this Vesuvius — was on fire; the fire was spouting from its top in terrific forms. Smoke, such as you have never seen it, leaped as the darkest thunder clouds upward, while melted earth and rock ran down the sides

ERUPTION OF VESUVIUS, 1880.

those great cities just as usual, an awful sound was heard like the firing of ten thousand of the biggest cannon; the earth shook as if it was going to pieces, then it grew dark like night. The sky was filled with flying cinders, or something like ashes; the air had a sulphurous smell. All the people wondered. Some ran into the of Vesuvius like a devouring flood. Before it, the gardens fled away. On it came, rushing, foaming, burning. It leaped upon the houses and buried them, whole streets at once. So suddenly it came that few of the people escaped. What a time was that!

Think of a whole city, like Philadelphia,

buried ten or twenty feet deep, so that in the place of the grand palaces, stores and temples, nothing was seen but a smoking furnace — red-hot lava!

Not a great while since people began to dig. They dug and dug, and after years of digging there were the streets again and buildings, the merchant selling his goods, babies sleeping in their mamma's arms, a bride and groom standing up to be married, a funeral procession coming from a house, a miser counting his money, a cruel father beating his child, a loving mother kissing her son, a marriage feast in this house, a dying parent in that. Just as the fierce, quick flood of lava found them, so it buried them, and so they were found after nearly two thousand years!

Since that awful day the volcano, Vesuvius, has been on fire again and again.　　　　L.

AURORA LEIGH.

(English Literature Papers.)

 OW many of my Pansies are acquainted with her? She is "a woman in a book," and the book was written by a woman of whom you have surely heard — Elizabeth Barrett Browning. I want you to know something about this story book and its author. There are those who think the story is too "grown-up" to interest children; but that is because they do not understand certain kinds of children very well. When I was a little girl of ten, I was very fond of narrative poems, and read some which were judged far above my understanding.

Would you like a picture of Aurora's room, as she describes it? Listen:

"I had a little chamber in the house
As green as any privet hedge a bird
Might choose to build in. . . .
The walls were green, the carpet was pure green,
The straight small bed was curtained greenly,
And the folds hung green about the window,
Which let in the out-door world with all its greenery.
You could not push your hand out and escape
A dash of dawn-dew from the honeysuckle."

Poor Aurora lost her mother when she was four years old, and her dear, dear father when she was just a little girl. Then she sailed across the ocean from her home in Italy to her father's old home in England. When she first saw English soil, this is the way she felt:

. . . "oh, the frosty cliffs looked cold upon me!
Could I find a home among those mean red houses,
Through the fog? . . . Was this my father's England?

I think I see my father's sister stand
Upon the hall-step of her country house
To give me welcome. She stood straight and calm,
Her somewhat narrow forehead braided tight
As if for taming accidental thoughts
From possible quick pulses. Brown hair
Pricked with gray by frigid use of life,
A nose drawn sharply, yet in delicate lines;
A close mild mouth . . . eyes of no color;
Once they might have smiled, but never, never
Have forgot themselves in smiling."

You cannot imagine, I think, any life more unlike what Aurora had been used to in her home in Florence, than the one to which she came in England. She describes her aunt's life as —

"A sort of cage-bird life, born in a cage,
Accounting that to leap from perch to perch
Was act and joy enough for any bird.
Dear Heaven, how silly are the things
That live in thickets, and eat berries!
I, alas, a wild bird scarcely fledged,
Was brought to her cage, and she was there to meet me,
Very kind! 'Bring the clean water; give out the fresh seed!'"

You wonder what sort of a little girl she was? She tells us:

"I was a good child on the whole,
A meek and manageable child. Why not?
I did not live to have the faults of life.
There seemed more true life in my father's grave
Than in all England. . . . . .
At first I felt no life which was not patience;
Did the thing she bade me, without heed
To a thing beyond it; sat in just the chair she placed
With back against the window, to exclude
The sight of the great line-tree on the lawn,
Which seemed to have come on purpose from the woods
To bring the house a message."

So quiet was she, and pale, and sad, that her aunt's friends visiting there, whispered about her that "the child from Florence looked ill, and would not live long." This made her glad, for she was homesick for her father's grave. But her cousin, Romney Leigh, a boy somewhat older than herself, took her to task for this. He said to her:

> "You're wicked now. You wish to die,
> And leave the world a-dusk for others,
> With your naughty light blown out."

Well, she did not die, but lived to be a sweet, proud, brave, foolish, sorrowful, glad, happy woman! You think my words contradict one another? No; they may belong to one life, and often do.

I do not mean that you will be interested in all her story—hers and "Cousin Romney's"—not yet awhile. Some day you will read it, study it, I hope, for the beauty of the language, and for the moral power there is in it. Just now, my main object is to introduce you, so that when you hear the name "Aurora Leigh," you may be able to say: "I know her; she is one of Mrs. Browning's characters—a little girl from Florence, who lived with an aunt in England." Or when you hear Mrs. Browning's name, you will say, or think: "She wrote a long poem once, named Aurora Leigh."

Why should you care to know that? Because, my dear, it is a little crumb of knowledge about English Literature, a study which I am hoping you are going to greatly enjoy by and by.

Oh! Mrs. Browning wrote many other poems, though the one about which we have been talking is perhaps considered her greatest. There are some which I think you must know and love. For instance:

> "Little Ellie sits alone
>   'Mid the beeches of a meadow,
> By a stream-side on the grass;
> And the trees are showering down
>   Doubles of their leaves in shadow,
> On her shining hair and face.
>
> "She has thrown her bonnet by,
>   And her feet she has been dipping
> In the shallow water's flow;
> Now she holds them nakedly
>   In her hands, all sleek and dripping,
> While she tosseth to and fro.
>
> "Little Ellie sits alone,
>   And the smile she softly uses
> Fills the silence like a speech;
> While she thinks what shall be done—
>   And the sweetest pleasure chooses
> For her future within reach."

There are seventeen verses; of course I have not room for them, but you will like to find the poem and read for yourselves. It is entitled "The Romance of the Swan's Nest."

Then there is that wonderful poem of hers called "The Cry of the Children." Surely you ought to know of that. It was suggested to her by reading the report which told about children being employed in the mines and manufactories of England. It is said that Mrs. Browning's poem was the means of pushing an act of Parliament which forbade the employment of young children in this way. The poem has thirteen long verses, every one of which you should carefully read. Let me give you just a taste:

> "Do you hear the children weeping, O, my brothers!
>   Ere the sorrow comes with years?
> They are leaning their young heads against their mothers,
>   And that cannot stop their tears!
> The young lambs are bleating in the meadows;
>   The young birds are chirping in the nest;
> The young fawns are playing with the shadows;
>   The young flowers are blowing toward the west;
> But the young, young children, O, my brothers!
>   They are weeping bitterly.
> They are weeping in the playtime of the others,
>   In the country of the free.
>   . . . .
>
> "'True,' say the children, 'it may happen
>   That we die before our time;
> Little Alice died last year; her grave is shapen
>   Like a snowball in the rime.
> We looked into the pit prepared to take her;
>   There's no room for any work in the coarse clay;
> From the sleep wherein she lieth none will wake her,
>   Crying 'Get up, little Alice! it is day.'
> If you listen by that grave in sun and shower,
>   With your ear down, little Alice never cries.
> Could we see her face, be sure we should not know her,
>   For the smile has time for growing in her eyes.
> And merry go her moments, lulled and stilled
>   In the shroud by the kirk-chime.
> 'It is good, when it happens,' say the children,
>   'That we die before our time.'"

It will never do to take more room with this paper, and I have told you almost nothing about the dear lady who voiced the children's cry so wonderfully, and to such purpose! Suppose you let me take her story, little bits of it, for the next PANSY. Besides, I want to introduce you to her dear "Flush."

PANSY.

MRS. BROWNING'S AURORA LEIGH.

BABY'S CORNER.

A GOOD TIME.

HIS is Trudy. She is all ready to go with papa.

They are going up in the woods to the "sugar bush."

It is April — a bright, sunshiny day, but the wind is cold, so she has to wear her warm coat and hood.

As Trudy ran along through the woods she saw a little bluebird singing on a branch, and she found yellow violets and tiny blue flowers

TRUDY.

pails were full of sap John, the hired man, brought it into the little sugar house and boiled it, and made nice cakes of maple sugar.

The house had a great fireplace. A bright fire was crackling there.

Trudy sat down on a stool and warmed her toes.

There was a big black kettle over the fire; it was almost full of sap. It bubbled and boiled and made a good smell.

John stirred it with a long wooden spoon. He stirred and stirred a long time, and the fire snapped and the sap boiled, and Trudy watched, and by and by it was done!

Then papa got a pan of snow, and John dropped little bits from the spoon all over the snow.

When it was cool Trudy put in her thumb and finger, and plump! went one of the little brown balls into her mouth. Oh! but it was good. Trudy thought maple candy was ever so much better than the pink and white stuff she bought at the stores.

She ate and ate, till papa said, "No more, dearie." So she carried the rest of it to little brother.

They rode home on the wood sled, drawn by two big oxen. Trudy said it was just the "beautifulest time" she ever had in her life.

She whispered to papa that she thought God was very good to make so many big trees full of candy just to please little girls and boys.

MRS. C. M. LIVINGSTON.

JOHN BROUGHT THE PAILS OF SAP.

with a long name. They had just poked up their heads through the snow. Brave little blossoms they were!

Wooden pails hung on all the maple-trees. The sap was running into them. When the

The Little Queen

THERE you have a fine Holland house, a palace rather. Come, let us go in. Just think, you have a royal invitation. Well, here we are. In this elegant room is a kingly throne. In that beautiful chair sits the little Queen of Holland.

Doesn't this Miss look like a wise sovereign, able to command armies and navies and make laws?

Now you laugh. But come out into her big back yard, and you shall see our little maid rule her subjects. See how obedient they are, running to her or fleeing from her as fast as their legs can carry them—and their wings too—

"Wings!"

Why, bless you, yes. This little Queen has one hundred and fifty cooing doves. She is their beloved mistress, feeding and fondling them, calling them by name, they laughing, singing, talking for her, after the dear dove fashion.

But look! there comes the Shetland pony, and quick as a cat she is on his back, and away they go down the road, gallopty, gallop, she tossing back a kiss to her mamma, the Queen Regent, who looks from the palace window. There she comes back, her face full of roses and laughter.

Twenty minutes more, and she is a student like any of you, with spelling-book, pen or geography, or thumbing the piano or reading aloud to her mother. She is her mother's constant companion. She is up at 7 A. M., and kneeling at her mother's knee, says her morning prayers.

She is often dressed completely in white, even to gloves and stockings. Watch and see what she will be in coming years.

L.

A WONDERFUL STONE.

A MR. MENINGER of New Orleans, while visiting in the town of Chilpanzingo, Mex., saw a rock there which he — and others — says foretells rain twenty-four hours in advance!

In fair weather it is grayish, very smooth and cold, but when it is going to rain it becomes a dingy red at the base, pink at the top, and it becomes warmer and warmer till the rain falls. If there is much lightning, the stone becomes charged (filled) like an electrical jar, so that you cannot safely approach it.

After the rain it goes back to its first state of color and coldness.

L.

THE FIRST CHRISTMAS.

WHY so soon with flocks returning?
  O, dear father, tell us why:
Scarce the night lamps ceased their burning,
  Scarce the stars dimmed in the sky
When we heard the distant bleating
  Of the flock come o'er the lea;
While the stars were still retreating
  Thou wert coming o'er the lea;
Home so early in the morning!
  Sheep and lambs so fast you're leading
To the fold at early dawning,
  At the time of sweetest feeding!

Ill, dear father, art thou? Surely
  Suffering art thou? Tell us true!
Has some lambie been unruly —
  Wandered far away from view?
Must thou go across the mountain,
  Starting in the morning gray,
Search by vale, and rock, and fountain
  For the lost one, gone astray?
But thy face is bright and beaming,
  And thy step is free and glad,
And thy eyes with joy are gleaming
  Surely nothing makes thee sad!

Thus she chattered to her father,
  Shepherd of Judean plain;
Eager for some reason given
  Which might satisfy her brain;
But the father, heart o'erflowing
  With the story he could tell,
Felt the spirit in him burning —
  Felt his soul within him swell —
And, with tender touch, down bending
  Gently drew her to his breast;
His life-calling sweetly lending
  Skill for what he loved the best.

Then his home flock, like the other,
  In the home fold where they dwelt —
Father, children, precious mother —
  All before Jehovah knelt;
Knelt to thank the covenant-keeping
  God of Jacob, who alone
In their waking and their sleeping,
  Safely shelters all his own.
This — and then began the story
  Of the night before that morn,

When the angels came from glory,
  Telling that the Christ was born.

(The story.)

On the hillside near our flocks were sleeping,
  While we, reclining by, our watch were keeping;
The sun had set in a glow of splendor,
And the stars looked down so pure and tender
That we felt a hush pervading
Every breast; for the fading
Of the day had been so slow,
And the twilight's gentle glow
Had left the earth so still
That over plain and hill
A gentle sleep seemed holding all
As quiet as beneath a pall

Of death. When every heart
Was hushed, and sure to start
At slightest move or sound,
From sky or earth or ground,
We would not break with song
The silence, which so strong
Had reigned supreme the while,
But sought we to beguile
With word of prophecy the hour,
Talking of Him whose conquering power
Our fallen Israel should restore,
And make her glory as of yore.

The Lord seemed wondrous near us then;
As when our father Jacob dreamed, or when
The great law-giver stood on hallowed ground
And heard Jehovah speak in words profound;
When, suddenly, burst on the ravished ear
A voice like music, or like trumpet clear,
And words most wonderful did there proclaim:
Tidings, glad tidings of the glorious Name!
He bade us haste to Bethlehem away
To find the Babe there born to us this day;
And then, when Paradise I see complete,
May it such strains to these glad ears repeat!
Then as from cloud the pealing thunder breaks
Till 'neath its voice the very mountain shakes,
So burst in chorus the celestial choir,
Each tongue aflame with heaven's own altar fire,
To celebrate, as by Jehovah sent,
The long foretold and now fulfilled event —
Our own Messiah's birth in Bethlehem town!
The Christ of God from heaven to earth come
  down!

The singing ceased, and all was still again
Save the sweet echo of "Good-will to men";
The choir had flown; our flocks were all at rest,
And could we, after such a vision blest,

Await the dawning to behold the Stranger
Which cradled lay in Bethlehem's lowly manger?
If we forgot our flocks, in haste to see the sight
Revealed to us by angel hosts last night,
Was it so strange, when honored thus were we
To be the first of all our race to see,
Worship and welcome to this world the King
Of whom the Prophets old did write and sing?
And so we hastened, sped, and tarried not
Until we found, O, joy! the very spot
Where lay this lily from sweet Paradise,
Angelic beauty there, before our eyes!

We bent, we worshiped, kissed the Babe so fair,
Then hastened back through all the perfumed air
To find our flocks by angel guards attended,
Better by them than by our skill defended.
Then each with gladness homeward sped away
To tell the tidings of this wondrous day.
The questions asked as round the father's knee
The children pressed in eager ecstasy,
I will not try to tell. I cease
My story of the "Prince of Peace,"
This only adding—though the talk was long—
There followed it this burst of sacred song:

(The song.)

O, thou Infant holy!
In thy cradle lowly,
Feeble stranger seeming,
Though almighty. Deeming
It thy pleasure,
Even in this measure,
In this casket fair
Human woe to share.

We thy praises sing;
To thy cradle bring
Love, and thanks and treasure,
Offerings without measure;
Just now come from glory,
We have heard thy story
Sung by angel chorus,
While God's light shone o'er us.

O, thou Baby stranger!
Hiding in a manger,
By crowded inn rejected,
By pilgrims all neglected,
For thee our hearts are burning
With a holy yearning.
Be thou our guest;
Our arms would now enfold thee,
Our hearts would gladly hold thee;
We love thee best.

G. R. ALDEN.

THE SPOOL-COTTON GIRL.

PART I.

 HE stood before a little old-fashioned twisted-legged toilet stand putting the finishing touches to her hair, looking, the while, into a queer little old-fashioned mirror which had been in the family ever since she could remember. Almost everything had been in their family a long while. Especially, Marion sometimes thought, her dresses had. "They do not wear overskirts like this any more," she had said to her mother that morning, as she was looping it.

"They do not wear overskirts at all," said Renie, the younger sister, looking up from her book. Renie always knew what "they" did.

"I know it," answered Marion, from whose face the slight cloud had already passed; "but we do, because, you see, it hides the pieced part of our dress, and the faded part, and various other blemishes. Why should not there be a what 'we' do, as well as to be always quoting what 'they' are about?"

Her mother laughed somewhat faintly. Marion's quaint bright speeches were always restful to her; but the fact was undeniable that the dear girl's clothes were old-fashioned and much worn, and the way to secure, or at least to afford new ones, was hedged.

You would not have called her pretty had you seen her as she stood before that little old-fashioned mirror, pushing in the old-fashioned comb into her knot of hair, and trying to make it hold the hair in the way the pretty new style fancy pins which the girls wore held theirs; but you would have liked her face, I think; nearly every one did. It was quiet and restful looking. She gave very little time to the hair, for she was late. There was so much to be done mornings that she was very apt to be late—I mean hurried. They never called her late at the store; she was always in her place before the great bell ceased ringing, but it required much bustling about and some running, to accomplish this. She was only thirteen, and most of the girls in her class in Sunday-school were students at the High School; but Marion had been for more than a year earning her own living. She had charge of the spool-cotton counter in one of the large stores.

It was a matter of some pride to her that she was a small saleswoman, instead of a cash girl. She had commenced, of course, in that way; but one happy day an unexpected vacancy had occurred at the spool counter, and she had fitted in so well that she had been kept there, although younger than most of the other salesgirls. Her face was quieter than usual this morning. Perhaps because it was such a rainy morning that she had felt compelled to wear the quite old dress, instead of the somewhat fresher one which had lately begun to come to the store on pleasant days. Marion had discovered that she needed special grace to help her through the rainy days and the old-fashioned gown.

Not very many people were abroad shopping; but Marion had her share of work, for those who came were in need of such commonplace useful things as spool cotton, or tape, or needles. She bent carefully over a drawer full of various colors, holding a tiny brown patch in her hand the while, trying to match the shade. "No," she said, shaking her head, "that is not quite a match, but I am afraid it is the best I can do. If I were you I would take a shade darker rather than the lighter; my mother always does."

The middle-aged woman, in a plain gossamer which covered her from head to foot, glanced up at the thoughtful young face and smiled.

"Does she?" she said. "I like to hear a young girl quote her mother's judgment; it is apt to be wise judgment, I have noticed, as I think it is in this case. Show me darker shades, please."

So another drawer was brought, and yet another, and the young head bent with the older one over them, and tried and tried again, and at last a satisfactory shade was found and the sale was made. Five cents' worth of thread for fifteen minutes' work!

"Why in the world did you putter so over that old maid and her patch? I should have told her I couldn't match it and sent her about her business fifteen minutes ago."

It was the girl whose stand was next to Marion who offered this bit of advice, while the "old maid" in question was but a few steps away from them looking at pin balls.

Marion turned a warning glance in her direction, and lowered her voice to answer: "Because I couldn't find a match sooner. We went over all the thread drawers on that side, but I think we secured the exact shade at last."

"What does it signify? Nothing but brown cotton. Wasn't the patch part cotton? I thought so. The idea of making such an ado over a match for cheap goods like that! I wouldn't fuss with such customers, I can tell you. Five cents' worth of goods and fifty cents' worth of bother. You couldn't have done more for her if she had been your sister."

Marion looked after the plain woman thoughtfully, then looked down at the tiny pin she wore. "I am not sure but she is. Anyhow, I was bound to endeavor to please her. I'm an Endeavorer, you know." She gave the pin a significant touch as she spoke. It was very small —almost too small to attract attention — but the letters "C. E." were, after all, quite distinct.

"O, bother!" said her neighbor, speaking contemptuously, "so am I; at least so far as wearing the pin is concerned. I wear it because it is pretty, and I have so few ornaments that I have to make the most of them; but as for putting sentiment into spools of cotton and balls of tape, I can't do it; the things don't match."

"They ought to," Marion said gravely. "If you and I don't put our pledges into spools of cotton and balls of tape of what use are they? Because we spend our days in just such work."

"I know it," with a discontented yawn; "I'm sick and tired of it. It is a slave life; I'd get out of it if I could. If there was any chance of getting promoted it would be a little different. Belle Mason has been transferred to the ribbon counter, and she gets more wages and sees other sorts of people, and has lots of fun; she hasn't been in the house as long as I have, either; it is just because she was put at a counter where she had a chance of pleasing people, and here we have just to poke over tape and cotton and pins, and such stuff. I think it's mean!"   PANSY.

SAYING HER EVENING PRAYER.

HELEN'S "APRIL FOOL."

MAMMA, is an April fool different from any other kind of a fool?" cried Helen Palmer, rushing into the sitting-room on arriving home from school. "Oh! good-evening, Mrs. Glenn," she added, as she noticed a lady who sat sewing with her mother.

"What does the child mean?" exclaimed Mrs. Glenn, returning Helen's nod, then looking her astonishment at Mrs. Palmer, who said: "What do you mean, Helen?"

"Why, the girls are all talking to-day about to-morrow being 'April Fool Day,' and they said a lot of things I don't understand, about calling people 'April fool.' They all agreed to see who could make the most fools and tell about it Monday. They said I must too, and I didn't want to tell them I did not know how to do it, or what it means."

"You don't mean to tell me, Helen Palmer, that you don't know anything about April fool?" cried Mrs. Glenn, in surprise.

"No," said Mrs. Palmer; "she doesn't. This is her first year at school, you know; I have taught her at home, and in our country home she heard very little but what we told her. I never saw any sense or fun in the custom of fooling on the first day of April, and did not instruct her in it when I taught her of Thanksgiving, Christmas, New Year, St. Valentine's Day, Washington's Birthday, Decoration Day and Fourth of July."

"But what is it?" insisted Helen.

"Well, my dear, it is a custom which I've read has come down hundreds of years, to send people on ridiculous errands on that day and call it an April fool. It is done all over Europe, and the Hindoos of India do exactly the same thing on the thirty-first of March. As I've always known it, people not only send others on foolish errands, but they often play practical jokes, silly and cruel, and actually lie to each other to fool them. It is a custom much better forgotten than kept."

"I should think so," cried Helen.

"But, mamma," she continued, "what shall I do? The girls expect me to tell my share on Monday."

"We'll see, dear, by and by. Go and put away your things now."

Mrs. Glenn went away after tea, and Helen began at once to coax her mother to tell her how to come up to the girls' plans without doing anything silly or wicked.

"I think, if I were you, I would spend the day surprising people with something good. Do things to help or please, and when they show their surprise say 'April fool!'"

"O, mamma! that will be delightful," cried Helen. "Tell me some things to do."

"No, my dear, that is your business."

All that evening Helen was very thoughtful, and next day she was unusually busy. At night she declared she had never been so happy. Monday morning she met the girls, and they began to tell their jokes.

"I fooled everybody around the house," said Carrie Andrews. "I filled the sugar-bowl with salt, and papa got a big spoonful in his coffee. You ought to have seen the face he made. He didn't more than half like it, even when I called out 'April fool!'" "I sent George out to pick up a package of sand I had dropped near the gate. I rang the doorbell and got Ann to go to the door, and there I stood and said 'April fool.' I sent a letter to Louise, and tied mamma's apron-strings to her chair."

Helen listened in amazement, as one girl after another told of such silly tricks.

At last they turned to her. "Well, Helen, what did you do?"

"Oh! I fooled every one in the family, but I did a lot of new things," said Helen.

"What were they?" cried the girls, in chorus.

"Well," said she, in a low voice, "I got up real early, and crept softly downstairs and set the table in the dining-room, while Jane was starting breakfast in the kitchen. She 'most always has it set at night, but mamma and the sewing woman were using the long table to cut out goods when Jane went to bed. She was hurrying as fast as she could, and rushed in, and when she saw the table set she threw up both hands, and said: 'Well, now, however did that table get set? Was it witches' work?'

"Then I jumped out from behind the door and cried: 'April fool!'

"'So it is,' she said; 'an' it's a fine one you've given me; I'll not forget it of you.'

"After breakfast mamma was just going to get Baby to sleep, and some one came to see her on business. She asked me to keep him till she could get back. I took him, and rocked and sung to him, and he went to sleep. I laid him down in his crib, and then hid to see what mamma would do. I heard her hurrying upstairs and into the room. Then she stopped and stared. I stepped up softly behind her and kissed her, and said, 'April fool!' She thought it was a nice one.

"Uncle Guy came in and asked mamma to mend his glove when she had time. As quick as I could I got my thimble and needle and silk and mended the glove; and when he came in again in a hurry and said: 'Well, I can't wait now for it to be mended,' he drew it on and said, 'Why, it is mended.' Then I called out, 'April fool, Uncle Guy!'

"'O, you little rogue!' he said; 'I'll pay you up.'

"Well, then I mended Frank's sails to his boat when he started to do it and papa called him away, and"—

"What did you do for your father?" asked Marjie Day.

"Oh! papa said he must hunt up some papers in the library at lunch-time, so I looked them up and laid them on his plate, and when he said: 'Why, how did these get here?' I said: 'April fool!' And that's all," added Helen, with glowing cheeks and sparkling eyes.

"Well!" exclaimed Carrie Andrews, "if that don't beat the Dutch."

"Wasn't it a good way?" asked Helen, almost crying.

"Of course, you little goose! but who else would ever have thought of it?"

"Mamma said she didn't like silly jokes, and said I had better try surprising people with pleasant things. I like it so well I am going to do it every day in the year."

"There's the bell," cried Belle Adams; "but hadn't we all better try it?"

F. A. REYNOLDS.

ABOUT PHILADELPHIA.

BY THE PANSIES.

ITS first name was Coaquenaque. I am glad they changed it to Philadelphia, because it is easier to pronounce; but I like Indian names. I went to Philadelphia once with my uncle. I think Broad Street is one of the nicest places in the world. I went to Germantown to see where Charlie Ross used to live, but I was so small I don't remember very much about anything, only Broad Street. I'm going again next year, and I'll look around and write you what I see. JOHN T. ROBINSON.

I WENT with father to Philadelphia three years ago; we staid near Washington Square; it is beautiful there. The trees are just splendid. Father told me it used to be a great burying-ground. I could not make it seem possible. A great many unknown soldiers, father said, were buried there; it was in Revolutionary times. How sad it must have been to live then! I like the little parks in Philadelphia that they call "squares." I saw the place where they held the Sanitary Fair, when they roofed over the entire square, and let the trees stand as pillars. LAURA CREEDMORE.

ONE of the most interesting places I visited in Philadelphia was Mr. Wanamaker's store. I did not know a store could be so large. It takes a hundred miles of steam pipes to heat it.

My uncle has a fruit farm of ten acres, and I used to think when I walked around it that ten acres was pretty big; but there are over fourteen acres of floor to walk around in Mr. Wanamaker's store! The different departments are fixed up beautifully. They have lovely parlors and dining-rooms and bedrooms all rigged up with beautiful furniture, to show people how to furnish their rooms, and every few days they change and give you another style. But the most interesting part of the store, to me, was the way the money is sent to the cashiers. There are eighty-one pay-stations in the store;

then there is a central cash desk where twenty-five cashiers are busy all day long receiving the money that is brought to them through the tubes. The clerk at a pay-station takes the money you give him, and starts it in one of the pneumatic tubes, and away it shoots to the central desk on the second floor; a cashier there looks at it, sees what change is needed, and shoots it back. I don't understand it very well,

FRANKLIN STATUE.

but I mean to. I am going to study the principles of pneumatic tubing, and Chris and I are going to have one to reach from my window to his. We are only about fifty feet apart. In Wanamaker's they have seven miles of tubing to carry their money around. We took dinner at the Wanamaker Dairy, right in the store; it

was jam full, and it will seat eight hundred people at once. Chris and I are going into partnership when we get to be men, and are going to have a store just exactly like it.

HENRY W. GILMORE.

I WENT to Philadelphia last winter and attended Mr. Conwell's church on Broad Street. It is very big — the biggest in the world, I guess — or maybe I mean in this country. It will hold thousands of people. Mother says she thinks Dr. Talmage's church is bigger, but I don't see how it could be. The people can't all get in; they have to have tickets and be let in by a door-keeper. The singing sounds just grand. There is a very large choir, and the organ rolls and rolls. I liked Mr. Conwell almost better than any minister I ever heard, except my own, of course. Then I went to Sunday-school; hundreds and hundreds and hundreds of children! I never saw so many together before. Of course I saw other things in Philadelphia, but what I liked the best was that church. It seemed so funny to see folks crowding into church on Sunday morning, and to have a big overflow meeting for those who couldn't get in. Where I live they have to coax the people to come to church, and there's lots of room always.

FANNY PIERCE.

ONCE I went to "Old Swede's" Church in Philadelphia. It is very old. There used to be a log church on the place where it stands; sometimes it was used for a fort. That was in 1677, but about three years afterwards the brick church was built, and that is the one I went to. In the churchyard are many very old graves, and some new ones. Some of the names on the grave-stones are so old I could not make them out. It seemed very strange to be in a church which was built almost two hundred years ago. Then we went to the queer little old house on Letitia Street where William Penn used to live. Great big buildings have grown up around it, and they make it look very odd. Then we went to the old London Coffee House; I had studied about that in my history, and I was disgusted to find it turned into a cigar store. It is a very queer old building. I saw

VIEW OF INDEPENDENCE HALL, PHILADELPHIA. *(See " About Philadelphia.")*

the house where the first American flag was made; that is on Arch Street.

HELEN STUART CAMPBELL.

My sister Helen has written all about old places and never mentioned Carpenter's Hall! She says that is because she knew I would. I went there with father and Helen. I think it is one of the grandest places in Philadelphia. It is the "Cradle of American Independence." That was where the first prayer in Congress was made the morning after Boston was bombarded. Before that some of the people had objected to having Congress opened with prayer, but after that morning nobody ever objected again. The inscription on the wall says it was here that "Henry, Hancock and Adams inspired the Delegates of the Colonies with Nerve and Sinew for the toils of war."

Then of course we went to Independence Hall, where the second Continental Congress gathered, and saw the old cracked bell which rung on the first Fourth of July. Helen says there was a Fourth of July every year before that time; but I mean the first one which was worth having. ROBERT STUART CAMPBELL.

I THINK the prettiest place in all Philadelphia is Fairmount Park. If I lived there I should want to stay in the park all summer. The drive out is just as lovely as it can be. We crossed the Girard Avenue bridge, which is a thousand feet long. You can walk or ride across, just as you please. There is a sidewalk on each side of the carriage drive sixteen feet wide, and beautifully paved. The railing around this bridge is trimmed with flowers, vines and birds, made in bronze. We saw the old house which was built by William Penn's son. And we went to the Zoölogical Gardens and saw the bear-pits and everything; then there is a part called the "Children's Playground," which is lovely. JAMES HURST.

[The above are some of the gleanings from the many letters received. Wish we had room for more. We are greatly pleased with your efforts to help on this department of THE PANSY. The main difficulty is, that many letters come too late to be of use. Notice the list of cities published in the December PANSY, and make a start three months ahead, then you will be sure to be on time. — EDITORS.]

THE SPOOL-COTTON GIRL.

PART II.

"WHAT did you say?" This last sentence was addressed to a customer who had been standing for some seconds. "Green braid? No, we haven't any to match that."

"Are you sure?" questioned the young girl anxiously. "Haven't you a little darker, then? that will do."

"No, we haven't!" sharp-voiced and spiteful. "Saucy thing!" she added, as the girl turned

THE LIBERTY BELL.

away; "I told her I hadn't; what business had she to ask again?"

"O, Nellie! I don't think you are sure. I think I found some in your upper row of boxes yesterday which would answer for the sample."

"Nonsense! as if you could tell without looking. I know I haven't; I tumbled the whole lot over yesterday for a fussy woman, and I remember every shade in it. It is of no consequence, anyhow; a seven-cent braid!"

"O, Jean! look here; let me see your photographs. Are they good?"

She had darted away to the counter below.

Marion stood for a moment irresolute, then

moved toward the girl. "Let me see it, please; I think I can match it."

The woman to whom she had sold a spool of thread turned at the sound of her voice and smiled on the girl. "Give it to her, Jennie, she will match it; she knows how," she said. Marion answered the smile; her heart was warm over the simple words of commendation. She sought among the upper row of boxes for the one which her memory associated with yesterday's shades, and found it. The girl made her seven-cent purchase and went away pleased, just as Nellie came back from her photographs.

"Such a stupid day!" she yawned toward its close. "Not a person of importance has even passed our counter. I've sold about a dollar's worth of goods to-day. How much have you done?"

"Hardly that," said Marion, smiling. "It has all been spools of cotton and darning needles. It has rained, you know, all day."

The next morning's sun shone brightly, and the large store was thronged early in the day with shoppers. Both Marion and Nellie were busy, the latter not much pleasanter than she had been the day before; it all seemed such trivial work to her.

"Are you sure you are not mistaken in the name?" one of the chiefs was saying, in a perplexed tone, to a lady who stood near Marion's counter. "We have but one clerk of that name, and she is the youngest in the store."

"This one is quite young, and she sells spool cotton," said the lady, catching Marion's eye and smiling a recognition. She had laid aside the long gossamer, and was carefully dressed. "I have a fancy to be waited on by her."

"Marion," said the chief, turning to her, "this lady wants to look at the light trimming silks; do you know anything about them?"

"Yes, sir," said Marion promptly; "I know the shades and prices."

"I thought so," the lady said, and Marion moved down the archway at her side.

"I have a fancy that you can match silks," the lady said; "at least I think you will patiently try. A girl who could do her best on a rainy day for a spool of cotton, can be depended upon for silk, I believe."

From the silk department they went to the glove counter, and from there to the millinery, in each of which departments the young girl with wide-open eyes and deft fingers and careful taste gave satisfaction. "You ought to be in this room," said the head milliner, smiling on her as she saw her select the right shade of velvet. "Where do you belong?" She laughed when told, and said that the spool-cotton department was fortunate.

"That Marion Wilkes," said the chief on Saturday evening, "what about her?" The clerk told briefly what he knew about her.

"Promote her," said the chief briefly. "Keep watch of her; if she succeeds in other departments as well, keep pushing her. She has been worth several hundred dollars to us this week. Miss Lamson told me she had expected to buy her niece's outfit over at Breck's, but was attracted here by that little girl selling her a spool of cotton on a rainy day. And Jennie Packard brought her mother here for the winter supplies for their family, because that girl matched her a dress braid; in fact, I have heard half a dozen stories of the kind about her. She is valuable; we cannot spare her for spool cotton."

It was four years ago that this true story happened. Last Saturday, as I stood near the spool counter in the fashionable store, I heard a voice ask: "And what has become of Marion Wilkes? She used to be here next to you, didn't she, Nellie?"

"Why, yes, she was the spool-cotton girl; but she didn't stay here long; she got to be a favorite with the proprietors somehow. I never understood it. She was a sly little thing; they promoted her all the while; you never saw anything like it. She gets the largest salary of any saleswoman in the store now, and I heard last week that they were going to put her at the head of the art department. That's just the way with some people, always in luck. Here I have been at this tape and braid counter for years, and expect to be until my eyes are too dim to pick out the stupid things. I told you I had no tape of that width; what is the use in asking again?" This last sentence was addressed to a little girl who was waiting to be served.   PANSY.

THE SPOILED FACE.

(Character Studies.)

ISN'T he lovely?" asked Miss Henderson, as we three stood in front of Charlie's portrait, which had just come from the artist's hand. "He has such great expressive eyes, so soft, and yet so full of intelligence. The artist has caught the very expression. I think I never saw a more beautiful boy."

"I think I never saw a greater nuisance," said Miss Maylie, speaking with a good deal of energy and with a slight frown on her face, as though some unpleasant memory was stirred by the sight of the lovely face in the frame. We both turned and looked at her in surprise.

"Nuisance!" repeated Miss Henderson. "Why, what can you mean? I have heard that his character is as lovely as his face. He is one of the most generous little fellows, always dividing his goodies with the children."

"Oh! I don't doubt it," said Miss Maylie; "but there are other traits in children to be sought after besides that of dividing their goodies." Then she laughed, as if half-ashamed of the warmth of her manner, and said: "I've been a recent victim to one of his habits, and feel somewhat deeply, perhaps. I had an important engagement with his mother yesterday — a business matter for which I had asked an interview — and told her I was pressed for time, and had but a half-hour. I suppose we had been together about two minutes when the door opened without the ceremony of a knock, and Charlie appeared to ask if he might go over to Uncle Harry's. He was told that he could not, it looked too much like rain; and he argued the matter, assuring his mother that the wind had changed and was blowing from the west; that the cook said it was not going to rain any more; that he would put on his rubbers and bundle up, and I don't know what else. He was listened to patiently by his mother, and impatiently by me, for my precious half-hour was slipping away. He shut the door at last with a frown on his face which, if it had been

painted, would have made this picture much less beautiful, but I am afraid more natural.

"It was certainly not five minutes before he was back, and this time it was, 'Mamma, may I call Jerry to bring in the kittens?'

"'O, no, dear! not this afternoon; you are dressed for dinner, you know.'

"'That won't make any difference; I won't soil my clothes. The kittens haven't been out in the mud. Do, mamma, let me.'

"'No, Charlie; I do not want them in the parlor, you know.'

"'Then I'll go to the kitchen and play with them; Jane won't care.'

"'Yes, Jane cares very much; the kittens annoy her. Charlie will have to get along without them this afternoon.'

"Another slam to the door, with the scowl deepened. But we were by no means to be left in peace. I was just in the midst of the most intricate part of my business explanation, when Charlie arrived again. Now he was hungry; could not wait another minute, and wanted some bread and butter and syrup, and a piece of cake and a glass of milk. It was carefully explained to him that dinner would be served within the hour, and that syrup was not good for him, the doctor said — to which he replied that he did not care what the old doctor said — and that cake would be given him at the table when it was passed to the others. To each of these explanations he returned an answer which had to be answered, and when all was settled, he began over again to coax for something to eat! The fourth time he came he wanted the gas lighted in the library, and the fifth he wanted a certain great book which he could not lift placed conveniently for him to look at the pictures. When at last even his mother felt the strain on her patience and told him he must run away and not interrupt her again, he burst into a loud howl, and slammed the door after him so that my nerves all shivered at the jar.

"I must say it would be difficult for me to admire his face to-day; my annoyances are too recent. Seven times during a single half-hour to be interrupted by a little boy, when you are trying to transact important business with his mother, has spoiled his face for me. If he had wanted one single thing which it was important to have at that moment, it would have made a difference."

"They all seemed important to him, I suppose," said gentle Miss Henderson, who always tried to apologize for everybody.

"Yes, they did," said Miss Maylie; "that is just the trouble; he evidently considered himself a very important person, and thought that his mother should leave her business and her caller and attend to him. I should call him a spoiled child." MYRA SPAFFORD.

CHARLIE'S PORTRAIT

MY LITTLE MAID.

THIS is my little maid, Eva ——, though that is not her Chinese name. She will be a woman one of these bright days, and who knows but she may become a real princess or empress of great China?

"What of that?"

Much every way, if she now loves the Lord Jesus, and grows up a noble Christian woman. Can't you see how she could help the Gospel

EVA.

among her people if she had the great power of an empress? I hope you remember how the good Queen of Madagascar led her nation to give up idolatry and choose the Bible. And now they are doing things so cruel to their neighbors who have become Christians we wish our little Eva were the grand good empress to stop these wicked Chinese doings.   L.

THINK well over your important steps in life; having made up your mind never look behind.

SACRED ANIMALS.

SOME nations think certain animals sacred; that is, they are so much better than other animals that they must not be harmed; of course they must not be killed. If they can they treat them almost as if they were human beings, dressing them up nicely, even richly. Just think of one of our bull-dogs dressed and fed and housed almost as well as a king!

"Why do certain tribes of Africa almost worship the Lion of Lhiamba?"

Perhaps because he is so strong and wise and terrible. He seems like a very god to them, they fear him so.

"Now maybe," they say to themselves, "if we respect this great, fierce beast, never lifting a hand to harm him, maybe he will not harm us."

"Does he ever harm them?"

Always, if they cross his path when he is hungry.

"Are there any other sacred animals?"

Yes; the bull, the white elephant, the monkey, even the serpent, and how many more it is hard to say.

Maybe you can guess which is sacred to the Egyptians, Chinese, etc.

We should not needlessly harm any animal. Shooting birds for mere fun is wrong. Animals have a hard time in this world. Let us not make it harder. But we must worship God only.

They are mere creatures, passing away after a short stay here; God lives forever. "Thou shalt have no other gods before me."

L.

EACH one of us is bound to make the little circle in which he lives better and happier; each of us is bound to see that out of that small circle the widest good may flow; each of us may have fixed in his mind the thought that out of a single household may flow influences that shall stimulate the whole commonwealth and the whole civilized world. — *Selected.*

THE LION OF LILANDA.

SADIE'S "HEATHEN."

OBODY knew or even dreamed how large a thought was puzzling the brains of little Sadie Wilmot. It had begun at family worship that morning. Or no; perhaps it began back of that, at the meeting of "Cheerful Givers," on Thursday. Mr. Wilmot said it was an absurd idea for such little dots as Sadie to be going to missionary meeting, but grandmamma quoted to him: "As the twig is bent, the tree is inclined," and herself dressed Sadie for the gathering. Then Miss Harlowe, the leader, had told a story about a little heathen boy who prayed to an ugly little wooden image, with a hideous face; she showed a model of the little heathen's god, and Sadie was shocked and distressed. She thought about the heathen a good deal that day. Now, this Saturday morning grandfather, at family worship, had read a Psalm. Sadie had not been listening very closely; in fact, it was hard for her to listen to Bible reading, some way, unless it had a story in it. This was not in the least like a story, and Sadie's thoughts were, if the truth must be told, upon her dollie's new hat and how she should make it, when she heard these words: "Ask of me, and I will give thee the heathen for thine inheritance." It was that word "heathen" which caught her ear. Who was talking? To whom were the heathen to be given? Had some naughty king given them away to a bad man, and was that why they prayed to ugly wooden dollies? Sadie's thoughts were in a turmoil; she could hardly wait until the prayer was over, before she was at grandpapa's knee questioning.

"Why, child," said grandpapa, with a puzzled air, for he was not used to explaining the Bible to little people, "it means what it says; the heathen are to be given to Jesus."

"Given to Jesus!" said Sadie, amazed, "then why do they pray to ugly wooden dollies?"

"Because He hasn't got them yet; they don't know they belong to him."

"Why doesn't somebody tell them?"

"They do. People are at work telling them. Did you never hear about the missionaries, child? I thought you belonged to a Mission Band?"

Of course she did, and had heard about missionaries, and assured her grandfather that she gave five cents a month to support them. He did not say that that was a larger sum than he gave regularly for the same purpose; for some reason he did not care to do so; he only said:

"Very well, then, you understand all about it. The Bible says the heathen will be given to Jesus, and the missionaries have gone over there to tell them about it, and show them how to serve the Lord."

"Has every single one of them heard it?" questioned Sadie, in great earnestness.

"Well, no," said grandfather; "I believe they haven't yet."

"Why don't they do it faster? Why don't lots more missionaries go, and take Bibles, and hurry? Because maybe some of them will die before they hear it."

Sadie was in intense earnest, but her father laughed, and said: "That's the question, father. Puts some of you Christians in a tight place, doesn't it?"

Sadie could not imagine what he meant; her grandfather sat at ease in his big leather-covered chair, and was not in a tight place at all. But she was disappointed at his telling her to run away and not ask any more questions for five minutes. If she only had a mamma, Sadie thought, she would ask her all the questions she pleased, for her friend Trudie Brown said that mammas never got tired of answering. But Sadie's mamma went to heaven when she was a wee baby.

She went away to think it over, as she had to do with so many of her puzzles, only to have it added to presently by words from her grandmother.

"I declare!" said that good woman, coming in from the back yard, where she had been talking to Tony, the errand-boy, "that boy is a perfect heathen."

Sadie nearly dropped her dollie with a china head on the floor, in her dismay. "Is he truly, Grandma?" she asked.

"Yes, he is," said grandmamma, with emphasis; "I don't believe there is a greater heathen in the depths of Africa than Tony. I have been trying to explain the simplest matter to him, and he does not understand me as well as a child of three ought to."

"How should he?" asked grandfather, to whom this sentence was chiefly addressed; "he has never had any chance to learn. The whole settlement over there where he came from live like heathen, and know no better."

Then came one of Sadie's startling questions: "Grandfather, is he one of those who were given to Jesus?"

"What?" asked grandfather, in astonish-

THINKING IT OVER.

ment. He had already forgotten the morning's questions.

"Why, isn't he one that you read about, out of the Bible, that was given to Jesus?"

"Oh!" said grandfather, "I suppose so; why, yes, child, certainly. Jesus came to save him, as well as other heathen."

"Does he know it?"

"What a child you are!" said grandmother; but as this was no answer Sadie waited, looking at her grandfather.

"I doubt if he does," he said at last, "or would understand if he was told."

"Why, then he ought to be told over and over, ever so many times, as you said you had to do with Bruce before he understood that he was to stand on his hind feet and ask for a bone, oughtn't he?"

Both grandfather and grandmother began to laugh, though Sadie had no knowledge of what there was to laugh about; she was often treated in this way, and did not understand it. She turned away with a dignified air, a trifle hurt that her logic should produce only laughter; but there was decision as well as dignity in the tone in which she said: "I mean to tell him."

That was the beginning of effort for Tony Black, as he was called for convenience, though his full name was Antony Blackwell.

Faithfully did Sadie pour information on him and ply him with questions until, from staring and being stupidly amused, and then half-vexed with her, he at last became interested, and listened and asked questions himself, and began to think. "Sadie's heathen," he was familiarly called by certain amused friends, who were told the story.

He was called so long after the name had ceased to fit him; for this is a true story of something which happened years ago. The years went by, and Tony Black became so utterly changed that people forgot that they had ever called him heathen, or even Tony. "Young Blackwell" was the name by which he began to be known; then, after a time, "Mr. Blackwell." And one evening, when there was a great meeting in one of the largest churches of a certain city, he was introduced as "The Rev. Mr. Blackwell, who is under appointment to go to Africa as a missionary." Who do you think went with him? Sadie herself! He told on the platform something of his story; of the time when he was called "Sadie's heathen," and of his joy and pride in having the name altered, until now, by her friends, he was called "Sadie's minister." But by mere acquaintances they were spoken of as Rev. and Mrs. Antony Blackwell.

MYRA SPAFFORD.

QUEER CREATURES.

THIS is a scene in Africa. Those queer creatures scampering up the tree, are monkeys, to be sure; the other big lizards are crocodiles, you see. The way of it was that one of the crocodiles was sleeping — or pretending to sleep — on the bank of the river, when along came a careless little monkey, and his eyes were not where they should have been, or they did not look sharply at this thing that seemed to be but a log; when, before he knew what he was about, this "log" opened his big mouth, and with a sudden flap of his tail, in went the thoughtless monkey. That was the end of that young monkey. That's about the way the saloons swallow folks. Don't go near them!

"But tell the rest. What did the mother monkey say?"

She was mad as — "a setting hen." She shouted at the top of her voice, and a great army of monkeys came galloping to her to know what was the matter. Now one monkey knows just how to tell the others what's the matter; so they all set up such a hue and cry as you never heard. They scolded and insulted the crocodile, and twitched their faces and shook their fists at him, and jabbered such a bedlam that all the crocodiles ran together to see what was to pay. Upon the bank out of the water they climbed, and with open mouths and loud hisses, hurried after the scampering monkeys; but those spry creatures bounded up that big high tree, and from the lofty limbs looked down and scolded with all their might and main, and again shook their fists and snapped their long finger-nails to show how they would tear every hair out of the crock's hide if they could get a chance — if there were any hair.

It would have been better if they all, monks and crocks, had come kindly together and asked one another's pardon and settled their differences, and signed a pledge never to eat or scold one another any more. Read this:

"We had a grand temperance rally here last night. The children marched around the neighborhood, before the meeting, with banner and song. The church was beautifully decorated with vines, branches of palm-trees, maidenhair ferns, calla lilies, white orchid blossoms, etc. The place was filled. . . . There were songs, dialogues, temperance catechism, temperance stories and speeches. Over twenty came forward and took the blue ribbon. One had been a 'hard case.' Among the natives pledging is almost equal to coming to

SCAMPERING UP THE TREE.

Christ. . . . Every day began with a sunrise prayer meeting. A chorus of young people, the girls dressed in white, occupied the platform. They enjoy music."

So writes Rev. Mr. Dorward of Umzumbe, Africa. You see there is a difference between the young folks of Africa and the monks and crocks. What is the difference? And which of the two meetings do you prefer?   L.

THE HARD TEXT.

(Matt. xiii. 57.)

YOU would think people would be proud of a neighbor who does well. They are often jealous of him. When he becomes very great they often are all the more jealous, and say hard things about him, and he must sometimes actually get away to get peace and respect. When Columbus told his neighbors he was sure he could get to the East Indies by sailing westward they laughed him to scorn. He asked his own nation for ships and men to sail away on a voyage of discovery. He got nothing but opposition. He was compelled to go away to Spain for honor and ships.

Jesus' neighbors ought to have been proud of him; but they drove him away. They tried even to kill him, so jealous were they of him. But he got honor elsewhere. So it usually is. Do you honor him or drive him away?   L.

WHAT HE COULD DO.

I READ not long ago of a little fellow who was employed in a Boston office as errand boy. Four young men had the office together, and liked to spend their leisure moments in teasing the boy, who was very small for his years.

One day, after they had been chatting together, and using many oaths, with which they were in the habit of mixing their conversation, one of them turned to the boy and said: "Dick, what do you expect to do for a living, anyhow? You can't be a business man; there is no sort of business that you can do; you are too small. The fact is you'll be a dwarf, and I don't see how you are to get your living."

Said Dick, "I can do something now which you four gentlemen can't do."

"You can, eh? What in the world is that?"

"I can keep from swearing," said the boy, in a firm, clear voice.

One of the young men laughed, another whistled, and all turned and walked away, leaving Dick master of the situation.

EASTER.

LONG nights she wept!
   Sad days and weary weeks went by,
And life resumed its routine mournfully;
The tasks that once were easy to perform
Did seem vast mountains to the strength so worn;
And if the sun did shine, or if it not,
In shadows dwelt her heart; no ray, no spot
Of light or hope did penetrate the gloom —
This life seemed sadder far than death or tomb.

And still she wept!
'Till to her tear-washed eyes there came,
Like "bow of promise" after summer rain,
A vision beauteous from that "other land" —
Sleep and a "maiden" walking hand in hand.
They passed among those homes of "silent dead,"
They found "her darling's grave," the "name" they read,
Then, bending on her soulful, tender eyes,
The "maiden" whispered: "Did our dear Lord rise?
Then wherefore fall these teardrops from thine eyes?
If 'Christ is risen indeed,' then shall not we,
His 'friends,' his 'heirs,' live through eternity?

"Why should the Christians fear, who thus believe?
Why will they not the 'Comforter' receive?
I come each year to raise the drooping head,
To whisper to the mourner, Is Christ dead.
That you so mourn your loved? Look upward, sing!
Behold yon butterfly on gorgeous wing!
Know that this grave is but the chrysalis —
Then light, and glory, where the Saviour is;
And 'where I am, there ye shall also be';
'Come, weary, heavy laden, come to me!'"

The vision fled,
But to her heart there softly came
Abiding faith in Jesus' precious name;
A joy, that all her sorrow she could rest
Upon her Saviour's sympathizing breast,
And, in the place of gloom and fear, was born
A perfect trust — on that fair Easter morn.
                              — *Exchange.*

HAVE A BITE?

SHALL I BITE OFF THIS BUTTON?

QUEEN ELIZABETH.

ABOUT three hundred years ago England's great queen died. She was not very beautiful. Some said this was a great trial to her, and that she took marvelous pains to "fix" herself up to look as well as any lady in the land. Fine feathers often make pretty birds, but all Queen Bess' efforts failed to make her handsome. However, as she had royal power she had many admirers. They called her "charming," "lovely," "lily," "rose," and such other words to flatter her. She liked it, and persuaded herself that after all her features and complexion were nearly exquisite.

However that be she had not a few offers of marriage. But none suited her, or may be she, as a queen, did not want to be bothered with a husband, who would be continually interfering in the government.

It is sad to think of some things this woman did. Of course you will read about it. Sometimes she would have outbursts of anger so great that she would actually box the ears of those around her, no matter how distinguished they were.

The great stain upon her character was her treatment of Mary, Queen of Scots, her own relative. Mary was imprisoned eighteen years, then put to death on charge of conspiracy.

But England arose to extraordinary prosperity under the long reign of "Queen Bess." There were great scholars in her day, and she encouraged all sorts of improvements. You Pansy girls must some day dress your P. S. President up in the Elizabethan style and say if you would like it nowadays.   L.

(Sent with the gift of a Canary Bird in Cage.)

In memory of the birdlings fair
    Who from your nest have flown,
To try in Heaven's serener air
    The wings earth could not own.
                    M. S. B.

ELSIE'S PLAN. — I.

(Something for Mamma.)

THE thought grew in Elsie's mind, nourished by three remarks made by her mother and sisters. They were all at work except Irma, who was trying to teach Leoline to jump gracefully from her shoulder, instead of giving such a rude bound. Leoline was the cat. Irma was not apt to be at work, if the truth must be told; she was the only one of the little household who did not seem to understand the need for being industrious. She was two years older than Elsie, but the grown-up sisters often said of her that Elsie was at least three years ahead of Irma in judgment. I have sometimes thought if they had said in conscientiousness it would have been nearer the truth.

At this particular time, while Irma struggled with the cat's education, Elsie took neat stitches in the apron she was mending, her face looking thoughtful the while. Margaret, the oldest sister, was sewing swiftly on a dress of Irma's, setting in new sleeves, and in other ways trying to make the half-worn garment look like a new one. Nannie came in, dustpan in hand, and with a handkerchief bound about her hair to protect it from the dust, just as her mother opened the door of the kitchen, with her hands filled with soiled napkins and towels.

"Mother, where can I put that roll of matting?" Nannie asked, a touch of irritation in her voice; "I have reached the end of my resources in tucking things away. If I ever do build a house I will have all the closets I want; good-sized ones, too — and if there is any space left for rooms, there may be a few tucked in; but the closets I will have."

Mrs. Harding sighed. "Closets are certainly very scarce in this house," she said wearily, "as well as many other things. I don't know what to do with the soiled clothes; we need a clothes hamper very much. There is a corner in the upper back hall where one might stand, if we had it." The sentence ended as it had begun, with a little sigh.

Irma echoed the sigh in a sort of groan. "I saw such a pretty one, mother, last night, at Turner's. It was only two dollars; I thought of you when I saw them unpacking it. And to think that we cannot afford even two dollars for a basket!"

"There are worse trials in life than even that, I suspect," said Nannie, darting an angry glance at Irma, as she saw the flush spread and deepen over her mother's face. Margaret made haste to change the subject.

"We each have our perplexities, it seems," she said, with a light laugh; "mine has to do with dress. I don't know what to do with that light sateen of mine; it is too gay to wear about the house at work, even if it were long enough, which it isn't. It is not worth giving away, it is too good to throw into the rag bag, and there isn't room for it in my closet. Now what is to be done in such a case?"

Then Elsie spoke for the first time, eagerly, a bright look flashing over her face, as though some perplexity had just then been delightfully solved. "O, Margaret! will you give the dress to me to do just what I please with?"

"To you, child! what can you do with it? It isn't just the thing for a dollie, I should say."

"No," said Irma scornfully, "I should think not. Do let us have our dolls dressed in good taste and decent style, even if we cannot afford anything for ourselves."

"I don't want it for my doll, Margaret. I have a plan, a real nice one, if you will let me

have the dress, and if mother will give me the matting Nannie cannot find a place for. Will you, mother? There is only a little of it left."

"Is it the yellow plaid, Nannie? Why, yes, dear, if there is any pleasure to be gotten out of that yard and a half of cheap matting, by all means use it; especially since there is no place to store it."

Then Mrs. Harding left the room, giving Nannie a chance to say what she was longing to.

"I never saw such a girl as you are, Irma; you omit no opportunity to remind mother of our poverty. Even so trivial a thing as a soiled clothes hamper must draw from you a woe-begone sigh. Why can't you remember that it is hard enough for mother, at the best, without trying to keep the thought of our troubles ever before her?"

"Why, dear me!" said Irma, "what did I say? Mother knew before I spoke of it that we could not afford even two dollars to buy a clothes hamper. I don't think she is very likely to forget that we have lost our money."

"Not if you are around," answered Nannie angrily. "I think you are a selfish girl; you do nothing but groan and regret, for your share. Well, I can't help it," she added, in answer to Margaret's warning look; "that child's selfish frettings do try me so!"

"We must not expect old heads on young shoulders, remember," Margaret said gently, as Irma put Leoline down with a decided bounce, and slammed the door the least bit after her, as she left the room.

"It is the contrast that makes one notice it so," answered Nannie, with a significant nod of her head toward Elsie. But Elsie neither heard the words, nor saw the nod; her mind was busy elsewhere.

"O, Margaret!" she said eagerly, "I have the loveliest plan. You know to-morrow will be mother's birthday, and I was all the evening wondering what I could give her; now I know. Nannie, I will take the matting out of your way. I mean to make a clothes hamper for mother out of that and Margaret's dress."

Nannie laughed outright, and even Margaret smiled as she said: "Why, dear child, how can you? I am afraid that is a very large undertaking."

"No," said Elsie positively; "I see just how I can do it. The plan flashed into my mind as soon as you and Nannie began to talk about the two things in the way. I almost know I can do it. If you will help to keep mother away from our room this afternoon, and she won't give me anything special to do, I can make it and have it ready for to-morrow morning. I know just how to go to work."

"Let her try it," said Nannie, with a wise nod of her head. "The child will make something; I never knew her to fail when she had undertaken to do a thing, and mother's birth-day ought to be noticed in some way, even though we cannot do as we used. I'm going to fix over her sewing-chair; I believe in useful presents myself. We will agree to keep mother in order, Elsie, and the sooner the matting disappears from the front hall the better."

So the little room occupied by the two younger girls was locked all the afternoon, while Elsie worked steadily, and Irma lounged on the bed with a book, encouraging her sister occasionally with: "You never can do it in the world, Elsie Harding! I don't see any sense in trying. For my part I would rather give her no present than a bungling thing like that. You can't sew matting decently; it ravels so." PANSY.

AN OLD-TIME MAY-DAY.

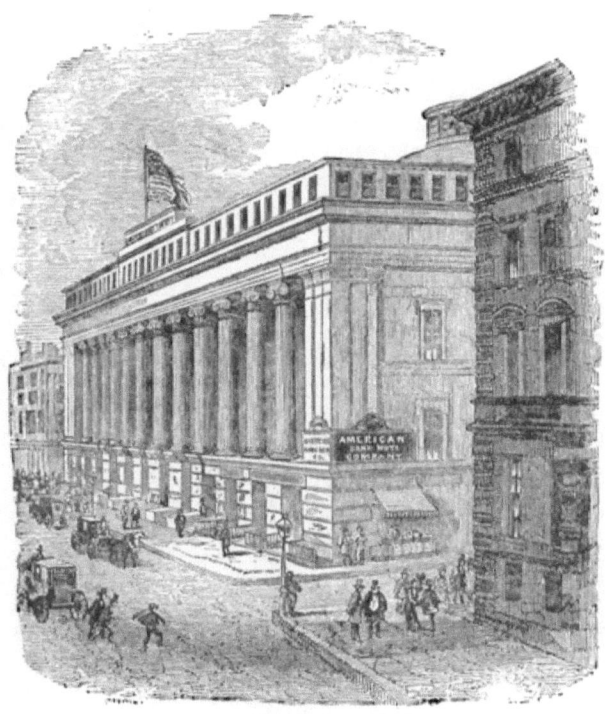

THE CUSTOM HOUSE, NEW YORK.

ABOUT NEW YORK.

BY THE PANSIES.

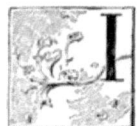 I READ about it when it was called New Amsterdam. A thousand people, and it was just a straggling little town. Pearl Street they called "De Perel Straat." The folks were very proud of this street; there were forty-three houses on it! One man thought his fortune was made because he had bought a lot two

There were no railroads to ride on; not a single train going out of New York City! That was in 1827. It seems strange that such wonderful things can take place in one century. I think this is the grandest century we ever had,

ROBERT CAMPBELL.

I SPENT a week in New York, and boarded very near Madison Square. I was on Twenty-third Street, pretty near to Fifth Avenue, and Broadway streaks across the city right there, so I had a chance to see almost everything; because those who know anything about New

COOPER INSTITUTE.

years before for fifty dollars, and was offered two hundred and fifty for it. And the lot was thirty feet wide and over a hundred feet deep! Think of a New York man to-day buying a lot of that size for two hundred and fifty dollars! My father says it would take a fortune to buy such a lot. HENRY STUART.

My cousin and I had great fun reading about a family who took a long journey from New York to Albany. They went on a river steamer; started at daylight and reached Albany at sunset, and thought they had done a big thing.

York City know that if you see what is on those streets, why, you have seen a good deal. It is Broadway and Fifth Avenue going criss-cross that make Madison Square. There are lots of hotels around there. The park is just magnificent; I like it better than Central Park, because it is right there, you know. There is a splendid fountain in the middle, and a drinking fountain somewhere else, and statues of Seward and Farragut. Seward is sitting down, and looks as though he didn't care.

If I had room I could tell you lots of things about Madison Square; but since you only let us have a few lines, what will a fellow do? I'm going to the Christian Endeavor meeting in July, and that will give a good chance to study up that part of the city, because the meeting is to be in Madison Square.

DAVID G. DUNLAP.

My mother used to be a pupil in Cooper Institute, and when I went to New York a few months ago father took me to see it. It is very large; it cost more than six hundred thousand dollars. Peter Cooper built it about thirty-five years ago; and then he gave three hundred thousand dollars to keep the free library going which belongs to it. They have all sorts of schools in the building. You can learn how to telegraph, and to write on the type-writer, and how to draw and paint. My mother was in the painting school, and she paints beautifully. We went up to the reading-room; it is on the third floor; there are rows and rows and rows of books! It makes me dizzy to think of so many. The books are all covered, so they don't look very pretty. There are long tables and lots of chairs; you are given a check made of brass, or tin, or something, when you go into the room; then if you want a book or magazine you go to the desk and ask for it, and give that check in return; you cannot get out of the room without that check, so you are apt to carry your book back when you are done with it, and get your check again. After all there are only about twenty thousand books on the shelves. I was disappointed; I thought there were millions. EMMELINE ANDREWS.

DICK WALTERS is in our "General Information" class, and when Trinity Church was talked about Dick declared he had been in the old building which was put there in 1697. I knew better, because my great-grandfather told about its being burned in the fire of 1776. But we couldn't make Dick Walters give up the notion that he was in the very identical church built two hundred years ago. At last Professor Townley explained that it was the old site, but a new church built in 1846. Since we had our fuss about it I have been there myself. It is a splendid building, I think, if it isn't two

hundred years old. The steeple is two hundred and eighty-four feet high, and the chimes are lovely. It is an old brown church, and looks solemn and still; it is right on Broadway, but when you step inside it seems just as still! You can hear the birds chirp on the trees in the churchyard, though there is a terrible roar of noise outside. Alexander Hamilton is buried in Trinity churchyard.

ROBERT PAXTON.

THE OBELISK.

I SUPPOSE everybody will write about Central Park; but I can't help it, I want to tell some things about it myself. I was there in June. We went up to Fifty-ninth Street and Fifth Avenue and took a carriage. We drove through the Scholars' Gate; this took us straight to the menagerie, and we saw the bear-pits and everything, though they say they don't have the menagerie there any more. We took a row on the lake, and we saw the Bethesda Fountain with its real angel — well, I mean a carved one, of course — bending over the water. Then we walked through The Ramble, which I think is the loveliest part of the park, only they won't let you break off the least little speck of a flower or leaf. There are lots of birds, and they seemed busier and happier than any birds I ever saw. We saw a sign directing us to the "Dairy," so we went there and got some splendid milk and some bread and butter. We children wanted to go to "The Carousal"; that is a sign which points out the way to the children's playground, where there are swings and everything; but father said we hadn't time, and that we could have " carousals" enough at home. LAURA J. WESTOVER.

LAURA has written a letter about Central Park, and hasn't mentioned the obelisk. Ho, ho! if that isn't just like a girl. I have studied up about it since I was there. They had an awful time bringing it over here from Egypt. They had to cut a hole in the bow of the boat that brought it to get it in; and then mend the hole, of course, before they could start. And when the steamer reached New York it took thirty-two horses to draw just the pedestal down to Central Park!

The carvings on the obelisk are called hier-

high, and it weighs three hundred and twenty tons. I don't exactly see what we wanted of it; but it is rather nice to look at it and think it came all the way from Egypt and was presented to us by Ismail Pasha.

REUBEN T. WESTOVER.

THE nicest ride I had while in New York was along Fifth Avenue. We started at Washington Square and went up to Central Park. It is almost three miles, and all the way there were such beautiful houses and churches to look at, and the road was as smooth as the floor. We passed the white marble house built by A. T. Stewart; it cost three million dollars, and the

VIEW OF MADISON SQUARE.

oglyphics, and used to mean writing; but scholars have had a great time trying to find out what the writing says. They don't agree about it, but they think it is a lot of stuff about some heathen gods. There are carved hawks on the top of the column, and these are said to be the birds that belonged to one of the gods, because they could fly the highest and could look at the sun. The obelisk is sixty-nine feet

people who now rent it pay thirty-seven thousand dollars a year for it. Only think! and we get three hundred a year for our house, and call it a good rent; but then, it didn't cost three millions. Then we passed the elegant Vanderbilt houses, and the magnificent Lenox Library building, and O, dear! I can't think what others. I thought I knew a great deal about them when I began, but they are so mixed up in my mind. But what I wanted to say was, that the drive from Washington Square away up to Eighty-first Street must certainly be the very splendidest in the world. I know I never saw so many beautiful buildings before;

THE MORROW.

OF all the tender guards which Jesus drew
About our frail humanity, to stay
The pressure and the jostle that alway

FIFTH AVENUE.

and I do like grand houses and grand churches and everything. KATE W. GLOVER.

[It has been very difficult to select items for this paper, because of the wealth of objects to choose from. We could make the article twice as long just as well as not, out of the material we have, if there were only room for it in the magazine. Also, some of the best and brightest items have been omitted, and others perhaps not quite so interesting chosen in their place, because they spoke of some building which we could show you in picture. The Pansies will understand, I hope, that we fully appreciate their efforts to help us, and that we enjoy the many items which we do not use quite as much as those we select. But do please be more prompt with your letters. — EDITORS.]

Are ready to disturb, whate'er we do, [through,
And mar the work our hands would carry
None more than this environs us each day

With kindly wardenship — "Therefore, I say,
Take no thought for the morrow." Yet we pay
The wisdom scanty heed, and impotent

To bear the burden of the imperious Now,
Assume the future's exigence unsent.

God grants no overplus of power; 'tis shed
Like morning manna. Yet we dare to bow
And ask, "Give us to-day our morrow's bread!"
— *Selected.*

MAJOR'S AUTOBIOGRAPHY.

III.

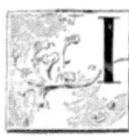IT is a nice light night, and if you youngsters have stared long enough at the moon, since neighbor Sport has come to call we will try to be a little more social.

Pet and Spot and Curley may play on the lawn if they choose, and have as good a time as they like.

You have come to ask my advice, have you, Sport?

Well, it doesn't cost much to give advice, but it isn't always so easy to take it.

What is the question in mind?

Have been slighted and abused, have you? Tell us about it.

Scolded you after you hunted birds all day for him, and then forgot to give you any supper. That was pretty hard; pretty mean treatment, I should say.

Had your master been drinking?

No? How came it about?

"Why, just before time to start for home I found a big flock of quail, and showed him just where they were; and he crept up, gun in hand, and tried to fire, but for some reason the gun did not go off.

"That put him out of humor, and he scolded the gun, and by that frightened the birds so they flew away.

"Then he sent me to find them, and I could get no snuff of them, hunt as hard as I could. Then he spoke to me as he never did before, and throwing the gun upon his shoulder started for the house, never noticing me by any word, whistle or sign.

"Well, I dropped my tail between my legs, and followed at a good distance.

"He didn't forget the cow, or the pig, or the pony, but took no notice of me, and I don't believe I could eat now if I had a chance."

Poor fellow! come here and lie down by me. Never mind, never mind; these men seem sometimes to have no heart for us, no matter how faithful we have been.

I am so thankful we have a master of another kind.

One of you run and bring some of that supper that was left.

We had a very nice supply this evening, and there is enough for two hungry fellows yet.

You just say no more till you have had the meat from that bone, and see if you don't feel better. Things hurt worse when one is tired and hungry.

There, now rest a while, and I will tell you a story about a great-uncle of mine, who lived in Groton.

He was pretty well educated, and did a great many things that some of his four-footed friends would not be trusted to do, even if they knew enough.

Well, Diamond — that was his name — was pretty good-natured, but a little sensitive. Being very affectionate, it was easy for those whom he loved to hurt his feelings.

His master was a mechanic, and had to go to his shop every day. The distance was so great that he did not come home to dinner; so his wife would prepare his dinner, put it in a pail, or in a basket, as it might happen, lay in the bottom a nice bone for Diamond, and give it all to him to take to his master. That he would do as faithfully as any one.

When the master had finished eating what had been brought, or as much as he wanted, he would take the bone, and any scraps left, and give them to his faithful carrier, who had been, the while, lying under the bench, patiently waiting.

But one day there was a break. The mistress said she was going shopping that day, and would take the dinner to her husband herself.

That rather hurt Diamond's feelings, though he said nothing, but followed on, and lay down in his usual place to wait for his bone. The master sat down to his dinner with no word for his faithful servant who was not permitted to bring the basket, finished his meal, closed the basket, and handed it to his wife.

No bone was there, nothing for the one who had been waiting, hungry, but patient. The only notice taken of him was a call to follow the lady and carry the empty basket. With a heavy heart and drooping tail he obeyed. When the purchases were made and put into the basket, Diamond was ordered to go ahead of his mistress and take the burden home.

On he trudged until he neared a bridge which they must cross, when a thought came suddenly into Diamond's mind, and quickly darting forward to the middle of the bridge he went to one side of it, and deliberately let the basket and its contents fall into the stream; then ran for home as fast as his four legs could carry him.

'I am not telling you this because I think he did right, but that you may see that others are treated as badly as you have been.

I suppose I am sorry that a relative of mine ever resorted to revenge; but it does sometimes seem very strange to me that more dogs do not revenge themselves in some way for the hard treatment they so often receive.

You would not like to be guilty of such an act as that?

Well, I am glad of it. Indeed, I think my kinsman was soon sorry for what he had done.

Let me tell you how he proved it. His master had been out nearly all day with Diamond hunting. The next morning he discovered that he had somewhere lost a key. So he showed Diamond another, and told him his trouble, and ordered him to go and hunt for it.

Off he went, and at three o'clock that afternoon returned, bringing the lost key.

He was tired and hungry, but a good dinner was ready for him, and kind words soon made him forget his fatigue.

In fact, I believe both master and dog were ashamed and sorry for the past, and inwardly determined to do right in the future.

Now after these true stories of my great-uncle, I hope you feel better, and will go home, not to plan how you can be revenged, but how you can be true and faithful, and, if possible, win better treatment in future.   R.

OF the four hundred and thirteen species of trees in the United States sixteen will sink in water. The heaviest is the black-iron wood of Southern California.

BARNYARD ILLUSIONS.

SOMEBODY in one of our exchanges tells an amusing story of his attempt at studying human nature in the barnyard. He placed a large piece of looking-glass against the trunk of a tree, and scattered corn in front of it, then took a convenient position and watched. Some of the hens came up with cautious tread, to meet what they supposed were new acquaintances, and were simply astonished and bewildered by the result. Others pecked at the glass, and were anxious to get up a fight with the supposed intruders.

The high-stepping rooster was bent on a victory. He advanced with skillful side steps, according to rooster fashion, and was amazed to lose sight of his enemy. Of course he had stepped too far to the left or right, and so gotten out of range of the glass, but this he did not understand. He gave an astonished crow, looked about him fiercely, saw no one, finally gave up and went back for a kernel of corn; behold, just in front of it was that other rooster, looking fierce. He made another attempt for a fight, with exactly the same result as before; but the second surrender to mystery brought him quite near to the mirror and his enemy. He ruffled his feathers, so did the other rooster. He made a dash forward, so did the other, and — the rooster was astonished; but you are prepared to hear that the mirror was broken into bits. The question which seemed to puzzle that rooster for hours afterwards was, What became of his enemy, that he could not find even a feather of him lying about the yard?

A GOOD man in France is said to have invented an instrument with a very fine tube to be inserted into the ear, by means of which sounds can be heard by the deaf.

Professor Dussouchet saw the experiment tried upon many deaf mutes, and in every case with success. Sounds are sent into a large bell-shaped contrivance; thence they pass down the fine tube and strike the tympanum (ear drum).   L.

A SONG FROM THE HEART.

I NEED A CHRISTMAS DINNER.

THE BOYHOOD OF TITIAN (*Tish'-yan*).

Pœta nascitur, non fit.

THERE, that is not Greek or German, but Latin, and some day your Pansy tongue will talk it off as readily, no doubt, as it now

STUDYING ITS CHARACTER.

casts English to your cat. Won't it be just splendid for you to be in the High School — and not at the foot of your class, either — reading Cæsar or Cicero or Horace?

"But what does that Latin mean?"

It means, "A poet is born, not made."

"So is every one ' born.' "

No, not born a poet, neither can be made into a poet by study; that is, a real true poet. Almost everybody can read poetry, and love it and make rhymes; but that is not being a poet.

You might just as well now learn that bit of Latin and surprise your mamma some day at the dinner-table by saying: "*Pœta nascitur, non fit.*" The next time you can say: "*Orator nascitur, non fit,*" for that is true too. It is true of an artist, and many, many others. We all have different gifts at birth. (See Rom. xii. 6.) Johnny Brown can sing and play upon almost any instrument. He is a born musician. His brother can't play even upon a jew's-harp, but he can make one. He can make a watch. His fingers can do all sorts of wonderful things such as Johnny's cannot. Boys differ; girls differ. They can't be made alike. One has one gift, one another.

Titian was born an artist.

What do you suppose he is doing there, one hand upon the limb of that tree?

"Going up for chestnuts."

No; try again.

"Going to climb for a crow's nest."

Not he. See that bit of a branch in his right hand. He is looking at it to see its shape, the form and color of the leaves, and all about it. He will paint that whole tree in a little while — no, no; paint one on canvas just like it. When he is a few years older he will paint portraits, then great elegant pictures.

He was an Italian boy, born in 1477.

Columbus was then about thirty-five years old. He had just made his great voyage to Iceland and got back when Titian was a baby. I guess Titian saw the born voyager and discoverer, and as likely as not painted his portrait or ships. But one of his masterpieces, or greatest works, is St. Peter, Martyr; another, The Presentation of the Virgin.   L.

HANNIBAL'S VOW.

MANY hundred years ago there were two magnificent cities on opposite sides of the Mediterranean Sea. One was Carthage and the other was Rome. But they were jealous of each other, and shook their fists at each other and went to war, each trying to do the other all the harm it was possible.

In Carthage was a man by the name of Hannibal. He hated Rome bitterly.

A little before his death he took his son out to the altar, where they burned sacrifice to the gods, and made him lift up his hands in a vow or promise to always hate and harm the Romans.

It was an awful thing for any one to do, but how dreadful for a dying man. So young Hannibal swore by the gods, Jupiter, Juno, Apollo, Hercules, Mars, Triton and Neptune, and all the other Dæmons.

The old man died. When young Hannibal was now twenty-four he was made commander of the troops, and, dressed in a coat of armor, he started from Carthage with a mighty army. Away he marched toward Spain, conquering and slaying his enemies on the way. On and on he went, over rivers and highest mountains. The Romans, when they heard that he was in Spain, laughed at the thought of his coming to Rome; they said none but gods could do such a thing. But they had not long to laugh. He and his conquering host clambered over the Pyrenees, then over the high steep Alps, then "down upon the soft and smiling plains of Italy." Then all was excitement in great Rome. Every one became a soldier of some sort. "To arms! to arms!" was the cry. The city was turned into a fort. Mighty armies went out to meet Hannibal, but one after another was slaughtered or put to flight. In one of the great battles forty thousand Romans were slain!

The Roman general, Fabius, was a great man, but he was compelled to retreat before Hannibal. But just then, when the people in the great city were trembling lest Hannibal would be upon them to burn the whole city and put the inhabitants to death, word came from Carthage that he must hurry home with his army and save Carthage from a Roman army coming upon it, led by a wonderful general, Scipio. Soon these two conquering hosts met at Zama, not far from Carthage, and here for the first time poor Hannibal was defeated, and in the course of time proud Carthage was utterly destroyed.   L.

THE WAR OF THE ROSES.

FIVE hundred years ago began very troublous times in England, and it went on many bloody years. You see, there were two great parties, as in this country, each struggling to rule. In this country they fight it out at the ballot box, with bits of paper upon which names are printed. The man or party which gets the greater number of ballots rules. In England years ago they fought it out with blows. The party which could strike the harder blows ruled.

The names of these two great parties were York and Lancaster. The Yorkers wore the white rose, the Lancastrians the red rose, so it was called the War of the Roses. Oh! the fierce battles, the groans of the dying and the banners rolled in blood; neighbors, sometimes brothers, killing each other.

And their homes, the mothers and children, what happened to them during all those hundred years? You must not know. But what must the Lord Jesus have thought of it all?

If it had been for some great good — to put an end to stealing, cruelty, drunkenness or some such dreadful thing — it would not seem so bad; but it was just to get upon a throne and then to be cruel to the defeated party. The great trouble was that this man or that wanted to be king just as in America a man wants to be president. Richard the Third wanted it so much that he caused his two little nephews to be smothered to death while asleep, lest they would grow up and trouble him! This was four hundred years ago.   L.

BABY'S CORNER.

COME TO SUPPER.

THE NAUGHTY ROOSTER.

ONE pleasant summer day Jamie's mamma said they would have tea out under the trees, because it was papa's birthday.

She spread a pink cloth on the table, and brought out some pretty dishes. Jamie thought it was fine fun.

He helped to carry out the biscuits and strawberries, and he put the knives and spoons by the side of the plates.

They had to hurry, because pretty soon the five o'clock train would come in, and papa would be on it.

When mamma went into the house to make the tea she gave Jamie a piece of cake and told him to sit down on the grass and rest his tired little feet.

Jamie liked to sit in that pretty spot. There were green grass and daisies and buttercups all about him, and oh! how good the cake tasted.

Pretty soon the old rooster saw that Jamie was alone, and that he had something good to eat.

So he called to his family: "Come quick! come to supper."

Then the gray hen and the yellow hen and the speckled hen and the white banties came running as fast as they could run to get some of Jamie's cake.

Old Speckle got the first bite. a great big one, and carried it off to eat it. Then Old Yellow came up one side and the rooster came the other side, and one took a bite, and the other took a bite.

Jamie began to cry. Mamma heard him. She came out, and said: "Shoo! shoo!"

And away went the chickabiddies as fast as

JAMIE BEGAN TO CRY.

they could fly, and no more supper for them that night.

MRS. C. M. LIVINGSTON.

OUT in the garden, wee Elsie
  Was gathering flowers for me;
"O, mamma!" she cried, "hurry, hurry,
  Here's something I want you to see."
I went to the window; before her
  A velvet-winged butterfly flew,
And the pansies themselves were not brighter
  Than the beautiful creature in hue.
"Oh! isn't it pretty?" cried Elsie,
  With eager and wondering eyes,
As she watched it soar lazily upward
  Against the soft blue of the skies.
"I know what it is, don't you, mamma?"
  Oh! the wisdom of these little things
When the soul of a poet is in them.
  "It's a pansy — a pansy with wings."
    — Selected.

THE HARD TEXT.

(Matt. xiii. 12.)

NO, it does not seem fair at all to give to him that has something, and to refuse it to one that hasn't anything scarcely, and even to take away what little that one has! Just think of giving a rich Pansy five hundred dollars more, and then snatching away the last penny from a poor Pansy!

Surely you don't suppose the loving, gentle, merciful Lord Jesus meant any such thing? Of course he didn't.

"What did He mean?" Why, simply this, my dear; that one who makes good use of his gifts will have more gifts. He will grow wiser and better, and go up higher all the time, just like a tree that uses well the good ground and good air and good dew around it. And the tree, that for some reason won't send its roots down and this way and that and set every one of its leaves to breathing, such a lazy tree will lose all its life and die, the first wide-awake tree sucking up that very life.

It may be just so with two Pansies. One is good, true, active, the other one isn't; how one will go up and the other down; how one will increase and the other decrease until one seems to have all the good, even the little the other started out with.

You borrow from a bank one hundred dollars and pay it back with interest when your note is due, and quite likely the bank will loan you two hundred dollars then, if you want it, and so on, increasing it just as you are faithful. But if you don't pay as you promised, because you were lazy, your one hundred dollars will be taken from you and loaned to one who may have ten thousand dollars, because he makes good use of it. We are all on trial. How happy we should be to be trusted by the Lord! It's a fearful thing when he will not loan us any more.   L.

GOOD temper, like a sunny day, sheds brightness over everything. It is the sweetener of toil and the soother of disquietude.

INASMUCH.

"IF I had dwelt"—so mused a tender woman,
  All fine emotions stirred
Through pondering o'er that Life, divine yet human,
  Told in the sacred Word—

"If I had dwelt of old, a Jewish maiden,
  In some Judean street,
Where Jesus walked, and heard his word so laden
  With comfort strangely sweet,

"And seen the face where utmost pity blended,
  With each rebuke of wrong;
I would have left my lattice and descended,
  And followed with the throng.

"If I had been the daughter, jewel-girdled,
  Of some rich rabbi there;
Seeing the sick, blind, halt, my blood had curdled
  At the sight of such despair.

"And I had wrenched the sapphires from my fillet,
  Nor let one spark remain;
Snatched up my gold, amid the crowd to spill it,
  For pity of their pain.

"I would have let the palsied fingers hold me;
  I would have walked between
The Marys and Salome, while they told me
  About the Magdalene.

"'Foxes have holes'—I think my heart had broken
  To hear the words so said,
While Christ had not—were sadder ever spoken?—
  A place to lay his head.'

      would have flung abroad my doors before Him,
  . nd in my joy have been
First on the threshold, eager to adore Him,
  And crave his entrance in!"

Ah, would you so?   Without a recognition
   You passed Him yesterday;
Jostled aside, unhelped his mute petition,
   And calmly went your way.

With warmth and comfort garmented and girdled,
   Before your window-sill
Sweep heart-sick crowds; and if your blood is
      curdled
   You wear your jewels still.

You catch aside your robes, lest want should
      clutch them
   In its imploring wild;
Or else some woful penitent might touch them,
   And you be thus defiled.

O, dreamers! dreaming that your faith is keeping
   All service free from blot,
Christ daily walks your streets, sick, suffering,
      weeping,
   And ye perceive him not!
      M. J. PRESTON, *in The Independent.*

I READ of a boy who had a remarkable
   dream. He thought that the richest man
in town came to him and said: "I am tired of
my house and grounds; come and take care of
them and I will give them to you." Then came
an honored judge and said: "I want you to
take my place; I am weary of being in court
day after day; I will give you my seat on the
bench if you will do my work."

Then the doctor proposed that he take his
extensive practice and let him rest, and so on.
At last up shambled old Tommy, and said:
"I'm wanted to fill a drunkard's grave; I have
come to see if you will take my place in these
saloons and on these streets?"

Harold laughed about his dream, but somebody who knew how Harold was being brought
up, said: "Do you know, I shouldn't be surprised
if of all the offers he accepted the last? He
has talent enough to become a judge, or a physician, or to make his fortune, but I am afraid
he will grow up to take old Tommy's place."

Who is willing to help fill "Old Tommy's"
place?

FROM BIRDLAND.

IF we only knew how
to understand bird
language, I fancy we
might be made ac-
quainted with a great
many pretty secrets
which now they keep
to themselves.

I have been reading
lately about a gentle-
man in New York who
has a collection of birds,
and who makes a study
of those who flit about
his home in summer.
At one time he had a
blind sparrow among his collection, and a little
bird named Dick seemed to have adopted it.
He waited at the door of its house for it to
come out, calling it with tender little chirps,
and when the blind one finally appeared he
would lead the way to the seeds and water.

When his friend was ready to return home
to rest Dick would shove him gently along the
perch until he was opposite his own door, then
give a chirp which seemed to say: "There you
are, jump in," and in would spring the little
sparrow, safe at home. Surely Dick ought to
be elected as at least an honorary member of
the "Helping Hand Society." What if he
hasn't any hands? He succeeds in being a very
efficient helper.   EFIL SREDNOW.

THERE are a few who make their life "a
      song,"
A silvery call to urge tired souls along,
   A clear bell o'er the cope
Of the steep mountain they have had to climb
With such a patience, they have made sublime
   The soul's forlornest hope.
And when these dear ones hidden pass adown
"The other side," beyond the mountain's crown,
   The silvery tinkling vein
Of gladness comes aback to touch us so —
New courage in our sinking heart doth grow,
   We urge us on again.   *— Selected.*

AN OLD QUACK.

ANGIE'S CROSS.— I.

(Character Studies.)

EVERYBODY said Angie Conran had a "perfectly lovely voice," extremely well cultivated for one so young. Her music teacher was in the habit of patting her hand in a patronizing way, at the close of almost every lesson, and saying, in broken French: "Mees Angie, you will make what you Americans call a mark in the world; remember I tell you."

Angie was a member of the choir, and a very faithful one; a member of the "Choral Club," and practiced early and late to help make it a success. On the particular evening of which I wish to tell you she was seated at the piano, giving a last half-hour of practice to the anthem before she went to rehearsal. Her mother and I sat in the back parlor, where we could have the full benefit of the music. How the exquisite melody filled the room, and how distinctly was every word spoken.

"Nearer, my God, to thee,
Nearer to thee,
E'en though it be a cross
That raiseth me;
Still all my song shall be,
Nearer, my God, to thee,
Nearer to thee!"

"That is as good as a recitation," I said. "How very distinctly Angie speaks her words."

"Yes," said the proud mother; "she prides herself on being heard. She says she would never have any pleasure in singing Italian songs; that she would want the words as well as the music to be uplifting. Angie prefers sacred music, I think; her heart seems to echo the sentiment of the words. What she is practicing now is to be sung to-morrow morning, just before the sermon. Our pastor requested it. This is a new arrangement, with solo and quartette, and Angie takes the solo. If the other parts are as beautiful as the soprano, I think it will be lovely. Angie dear, isn't it time you were going?"

"In a minute, mamma; I want to try this minor strain first." The sweet, tender sounds filled the room:

"Though like a wanderer,
Daylight all gone,
Darkness be over me,
My rest a stone."

"Isn't that exquisite?" whispered the mother, when the last notes had died away. Then, in almost the same breath, "Angie dear, it is beginning to rain; are you prepared for rain?"

"O, dear, how provoking! No, ma'am, I can't say I am in the least prepared for it."

The mother arose and moved toward the music-room. "Why, dear child!" she said, in surprise, "you ought not to have that dress on to-night. Even if it were not a rainy evening it is not suitable to wear to a rehearsal."

"Why not, pray? ever so many people come to the rehearsals. I want to be as well dressed as I am on Sunday."

"My dear, that is a pretty evening dress, and the rain will spot it, you know. You would have to wear your gossamer, and that would crush the trimmings. Besides, it doesn't look at all suitable for this evening. If you were going out to a social gathering you could not dress more than that. Do go and change it, dear; it won't take you long."

"I assure you, mamma, it is quite out of the question that I should change my dress now. It is already late; you just said I ought to be going. It was quite a work of art to get this dress on, and I haven't the least desire to change it; I am not at all afraid of it."

"But, my dear child, just consider how unsuitable it is. Those laces at the neck and wrists are real, you know, and as fine as cobwebs; you certainly could not dress more than that if you were going to a reception."

"O, mamma! how absurd. As though anybody would take notice of me, or care whether my laces were real or not. They fit the dress, any way, and as long as I don't object to them I don't see why anybody else should."

"My daughter, your mother objects to them. Moreover, the dress is lower in the neck than you have been wearing all day, and it is quite a cool evening; that in itself should be sufficient to make you change it. I really must insist on your putting on a more proper dress."

Angie's pretty fingers came down upon the keys with a crash which made me start in my chair; then she whirled herself about on the music-stool. "Really, mamma," she said, and the voice was so sharp it hardly seemed possible that it could be the same which had filled the room with melody, "I should think I was old enough to decide what dress to wear; I am almost fifteen, and I think I might have the privilege of choosing my own clothes once in a while."

"Do not speak in that tone, dear," said her mother gently. "You shall have all the privileges I can give you; but we haven't time to discuss it now. Run and slip on your gray cashmere, it is in order; I fixed that place in the sleeve this morning, and brushed it and got it all ready to put on."

"Mamma Conran! that old gray cashmere. As if I would go out in it to-night! Why, the Barnards come to rehearsal, and the Needhams, and their cousin from New York. The idea of rigging up in that old thing and standing out there to sing, the most prominent person in the choir. I just can't do it! If I can't wear the dress I have on I'm not going at all."

"My daughter, don't be so foolish; the rehearsal surely doesn't depend upon the dress you wear. You are wasting time; I cannot think of letting you go in that dress. If I had noticed it before I should have called your attention to it; but I hadn't the least idea you would think of putting it on. The gray cashmere is entirely suitable, my dear. Your mother has not lost all sense of propriety, even

though she is older than fifteen. You must allow yourself to be guided by her. I would not make a scene if I were you, and spoil the beauty of the music you have given us. There is ample time just to slip on another dress. Run along, and I will get out your wraps and have them ready for you when you come down."

"Mamma, I'm not going to do it. I told you if I had to wear that old cashmere dress I shouldn't go out of the house to-night, and I meant it. Other girls can wear decent dresses. Carrie Wheeler wears a white silk to rehearsal often, and here I have got to rig up like an old woman and sing the leading part. You don't know anything about it, mamma; it is so long since you were a girl you don't realize how girls dress now. I wouldn't hurt this dress and you know it. It is just too mean for anything. You always spoil my pleasure."

"Angeline!"—the mother's gentle voice was growing stern at last—"I cannot allow you to speak to your mother in that way. There are the Wheeler girls coming up the walk now, to call for you. If you will go immediately and change your dress I will explain to them that you will be down in a few minutes."

A loud, angry cry from Angie, a sound like that from a naughty child who had lost all control of herself, and between the sobs she managed to get out: "I won't go a single step, and you can tell them so; and you can tell them the reason, if you choose; then they will understand just what hard times I have." And with another jarring crash of the keys the angry girl left the room, slamming the door after her.

MYRA SPAFFORD.

THE SCHOOL-GIRL OF 1830.

THE BLOSSOMVILLE BAND.

ELSIE'S PLAN.—II.

(Something for Mamma.)

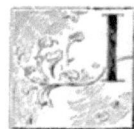'M going to stop its raveling," said Elsie serenely. "I'm going to overcast it, as mother does dress seams, and then line it with Margaret's dress skirt; that is real strong, and will make it stand up beautifully."

Sure enough, by dint of patient, painstaking effort, a circle of matting measuring nearly a yard around was cut off, the raw edges "overcast" with a large needle and strong linen thread, then the dress skirt was ripped and carefully smoothed. A journey to the kitchen, where Mrs. Hobbs, the woman who washed and ironed on the same day for this fallen family, was at work. Elsie hinted that it would save her time if Irma would see to the ironing, but at that moment Irma was in the depths of her book, and seemed to be deaf. Back again with her ironed skirt, the yard of matting was laid on the floor, the cloth spread over it and neatly tacked at sides and ends; then the long side seam was sewed, amid statements from Irma that it could not be done, because whose arms could be expected to reach down such a ridiculous cylinder as that to sew! It was hard work. Twice Elsie gave up with a sigh, and once was on the point of going to Margaret for advice, but the strong desire to do the work herself held her, and she actually did accomplish it! To stand the cylinder on one end, and draw with white chalk a "head" for it, and then another a trifle larger for a cover, was comparatively easy. These two were lined by cutting out a circle of cloth three inches larger than the matting circle, running a strong gathering string around the edge, and drawing it up around the matting.

"What is the use of that?" Irma demanded; and upon being informed that it was for strength and also to give something substantial to sew to, she said, with a little sniff, "Such a lot of trouble for what will only be an ugly bungle when you get it done."

"It will be a bungle that will hold the clothes nicely," Elsie said merrily.

She was so sure now of succeeding that she could afford to be merry.

The small patient fingers sewed away, and Irma, watching, grew interested in spite of herself. "You are not making a true round for the cover," she presently exclaimed. "The thing wiggles in and out so, it is hard to make a true circle; you ought to cut a paper pattern first, and work at it until you get it true, then cut the matting by it. Here, I'll make a pattern for you; and if I were you I would wire the creature around the top; that would make it stay in place."

"That is an excellent idea," Elsie said, "and I know just where there is a bit of wire that will do; I'll run and get it." She smothered a wee sigh as she went; it was a good plan to cut a pattern, and Irma's eye for cutting was better than her own, but she had wanted to do this work entirely herself. The pattern was troublesome, but at last a fair circle was made, an edge of matting four inches deep sewed around it, the whole carefully lined, and the thing was done.

"It really looks very well," Irma said, "and will do to stand in the back hall. That wire around the top was a good scheme."

"Yes," said Elsie heartily, "it was."

Mrs. Harding gave no faint praise the next morning when the matting "hamper," duly addressed and wrapped, stood close to her seat at table. She examined the workmanship most minutely, declared that the idea was original, and the completed work most useful.

"You have no idea how much more precious it is to me than anything bought with money could possibly be," she said, kissing again the rosy cheeks of her youngest daughter, while the others looked on, smiling. Then truthful Elsie bethought herself. "Irma helped me," she said quickly; "she made the circle true, and planned the wire for the top; it would not have been nearly so nice without her help."

"I didn't do the least thing, mother, except to cut a paper pattern for her, and to propose that some wire be sewed around the top. She had it nearly done before I said a word. It is all nonsense to say I helped. All I did was to give a little advice."

The older daughters laughed merrily, for Irma was very fond of giving advice; but Mrs. Harding drew Irma to her side and kissed her lovingly, while she said: "There spoke my truthful girl. She is not going to be commended for what she has not done."

"Oh! but, mother, she did truly help," was Elsie's eager explanation.

"Of course she did," declared Margaret; "I have seen the time when I needed a little good advice more than any other kind of help."

PANSY.

MAJOR'S AUTOBIOGRAPHY.

IV.

 AM glad you do not get tired of my talking so much about myself, and what I have seen and heard. It shows how you have been brought up, so far; and if we old dogs live a great deal in the past you may pick up a little wisdom from us, after all, and be none the worse for what we say, if you only learn to profit by our experiences and avoid our mistakes.

You want to hear more? Well, let me see, what shall I tell you about this time? I am reminded by the talk I overheard about the family going to the seaside, of the summer when I was two years old. I spent it with my old master at a place on the New Jersey coast. There did not seem to be any one with whom I could well stay at home; besides, my young master's little girl was very anxious to have me go with them, so they finally agreed to it, and were not sorry afterwards.

As I remember, I enjoyed the bathing as well as any of the party, or would have done so had I not been anxious all the time about little Lucy's drowning. When those big waves would roll in, it seemed to me they meant to carry my little friend out of my sight forever.

The summer proved to be one which we could all remember without trying. For the first few weeks there was nothing very unusual happened, and some seemed to think it was going to be very dull and monotonous. But it "is a long road that has no turn," and a "turn" finally came which was exciting enough for all of us.

The old settlers near the beach said we were to have a storm which would afford us a chance for a vacation in our bathing, and give us a sight of some "big seas," for we would probably see the Atlantic in one of his angry moods before many hours.

We felt ready for the change, and lay down at night thinking what a good time we would have the next day looking at the great waves roll in.

I knew the wind was blowing pretty fresh, but had such a protected place that I did not know how the storm had arisen until towards morning I heard the sound of a big gun. It sounded again and again, and then there was a noise in the house, and a general turn out and rush for the beach. Of course I followed the crowd, and soon learned what was the matter. There was a ship in distress, and being driven upon the shore.

The men were there with the life-saving apparatus, and soon a line was got out to the ship, and they were running a kind of boat back and forth upon it, bringing the passengers from the ship to the shore.

Well, the people were all safely landed, but there was a splendid big dog on that ship, and no one had seemed to think of or to care for him. O, yes! he knew how to swim, but that was a terribly angry water, and the distance was great, and they said there was an ugly undertow. That means that water which has come pouring in upon the shore runs back on the bottom with such power sometimes as to carry anything with it that it can get hold of.

Poor Hercules — that was the dog's name — had seen himself left there alone, the while the great waves were breaking all over the ship. If the poor fellow had been a fool he might have suffered less, for he would have thrown himself into the water at once; but as it was he knew the danger. Why, we could hear his howl above the noise of the breakers! and some of the men were almost wild with anxiety to try to save him. I suppose none of them thought the poor dog would know enough to get into that little car which had brought the people to the shore; and if he had he could not have shut himself in. So there he was. His owner, having several children besides his wife and the nurse to look after, had entirely forgotten the dog.

Hercules ran up and down the deck until there finally came a wave much bigger than any which had preceded it, and he was washed

HERCULES.

overboard. Of course he did then the best he could, and that was saying a great deal, for he was a powerful fellow; but those were terrible waves, and what could anything but a fish do in such a sea? We could see him now and then upon the crest of a wave, and then he would disappear. Every time we saw him he seemed to be nearer the shore, and we had a little hope that some big sea would throw him near enough for us to help him.

But the women and children must be cared for, so the people were soon gone, only a few of the boarders remaining to watch the sea,

all believing the four-footed passenger to have been drowned. Looking steadily, I thought I caught sight of the fellow once, then again, and much nearer the shore. Yes, there he was, and a big wave landed him so near that his body actually rolled over on the sand, as the waves ran back to their home again. He was too weak to help himself; but I ran down, and before the next wave came seized him by the back of the neck and stopped his rolling; but he was too heavy for me to drag alone. My presence, however, seemed to give him courage, and he got upon his feet again; then came another wave and covered us both. This did not prove to be so heavy as most of them, and the men came to our assistance, so brave Hercules was saved.

Those who had remained to see this part of the scene sent up a rousing shout, and both of us were petted at a great rate.

I have never seen many happier moments in my long life than those which followed for a little while. I was so glad to see this stranger safe, and glad that I had been able to help save him!

He understood it all, too, though he did not understand English very well. I need not tell you that we were together that summer all we could be. The man who owned the dog had gone off and left him, and my master said that Hercules belonged to him more than to any one else, because I had been the means of saving his life.

But after a while the dog's master came down there from New York to look after the wreck, and see if he could not find anything of value washed ashore which belonged to him. The place proved so pleasant that he sent for his family to come and spend a few weeks. They had experienced such a fright from the ocean the day of the wreck that at first they were very shy of the water, but it was not long before they were in with the others, enjoying the bathing.

This lasted for some time, and the children became very careless, venturing out where they ought not. My new friend and his master had not met since the day of the storm, as they were bathing at another part of the beach. For some reason my master decided not to go into the water one day, and we took a stroll along the beach to where those people were bathing. We had hardly reached the place, and my master seated himself in a comfortable position to watch the bathers, when Hercules gave a loud bark, as much as to say "Come," and bounded into the breakers. Of course I followed fast after him, on, on, out into the sea; and he had his master's little Gretchen by the back of her bathing-suit and was starting for the shore. It was a hard struggle; it was all both of us could do to save her.

The poor child was almost gone when we got to her, for no one had noticed her trouble and danger except Hercules.

Well, there was a scene on the shore again, and for a time one could hardly tell which the father was most rejoiced over, the saving of his child, or the sight of the dog who had saved her life.

Yes, we had a good time the rest of the summer, and then we had to part; for of course the man had his dog back again.

How I have wished I might see the brave fellow once more. I think he will never be forsaken again.

They went away from the coast a little earlier than we did. The children all bade me good-by, and Hercules' master invited me to go with them. We had a long visit the night before they went, and both of us felt very sorry to part company; but some way people do not think that we dogs have much heart, or ever mourn for absent friends. There, excuse that tear, but it always makes me feel badly to talk of Hercules, and that delightful summer by the sea. R.

FLY-LEAF WISDOM FOUND IN AN OLD BOOK.

READ slowly, pause frequently,
    Think seriously,
Keep cleanly, return daily,
    With the corners of the leaves
        Not turned down.

ABOUT CHICAGO.

BY THE PANSIES.

I THINK it is great fun to go to Chicago on a visit, and then come back and hear about it as it used to be. My grandfather went there in 1833. He was just a boy, but he remembers lots of queer things. He went to church in a kind of a barn; the front part was the church, and there was a curtain in the middle, and behind it the minister lived — slept, you know, and ate, and everything. Think of that for Chicago! There was a school kept in a little room on Water Street; the woman who taught it had twenty scholars. The mail was brought once a week by a man on horseback, and the postmaster had a row of old boots nailed up on the wall for mail boxes. Grandfather says the place had begun to grow real fast when he went there, and as many as two

CHICAGO IN 1820.

hundred frame houses were built within a short time. He was there when they voted to make it a regular town, with officers and laws. One law was that pigs must not run in the streets, and that people must not cut holes in their outside walls and poke stove-pipe through them.

ROBERT CHAPPELL.

THE word "Chicago" used to be spelled "Chicagoux." Some people think it was named for the "Cheagomeinan River," which is the Indian name for the Chicago River. The

Indians called the Mississippi River "Chacaqua," which means "divine river," and I think they worked the name Chicago out of all these notions. My uncle says the name of the French fort in 1688 was Fort Cheeagou. I like to study about names, and find what they mean, and how many changes they have had before we got hold of them. I have never been to Chicago, but I expect to attend the Columbian Exposition. If you will wait until after that I will tell you something about the city. It is larger than it used to be.

THOMAS L. WOOD, JR.

My father knows about a man who bought a lot in Chicago in the year 1832 for one hundred dollars, and sold it again about three years afterwards for fifteen thousand dollars! I think that 'tells a boy better than anything else could, how fast the town grew for a while. Of course it was a nice choice lot, in what suddenly became the business part of the town. I know I should like to have been its first owner.

ROBERT TOWNSEND.

I READ about how Chicago came to be called the "Garden City." It grew out of hard times. They had what is called a business panic, when everybody owed everybody else, and could not pay them, and business was awfully dull, and people thought the town was going to ruin. The most people had to do was to take care of their grounds. They whitewashed the fences, cleaned up the yards, planted fruits and vines, and did everything they could think of to make their places look pretty. I suppose they hoped somebody would come along and buy them. And that is the way they got the name of "Garden City."

ALICE PETERSON.

THE people who lived in Chicago about the year 1843 certainly could not have had so high an opinion of the city as people do who live there now. A Mr. Miltimore built a schoolhouse on Madison Street which was called "Miltimore's Folly," because people did not believe that there would ever be children enough in the town to fill so large a building. The

mayor of the city urged the Council to have it turned into an insane asylum, or sold, and the money from it used to build and care for a smaller building, suited to the present and future needs of the city! I don't think he could have been a very bright man, because in less than four years from that time the building was not only crowded with scholars, but three others had to be opened in different parts of the city.

ROGER SHERMANN.

CHICAGO is a great place for manufactories. It seems to me as though almost everything was made there. I know they make brooms, and bricks, and boilers, and hats and caps, and saws, and scales, and nails, and paint, and gloves, and carpets, and I am sure I don't know what else; I guess they make everything. Once I went to the car-wheel factory where they make three hundred wheels every day. It was great fun to see the men work. I like to see things made, and that is what I am going to do when I am a man.

ROBBIE WILSON.

[We are almost certain Robbie means that when he is a man he is going to help make things; not merely stand still and see them made. Good for Robbie! What would become of us if all the people who are hard at work making things should grow tired of their work, and conclude to — write books, for instance, instead? — EDITORS.]

WE are reading in school about the Chicago fire, which was in 1871. I think it is perfectly dreadful to read about it. Just think! it all came from a woman milking after dark, when she ought to have done it before, I suppose; or maybe her little boy ought to have done it for her, and did not come home in time — well, the cow kicked her lamp over and set the hay in the barn on fire, and all that awful ruin came!

I think that woman must have felt dreadfully. As for the cow, I don't suppose she cared a bit.

LAURA JONES.

I KNOW a man who was in Chicago at the time of the fire, and he paid fifteen dollars for

PICTORIAL CHICAGO.

a hack to drive him half a mile! He says a hundred thousand people were made homeless that night. Folks ran through the streets as if they were crazy. Everybody was trying to carry something of theirs to a safe place. One woman tried to save her sewing-machine; she dragged it through the streets a long distance. One man walked along quietly, carrying an ice-pitcher. He said it was all he had left in the world.

The poor man had been made crazy by his losses, and did not know what he was about.

THOMAS JONES.

WE lived in Terre Haute, Ind., at the time of the great Chicago fire — at least my folks did — and my father says that on Monday, the ninth, while the fire was still burning, a train loaded full of provisions went out of Terre Haute for them. I think that was nice. There is a boy in school who says that his folks, who lived in Pittsburg, raised a hundred thousand dollars before Wednesday night, and sent it to the Chicago sufferers, and another fellow said that was nothing; that his uncle in Louisville raised most a hundred thousand within ten hours after the fire began! He talked as though his uncle did it all, but I suppose some others helped.

WILLARD J. MOONEY.

I THINK the great big splendid temperance temple is the grandest building in Chicago, and I helped build it. I gave two dollars and seventeen cents that I earned myself, for it. In 1893 I am going to see it, and some other things. I think you ought to have waited until after the Columbian Exposition for letters about Chicago. Then we could have told lots of things.

MARY CLARKSON.

I WENT to Chicago with my grown-up sisters when the Y. P. S. C. E. had its big meeting there. We stopped at the Sherman House. That is one of the nicest hotels in the city. At seven o'clock Sunday morning we had a prayer meeting in the billiard-room; more than a hundred young ladies and gentlemen spoke at that meeting in less than a half-hour, and the sing-

ing was lovely. The big meetings were held in Battery D. Ever so many thousand people were there all the time. Some of the speeches were splendid. Chicago is very large. My cousin and I took a ride on a street car as far as it went, then got out and took another line and went as far as its route, just to see the city. They have very tall buildings. I went to the Herald office; that is the handsomest newspaper building in the world, I guess.

LUCY J. HARTMANN.

ONCE I went to the church where Mr. Moody used to preach. I heard the Rev. Charles Goss; he is young. I liked him. I went to a splendid store, but I don't remember where it was. There was a newsboys' dinner given while we were there, and I went to look at the boys eating their cake and cream. There were hundreds of them, and they ate fast and seemed to like it.

A great many benevolent things like that are done in Chicago, but I think they need a temperance temple; I saw lots of drunken men, and one drunken woman.

ALICE PETERS.

[We have still more, about incidents which happened in Chicago rather than about the city itself, but we have already crowded our space. If the Pansies could be induced to get their letters in earlier they would stand a better chance of being selected from.— EDITORS.]

THINGS WHICH SOME PEOPLE REGRET.

HOW many of the Pansies have heard the "silver-tongued orator" lecture on his special theme, Temperance? All of you who have will be sure to hear him again at the first opportunity. Those of you who have not, let me urge to keep on the watch for a chance. Meantime, listen to his hint, which ought to help every boy who reads it to be a better educated man.

"I regret that the many hours of youth I gave to idle pleasures were not used in storing my mind with useful knowledge."
Yours truly,
GEORGE W. BAIN.

THE LAPPS.

FRANCE is "sunny." It loves shade-trees, fans and fountains. Laplanders must need have furs and fire and fat food. Of course you know why. Those Lapp faces would look equally well as Mr. William's, if they were to exchange dresses, putting a Lapp where the Emperor now sits so loftily. Give the Lapp the very same chance, and maybe he would make just as wise a ruler of Prussia. People are not so unlike, after all. When God would raise up the greatest Prophet that ever appeared on the earth, he found him in the despised Nazareth. Maybe he is nursing a little child

INTERESTING FACES.

of one of these Lapps who will one day be as great as young Master Wilhelm of Prussia.

L.

ALTHOUGH the printing presses at Beirut are working night and day they cannot supply the demand for the Arabic Bible.

EDMUND SPENSER.

(English Literature Papers.)

JUST three hundred years ago, and just one hundred years after Columbus discovered America and planted his flag on San Salvador, there stood in the middle of a wide, boggy Irish plain a building better than most of those anywhere near it, called Kilcolman Castle. It was a time when the English Government was having a hard time to keep the Irish under their control, and we shall see after a while how the poor people of the castle suffered on account of this fact. But there lived at Kilcolman, in those days from 1586 to 1598, one of the most celebrated of the poets about whom we shall talk in our English Literature Papers. It was Edmund Spenser, and the old picture of him that has come down to us shows him to be a kind, gentle looking man, with a long thin nose and a high forehead, dressed in a black robe, and with a great lace collar coming up above his ears, which must have been very uncomfortable in warm weather.

Spenser was born in a part of London called East Smithfield, right under the shadow of the great Tower; and it is a very disagreeable fact to one who is trying to write about him, that we know almost nothing about the little events of his life, and especially of his boyhood. Three hundred years ago, you know, people did not take notes of themselves so much as we do nowadays, or as they did even in the last century; or if they did they have not been kept for us. Just a few people have told us anything about Edmund Spenser, and the probability is that even his picture is not any better than many of those which we see nowadays in the newspapers.

One of the few things which we find about him was that he entered one of the colleges at Cambridge when he was seventeen, as what was then called a "sizar." These sizars were the poorer students, who had to work for their living in a much more disagreeable way than any students do now, by waiting on the older and richer ones at their meals and elsewhere, and were paid by their tuition in the college and the fragments of food which their employers left for them. I suppose if the student on whom Edmund Spenser waited could come back to earth for a little while he would be considerably surprised and perplexed to find that the only reason why the world would like to know more about him would be on account of the little sizar whom he used to have at Cambridge!

When he had left college, in which we find that he was a very good scholar, Spenser taught for a while in the northern part of England, and began to write the first poetry which made him at all famous; it was a long poem in twelve parts, about the twelve months of the year, and he called it at first "The Poet's Year," and afterward the name by which we know it, "The Shepherd's Calendar." It was a very pretty poem, and described the scenery and the country life of England in a way that made all good Englishmen like the author. So Spenser fell in with some good friends, and was introduced to Queen Elizabeth. It is a curious thing that in those days the best writers did not depend for their payment upon the number of books which were sold, or what their publishers paid them; but it was the custom of the king or queen, whenever an especially good writer appeared, to support him at the royal court or elsewhere, in return for which the writer served his sovereign in any way he could, especially by paying him any number of compliments in his writings. It is as though whenever a promising young author

should appear in New York or Boston, he should find a Congressman who would introduce him to the President at Washington; and if he found that he was likely to be a pleasing writer and a convenient friend to have near him, he should invite him to stay in the city, and should see that he had all the money he needed.

THE AUTHOR OF THE FAERY QUEENE.

But we shall be sorry to find that although Queen Elizabeth received Spenser very pleasantly, and although he paid her any number of pretty compliments in his after life, she never did very much for him. The first piece of good fortune which seemed to come to him was when he was appointed secretary to Lord Grey de Wilton, who was the Governor of Ireland. After that he was also given Kilcolman Castle, which we spoke of at the beginning, where he spent so many years. We shall see that he did a good deal of writing while there, and also acted as the agent of the English Government, in looking after whatever matters needed his attention. It was this that probably made the Irishmen dislike him, rather than any one thing which he did, for when he had been there twelve years there was a rebellion among them, and they burned the castle and forced the poet to run away to England. The saddest thing about it was that his baby was burned at the same time, and they tell us that the lonely father never recovered from his sorrow over this event. At any rate he died the next year in London, in a small lodging-house, and probably with very little money left. It was with him as with so many, many others, both in those days and now: the people did not begin to think enough of him until he was dead, and then they gave him a magnificent funeral, and buried him in Westminster Abbey, where the graves of all the greatest Englishmen are.

We know nothing but what is good about Edmund Spenser; he seems to have been a kind man, loving everything true and beautiful, and when we have a chance to read his writings we shall feel certain that this is so. Besides the "Shepherd's Calendar" he wrote a book in prose about Ireland while he was there, and it was also at Kilcolman Castle that his great poem, "The Faery Queene," or as we should say "The Fairy Queen," was written. This is a long, long poem, and was planned to be written in twelve parts, but it is probable that only six of them were ever finished. At any rate that is all which has come down to us; and some one has said that in this work "the half is better than the whole," meaning that although Spenser wrote six very nice books, he could scarcely have written six more anywhere nearly so good.

The "Fairy Queen" is what people call an allegory; those of us who have read "The Pilgrim's Progress" have probably found out what is meant by that. In allegories the story seems to be about real people, but all the time the people stand for good or bad qualities, or something of that sort—like Christian and Mr. Greatheart, or the Fairy Queen and the Red Cross Knight. If we look in Webster's Dictionary under "allegory," we shall find that the "Pilgrim's Progress" and "The Faery Queene" are spoken of as the most celebrated examples.

I am sorry to say that we shall find the "Faery Queene" rather hard reading; not because the story is not interesting, but because there were so many good English words in those days that we have forgotten all about now. Then the spelling, as we have already guessed from the name of the poem, seems more like one of our PANSY "Queer Stories" than anything else. We will try to read just one very pretty verse, at the beginning of the second Canto, which describes the sunrise. Spenser put quaint little rhymed headings at the top of his cantos; the one here is—

"The guilefull great Enchaunter parts
The Redcrosse Knight from Truth:
Into whose stead faire Falshood steps,
And workes him woefull ruth."

In reading the description of the sunrise we shall want to remember that there was an old story that the sun was a golden wagon driven up the sky by the god Phœbus, and also that "chaunticleer," or "chaunticlere," was the old-fashioned word for rooster. Here is the verse, and we will bid Spenser good-by with it :

"By this the northerne wagoner had set
His sevenfold teme behind the stedfast starre
That was in ocean waves yet never wet,
But firme is fixt, and sendeth light from farre
To all that in the wide deepe wandring arre:
And chearefull Chaunticlere with his note shrill
Had warned once that Phœbus' fiery carre
In hast was climbing up the easterne hill,
Full envious that night so long his roome did fill."

ELIZABETH ABBOTT.

AN Englishman visiting Sweden and noticing their care for children, who were gathered up from the streets and highways and placed in school, inquired if it was not costly. "Yes," was the answer, "it is costly, but not dear. We are not rich enough to allow a child to grow up in ignorance, misery and crime, to become a scourge to society as well as a disgrace to himself."

A COMING RULER.

THE little fellow at the left of the man on a big dark horse, is the one for you to study. He looks like a prince already. He certainly rides like a soldier.

What is the color of his eyes, the shape of his nose, or the kind of clothes on his back, and many more such things of Prussia, one of the most powerful nations of Europe.

His grandfather, Emperor William, died a few years ago, at a great age, greatly beloved by all Germans, and respected by other nations.

That man, sitting in the carriage, dressed like a soldier, with folded arms and a stern look on his face, is the present Emperor William.

There is the mother, the Empress, with the other children. Their faces are all turned

A STATELY RIDER.

you would like to know. Perhaps you will know these and many more things about him when you see him in Boston, New York, San Francisco or at the Chicago World's Fair.

"Will he be there?"

As likely as not.

"But who is he?"

Ah! now you ask something. He is Master Friedrich Wilhelm, the Crown Prince of Germany. If he live long enough, he will do something more than hold the reins of that pretty, proud white pony; he will hold the reins toward you, so you can get a good look at them. But you need not expect to see so many princes and princesses at Chicago.

It is the fashion nowadays for kings, rulers and coming rulers to visit other lands. Which of our presidents went around the world?

L.

It is said that the native Christians in Japan, with less than one shilling a day as an average for wages, contributed last year twenty-five thousand dollars to mission work.

JUST MOVED IN.

BABY'S CORNER.

ROSY POSY.

 AT last July came, and Rose went to grandpapa's to stay a week.

She loved to go to the farm, because grandmamma let her work.

Rose could shell peas and sweep the floor with a pretty little broom. She took up the dust on a bright new dust-pan.

The first day she went out in the field with grandpapa and raked hay. Then she took a little watering-pot and wet the flowers.

By and by Grandmamma put the kettle on to boil.

"Now we will get supper," she said.

 She spread a white cloth on the table, and Rose put on the cups and plates and spoons and knives and forks. They had apples and cream for supper. When the clock struck eight Grandmamma lighted a candle and went upstairs with Rose to put her to bed.

 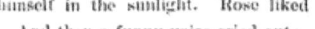  Grandpapa said, "Good-night, dear Rosy Posy."

Rose lay still as a mouse, and soon she was fast asleep.

In the morning when Rose opened her eyes the sun was shining in at the window. There was a big fly buzzing about trying to warm himself in the sunlight. Rose liked to watch him.

And then a funny voice cried out: "Get up, Rosy Posy."

It was Poll. Grandpapa had taught her to say it.

MRS. C. M. LIVINGSTON.

HEROD seemed to think one must keep a promise, no matter what it is, so he put good, honest John the Baptist to death! One reason he gave was because of what his guests would say. But how did he know but they would say it was right for him to break such a bad promise? But why did he not think: "What will people all the coming years say to this wicked deed? What will the angels say? What will the holy mighty God say?"

"But shouldn't one keep his promises?"

You see Herod should not in this case. Suppose the girl had said: "Give me your crown," or "Let me cut your head or tongue off," how then about Mr. Herod's keeping his promise? Guess he would have found a way — not to keep his oath.

No, it is never right to keep a wrong promise. That would be doing two wrong things instead of one. Herod had no business to take such an oath. How could he know what this artful dancer might ask? No one may make a promise about which one cannot know.

Don't ever do such a thing.

"If you have done it?" Break it. Break it, and repent over your rashness. Beware of the state of your mind when you make a pledge. See that you know what you are about.

Perhaps Herod would never have taken such an awful oath had he not been intoxicated with wine and this dancing girl. "When wine is in wit is out." Many a person has lost his reason and committed some great crime by being in such society. Wine and dancing never helped any one heavenward.

Take care!   L.

MANY blessings will occur to him who is in search of them. Let us dwell lovingly and gratefully upon these; let us weigh and consider how to make the most of them, by neglecting no opportunity and shutting out nothing from our life that can brighten and invigorate it.

I WAS sorry for the mother, I heard her gentle, troubled voice in the hall, trying to make explanations. "Not going!" was the startled response of the girls; "what is the matter? O, dear me! what shall we do without her? Celia Lewis might sing the part if she had only known; but she thought she wouldn't be needed, and she isn't feeling very well, so she didn't come out. Dear Mrs. Conran, cannot you coax Angie to come? I am afraid we shall have to give up the anthem altogether if you don't. Harold says he cannot sing it without having one rehearsal."

"I am very sorry," said gentle Mrs. Conran, "but I am afraid it is quite out of the question, Angie is so sure she cannot go to-night. Perhaps you can arrange a rehearsal early in the morning?"

"No, ma'am, we can't do that, because the Bible classes occupy the room, you know, until the last minute. O, dear! how I wish we had known it before. I don't know what we shall do. Is Angie feeling very ill, Mrs. Conran?"

"N-o," said the mother hesitatingly, and I knew that her face flushed to her temples; "she isn't sick, but she is very much — out of sorts. I regret it exceedingly, but you know how Angie is. When she once settles in her own mind that she can't do a thing it doesn't seem possible for her to get the consent of her will to do it."

"Well," they said, turning away, "it seems too bad, when Dr. Brand asked for that particular anthem, and Angie is the only one who has sung it; but I suppose we shall manage some way. Good-evening."

Mrs. Conran closed the door after them and came slowly back to the parlor, I, meantime, wishing there had been some excuse for me to slip away, so that she need not have the embarrassment of meeting me. There was a weary attempt at a smile on her face, which had grown pale again, and she said apologetically :

"Poor Angie! she is the victim of her own strong will. I sometimes feel very sorry that she matured in some things so early; she has an idea that her mother does not know what is suitable for young people to wear, and is growing a little too fond of dress, I am afraid. She has been put forward so much in her music that it has injured her. It seems strange that a sweet voice should lead one into temptation, doesn't it?"

I murmured something about girls being fond of their own way and about their having to learn by experience, the more to give the mother a chance to recover herself than because I felt that I had anything worth saying. I do not think she heard all I said, but the words "learn by experience" caught her attention.

"Yes," she said, after a moment, speaking with a long-drawn sigh, "that is it. Poor child! she must learn by experience, and experience is a bitter teacher sometimes. Often, when I hear her sweet voice roll out on those solemn words:

> "'Nearer, my God, to thee,
> . . . .
> E'en though it be a cross
> That leadeth me,'

I wonder what the 'cross' will be that will lead Angie to think less of her own will and more of Christ. She is so strong-willed, so passionate, and has such a way of giving vent to the thoughts that come into her mind at the moment, without stopping to realize how they will sound.

"In some way the child must be taught. It seems to me I have tried hard to teach her, but I have failed. I do not often speak in this way of her," she added, with a sad smile; "I do not like to talk about her faults before any one, but to-night you heard all the talk, and I want you to understand that her words do not mean all they seem to. She would be startled and frightened at herself if she could have them photographed in some way and spread out before her.

"But every exhibition of this kind only proves to me more clearly that she is in need of a solemn lesson, and I do not know how it is coming.

> "'Though like a wanderer,
> Daylight all gone,
> Darkness be over me,
> My rest a stone.'

"It makes my heart ache sometimes to hear her sing those words, because I cannot help wondering if she must have the 'darkness' and the 'stone' to bring her to the true Light."

I did not know what to say to the pale mother, so I said nothing; but as I thought of her unnatural pallor, in sharp contrast with the two burning spots on her wasted cheeks, and remembered how constantly that little cough annoyed her, I felt sorry for Angie. I thought I could see the way in which the "cross" must come.

I could feel how much heavier she was making it for herself; because some day, perhaps soon, her memory would recall with bitter tears the harsh, cruel words she had spoken to her mother, absorbed as she was in the eager desire to have her own way. If she would only consent to be led "nearer" by a pleasanter path!

MYRA SPAFFORD.

THINGS WHICH SOME PEOPLE REGRET.

NOW we have something unique. Read the "Regrets" over carefully, and you will discover that we have had nothing like this. You recognize the writer, I presume, as an author who has interested a great many people. Let us hope that he will never have occasion to regret the regret which he has so kindly given us.

"I have regrets for the past, of course; but I have rarely expressed regrets without afterward regretting that I had expressed them."

Yours truly,
GEORGE W. CABLE.

WHO'S AFRAID?

THE FIRST FLAG.

WOULD the Pansies like to see a picture of the first United States flag which ever floated from a vessel? Count the stars. Why do you suppose there are only twelve, when everybody knows that thirteen was the original number? The explanation is said to be that at the time this particular flag was made — that is in 1779 — the Legislature of Maryland had not yet formally joined the Union, so her star was omitted.

The flag was made by some Philadelphia ladies, and presented to Captain Jones. For a time it sailed proudly up and down the Schuylkill, fresh and beautiful. Then it went to war, and was shot and fell into the sea. A young lieutenant, Stafford by name, jumped overboard to save the flag. When it fell the British thought the Yankees had "struck their colors," but in a little time it waved aloft again, trimmed with bullet holes. You must read in our United States history about the great victory which Captain Jones and his brave vessel, the *Bonhomme Richard*, gained at that time.

When the war was over the flag was sent to Lieutenant Stafford as a memento of his faithfulness and bravery. It has been kept in the Stafford family ever since, although they have been urged many times to sell it, and as many as three thousand dollars have been offered for it.

When the lieutenant's daughter Sarah died the old flag was draped about her coffin. When President Harrison was inaugurated it came to Washington, and was carried by one of the Stafford family in the procession.

We show you, also, the picture of Mrs. James Bayard Stafford, the wife of the lieutenant. She was over eighty years old when this picture was taken, but the face shows a sweet brave woman, strong for the right and the true, which was the character she bore. I do not know whether she is still living, but a few years ago she was the light of the home in Cottage City, Mass., and guarded the old historic flag as a sacred relic. PANSY.

AN Indian arrow is quite a work of art. The head, or point, is made from a barrel hoop about three inches long, tapered to a point, and sharpened on both sides. In a bunch of arrows these points are absolutely uniform. The shaft is made of ash about twenty-three inches long. The feathers are glued on and lashed at each end with sinew. The head or point is inserted in the wood, and also lashed

PAUL JONES'S "STARRY FLAG."

with sinew. And running along the arrow are three wave-like grooves from the head to the feathers. This, the Indians explain, is to make the arrow go straight. The bow is also made of ash, and with a string of twisted sinew taken from along the back of a beef. So that with an ordinary butcher knife and a file, if it is to be had, an Indian can make his own arms.

The penetrating force of an arrow is wonderful. An Indian can shoot an arrow right through a buffalo. I have heard it stated that bows and arrows would be much more effective weapons in the hands of Indians than such guns as they surrendered to General Miles. — *Selected.*

AN UNWELCOME BILL.

ABOUT BUFFALO.

BY THE PANSIES.

 I HAVE been waiting for the time to come to write about Buffalo, because I knew something queer to write. Three of the nice streets there are named Niagara St., Erie St., and Church St.; but their names used to be Schimmelpenniek Avenue, Vollenhoven Avenue and Stadnitski Avenue! Isn't it a good thing they were changed?

SARAH L. JOHNSON.

THE Indian name for Buffalo is Teosahway. I think it is much prettier than Buffalo. Some people say the city was named for an old Indian chief who lived in a hut in the center of where the main business part is now located; the Indian's name was Buffaloe. But others think it was named after the "creek," where the buffaloes used to come in droves.

HENRY RICE.

THE city of Buffalo used to be spelled with an e, and the citizens had a great time getting rid of that final e. Father says that years after it had been dropped the city of Binghamton, N. Y., which used to be spelled "Binghampton," set to work to get rid of that unnecessary p. Buffalo, forgetting the trouble it had had, was the last to remember the change; long after others were pretty well educated, the Buffalo postmaster would send the Binghamton mail in a package marked "Binghampton." At last the Binghamton postmaster made up a package for Buffalo and addressed it in very large letters, "Buffalop," then wrote underneath: "If you are so fond of the letter p take it." Father says he believes this cured them.

SARAH H. ATCHISON.

MY grandmother used to live in Buffalo when the water supply was very different from what it is now. There used to be an old man whom they called "Water John." He had a cart and an old horse, and he used to fill a hogshead with water at the lake, and go through the streets peddling it for a shilling a barrel. A shilling was twelve and a half cents. Grandmother says they always used to have to give Water John thirteen cents; and I don't see why they did not call it thirteen cents a barrel, instead of a price which nobody could exactly pay.

LAURA HOLMAN.

I HAD a great-uncle who used to live in Buffalo when there were only about forty houses there, all built of logs; and I have an uncle living in Buffalo now who went there in 1825, when there were about two thousand inhabitants, and has seen it grow to its present size — about two hundred and fifty thousand; some say more than that. It must be a great thing to be able to look back on such changes.

JAMES CAMPBELL.

MY grandmother went to Buffalo when she was a little girl and took a ride on the "Black Rock Railroad"; that was what they called it, but it was just a street car. Grandmother thinks it was the first horse railroad used in this country. There was a car for pleasant weather and one for storms. The pleasant weather one was like a great box, with an outside seat for the driver. The seats were just boards with straight backs. There was no cover, and the sun could pelt down on you as much as it pleased. For bad weather they had one with a top, and canvas curtains that buttoned down. The car was drawn by one horse, and Grandmother says they did not use any time table, but came along just whenever it happened. The fare was a shilling.

LUCY STEVENSON.

IT is great fun to read about Buffalo as it used to be. I was there last summer and stopped at an elegant hotel. I forget its name, but I know they said it was the handsomest in the city, and it was just splendid, I tell you! A little while after I came home I read about "The Farmers' Hotel," which was the grand hotel of Buffalo in 1832. I saw a picture of it; the queerest looking little old building you ever saw, with a bell on the top, like a great cow bell; it was rung by a rope, and that is the way people used to be called to their meals. The book I was reading said it was a very useful bell, for it not only told when breakfast or dinner was ready at the Farmers' Hotel, but was useful as a time-keeper in every house in the neighborhood; for there were very few people indeed in those days who carried watches, and clocks were very rare and costly.

REUBEN S. BENTON.

I HAVE a letter which was written to my grandmother in 1836, by a lady who lived in Buffalo. Grandmother lived in New York, and the amount of postage which it took to carry the letter from Buffalo to New York was two shillings. This was marked in red ink on the outside of the letter; not on an envelope, for none were used, but one side of the paper was left blank, and the letter was folded in a curious way, and marked "Paid 2 s." Grandmother said her sister in Albany used to get letters from the same lady, and hers were marked: "Paid 18¾." At that time it cost less to write from Buffalo to Albany than it did from Buffalo to New York; and I must say that seems reasonable. Why should letters be two cents now, whether they travel ten miles or a thousand? But I am glad they are not twenty-five cents.

CARRIE FOSTER.

BUFFALO is a great city. You can start from it and go anywhere you want to, at most any hour of the day or night. There are as many as thirteen different railroad lines to choose from, to say nothing of steamboats and all that sort of thing. But it is the queerest laid out city in this country. A man Ellicott planned it almost a century ago, and meant to build a palace for himself right in the center, but he never did.

JOHN JONES.

MOTHER says I ought to be able to write you a letter about Buffalo, because I've been there lots of times. But I can't. What is there to write about a city, I should like to know?

They are all alike; great long streets with big houses on both sides, or big stores or something, and churches every little way, and crowds of people in the streets getting in a fellow's way all the time, and carts running over you, and carriages that you want to take a ride in and can't; and an awful noise and smoke and hurly-burly. I'd rather spend one afternoon in the country in an apple orchard or a strawberry field, or by a trout stream, than to be a whole week in any city I ever saw. Buffalo has some splendid-looking houses and parks, and there is a lunatic asylum that I was interested in, because the people acted so queer. I don't like Buffalo, however, nor any other big place.

TOM HURST.

I THINK they must make flour enough in Buffalo to supply the world with bread. My father says that twelve years ago there were eleven great flouring mills there, and he doesn't know how many more have been started since. At that time they made every year about two hundred and fifty thousand barrels of flour; but dear me! it would take more flour than that to feed the world, wouldn't it? What a lot of things we do have to eat!

JIMMIE TUCKER.

I SHOULD think Buffalo would be called the "City of Churches." There must be hundreds of churches there. I went with my uncle and brother to look at different ones, and it took us two days just to see those which were on three streets of the city. Some of them are lovely, and some were great, dark-looking buildings, like jails.

LUCY STONE.

[On the whole we consider these Buffalo letters decidedly unique. A little ahead of anything in that line which the Pansies have yet given us. Certainly some rather original ideas in regard to cities in general have been advanced, and we have been given a better chance than usual to mark the progress which time has made. We are somewhat surprised that no one has described a ride to or from the city on one of the canal packets. That is a vivid memory of our childhood which we would like to tell you about were there time.

Our material is as usual not exhausted, but our space is. I presume Buffalo will fare like the cities which have preceded it — that is, some of the best letters will come too late to use. If our Pansies could only learn to start three months ahead! — EDITORS.]

MAJOR'S AUTOBIOGRAPHY.

v.

THIS is a beautiful moonlight evening, but you would rather listen to me than bark at the moon?

All right; I don't mind talking when I have good listeners, but to try to tell a story and be constantly reminded that those to whom you talk are thinking of something else, is not pleasant.

What shall I talk about to-night?

"Something concerning our relatives away back?"

So you want to know what kind of blood there is in our veins? That is an interesting theme for some, and why not for us?

It is not three days since I heard our master boast that he had descended from the Pilgrim Fathers. We do not all claim to be related, but we are of one family now, and so interested in each other.

I like to think that some of my relatives have done good and been faithful; so I think I will tell you what one of my great-great-great-uncles did a long time ago.

His name was Sport, and at the time to which I refer he lived with a man by the name of Stillman. He was thought much of for hunting, and because of his skill in this direction he had a chance to earn the reputation which so many envied; that is, to earn it in just the way he did.

I want my young friends to remember that the way is always open for any dog to get a good name if he will only try. Why, even a little insignificant poodle can be of use. There is our neighbor, Mr. Fellows; he had two or three dog sentinels all about his place, and the other night a man got clear to his front door, and none of these big fellows said or knew anything of it; but the moment the man reached the door little Tip, the poodle, notified the whole house.

Well, this dog Sport was taken by his master, one fall, away off into the wood. They went miles and miles beyond where anybody pretended to live, and there in a little hut they staid for days and days, the master hunting and fishing and resting.

This was all well enough so long as nothing unusual occurred, though it was pretty lonesome for the four-footed one. The master seemed to take it for granted that his dog knew nothing but how to follow game, so said little to him, sometimes hardly noticing him from morning till night.

As I said, matters moved on very well for a time, but there came a change. Mr. Stillman awoke one night feeling very ill, and by morning was sick enough.

He took such medicine as he had, but grew worse and worse. The poor man could not sit up to write, and if he could have written, who would be mail carrier for him?

He lay there and thought, and tried to plan. "If I only had a St. Bernard dog I might send him for help; but Sport is nothing but a hunting dog, and he cannot understand anything but how to follow a track."

In the meantime Sport was feeling badly, and trying to think what he might do, for his master was getting worse all the time. Walking around the room he saw an envelope with something in it, and while his master was seemingly asleep, he took the package in his mouth and started upon the run in the direction in which they came into the woods.

He made pretty fast time for eight or ten miles; then he came to a trail, and knew a party had passed there not long before. So, putting his nose to the ground, he soon learned which way they had gone, and followed them at good speed.

Fortunately he came upon them where they had encamped for the night. It proved to be quite a large party with an experienced guide.

Sport dashed in among them and laid down his package and barked, to call their attention to it. The men examined the writing, and while it did not tell them how it was sent — it not having been sent — it seemed to be an attempt of some one to leave on record the condition he was in, his name and address, so that if he should die, any one finding this might be able to inform his friends.

No one of those who first composed the party knew what to think of the paper, for there was little of it which could be read, more than the name; but the guide was not long in interpreting Sport's meaning, and told them that the faithful dog had without doubt come from some one in distress, and that they must try to find him.

"If I don't miss my guess by a shot or two this four-legged mail-carrier will be dreadful glad to pilot us back the way he came; won't you, old fellow?"

Sport showed his readiness by jumping up and starting; but Simpkins — that was the guide's name —called him back, patted him on the head, and gave him something to eat, promising to go with him pretty soon.

The guide told the party to remain there, all but one or two,

hesitated; and the men probably preferred following him to being left alone.

As they neared the place on the main trail, Sport would run ahead and bark, and then come back to the guide and whine.

Well, they got to the hut at last, and it appeared as though the sick man had not moved while his faithful friend was gone; and what is more, the doctor said he never would have moved if help had not come.

The men rubbed him and gave him medicine,

SPORT BEFRIENDS HIS MASTER.

till he should return. One of their number was a doctor, who was taking his vacation, and he volunteered to be one of the company to make the search for the supposed sufferer. Although all had believed themselves to be tired, yet they were soon off, Sport taking the lead, and so eager that he let his followers only just keep in sight. It was dark some time before the little hut was reached.

When the men told the story afterward, they said it was a great wonder they kept on following a dog in that way, though the guide never

and towards morning he opened his eyes. It took him a little while to make out what it all meant, but when Sport heard his voice he sprang to his side, and seemed wild with delight.

There is a great deal more to this story which I will not take time to tell. The doctor tried hard to buy Sport after that, but his master said he would sooner let him have one of his hands; he kept him until he died of old age.

Before he died Mr. Stillman had his picture painted by a fine artist. Master and dog have been dead for years, but I have seen both their pictures, made by the same man. Saw them often when I was little. Our folks used to tell the story to people who visited them, and then point to me and say: "This little fellow is related to that noble dog, and we hope he will be like him." Then I would be so proud of the relationship, and resolve to be just as good if I could not be as smart.

Now it is time to look around and see that everything is all right. If they have not forgotten to shut the hen-house door, we can take our places as usual till morning.

No, I never had such a chance as old Uncle Sport had for making a name, but I have done what I could, and my master is not slow to show that he loves me.

R.

JACK'S DECISION.

JACK was in a very doleful frame of mind. It was Sabbath morning, and as bright a day as even July could furnish to that part of the world. The birds in the trees, the leaves as they rustled, and the sweet odors in the air, all seemed to whisper that it was a perfect Sunday. Jack wanted to go to church. Not that he was devoted to church-going, either. The sermon often seemed long to him, and he sometimes grew very tired of counting the bits of stained glass of which the large round window was made; but on this particular morning, as he sat curled up in the large armchair with a great pillow at his back, he made himself believe that there was nothing in life he wanted so much as to go to church that day. It was not simply that the new carriage was to be used for the first time, and that Prince and Tony were harnessed together before it, and would look splendid, but in addition to these excellent reasons Jack had not been out of the house for nearly a week, and had not had a ride since last Sabbath, and it seemed to him he should fly if he had to stay in much longer. But then, Jack had the mumps, so it couldn't be helped.

Uncle Jack was to stay with him; or rather

he was to stay with Uncle Jack, which was pleasant, for although this favorite uncle always staid at home on Sundays, and could not take a single step without somebody on either side to help, yet his nephew considered him the "jolliest kind of a companion." This may have been partly owing to the fact that Jack the uncle was quite young to have that title — only a boy of twenty — and he was as sunshiny, in fact more so than many boys of ten contrive to be.

On this particular day he exerted himself to his utmost to entertain his namesake, and succeeded so well that when the clock struck twelve the boy said, in round-eyed wonder: "Why, who would have thought it was so late? They will be home in a little while, won't they?"

"That's a fact," said Uncle Jack. "I think there will be just time for us to have our Bible story together, and a little talk about it before they come. You know that was to finish the morning's programme, Jack."

"All right," said Jack, settling back on his pillow, "go ahead; I like to hear you read the Bible better than anybody else, except mother, of course."

This was no wonder, for Uncle Jack had a way of reading between the lines, something after this fashion: "'And a certain man, lame from his mother's womb, was carried.' Just think of that, my boy! Forty years old, and never had walked a step! That is worse than being lame for two years, isn't it?"

"How do you know he was forty years old? It doesn't say so."

"It does in another place; I hunted it up once, to see how long he had been a burden on his friends. And just listen to this as the best they could do for him: 'Whom they laid daily at the gate of the temple, which is called Beautiful, to ask alms of them that entered into the temple.'"

"They were a mean lot," said Jack; "they might have kept him at home and taken care of him."

"Ah, my boy! that is much the way it is to-day in countries where Jesus Christ does not reign; still, we must not be too hard on these friends of his; they may have been miserably

DOLEFUL JACK. — (See "Jack's Decision.")

poor, and to carry the man to the gate and leave him there may have been the utmost that was in their power to give."

"Then they ought to have taken him to the hospital."

"There was none, Jackie. No provision whatever was made in that country for the suffering poor; such things belong to Christianity. Well, ‘Who, seeing Peter and John about to go into the temple, asked an alms.’ He liked the appearance of those ministers, I fancy. I suppose he said, ‘They look kind, and I shouldn't wonder if they would give me quite a lift.’"

"I should say they did," chuckled Jack, who knew the outcome of the story. Reading in this way you can see how long it might take them to get through with even a short story; but Jack thought it a "tip-top" way to read.

He sat lost in thought for some minutes after the lame man had gone leaping into the temple, then said, half-doubtfully, as though not sure whether it were just the proper thing to say: "Uncle Jack, wouldn't it be a splendid thing if Peter were alive now, and should come home from church with the folks, and cure you so you could run all around?"

Uncle Jack turned bright smiling eyes on his nephew. "You forget," he said briskly; "it wasn't Peter who did it; he was only the instrument. You might as well call the cup in which you take your beef tea the food, as to call Peter the physician in this case."

"Well, then," said Jack, looking resolute, "I don't understand why he doesn't cure folks now — Jesus, I mean. People say he is here all the time, though we can't see him, and that he is just the same as ever he was; why don't he cure you, Uncle Jack, just as he cured the man at the temple gate?"

"He has," said Uncle Jack promptly; "He has performed a much greater cure for me than He did for the man at the gate."

And then Jack looked astounded. As though he did not know that his Uncle Jack had not taken a step in two years, and even the great surgeon from the city could not be sure if he ever would.

The gay young uncle laughed over his astonishment, then said: "I see I shall have to tell you something, Jackie. Before I was hurt I was in a bad way — lame not only in my feet, but in my will power, which is much worse. I was making a headlong rush toward ruin, and when the accident happened which laid me flat on my back, I knew before many weeks that it was Jesus Christ trying to cure me."

Little Jack stared. "Couldn't He have done it without that?" he asked.

"No," said his uncle confidently; "I don't believe He could. I wouldn't let Him, you see. He had called me hundreds of times, and urged me to let Him do the best things for me, but I wouldn't. My will power, as I told you, was lame, sick — deathly sick; I couldn't seem to want to be cured, nor to do any of my part of the work. There is always our part to do in a cure, you know." Jack nodded, and remembered the bitter medicine which he had rebelled against swallowing. "Well, I wouldn't do my part; refused out and out, and kept on refusing until I was placed on my back. I suppose the Lord Jesus knew that that only would bring me to my senses, and give him a chance to cure my heart sickness, so he let it come to me. Understand?"

Jack was not disposed to answer. He was thinking. "Why doesn't He cure your back now?" he asked, speaking part of his thought.

His uncle's voice was a trifle lower, and hinted at strong feeling which was being controlled. "I believe he will, Jackie, just as soon as it is best for me to be cured. I think I am going to get quite well; indeed, I may say I am almost sure of it, though the surgeon is not. I believe the Lord Jesus has decided to let me be well and strong again, so I can be a witness for him, as the lame man was, you remember. Why, we didn't finish the story, did we? And there is no time now. Here come the people from church. You look that up, Jackie, in your Bible sometime, and see what an unanswerable argument the man was."

Jack the younger thought over the entire story later, while he was eating his beef tea. Thought and thought, and by a way which was clear to himself, came at last to this point: "I wonder if He let me have the mumps so as to stop me from doing different from what mother says? If I hadn't thought it wouldn't do any harm to run into Judge Howell's a few minutes, even after she had told me not to stop anywhere, why, I suppose I shouldn't have had these horrid old mumps. Maybe He knows it was the only way to cure me. Well, I tell you what it is; I believe I'll be cured. I guess, after this, I'll do just exactly as I'm told, and be a 'witness' myself, so that folks will begin to say of me: 'Jack Campbell won't do it; his folks told him not to, and you can't move Jack after that any more than you could a stone wall.' I declare, that will be tip-top fun. I'll do it!"

PANSY.

JACK THOUGHT AND THOUGHT.

MY PRETTY DEER.

ONLY ONE LEFT.

CLAUDE'S STORY.

CLAUDE TALMAN was ten years old. He lived in a marble house. Its floors had costly carpets, and all the furniture was elegant. His clothes were fine and rich; his food came from almost all parts of the world. How soft was his bed. Tenderly was he watched over. He seemed to have more than heart could wish — not his heart, however.

One day as he looked from his elegant window he saw a poor boy passing drawn in a little thing that he (Claude) didn't have? His mother reasoned with him, but all to no purpose; he stormed about, stamping his foot, saying he would have it if he had to kill the boy to get it. When he got over his rage somewhat his mother said: "You remind me of another Claude, only his real name was Claudius."

Then Master Claude quieted down and listened, for he was fond of stories, and now he knew his mother had one for him. So she went on thus: "Two thousand years ago there lived a large family in the country that is now called England. Their name was Briton. They were

CARACTACA BEGS TO BE SENT HOME.

wagon by a goat; then he set up a loud cry that he must have that very wagon and goat. It did no good for his mother to promise him just as good an one if it could be found in the Central Market, where almost everything could be bought. No, he must have that. That boy must sell it to him or it must be taken from him. What right had that poor boy to some- not the handsomest or wisest folks in the world, nor were they always gentle among themselves. Their houses were mere huts and their dress was the skins of wild animals. They were a brave people, but generally minded their own business. The great father of this family — I should say one of the big brothers — was Carac-tacus. He was strong and fearless, and very wise and good in his way. When they were in trouble they went to him, and somehow he always knew just what to do. So they thought of him just as American people think of Washington.

"Miles and miles away across the great waters lived another family in an elegant marble palace " —

"Now you are going to tell a story about me," interrupted Claude.

— "in an elegant marble palace. Everything without as well as within this beautiful mansion was costly and wonderful. There was nothing just like it on all the face of the earth.

"But they were unhappy. They wanted something more. One day while they were sitting and feasting, dressed in purple and fine linen, and bands of music were playing, word came from one of thei· travelers about a fair island far away, and about this Briton family who owned it, and were living there so contentedly.

"Then uprose the father of the Roman family — for that was their name — and the music ceased, the feasting was over, and the men put off their showy dress and put on their soldier clothes, and the father or big brother, whose name was Claudius " —

"Now, mother, more about me?"

"His name was Claudius, and he mounted his war horse and blew a loud blast that made the marble halls ring again, and with waving banners and peals of music away marched this Roman family to conquer the Briton family and make them give up their" —

"Little wagon and goat?"

— "give up their beautiful farm. On they went on foot and on horse and by boats till they landed one dark night and stole up to the back yard of the Britons.

"Then of a sudden the dogs set up an awful barking. The Britons — women as well as men and children — sprang up in a jiffy, and a fierce fight followed. Sometimes the Romans got the better, sometimes the Britons; but after a long, long time, when many were killed on both sides, six of Claudius' biggest brothers saw Caractacus fall, and the blood was streaming from his side by an arrow wound, and they leaped upon him

and bound his hands behind him, and led him as best they could to Claudius. But Caractaca, his poor wife, followed, begging the soldiers not to harm her suffering husband.

"When the brave Britons saw their leader fall, and knew he was now a prisoner, their hearts failed them, and they fled, many of them, far away into the forests.

"But Caractacus and his sad wife were taken from their home and carried far away to the Roman palace as prisoners.

"Now when they looked around this grand home and saw all its richness and glory they drew a deep sigh, Caractaca begging Claudius to send them back to their home, the brave Caractacus only saying he did not see why such a rich family cared for the plain hut he lived in."

Master Claude never again insisted upon having the littl· wagon and goat. Nay, he helped him to b·tter ones.   L.

THE LONGEST DAY.

IT is quite important, when speaking of the longest day in the year, to say what part of the world we are talking about, as will be seen by reading the following list, which tells the length of the longest day in several different places. How unfortunate are the children in Tornea, Finland, where Christmas Day is less than three hours in length!

At Stockholm, Sweden, it is eighteen and one half hours in length. At Spitzbergen the longest day is three and one half months. At London, England, and Bremen, Prussia, the longest day has sixteen and one half hours. At Hamburg in Germany, and Dantzig in Prussia, the longest day has seventeen hours. At Wardbury, Norway, the longest day lasts from May 21 to July 22, without interruption. At St. Petersburg, Russia, and Tobolsk, Siberia, the longest day is nineteen hours, and the shortest five hours. At Tornea, Finland, June 21 brings a day nearly twenty-two hours long, and Christmas one less than three hours in length. At New York the longest day is about fifteen hours, and at Montreal, Canada, it is sixteen. — *Selected.*

THREE YOUNG MISSIONARIES.

"WHO are they?"
The one with his hat off and flag in hand — his name is Judson. The neat little Miss, her fingers tucked in that warm muff, and her satisfied face saying: "See what a nice big snowball we've made," she is Miss Emily Chubbuck, to be sure. The third — wouldn't you give a penny to see his face? — he looks like a young Scotch Highlander in plaids. He it is who fixed up the funny mouth, nose and eyes, and is now putting something sweeter than a nasty cigarette into his snow mouth; well, this one is Master Carey. Now they look only like children having fun. Not a hundred years after they became missionaries. Heard you ever of Carey? Of Adoniram Judson? Of his wife, Emily Chubbuck? L.

FIRST TIME AT CHURCH.

A GRAVE sweet wonder in thy baby face,
And look of mingled dignity and grace,
Such as a painter hand might love to trace.

A pair of trusting innocent blue eyes,
That higher than the stained-glass window rise,
Into the fair and cloudless summer skies.

The people round her sing, "Above the sky
There's rest for little children when they die."
To her, thus gazing up, that rest seems nigh.

The organ peals; she must not look around,
Although with wonderment her pulses bound —
The place whereon she stands is holy ground.

The sermon over, and the blessing said,
She bows, as "mother" does, her golden head,
And thinks of little sister who is dead.

She knows that now she dwells above the sky,
Where holy children enter when they die,
And prays God take her there too, by and by.

Yet, may He keep you in the faith alway,
And bring you to that home for which you pray,
Where all shall have their child hearts back one
day! — *Selected.*

AN IDEA THAT GREW.

 IT was Nancy and the book together which put the idea into Clara's mind. They were slipping along in the shadows of the quiet river, she and Wallace. It was the Fourth of July, and most of the boys and girls of the region were busy with what firecrackers they could get — those of them who had not taken a five-mile tramp to the village to attend the celebration.

But Clara was too old to care for firecrackers, and Wallace had had enough of them before he came; he was only here for a few days, and preferred a visit with his sister to all the Fourth of July celebrations that could be planned. She was reading aloud to him bits from a new book which he had brought her as a birthday present; for the Fourth of July was not only the birthday of freedom, it was also Clara's birthday.

"O, Wallace!" she said, "this is a lovely book." She had said the same thing at least a dozen times that day. "Just see what queer ideas she had," Clara continued, meaning the girl in the book; "she was very good — better than anybody I ever knew. I should think it would be lovely to do half the nice things she did. One plan was to pick out a friend — another girl — and try to help her in every way she could. Pray for her, you know, and talk with her, and influence her, until at last the girl would be converted; then they two would choose two others to help in the same way, and they were going to see how large a circle they could make of that kind. She thought perhaps she could reach all around the world; she was only a young girl, and she thought if she lived to be a woman perhaps she could. Wallace, what are you laughing at?"

"At the modesty of the young woman and her ideas," said Wallace, laughing afresh. "She hasn't gotten around the world yet, I take it; I've never seen anything of her."

"I am sure the idea is beautiful," said Clara, half-inclined to be vexed with Wallace for making sport of it. "And of course one could do a great deal of good in that way. I would just like to try it."

"Why don't you?" Wallace asked, his eyes twinkling; "I'm sure you have a good field for work of the sort here among the natives. Look at that specimen on the bank at this moment. Her eyes are as large as sunflowers, and she looks as though she might take any amount of doing good to and not be hurt by it."

Clara turned around and stared back at Nancy on the shore.

A little girl with a sallow, wistful face, and great mournful-looking eyes. She had on a worn and faded dress, an apron which was much too long for her, but seemed to have been put on to cover the deficiencies of the dress. She wore neither shoes nor stockings, and was hanging tightly by the two strings to her pink gingham sunbonnet, and gazing at the people in the boat with the most unutterable longing in her eyes that Clara had ever seen.

"Poor thing!" said Clara; "she envies us our row. I wonder if she never has a chance to take a row on the river? Only see how hungry her eyes look."

"It is more probable that she envies you your hat and dress," said Wallace; "she keeps her eyes on them. She has an eye to the beautiful, that is what is the matter with her. I am not sure but it is your hair she wants most, after all, though hers is arranged elaborately. She would make an excellent beginning for your scheme, Clara."

"I am not sure but she would." Wallace was teasing, but his sister was grave and in earnest. "Row toward the shore, Wallace, and let me speak to her; I never saw a child who had such a wistful look.

"Good afternoon, little girl," she said pleasantly, as Wallace obeyed directions and the boat drew near, "are you having a pleasant Fourth of July?"

"No," said the child, without hesitation or ceremony.

"Not? I am very sorry. What has been the trouble?"

"Nothing," said the child, as promptly as before. Then, seeming to consider something more necessary, added: "Nothing more than

always is. We don't never have no pleasant times to our house."

"You see," said Wallace, in low tones, nodding significantly to his sister, "she is in perishing need of being chosen."

"So she is. Wallace, you are simply making fun, but I am in earnest. I wonder what I could do for the poor little thing? I have been here for two months, and haven't done a thing for anybody. I have tried to get acquainted with a few of the girls of my age, but they are shy of me; this child does not seem to be shy."

"Not in the least," said Wallace. "Very well, how shall we commence? Shall I invite her to sail with us this afternoon as a sort of entering wedge?"

"Do you mean it?" Clara asked, well pleased, and she turned again to Nancy. "Do you ever go rowing on the river?"

"No."

"Why not? Would not you like to?"

"Never had no chance. We ain't got no boat, and nobody won't lend us poor folks any; and we don't never go nowheres, me and Billy."

"Poor little girl! Who is Billy? your little brother? Would you like to take a ride with us this afternoon? If you would you may come down to the landing and get in the boat."

The child stared for a moment as though she felt her ears were not to be trusted, then turned and made a dash for the landing below. Wallace laughed and steered the boat in the same direction. A few moments more and they were off, with the barefooted Nancy seated comfortably beside Clara.

It is only the very beginning of this story that I have space for. I am wondering if you Pansies cannot sit down thoughtfully and think it out for yourselves, perhaps write it out. The story is true, and it happened years ago. Such a girl as Clara, who was spending a summer in a backwoods region, for reasons which I need not stop here to explain, and such a girl as Nancy met first in the way I have described; and in the course of that afternoon ride Clara heard enough about the home where they "never had no pleasant times," to make her heart ache. The beautiful idea in the book kept coming to her, or rather staid with her and kept asking if she could not do something of the kind with this Nancy. To be sure Nancy was not like the girl chosen in the book; she had been of about the same age and station as her friend. "But then," said Clara to herself, "she did not need help half so much as this one does; and I think with this kind of people I might help one younger than myself better than one

ON THE QUIET RIVER.

of my own age. At least I can pray for her."

Now the story for you to work out is begun, and I will give you just a few more facts, and then jump to the end of it — that is so far as I know it — leaving you to fill up the blank space. It was a stony, hilly, desolate country side, where the people were very poor, and were cursed with more rum saloons than with any other form of business; where the nearest

church was five miles away; where there was no Sunday-school, and no day-school except for three months in the winter. And Nancy, being questioned, showed that she not only did not know what Fourth of July meant, but she did not know what Sunday meant in the true sense of the word; nor did she know about Jesus Christ, save as she had heard "Pap swear his name sometimes!" Did ever girl need helping more?

Now for the end, so far as it can be said to be ended, for the people are still living. Nancy is a young woman who wears the neatest of dresses and hats, and the nicest fitting boots and gloves. She is herself a teacher in the day-school in that part of the country where her home has always been. The school is in session nine months of the year. She is a teacher in the Sunday-school, which has a room of its own, opening from the pretty church where every Sabbath day the people gather to hear of Jesus Christ. And Nancy's father is the superintendent of the Sunday-school! And there is not a saloon left within two miles of the neighborhood; and the change began that Fourth of July afternoon, when Clara, reading from her new book, caught an idea which grew.

You will perhaps be glad to hear that Wallace, although he professed to be only amused, was much more than that, and helped to form Clara's "circle" so effectually that he preaches in the little church whenever he comes to this part of the world for a few weeks of vacation. "You haven't reached around the world yet," he said to Clara not long ago; "but I am not sure but you will. Do you know that boy Billy wants to be a missionary and go to China?"

Billy is Nancy's youngest brother.

Now see if you can plan ways by which Clara may have helped to bring about such changes. No, better than that; look about you and see what you can do to make a circle of good that shall reach — as far as it can.   PANSY.

THREE YOUNG MISSIONARIES.

TEACHING THE CHINESE.

AND so you thought the Chinese do not know anything?

Look into this school; see wise Mr. Ah Lee sitting before his thirteen youngsters. See how bright they look. And surely they know how to get as much fun out of a cat's tail and get rapped over the knuckles

mastering Chinese so they can converse with the people and preach the Gospel to them. The trouble is that a word may mean one of a dozen different things, just as you happen to give it this tone (sound) or that.

A Mr. Meadows once wished to say "bargain money" to a Chinaman. He used the proper Chinese word for it, but pronounced it as though it meant to the Chinaman "Do you hear? do you hear?" And what said John

A CHINESE SCHOOL.

as hard as any American boy. Yes, they sit upon the floor, and they don't seem to have blackboards and maps and many other nice school contrivances, but they manage somehow to learn one of the most difficult languages in the world.

Our poor missionaries do have such a time in

Chinaman? Just nothing at all, but came nearer and nearer to Mr. Meadows, turning one side of his head then the other to listen.

Once Mr. Pohlman asked a Chinese family if they drank wine, but he pronounced the word wine (*tsёn*) so it sounded to them like their word for land (*t'sёn*).

At another time he asked a mourning family if they had buried (*tai*) the body of their dead grandmother. But he sounded it *t'ai*, which means to kill. Imagine their looks.

But the missionaries work away at the queer Chinese words and tones until they can tell the "old story" plainly — and hundreds have heard and understood, and now believe.

You know how hard it is for the Chinaman to speak our language. He says "Amelican" for American, our *r* is so difficult for him to get.

But the time is coming when every one of God's family will know the one great language, and there will be no hard schoolmaster to scold or whip it into them.   L.

WHEN HE WAS TWELVE YEARS OLD.

OUR little lad, our bonnie twelve-year-old,
   Has journeyed to the city of the King;
Our happy boy — ere heart could grow a-cold,
   Or soul turn bitter — in youth's joyous spring,
Went up to keep the feast in that bright place,
   City of Peace, where restful mansions be;
And straightway looking on the dear King's face,
   Remembered naught but joy that face to see!

Long time ago, when He was twelve years old,
   The Holy Child climbed fair Judea's hills,
And his young mother in her heart did hold
   Strange words concerning him, whose mystery fills
Her soul with wonder. — On their homeward way,
   The reverent pilgrims haste; and sorrowing
She seeks her Son, and lo, in calm delay,
   He lingered in the temple of the King!

She, coming to the sacred portal, waits
   With tear-wan face; her fair first-born she seeks;
Weary and grief-worn, at the shining gates,
   With faltering lips his sweet home-name she speaks,
And He is in her arms! — With tender word
   Of gentlest chiding, each to each revealed
The love that to the depths of feeling stirred
   Hearts that brief absence near and dearer sealed.

O mother, mourning for thy fair first-born,
   He tarries in his Father's House of Light,
With God's beloved; and thou in some glad morn,
   Finding the glorious gates beyond the night,
Shalt breathe his name, and ere it leaves thy lips,
   In thy dear arms, aglow with life and joy,
All strong and beautiful — death's long eclipse
   Forgotten in the first kiss of thy boy!
           Rosa Evangeline Angel.

MISS HALSEY read a letter from Miss Patton, of India, who after wittily describing some of the daily trials of housekeeping there, between her rising hour, five o'clock, and that of reaching her first school, says:

"This school, over a mile away, is upstairs in a large house in an alley. The children looked so nice and bright this morning, I wish you could see them. Prayers are over, so I begin by taking the wee tots in the first class and teach them the Lord's Prayer. Then I take class after class until half-past nine, when with pony and queer little two-wheeled tonga I go on about half a mile to the other school. There I teach until nearly eleven and then drive home to breakfast, after which we have English prayers. By that time the gun has gone off, and that means twelve o'clock. The gun is the signal for our servants and native Christians living near to come in and have Marathi prayers.

"Then I teach my servants to read, and ask a few questions in the Catechism, then teach the Christian girls and young women whom we want to train for Bible women, from two until three P. M. At three o'clock we have a cup of tea and some bread and butter; then I am free to settle 'cases' and hear 'tales of woe' until half-past four, when I go into town to teach the women and girls in the zenanas. I get home in time to have a good bath and get into a fresh dress before dinner at half-past seven. After dinner we talk over our experiences and plans of work, and sometimes one reads aloud while the rest of us sew until it is time to retire, generally an early hour." — *Interior.*

AN OLD-TIME WARRIOR.

THE MILKY WAY.

YOUNG FOLKS OF ALASKA.

THIS face is not like yours, but more like some of the young folks of Alaska. Of course you want to know a bit about the boys and girls away off there.

Here it is from Mrs. Cady, who was there not long ago :

"Mr. Austin, the missionary, and these boys dragged all the timber by ropes to build the first house.

"The Sabbath evening service was opened by a fine anthem, these boys and girls being among the singers. Mr. Austin read a Psalm in English, which was interpreted by a boy fourteen years old.

"He asked a girl twelve years old to offer the closing prayer, and she expressed it beautifully in English.

"They are very polite. If a boy taps at the door his hat is off before the door is opened. Their table manners are good. One boy is head waiter.

"He can offer thanks or call upon some other boy to do so, or sing a blessing."

Of course you ought to know just how the

AN ALASKA CHILD.

grandmothers of these bright Alaska children look. Our picture will enable you to judge somewhat of their appearance.   L.

ALASKAN WOMEN.

BABY'S CORNER.

POOR TABBY.

TABBY thought she was a very smart cat, but there were some rats living in the barn who knew almost as much as Tabby did herself.

One morning Tabby went to the barn. She

Now Tabby had never seen a trap, and she said to herself:

"Why, here is a pretty little house! It must be for me; I will walk right in. How nice!"

So she stepped in. Snap! went the door, shut! and there poor Puss was in prison.

She tried to get out, but she could not. She cried, but nobody came to let her out.

While she sat there feeling sad, two rats

THE GRAY RAT TANTALIZES TABBY.

had tried for days to catch a rat, but just as she got her paw out to strike one off he scampered. "To-day I shall get the old gray rat, see if I don't," said Tabby to herself as she walked down the path.

She stepped softly into the door. But what was this new shining thing she saw?

Why, Farmer Jones had put a big trap there to catch the rats.

came and looked at her. The old gray one, as he stood on his hind legs, said:

"Aha! I see; I see! Anybody who goes into that door does not come out. I shall never go in."

By and by Tommy Jones missed his pussy and went to the barn to look for her.

Oh! was not Tabby glad to see him coming?

MRS. C. M. LIVINGSTON.

DAVIE'S WITNESSES.

DAVIE'S WITNESSES.

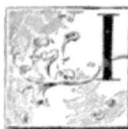 IT was Fourth of July morning, and Davie Carson had been up since a good while before the sun, not firing crackers and torpedoes, nor watching the firing of the great cannon, but doing the chores. He was in tremendous haste. An entire holiday was a thing he did not have twice in a year. A hard-working boy was Davie, with not only his own bread to earn, but with a great longing in his heart to help earn the bread of two sisters and a brother younger than himself. He lived in a small village where there was little chance of a boy of his age earning much. The best that he had been able to do, so far, was to seize odd jobs as they happened along; or rather as he hunted them out. Not very pleasant jobs, all of them. Davie liked horses, and was glad of a chance to lead Dr. Bristol's to water; but to like to clean out their stalls was another thing. But he knew how to do this work, and did it well, and had put on his great work apron this morning for the purpose of taking that job next.

It was his last one for the morning; after that breakfast, and then a four-mile brisk run to the next village to the Fourth of July celebration. His mother had not made the least objection to his staying to the celebration. On the contrary she had said heartily: "I am glad the doctor wants an errand done there; it will give you a good excuse for going. Of course you may stay, and welcome; and I'll put you up a nice Fourth of July lunch; and if there is something to see, or to buy, that doesn't cost more than ten cents, you just have it, or see it, whichever it is. You deserve a treat, Davie."

Davie laughed gleefully. It was pleasant to hear his mother speak such words, but he had a very different plan. Hurried as he had been that morning, he leaned on his spade and thought it all out. In the village where the celebration was to be was a large book store, where he had once or twice been sent on errands for Dr. Bristol, and had feasted his eyes upon the rows and rows of books and magazines, and thought what a thing it would be to have a

chance to handle them. The day before, while holding the horses and waiting for the doctor, his eyes had rested on an advertisement in the paper — WANTED: A BOY. Then had followed a brief statement of the kind of boy, and what his duties would be, and the whole was signed by the proprietor of the book store.

Davie's cheeks had glowed so while reading it, that the doctor, returning just then, had looked hard at him, and asked him if he was getting up a fever. The splendid plan which the boy had thought out leaning on his shovel was, that he would clip around to the book store the moment the doctor's errand was done, and try for that place!

To be sure there was hardly a possibility that he would succeed, but then he might, and certainly he would never accomplish anything if he did not try. But he did not mean to let any body know of his ambitions, so he had only a laugh for his mother's suggestion.

"If I get a chance to see the procession and hear the music and a few such things it will be all the lark I want," he said cheerily, "except the lunch; I'll be sure to want that. You are sure you can get along without me for such a long time?"

"O, yes, indeed!" the mother said, smiling back on him. It was so like her Davie to think of mother.

Davie made good speed over the road, though it was up hill and dusty, and the day was warm. He believed himself to be in ample time to see the parade which was to be made in honor of the day. At the corner he halted and glanced wistfully toward the book store; it was within half a block of him, and who knew but that if he should appear so early in the day he might get ahead of somebody?

"No, it can't be done," he said at last, speaking aloud and firmly. "Davie Carson, I am ashamed of you! A package of medicine in your pocket that the doctor said an old lady was anxiously waiting for, and you thinking about stopping on an errand of your own. Just march down to Coleman Street as fast as your feet can carry you!"

And the order was meekly obeyed. Here he was detained for minutes which seemed like hours to him. The sound of martial music was heard in the near distance, and people all along the streets were dodging to the doors to see if anything was to be seen; but the old lady's daughter wanted to write a note to the doctor to send back by Davie. She would not be a minute, she said; but she was.

"I might call for the note on my way home," Davie timidly suggested. But she said, "O, no! that was not worth while; she could just as well write it now, and make sure of it; she would have it ready very soon." And the sound of music drew nearer and nearer, until it passed the corner and faded in the distance; and the note was ready at last.

Davie crowded it into his pocket, tried to listen respectfully to several messages besides, and went down the stairs three steps at a time to follow that fading music. The street was nearly deserted; all the boys had rushed out of sight with the procession. Davie took long strides in the same direction, and wondered if it would be improper to break into a run.

Appearing at that moment around the corner ahead of him was a belated group — a father, mother and two children; odd-looking people, queerly dressed, and seeming to be entirely out of place in a town.

"Halloo! what's the matter now?" Another corner had been reached and turned by the people ahead of him, with the exception of the youngest of the group, who had tumbled down; it was her outcry which roused him. He picked her up, brushing the dust and soil from her clothes, straightening the much bent sunbonnet, and urging her not to cry, that they would find the others in a jiffy. She stopped crying the moment she discovered herself in kind hands, and looked confidingly at Davie out of great blue eyes, and slipped her small brown hand into his with great satisfaction. Then they two turned the corner, and were at once in a crowd. The thing which astonished and troubled him was, that the father and mother and older sister of his little girl seemed to have disappeared. For a weary half-hour the two jostled against the crowd and stared and hunted. At last there darted toward him an angry father, talking broken English in loud tones, followed by an

angrier mother and a crying little girl. "What was he doing with Gretchen? How dare he steal their Gretchen and make off with her! Bad, wicked boy! The police should know all about it, that they should!" In vain Davie tried to explain; they were too excited and frightened to listen to explanations. In the midst of Davie's attempts two well-dressed boys standing near, broke into laughter, and so confused him that he stopped short, and the enraged family trudged away, his little girl in his arms, and the father shaking his head at Davie. But the little girl looked back and smiled lovingly on him.

Then Davie found that the crowd were trying to get near the band stand.

"Come this way," said one of the boys who had laughed, touching his shoulder; "there is a chance to slip in behind here and get a first-rate position." Davie thanked them, and was just going to slip in, when a little girl who was flying past, going in the opposite direction from the pushing crowd, jostled against him, and as she did so dropped from under her arm a small package. Davie picked it up and looked eagerly after the girl, shouting, "Hold on, you've lost something!" But she flew like the wind.

"You can't catch her," said a man; "she is lost in the jam by this time. You may as well pocket the bundle and call it Fourth of July luck."

"And you will lose your chance in here if you don't come this minute," said one of the boys, trying to keep a way open for him.

"Thank you," said Davie, "but I think I ought to find the little girl." saying which he struck into the crowd, and began his search.

It was several hours afterwards that a boy who was very tired, and who, if he had not been so disappointed, would have been hungry, came out of the handsome book store and with slow steps started for his long walk home. He had delivered the medicine for which he came in the first place; he had the note for the doctor safe in his pocket; he had picked up a little German girl, and after much trouble given her back to a father who was angry at him about it; he had followed a little girl, or rather followed the road over which she vanished, for two weary hours, and at last found her and restored the lost parcel, only to hear her laugh gleefully and declare that there was nothing in it but some dried-up sandwiches, which he was welcome to if he wanted them. And not a glimpse of procession, or sound of martial music or voice of public speaker had he seen or heard that day, save the few strains in the distance which had lured him in the morning.

Moreover, he had called at the book store only to have the proprietor shake his head and say: "Of course, my boy, I couldn't engage you for such a place as this without references. For whom do you work when you are at home?"

Davie explained that they had been but a short time in that part of the country; he had no regular place, but did odd jobs for Dr. Bristol — cleaned out the stable and such things. No, Dr. Bristol did not know much about him — nobody did but mother — and he had not known that a recommendation would be needed.

"I might just as well have staid at home and helped mother," said Davie, as he walked slowly, with head down. "I've lost a day, and gained nothing at all. I wish I had — no, I don't either. I did what I thought was right. I'm glad I did it." Whereupon Davie whistled.

"Who was that boy, father, and what did he want?" A young man asked the question of the bookseller as he came back to his parlor; he liked the looks of the boy.

"Do you know anything about him?" replied the father, and before he could answer a bright-faced little girl chimed in: "O, Unc'e Edward! what is his name? Don't you know? I'm so sorry if you don't; papa wants to know it."

"No, sir," said the young man; "I don't know him; but he is the chap I was telling you about who wandered around with that little German girl, and took patiently a hard scolding from the father afterwards, and a laugh from two well-dressed, thoughtless boys."

"Is he, indeed?" said the father; "I wish I had known it."

Then the little girl: "And O, Uncle Edward! don't you think he is the very same boy who hunted after me for two hours to give me those sandwiches. Papa said I was a little dunce not to ask his name; that he ought to be rewarded for honesty and faithfulness."

"I know his name," said Uncle Edward, "and I believe I will reward him."

The next morning, when Davie was out in the little garden hoeing and whistling, a strange thing happened to him; he received a letter — the first letter with his name on the envelope which he had ever received. It was short and to the point:

After you left me yesterday two witnesses to your honesty and faithfulness, as well as to your good temper under provocation, called upon me, and made me decide to give you a month's trial in the store if you still wish the situation. Call on me to-day if possible; if not, to-morrow will do.

Yours sincerely,   EDWARD HAMMOND.

"Mother," said Davie, as they went all over the plans for the third time, "who could have called on him who knows anything about me? I can't imagine."   PANSY.

A SUMMER DAY IN THE COUNTRY.

A STITCH AT A TIME.

ABOUT ST. AUGUSTINE.

BY THE PANSIES.

THE way it came to be called St. Augustine was this: it used to be named Seloy on the river Dolphins. That was when it belonged to the Indians. The French people named the river, and they gave it that name because they saw a great many dolphins playing in the mouth of the river. After awhile the Spaniards came and took the town on the day which was sacred to their saint, Augustine, so they named both town and river San Augustin.

RUFUS HUNTER.

In the American Revolution Florida was the only colony which was loyal to the king. When they heard the news of the Declaration of Independence they burned John Hancock and Samuel Adams in effigy, calling them rebels. After that some of the "Liberty Boys," as our soldiers were called, stole powder from the British brig *Betsey*, which lay at anchor at San Augustin and slipped away with it, to be used at Bunker Hill.

HARVEY DENNISON.

I READ about the services which they used to hold in St. Augustine on Palm Sunday. They marched from the church to the platform of the convent, where was a beautiful altar trimmed with flowers and fruits. The congregation knelt on the ground while the priest said mass, then the nuns took baskets of rose petals which were brought by many little children in the procession, and strewed them before the altar in honor of the Virgin.

LAURA EASTMAN.

I LIKE to read about St. Augustine when it was a walled town with earthworks and batteries; when you had to enter the town through the great gate or by the drawbridge. At sunset a gun was fired, which meant that the bridge was raised, the gate barred, and both were guarded by soldiers. I can imagine them pacing back and forth challenging people who passed. "*Centinela alerta*," they said, and "*Alerta esta*," answered the outsider if he knew enough. I think it must have been great fun. I should like to understand the Spanish language, the words have such a musical sound. But the outsider might say "*Alerta esta*" as much as he liked, after the gates were closed he could not get into the town until next morning, no matter if his home was just the other side of the gate. Once in a long time came a messenger with news for the governor so important that for him they would open the gate; but this was very unusual.

JOHN L. PARKER.

THEY had one fashion in St. Augustine in the early days when the town was ruled by Spaniards which might work pretty well nowadays in some places. When a fellow became a great nuisance, would not work, and disturbed people by making noises in the streets, and things of that kind, they used to make him dress himself in some ridiculous fashion, put him at the head of a procession made up of anybody who wanted to join it and help make fun of him; then the drum and fife started up and he was marched out of the town, and he could not come back again.

HELEN DUNNING.

I WENT with my father and mother to St. Augustine only last winter. We went through the Ponce de Leon, which I think must be the finest hotel in the world. It is built of some kind of stuff that glitters in the sun, and looks in the shade as if it were blue, and the trimmings are of terra cotta. The floors of the halls are inlaid with little bits of marble, and the marble columns everywhere make you think for a minute that you are stepping into an art gallery instead of a hotel. The rotunda is just lovely! It has eight oak pillars to support it, each beautifully carved. The rotunda is four stories high, and has corridors on each story with more columns and lovely arches. The dome has wonderful paintings and carved figures, giving in pictures the history of Spain and France. You can look straight up through an opening to the great copper columns which form the lantern at the top. The large parlor is perfectly splendid. It is a hundred and four feet long, and fifty-three feet wide; but there are arches and portières, so that it can be divided into five rooms whenever the people wish. It is magnificently furnished. I think, however, that the great dining-room is really more beautiful than the parlor. More than eight hundred people can take dinner there at one time, and you can look out of the windows at lovely orange groves, and hear the mocking-birds singing, and there is a band of music which always plays while the dinner is being served.

ANNA WHEELER AUSTIN.

A BAND of singers used to go about the streets of old St. Augustine on Easter eve, playing on their violins and guitars, and stopping under the windows to sing:

> " *Disciarem lu dol,*
> *Cantarem anb alagria,*
> *Y n'arem a da*
> *Las pascuas a Maria.*"

It seems almost impossible to sing such queer-sounding words, but translated they mean:

> "Ended the days of sadness,
> Grief gives place to singing;
> We come with joy and gladness,
> Our gifts to Mary bringing."

MARY GEDDIS.

IN the year 1821 Spain gave Florida to the United States, the old yellow flag of Spain was taken down forever, and in its place our own beautiful stars and stripes floated over the old town. I wonder if the people living there knew enough to shout for joy?

HENRY STUART.

IT is all very well for my brother to talk about the people shouting for joy when the stars and stripes floated over their town; but I guess he forgets what an awful time they had only about fifteen years later, when the Seminole War broke out. That was because the new people who had come in wanted the lands which had always belonged to the Indians, and

wanted them driven further West. For the next seven years I think the people had reason to be sorry that they had ever seen the stars and stripes. Not but that I love the old flag as well as my brother does, but I think the Indians were ill-treated. It makes me very sad to read how they were at last cheated into a surrender, and carried away by force from the land they loved so well.

CHARLES MORTON STUART.

MY sister Anna thought the hotel was the nicest part of St. Augustine, but I liked the old fort the best. It used to be Fort San Marco, but when the United States got hold of it they named it Fort Marion, after General Francis Marion. I would like to describe it, but I don't understand just how. It is in shape what is called a polygon, and has a moat all around it. The stone or shell of which it is built is used a great deal in St. Augustine, or used to be; it is called coquina. I think the narrow streets and queer-looking old houses are much more interesting than the new streets, which are just like any other city. At least I liked them better; but girls always like elegant hotels and splendid furniture and all such things.

GEORGE WHEELER AUSTIN.

MY mother used to live in St. Augustine years ago. She has told me a good deal about the streets, and the sea wall, and the little old houses. She has described St. George Street and Tolomato Street until it seems to me I could find my way up and down them almost as well as she could. But mother says things are very much changed since she was there; she reads in the papers about the beautiful new hotels, and says it does not seem possible they are in old St. Augustine. The old streets were very narrow; I suppose they are still. Next winter I am going there to see things for myself.

SARAH CASTLETON.

[The Pansies have seemed chiefly interested this month in the history of old St. Augustine, rather than in a description of the city. But I think our readers will agree with me that they have managed to crowd a good deal of information into a small space. Sorry we have not room for all they said.— EDITORS.]

REUBEN AS AN ERRAND BOY.

(Character Studies.)

REUBEN MINOR was in his own room in his shirt sleeves, and the sleeves rolled to his elbows. His paste pot was on the table, sheets of paper and scraps of pasteboard were on the floor, and Reuben, with a queer-shaped box before him, was in what Maria called "a brown study."

"IN A BROWN STUDY."

The stair door opened, and his Aunt Mary's voice called, "Reuben!"

"Yes'm."

"Don't you forget those errands that you've got to do in town. Have you got 'em all in your mind?"

"Yes'm."

"There's only the eggs and the kerosene and the vinegar, you know, so you won't need to have 'em written down — just three things."

"All right."

Silence for a few minutes, during which Reuben turned the box endwise and squinted at it. "Let's see," he said, leaning his elbow on the table and his head on his hand, "I wonder how that would do?" Then he started for his row of shelves, seized upon a good-sized book in the corner, and dived into its pages. Something was not clear. The stair door opened again, and his aunt's voice sounded : "Reuben!"

"Yes'm."

"You must take that next car, you know, because there isn't another for an hour, and I'm in a hurry for the eggs; if I don't have them by noon there'll be no pumpkin pie for Sunday. Are you all ready for the car?"

"I will be in a minute, Aunt Mary."

"Well, you better get ready right straight off, then there won't be any mistake; it will be along now in a little while."

There was no reply to this, and the door closed again, Reuben, meantime, deep in his book. Ten minutes, fifteen minutes, then a sudden, sharp call from below : "Reuben, there's the car coming. Hurry, now! don't you miss it for anything."

Reuben hurried. He made a frantic dash for his coat, ran his fingers through his hair by way of combing, concluded to go without a necktie, and tore down the stairs and out of the kitchen door and across the lawn, to the tune of his aunt's words : "I believe in my heart you'll lose that car, after all!"

No, he didn't. He hailed it, panting and breathless, some minutes after it had passed the corner, and at last was seated in it, mopping his wet forehead, for the morning was warm. But he had not forgotten the big book. Four miles in a street car, with not many passengers at that hour, gave him a good chance to study up that puzzling portion which he could not get through his mind. So he studied and puzzled, and the car rumbled on, and stopped, and went on again many times, and people came in and went out, and Reuben knew nothing about them. At last he looked up; he believed he could make that box now, partitions and all, if he were only at home. Halloo! they were in town already, and were passing Porter's. Why! then they must have passed the corner grocery where Aunt Mary always traded. What a nuisance! Now perhaps he could not get this car on its return trip. He must try for it. So he pulled the check, and made what speed he could back, three, four, five blocks, to the corner grocery. As he left the car he wondered how they managed the flap that made the fastening of the inner box, and still puzzling over it, presented himself at the counter of the city grocery.

"Well, sir," said the clerk, after waiting a minute for orders, "what can I do for you?"

What indeed? Reuben stared at him, grew red in the face, stammered, mopped his face with his handkerchief, gazed up and down the rows and rows of crowded shelves, gazed about him everywhere. What had he come for? That was the awful question. What had Aunt Mary said? She had said several things, he remembered. He tried to recall the all-important one. Butter? No, of course not; they made their own butter. Flour, perhaps, or starch — women were always wanting flour and starch — or it might have been tea. He was sure he did not know, and the longer he thought the more confused he seemed to get. And there was the return car! Unless he took that he would have to wait a solid hour, and for what? Was there any likelihood that he would remember? Reuben asked himself that question in a most searching manner, then sorrowfully shook his head as he owned to himself that he did not believe he ever knew; he had not paid any attention to that part of the business.

Aunt Mary was watching for the return car. "Reuben has come," she called out to Maria in the kitchen, as she caught a glimpse of him. "I must say I am relieved; I don't know how we could have managed without those eggs. If

I ever get hold of any hens that lay again, I'll venture to say I won't sell all my eggs to my neighbors and have to depend on store ones for myself. Why, what in the world has the boy done with them? He seems to be empty-handed! Hurry up, Reuben, we are waiting for the eggs. Where are your things?"

Poor red-faced, shamefaced Reuben! It was hard work, but there was nothing for it but to own that the first he had heard of eggs was at that moment; and as for the "things," he had no more idea than the man in the moon what they were. ·

"I believe that boy is half-witted," the clerk at the corner grocery had said, after watching him for a few minutes, and seeing him make a dash for the return car, not having bought a thing. But bless your heart, he wasn't. He had wits enough. "Too many of 'em," his Aunt Mary said. The trouble with Reuben was that he had never learned to withdraw his thoughts from the thing which wanted to absorb them, and fix them for the time being, instead, on the thing which ought to claim his attention.

MYRA SPAFFORD.

THE ADOPTED FAMILY.

IT was a beautiful summer day when the Westwoods arrived at their country home, most of them very glad indeed to see the dear old place. They had staid in town very late this season, Mr. Westwood's business being such that there was a time when he feared he could not get away at all. Now here they were turning the corner which brought the house into view; the great wagon following close behind, piled high with baggage, and every one was glad, save Herbert. He was eleven years old, and fond of his city home, and of the school which he attended, and of the boys in his class, and felt very lonely and desolate. He "did not know a single boy out here," he confided to his mother, "that he ever cared to see again." "And when a fellow hasn't any friends," he said dolefully, "it is very lonesome."

"Poor boy!" said Mrs. Westwood, when he was out of hearing, "I am sorry for him; I wish he liked the country as I used to; the long bright summer days were just crowded with happiness for me; but then I had sister Fanny to play with, and brother Will. Perhaps it would have been different if I had been all alone."

"Children must learn to make friends of the birds, and the squirrels, and all sorts of living things," answered his father. "When I was Herbert's age, I used to know the note of every bird in the woods, and I don't believe he can tell even a robin when he sees it."

"No," said his mother; "he has but little chance for that sort of education; and moreover he has no taste for anything of the kind; I wish he had."

The carriage which had been winding up the drive, stopped in front of the old-fashioned, wide piazzaed country-home. It did seem a pity that anybody should feel doleful coming to such a pleasant place as that; but Herbert felt doleful; as he stood with his hand in his pockets, and stared down the country road, he winked hard to keep back the tears, when he thought of the boys in town having their military drill at this hour. Meanwhile his father and mother, and Peter and Hannah, bustled about, opening doors and windows, and planning where the luggage should be set down. Presently Herbert heard an exclamation from his mother. "For pity's sake!" she said — and in the next breath —

"Herbert, come here and see what I have found!"

So Herbert swallowed hard, and brushed away a tear or two, and went round to the side piazza from where his mother's voice had sounded, and saw a sight which made him go on tiptoe and gaze in delight.

Pushed back, well under shelter from the summer storms, in the southeast corner of the piazza, was an old, somewhat dilapidated willow chair, large and very comfortable in its time, but which had long since been assigned to the piazza, and not considered worth bringing in out of the dews or the rain. In the fall when the family closed the house, the old chair

had been forgotten. It had stood there all winter, deserted and lonely. But in the spring it had evidently been mistaken by a certain family as a house which was for rent, and they had rented it and moved in and set up housekeeping on a splendid scale; the consequences were, that fastened ingeniously to the back of the chair was a luxurious nest, most carefully woven, and within it at this moment were three of the prettiest speckled eggs that Herbert had ever seen. In fact his knowledge of birds' eggs was limited; he had seen but very few.

"O, mother!" he said softly, "how pretty it is. There is one of the birds on the branches near by — a splendid fellow. Where is his mate, do you suppose?"

"Not far away, you may depend," said his mother. "What a cunning place it is in which to build a house. How fortunate that the chair is so near that door instead of the other one. We can get along for awhile without opening that door at all, and they can raise their family without having trouble. If I were you, Herbert, I would adopt them and look after their interests and help to bring up their young ones; wouldn't that be fun?"

"Well," said Herbert, with more glee than he had shown since he had left his city home, "I believe I will. I will call that fellow up there on the bush Denny, and he and I will be companions this summer."

"That will be splendid," said Mrs. Westwood, very much pleased, for Denny was the short for "Denison," her boy's best friend in town. It was certainly a delicate compliment to name the bird after him, and showed to the mother the degree of friendship which Herbert meant to cultivate.

"We shall get along comfortably now," she said to her husband laughingly; "he has adopted the birds in the old chair, and named the singer 'Denny,' so he will not lack for companionship."

Ah! I wish I could tell you about the lovely summer. Never was a brighter, more congenial companion than Denny. He sang his sweetest songs for the lonesome boy, and accepted his overtures of friendship in the most genial manner possible. Before the season was over not only he but his wife would allow Herbert to come close enough to the old chair to drop special dainties into the nest for the children, and were voluble in their thanks. More than that, Denny actually learned to come and perch himself on Herbert's finger and eat sugar out of his hand. And one of the children grew so fond of Herbert that she took many a walk perched on his shoulder, chirping occasionally to let him know that she was there, and was happy.

"I never knew that birds could be so pleasant," Herbert said to his mother; "they are better than boys and girls in some respects; they never get vexed at a fellow, you know, and refuse to speak to him for days together. Even Denny got mad at me once, and wouldn't speak for a whole day. Now this Denny never forgets to say 'How do you do?' even if I haven't been out of his sight longer than five minutes."

On the whole the birds did a good thing for Herbert Westwood that summer; they turned what they thought would be a weariness into a season of great delight, and of daily increasing interest. More than that, he did a good thing for the birds. Before the season was over he had made the acquaintance of dozens of boys in the neighborhood and formed a society, the pledge of which was protection to the birds. No stones were to be thrown, no snares to be set by these boys or any whom they recognized as friends; neither were any nests to be molested, and not a few of the boys became so interested in Denny and his family that they determined for another season to adopt a family of their own, and study birds.

"They are wonderful creatures," said Herbert thoughtfully, as he was reporting to his mother some of the bird stories which had been told in the society that afternoon, "just wonderful creatures! I don't know how I ever came to pass them by without thinking anything about them. I tell you what, mother, God must have thought about them a great deal."

EFIL SREDSNOW.

GOD'S promises are fulfilled a hundred cents on a dollar.

A PRETTY GIFT.

(Something for Mamma.)

 THE materials needed for this gift are a smooth thin board about two feet long and six inches wide, some bright-colored plush, some pretty cretonne, a dozen or more brass hooks of varying sizes, none of them very large, a couple of "cock eyes" such as are used for hanging small picture frames, and a yard or two of ribbon, color to match the plush, or contrast nicely with it.

The smooth board is to be covered on one side with the plush, on the other with the cretonne, the edges neatly sewed; then the hooks are to be screwed in at regular intervals on the plush side, the ribbon drawn through the rings or "cock eyes," and tied in a bow ready for hanging, and your work is done.

When it comes into mamma's possession she will select a convenient spot on her wall, and hang it as though it were a picture. Then on the little hooks she will hang her glove buttoner, her small scissors which are forever slipping out of sight, her shoe buttoner, her watch, perhaps, when it is not in use, and it may be her favorite ring which she removes when she washes her hands. I am sure I could not enumerate the little bits of useful articles which she will be only too glad to hang on such convenient hooks, that she will find not a disfigurement but an ornament to her room.

Now having told you just what and how, let me go carefully over the story again and remind you of its possibilities. For I can well imagine a little girl who wants to make her mother a neat and convenient present, but who has no plush nor ribbon, and does not even know how to get the right kind of a board.

My dear, you are just the one I want to help. About the board; it need not be exactly two feet long and six inches wide; it may be of the length and width which you find convenient, and which you decide will look well in the space where it is to hang. There are light boards used by wholesale merchants in packing certain goods which are just the thing, and they can often be had for the asking at the store where your mother does most of her shopping. Neither is plush a necessity. I have a friend who made a pretty "Wall Toilet" such as I have described, out of a bit of soft silk a friend had given her to dress her dollie. The silk was old, but she smoothed it neatly, padded it with a sheet of white cotton padding, and it looked very nice; but you may not happen to have the silk? Never mind, don't you remember those pieces of turkey red calico in your auntie's piece bag? They are just the thing, and your little friend who wants to make one, and has no turkey red calico, has some bright blue cambric which will be very pretty. All

thin material will look better if the board is first padded with the cotton I spoke of. The brass hooks are quite cheap, and so useful that I think we must have them; but a red cord, or a neat band of cretonne, or some tidy cotton twisted into a cord, finished with tassels made out of it, will take the place of the ribbon very nicely indeed. In short, the old motto, "Where there is a will there is a way," will serve you well in making this gift, as indeed it will in almost any emergency in life.

I know by experience how useful the little contrivances are, and I earnestly hope that many a mother will have her birthday enriched this season by one of them, made by her own little daughter's thoughtful hand.   PANSY.

AS WE USED TO DRESS.

A DEER CHLIS

OR MISS MOON'S FACES.

TRUTH to tell she does make up faces, very different and queer ones, and no one Pansy sees exactly the same one at the same time, and since there are ten thousand Pansies, more or less, you see Miss Nancy Moon is smarter in "making faces" than some of you.

Another "truth to tell" is that the "moon's phases" means appearances, or looks, and so why is it not quite the same as Nancy Moon's faces? We'll think it is.

Every Pansy knows some astronomy or — ought to. Come, then, and from this time on till you are a hundred years old know that astronomy means star-law, or all about the bright worlds in the sky. Now you know some astronomy. The moon is one of these worlds, and is very near our world — only two hundred and forty thousand miles away — and is one of the lamps to light it up. You must begin to learn about it. That you may call moonology. One of the first things to learn in moonology is how she makes so many faces; once a month a long, narrow bent face, then a little fatter, and so on till it is full as a — beer keg. Of course you mustn't think she really drinks that stuff. I guess there is no license in Moontown.

If you will study the picture with all your might and main a half-hour to-day, another to-morrow, and so on, and then get grandpapa to put on his specs and help — you'll surely answer the riddle, how the faces (or phases) are made.

Then some day you may become a great astronomer — like Tycho Brahe or John Kepler.

L.

WHEN you've got a thing to say,
Say it! Don't take half a day.
When your tale's got little in it,
Crowd the whole thing in a minute!
Life is short — a fleeting vapor —
Don't fill up a ream of paper
With a tale, which, at a pinch,
Could be cornered in an inch!

THE MOON'S PHASES.

Boil it down until it simmers;
Polish it until it glimmers.
When you've got a thing to say,
Say it! Don't take half a day.
— *Selected.*

AT THE PARIS OBSERVATORY.

BABY'S CORNER.

JOHNNY'S PILLOW.

ONE day Johnny was taking a walk in the orchard with Nurse.

He was hunting for berries, and what do you think he found?

He found some big white eggs hidden in the tall grass!

Johnny wanted to put the pretty eggs in his basket and take them home to mamma.

But Nurse said:

"No, no, come away, dear. That is a nest. Hush! there comes the old goose. She will sit on the eggs and keep them warm, and by and by she will have some pretty goslings."

After that Johnny went with Nurse every day to take a peep at the gray goose sitting on her eggs.

She sat and sat a good many days, and then one morning when Johnny went to look, sure enough, the goslings had come!

They had no feathers on, and they had long, ugly necks and big feet.

"I don't like 'em," said Johnny.

The little goslings grew fast. They had a nice farmyard to live in, and a little brook to paddle in.

At night the farmer shut them up in the barn, so that the cats and dogs could not eat them up.

In a few days they were all covered with pretty feathers.

Then Johnny liked them.

By and by the little goslings were old enough to go with their father and mother and aunts and uncles to swim in a big lake. That made them very, very happy.

Then they grew to be big geese, and wore a lot of feathers, and Johnny had a pillow, which he enjoyed very much, made from the soft down that grew on their white breasts.

MRS. C. M. LIVINGSTON.

WHO WAS TO BLAME?

"OW you see, Emeline Frances," said Celia, pushing herself up among the pillows and speaking in slow, stern tones to the dollie lying on her arm, "it is really your fault, and no other person's; if you hadn't been bound and determined to go out this afternoon, why, we shouldn't have gone, that's all. It had been raining, of course it had, and the walks were all damp, and you had no rubbers to wear over these shoes. Besides all that, you had been told that you must not go out this afternoon; but you were so vain of your new dress and hat, and so anxious to show them to Lulu Parks, that you would insist on going, and making me get my feet wet. Now here we are! A whole hour yet before it will be dark, and just a lovely time to play, and company downstairs in the parlor, and just the kind of cake for tea that I like the best, and we have to come upstairs and go to bed! I hope you are satisfied, Emeline Frances, with your afternoon's work. I shouldn't have thought of going out if you hadn't have been so crazy to show your new hat. It is just a pity that you think so much of fine clothes. The dampness took the curl all out of your new feather, and it will never be so pretty again; but you had your own way, and will have to take the consequences. The worst of it is that you make me suffer with you. If this were the first time you had disobeyed perhaps I shouldn't feel so badly, but as it is, I am almost discouraged. I do not see how you can be so naughty and forgetful."

The lecture closed with one of Celia's longest sighs. The door which led from her room to her brother Stuart's was ajar, and he, sitting at his desk supposed to be studying his Latin for the next day, listened with the most unqualified amusement to the whole of it. He repeated the story downstairs at the tea-table, amid bursts of laughter from the entire family, his mother excepted.

"Mamma looks as grave as a judge over it,"

Stuart said at last, when the laugh had subsided. "What's the matter, mamma? Don't you think the poor baby's version of her troubles is funny?"

"It has its funny side," said Mrs. Campbell, with a grave smile upon her face, "but really, it has its sad side too. You are a very good mimic, my son, and gave Celia's voice and manner to perfection, in doing which you have reminded me of her besetting sin. Have you never noticed that the child, in her own estimation, is always led into trouble through the fault of others? If she cannot blame Nora, or Josie, or some of her playmates, why then poor Emeline Frances has to bear it. I am really very much troubled by this habit of hers.

CELIA TALKS TO EMELINE FRANCES.

To judge from Celia's statement of the case, she is forever led astray by the evil propensities of other people. If it were true, it would be sad enough, to have a child so easily led in the wrong way; but sometimes there is as much foundation for her theory as there is in this case, when the vanity of poor Emeline Frances is supposed to have caused all the trouble. I have tried to reason the child out of such excuses, but when she reaches the folly of actually blaming the doll for leading her astray, I hardly know what to think of her."

"It is a curious development," said Celia's father, "but I have known older and wiser people than she to indulge in it; I knew a young man once, who charged a moonlight night of unusual beauty with all the folly of which he was guilty that evening."

After this sentence Stuart Campbell finished his supper in silence, with his eyes on his plate; but perhaps no one but his father knew that his cheeks were redder than usual.

PANSY.

A VERITABLE POEM OF POEMS.

A LADY of San Francisco is said to have occupied a year in hunting up and fitting together the following thirty-eight lines from thirty-eight English-speaking poets. The names of the authors are given below:

1. Why all this toil for triumphs of an hour?
2. Life's a short summer, man a flower;
3. By turns we catch the vital breath, and die;
4. The cradle and the tomb, alas! so nigh.
5. To be is better far than not to be,
6. 'Though all man's life may seem a tragedy;
7. But light cares speak when mighty cares are dumb,
8. The bottom is but shallow whence they come.
9. Your fate is but the common fate of all;
10. Unmingled joys here to no man befall.
11. Nature to each allots her proper sphere,
12. Fortune makes folly her peculiar care;
13. Custom does often reason overrule,
14. And throw a cruel sunshine on a fool.
15. Live well, how long, how short, permit to heaven,
16. They who forgive most shall be most forgiven.
17. Sin may be clasped so close we cannot see its face —
18. Vile intercourse where virtue has not place;
19. Then keep each passion down, however dear;
20. Thou pendulum betwixt a smile and tear;
21. Her sensual snares, let faithless Pleasure lay
22. With craft and skill to ruin and betray;
23. Soar not too high to fall, but stoop to rise.
24. We masters grow of all that we despise.
25. Oh! then, renounce that impious self-esteem;
26. Riches have wings, and grandeur is a dream.
27. Think not ambition wise because 'tis brave,
28. The path of glory leads but to the grave.
29. What is ambition? 'Tis a glorious cheat,
30. Only destructive to the brave and great.
31. What's all the gaudy glitter of a crown?
32. The way to bliss lies not on beds of down.
33. How long we live, not years, but actions tell;
34. That man lives twice who lives the first life well.
35. Make, then, while yet ye may, your God your friend,
36. Whom Christians worship, yet not comprehend.
37. The trust that's given guard, and to yourself be just;
38. For, live we how we can, yet die we must.

1, Young; 2, Dr. Johnson; 3, Pope; 4, Prior; 5, Sewell; 6, Spenser; 7, Daniel; 8, Sir Walter Raleigh; 9, Longfellow; 10, Southwell; 11, Congreve; 12, Churchill; 13, Rochester; 14, Armstrong; 15, Milton; 16, Baily, 17, Trench; 18, Somerville; 19, Thompson; 20, Byron; 21, Smollett; 22, Crabbe; 23, Massinger; 24, Crowley; 25, Beattie; 26, Cowper; 27, Sir Walter Davenant; 28, Gray; 29, Willis; 30, Addison; 31, Dryden; 32, Francis Quarles; 33, Watkins; 34, Herrick; 35, William Mason; 36, Hill; 37, Dana; 38, Shakespeare.

LITTLE LENA.

DID the Pansies read in the papers about Lena Haupt?

She was only five years old when her mother died, and three months afterwards her father, who had kept her with him by the kind help of a neighbor, fell from a building where he had been working, and was so badly injured that in a short time he died. He had his little girl with him a few hours before his death, and explained to her as well as he could that he was going where her mamma had gone, but could not take her with him yet. She must be a good little girl; she had an uncle and aunt and little cousins in Chicago, and they would take care of her and love her if she was good.

Only a few days after that Lena started alone on her long journey. Her uncle had telegraphed to "send her on," and he would meet her at the Chicago depot. There was a card tied around her neck by a ribbon, and on the card was written: "Please take care of me." There was a letter, also, fastened to the same ribbon, which told Lena's sad little story, and asked the passengers to be kind to her, but to please not give her any candy. She had a wee purse fastened to the buckle of her belt which had nearly two dollars in it.

As for her ticket, it had been bought and paid for, and the conductor had it in charge. Before night of that long day almost every passenger on the crowded train had called on Lena, and her wee purse was filled to its utmost capacity with shining quarters and half-dollars. She herself made a great many journeys in the porter's arms to the parlor car, to visit with some ladies. And at last, as night was coming

IN THE MIDST OF HARVEST.

on, and Lena's eyes were beginning to droop, and the conductor was considering how he could make her comfortable for the night, came a lady and gentleman and begged to have her transferred to their sleeper, where they bought a berth for her and put her to bed.

And all along the line little Lena found loving friends. I think her father and mother in Heaven must have been glad to see how warm were the hearts of even strangers toward their darling.

POSITIVE PEOPLE.

I WANT to call the attention of all Pansies to a statement made by Benjamin Franklin in his story of his life. He says he tried to form the habit of expressing himself always with great modesty. He was careful not to use the word "certainly" or "undoubtedly," or any of those words which give an air of positiveness, when the subject was one which might be disputed. He tried always to say, "It appears to me," or "If I am not mistaken," or "I should think that," etc. He declared this habit to be of great use to him in persuading others to think as he did, and that moreover it gave him a chance to learn a great deal more than he would otherwise have had; for he said he had noticed that people did not care to give information to those who acted as though they already knew all that it was possible to learn.

In many respects Benjamin Franklin was a wise man, and perhaps in no small way could he have shown his knowledge of human nature better than by adopting such rules. But I really do not think he has many followers. Just watch the conversation of even quite young people for awhile, with this thought in mind, and see how many of them seem to be absolutely sure of their position, even in regard to subjects where wise men differ. If we could have more doubt about things which have not yet been decided, and more certainty about things which God and the Bible have decided for us, we should have a much better, as well as a much pleasanter world.   HANNAH HEARALL.

OFF FOR BOYLAND.

HO! All aboard? A traveler
    Sets sail from Babyland!
Before my eyes there comes a blur;
    But still I kiss my hand,
And try to smile as off he goes,
    My bonny, winsome boy!
Yes, *bon voyage!* God only knows
    How much I wish thee joy!

Oh! tell me; have you heard of him?
    He wore a sailor's hat
All silver-corded round the brim,
    And — stranger e'en than that —
A wondrous suit of navy blue,
    With pockets deep and wide;
Oh! tell me, sailors, tell me true,
    How fares he on the tide?

We've now no baby in the house;
    'Twas but this very morn,
He doffed his dainty 'broidered blouse,
    With skirts of snowy lawn;
And shook a mass of silken curls
    From off his sunny brow;
They fretted him — "so like a girl's,"
    Mamma can have them now.

He owned a brand-new pocket-book,
    But that he could not find;
A knife and string were all he took.
    What did he leave behind?
A heap of blocks, with letters gay,
    And here and there a toy;
I cannot pick them up to-day,
    My heart is with my boy.

Ho! Ship ahoy! At boyhood's town
    Cast anchor strong and deep.
What! tears upon this little gown,
    Left for mamma to keep?
Weep not, but smile; for through the air
    A merry message rings —
"Just sell it to the rag man there;
    I've done with baby things!"
                    EMMA HUNTINGTON NASON.

ON THE LOOKOUT.

THE OLD WORLD TOO.

AMERICA is still the "New World." Each day pick up something new about it. It is your world now. But there is an "Old World." You must know about that too. If you could go and see it, so much the better. The eye is a little contrivance, but large enough to take in all England, Ireland, Scotland and any other land it gets a chance to see.

If you go abroad you must sail. There is no railroad or cable to carry you yet. A hundred years hence people may cross the Atlantic in balloons. But you can't wait so long. Why should you? Here is the good ship Majestic — not exactly the one shown in the picture on the first page — which will take you over from New York to Liverpool in less than six days.

Once it took weeks. Sometimes a big iceberg came sailing along right across the ship's path. Then there was a crash. Perhaps the poor little ship went to splinters and the passengers — well, you know what happened then. Sometimes a dreadful storm came down upon the ocean and the waves went up and down, looking like mountains and valleys. Not every frail ship could stand it. There was a wreck. But in spite of all these dreadful things most passengers get there and see the sights, and have a good time and get safely home. A friend has crossed the Atlantic nearly seventy times safely.   L.

CASHMERE SHAWLS.

IT is said that sixteen thousand looms are kept in constant employment in Cashmere, producing annually about thirty thousand shawls. The shawls are woven on rudely-constructed looms, a pair of shawls sometimes occupying three or four men a whole year in weaving. The Cashmere goat, which furnishes the material, is found in Thibet, the hair of it being fine, silky and about eighteen inches long. It takes the fleece of ten goats to manufacture a shawl a yard and a half square. — *Selected.*

MAJOR'S AUTOBIOGRAPHY.

VI.

WHILE the folks are gone to the fair, and we have nothing to do but watch around the place and see that no tramp gets in, we might as well have a good time, and I will tell you about my brother Nero. You must not forget, though, but keep eyes, ears and nose open while I am talking.

To begin with, there was a very large family of us, or would have been if we had all been kept together. There were brothers and sisters older, and a good many younger than we. We were of the same age, and there were three others just our age, too; but they had gone to live with other families, and Nero and I were all there were left with mother. Poor, dear mother! I remember well how she used to feel when her children were taken away from her, though I was too young at that time to realize it.

When we were alone she would sigh, and many a tear have I seen fall from her eyes, as she would lap us and think of her darlings whose faces she knew not that she would ever see again.

She, poor mother, seemed to lavish all her love upon us after the other three were gone.

Mr. Bryant, our master, had a daughter — only one — whose name was Fanny. Her father and mother seemed to think the world of her; and the thing that puzzled mother was, that Mrs. Bryant, being a mother herself, should not feel more for her four-footed friend, who was a mother also. She fed us enough, and never abused us in the ways in which so many abuse their dogs; but when it came to parting mother and children it never seemed to occur to her that a mother with four feet, and that couldn't talk, could have any motherly feelings, or care what became of her little ones.

I remember little Fanny was not so. She would cry every time one of my brothers or sisters was taken away, and after one was gone would come out with us and put her arms around mother's silky neck and cry as though her heart would break.

Well, one day while we were quite small a man came to the house. I think he was some kind of agent. He saw mother, and could not help admiring her glossy coat and beautiful eyes, and so was anxious to get one of our family. He wanted mother herself, but soon found that money could not buy her. Fanny overheard them talking about us, and then slipped quietly out of the room, and came in great haste to where we were, and with one of us under each arm fled to a place of safety. Down through the orchard she went till she came to an old building which was used to store hay in; there, in a hole which she and some of her playmates had made to hide in, she put us, and covered us up with soft straw, and fixed it so that we could not possibly crawl out, then closed the door and went off under a sweet apple-tree to hunt for apples as though nothing had happened.

Now I suppose men will think she did not act just as she should, and perhaps she was guilty of disobedience for not telling where we were when they were hunting for us; but we were very grateful to her, and whined with delight when we heard the man drive away, and learned that he was not likely to come over that road again.

Fanny felt badly about it, and that night when she was going to bed told her mother what she had done, crying almost as hard as though we had been sold.

Fanny's mother explained to her how it was wicked to be disobedient, and that it was disobedience to not do what she would be required to do, if all the circumstances were known, and that doing wrong that good might come of it was never right.

Then after Fanny was asleep her mother told Mr. Bryant why they had failed to find us, and after he heard the whole story he said: "Bless her dear heart; for her sake we will keep the little fellows, and Bess" (that was mother's name) "will look at us with less sadness in her great eyes."

So Mrs. Bryant told Fanny that they had decided to keep us both until we were much

bigger, at least, and she need not worry any more about our being sold.

When they told mother you should have seen her leap for joy; she sprang up upon her hind feet, and put her fore paws upon Mr. Bryant's breast, forgetting in her great joy that her feet were not clean; but he, good man, only patted her and let her lick his cheek, and called her "Good old Bess," and then told her to go and look after her children and give them their supper.

I heard her say to one of the neighbors some months after, as she was telling her experience with us, that that was the first time she had lain down with any peace of mind for weeks.

Well, the bigger we grew the more Fanny loved us, and so we did her. We never let her go down in the orchard, or out into the woods, or to fish in the brook but what we went with her, and we drove everything and everybody away, unless she told us not to.

After awhile she decided that she wanted one of us in her room nights. To that arrangement her mother at first strongly objected; but her father plead for her, and the mother finally consented.

When the cold weather came on Fanny got a rug, and had Nero sleep on that rug on the foot of her bed, "to keep her feet warm," she said.

This had been going on for some time when Mr. and Mrs. Bryant went out to visit a neighbor's at some kind of a gathering, and left mother and me outside in our kennel to watch, and Nero to remain in the room with our little friend Fanny.

The hired man and the cook, instead of remaining at home as they were expected to, went to spend the evening with a neighbor, thinking it would be all right with Fanny, as she was asleep. But it had been ironing day, and the clothes had been left hanging in the kitchen to air, and how it was no one will ever know, but in some way they took fire. Mother was the first to discover it, and began to bark with all her might to awaken Fanny and Nero. I remember that I barked too, just as hard and loud as I could.

Soon Nero heard it, and began to feel that something must be the matter somewhere. His first thought was that he ought to awaken his young mistress, and he went at the job as best he knew. But she was too sound asleep to be awakened by barking, do the best he could; so he sprang upon her shoulder and began to pull at her nightdress, and finally took her by the ear, and pulled so hard that it almost started the blood. Then she awakened in a great fright, for a bright light was shining so she could see everything in her room.

Pulling on her shoes and stockings, and wrapping around her some of the blankets from her bed, she opened the door, which fortunately was near the stairs.

With the help of Nero she made her way through the smoke to the street, about the time the neighbors began to arrive. They were too late to have been of any help to Fanny, for the flames would have overtaken her before they reached there, but for Nero. By the time Mr. and Mrs. Bryant reached home the house was far gone. When they saw the flames they

seemed almost crazy with fright; for they remembered that they had left their only child asleep in the second story. It was some minutes before they could be made to understand that Fanny was safe.

She and Nero had been hurried to the house of a neighbor, and when they found them Fanny had her arms around Nero's neck.

When Fanny was being tucked into bed for a second time that night she said to her mother: "Are you not glad that I kept Nero from being sold? Because if he had not been there to wake me up you wouldn't have had any little girl now."

From that time Nero was a great pet, and I was very proud of him, though I could not help being a little bit vexed because nobody gave mother and me any credit for awakening him. One day I said something about it to her, and she said: "Never mind, Major; we know ourselves that we did our duty, and that is the important thing."   R.

SOME OF OUR EARLIEST SETTLERS.

A "MIDSUMMER NIGHT'S DREAM."

HOW TO MAKE A SCREEN BAG.

(Something for Mamma.)

IT is my opinion that the little girl who makes this convenient thing which I am about to describe, will need to have an accommodating brother who owns a box of tools and knows how to use them. Or she may have a good friend among the carpenters who are at work on the next corner. Still another way would be to get papa enlisted and agree to divide mamma's birthday present with him; that is, let him share the honor of getting it up.

However that part may be managed here is yours, my dear, industrious little girl.

The name of the article is Screen Bag. I have no doubt you know how fond mamma is of bags, of all shapes and sizes, for keeping her unmended stockings, or perhaps, more truthfully speaking, your and your brothers' and sisters' unmended stockings, for balls of cord, and rolls of tape, and papers of hooks and eyes, and I have not room to tell how many other things. Well, this Screen Bag is just the thing. First get your frames made of common pine wood, three of them, of about the right height to furnish a comfortable screen for mamma if she wishes to keep the wind from blowing on her, or the firelight from burning her face. Indeed, you must decide where she will be likely to want to use the screen, and plan its size accordingly. Then you want some bright cloth of a pretty color; perhaps red, if that harmonizes best with the colors in your mother's room, or possibly blue or a soft rich brown; what you will, so that it is strong. Cretonne is good, so is the striped cotton furniture cloth which may be found at any upholsterer's, and in nearly all large city stores. You want two kinds; one for the front and one for the back of your screen. The back or lining side need not be made of such strong material. English cambric or common calico will do nicely. Of course the amount of material needed will depend upon the size of your frames; some careful measurements with a tape line will be necessary. Now get your "pockets" ready, as many as you have room for, and of whatever size you think the most useful. The first or lower row should be a little larger than the ones above. The screen I have in mind had two good-sized pockets below, three smaller ones above, four above them, and five tiny ones at the top. These may be made of the same cloth as the screen, or of different colors, according to your taste and the variety of material at command. They should be hemmed neatly at the top and stitched firmly to the cloth; first basted, then sewed in the machine, to insure strength; or, if you do not understand a sewing machine, and want to do all the work yourself, you can take strong thread, and make a back stitch for every third or fourth one, and do the whole by hand.

Now you want some brass-headed nails — round heads, you know. Finally, your frames are ready for the brass hinges on which they are to swing. You will need four of these, and when they are screwed into their places your Bag Screen will be finished. Fifty-two pockets! My word for it, if your mamma does not feel richer than she ever did in her life, after she has her conveniences packed away in those delightful pockets, which besides holding them, are at work screening her from the heat, or sun, or wind, I shall be very much astonished.

I shall hope to hear that some of the Pansies have tried this experiment.

PANSY.

ABOUT MINNEAPOLIS.

BY THE PANSIES.

GOOD many years ago there used to be a city named St. Anthony. It was built on the east side of the Mississippi River; then a city grew up on the west side named Minneapolis, and after awhile it swallowed St. Anthony and made one big city of itself on both sides of the river. I think St. Anthony would have been a prettier name for the city, on ac-

count of the Falls of St. Anthony being right there. But Minneapolis is pretty, too. I have never been there, but my brother has, and some day he is going to take me a long journey all over the West; then we will visit Minneapolis, and I will write to the Pansies about it.

HELEN M. LEEDS.

THE flouring mills of Minneapolis are the largest in the world. They can make thirty-eight thousand barrels of flour in a day if they want to; and I guess they want to, for their flour is famous all over the country. I order flour for my grandmother, and she won't have a barrel which does not say "Minneapolis" on it. I should think the coopers would all get rich out there. I read in a book that in one year they sold pretty nearly three million barrels!

JOHN WILLIS LEEDS.

I DON'T know what I can write about Minneapolis. I think it is just like any other great big city, with electric lights, and street cars, and parks, and all those things, of course. I think cities are all alike; I like the country myself. But Minneapolis grows faster than many cities do. My grandfather was there in 1860, and there were only about six thousand inhabitants; now there are two hundred and twenty-five thousand. Some say more, but I think that is enough.

HARVEY CAMPBELL.

I AM so glad it has come time to write about Minneapolis, because I went there myself only a year ago. I do think it is the loveliest place I was ever in. It seems more like a great big beautiful town than a city. The houses are not crowded together in great ugly-looking brick rows, all just alike, as they are in Philadelphia, and on some streets in New York; but almost all of them have lovely grounds, and trees, and flowers, and pretty lawns. Oh! I liked it all so much. We had a picnic out at the Falls of Minnehaha, the prettiest place I ever saw in my life. There is a magnificent park out there of more than a hundred acres, and the drive all the way through the city to

the park is perfectly beautiful. Then of course the falls themselves are just too lovely! We had Mr. Dickson the elocutionist with us, and after lunch he recited parts of Longfellow's poem about "Minnehaha, Laughing Water." I had never read "Hiawatha" then, but I have since, and I know several pages of it by heart. But you cannot think how lovely it was to have Mr. Dickson recite it right at the falls. We took a great many lovely drives while we were in the city. We stopped at West Hotel, which is one of the finest in the United States, or for that matter in the world. It can accommodate twelve hundred guests, and it seemed as though there must be that number in the house while we were there. When we met in the great dining-room it seemed queer to think that there were more people there than can be found in the village where I live. Still I like our little village in the summer, and would not exchange it for a city. I would like to describe West Hotel, but I cannot, except to say that the furniture was grand, and everything was elegant. We rode past Senator Washburn's house a great many times. It is out on Twenty-second Street and Third Avenue, and has ten acres of the most charming grounds, so that it is just the same to him as living in the country. The house is built of a kind of stone which is called kasota, and is very beautiful. I did not mean to make my letter so long, but there is a great deal to tell.

ALICE WASHBURNE MILLS.

I HAVE an aunt who is very fond of visiting churches. When she goes to a new place, if it is only a village, she wants to see all the churches and know about them. When she was in Minneapolis first, years ago, it was a little bit of a place, and my aunt is an old lady, and does not read the newspapers much, and did not realize that Minneapolis had grown a great deal. She went there last spring to visit a nephew. She reached there in the night, and was taken in a carriage to her nephew's house, and did not realize the changes at all. The next morning at breakfast, when her nephew asked her what she would like to see in the city, she said she would like to visit the different

CITY HALL AND COURT SQUARE.

to an old lady. She saw a good many of the churches, among them Dr. Wayland Hoyt's, which she said she liked the best of all. It is the First Baptist Church of Minneapolis, and cost two hundred thousand dollars. It will seat about fifteen hundred people. I thought the Pansies would like to hear about it, because Dr. Hoyt wrote one of our "Regret" letters for us.

MINNIE ANDREWS.

My uncle is a lawyer and lives in Minneapolis. He says the City Hall is just splendid. It cost three million dollars. Its great tower is three hundred and forty-five feet high, and there are only two others in the United States which can get above that. There isn't any danger that this building will ever burn up, for it is made fire proof. I wonder why they don't make all buildings fire proof? Then we would not have to buy engines, and pay firemen, and keep great splendid horses doing nothing all day long but wait for fires. This City Hall which I began

churches if she could, and that perhaps as the day was pleasant they could go that morning.

"Very well," said her nephew; "to which ones shall we go?"

"Oh! to all of them," answered my aunt; "we can take a few minutes for each and see them all this forenoon, can we not?"

"Certainly," said her nephew; "just as well as not. There are only about a hundred and sixty, I believe."

And that was the first time my aunt knew that she was in a big city instead of the little town she had left thirty years or so before. But I don't think her nephew was very polite

PUBLIC LIBRARY.

to tell you about is three hundred feet square, and fills up a great block on four streets. I should like to see it. My uncle has a photograph of it, and it looks magnificent. I am going to be a lawyer, and I shall have an office in Minneapolis.

HARRY DENNING.

My father was acquainted with Governor Washburn, who gave three hundred and seventy-five thousand dollars for the Washburn Memorial Orphan Asylum in Minneapolis. My father has been there to see the asylum. He says it is in a beautiful place, with lovely trees and plants in the grounds. There were fifty-seven orphans there when father visited it. I am glad they have such a nice place. I would like to be rich, like Governor Washburn, and give lots of money to something. I think I shall be, and I shall found an orphan asylum somewhere, but not in Minneapolis, because they don't need another.

HORACE WEBSTER.

MINNEAPOLIS was started about the same time that St. Anthony was. They grew about the same for awhile, then Minneapolis got to growing so fast that about all which could be heard in that city was the pounding of hammers. Afterwards St. Anthony and Minneapolis were united.

Minneapolis was naturally a very pretty place, and until the last few years it was called the prettiest city in Minnesota, but now St. Paul is prettier.

MILLIE ROWELL.

I ATTENDED the International Christian Endeavor Convention when it met in Minneapolis. I was a Junior delegate. We had a splendid time. The convention was held in the great Exposition building, which is three hundred

and fifty feet square. That is, they made a big hall for the convention inside the building, and it held more than ten thousand people.

My sister and I visited the Public Library. It is a very handsome building. They say it cost a good deal over three hundred thousand dollars. We sat in one of the elegant reading-rooms and read books while our uncle was looking up something in books of reference. There are thousands and thousands of volumes

THE FALLS OF MINNEHAHA.

there; I did know how many, but have forgotten. The street cars in Minneapolis are all electric. My sister did not like to ride on them when there was a thunderstorm, but I was not afraid. There are lots of lakes all around that part of the country, and of course the Falls of St. Anthony are there. It is queer to have a splendid falls in the midst of a city.

I think I like Minneapolis better than any

place I was ever in. I may go to stay with my uncle and attend the University of Minnesota, which is there. That is what I want to do. If I go I shall know more about Minneapolis, and will write again.

THOMAS BAILEY ATWOOD.

THE OSBORNE HOME.

(*Character Studies.*)

LL day long the Osborne home had been in a state of excitement. It had been very difficult for the family to attend to its usual duties. The little girls had at first declared that they could not go to school at all; and then, being convinced that they must, it had been nearly impossible to get them ready in time. Even the baby had caught the unrest, and refused to take his long morning nap and give the seventeen-year-old sister Mary a chance to attend to the work. The explanation was that mother was coming home. She had been away a whole month, an unheard-of thing in the history of the family before this season.

The fact is, Mrs. Osborne was one of those mothers who would never have been persuaded to leave her home and her children had it not become a serious duty to do so. She had been in poor health for several months, and grandmamma had written and coaxed and urged, and at last almost commanded that she should come back to the old home and the old physician, and see if he could not help her. One terrible thing about it was, that this same physician refused to allow her to bring her baby along. "I know just how it will be," he said, shaking his gray head and looking wise. "The baby is a strong, healthy little fellow, and a perfect tyrant as they all are, and he will be carried, and put to sleep, and fed, and petted by his mother and nobody else; he will be more positive about it than usual, being among strangers, and he will just keep her worn out. There is no use in talking, Mrs. Fuller, I know your daughter Mary of old, and I will not consent to try to

help her unless she will leave that fellow at home and come away from all care for a month."

Well, the doctor had had his way, as he nearly always did, and Mrs. Osborne, having declared that it would be utterly impossible to go away from home and leave Baby and the little girls, and only Mary to look after them all, had been gotten ready and carried to the cars. And a whole month had passed, and she, wonderfully improved, was coming home to-day. Father had driven to the depot three miles away to meet her, and the house was in commotion.

Mary, the housekeeper, nurse and mother-in-charge, had had a busy day. There were still a dozen things which she meant to have done before mother came, not the least among them being to get herself in order; for her apron was torn, her slippers were down at the heel, her hair was what her father called "frowsly," and, in short, she did not look in the least as she meant to when the mother should put her arms around her. Then there were last things to be done all over the house, and the table to be set for the early tea-dinner which was to do honor to the traveler's newly-found appetite. Yet, notwithstanding all this, Mary, feeling sure that the time must now be short, allowed herself to drop down into the chair which she had been dusting, draw from her pocket the mother's last letter, whose contents she knew by heart, and glancing at it, go to studying for the dozenth time the possibility that her mother might have meant the evening train instead of the afternoon, in which case she would not be there for several hours.

"Let me see; I almost believe that is the way, after all," she said, biting the feather end of the old quill which she had picked up somewhere in her dusting, and looking vexed and disheartened. "I am sure I don't know how I am to keep the children from growing wild, if they have to wait three hours longer."

Meantime, the children, in the other room, were in various stages of excitement. Helen, the older of the three, in whose charge Baby Joe was especially put, occupied herself in racing to the front gate every few minutes to see if she could not get a glimpse of her father's horse and wagon climbing the hill; and Baby Joe, each time she went, either reached after and tumbled over something which he ought not to have touched, or tumbled down, in his eager haste to follow to the gate. In this way the room was being put into more or less disorder.

"How perfectly silly you are!" said Jessie, looking up from the book she was reading, as Helen came back panting for the third time. "Just as though racing to the gate every few minutes would bring them any quicker! and look at Joe; he has tipped the spools all out of mother's box. A nice tangle they will be in."

"Why didn't you keep him from them then?" asked Helen irritably; "you are doing nothing but pore over a story book. I should think you would go and comb your hair and change your dress. Mother will not like to see you in such a tangle, I can tell you."

"There is time enough," said Jessie, yawning. "I can't do anything but read a story book; it is impossible to settle to anything when mother is so near home as she must be by this time. I haven't done a thing this afternoon; I couldn't. I don't see how Elsie can bend over that stupid History, just as if nothing unusual was going to happen."

This made Elsie raise her eyes; they were pretty brown ones. She was a little girl of about ten, in a neat blue dress, and with her hair in perfect order. "I thought it would be a good plan to get my history ready for to-morrow while I was waiting," she said, "then I will not have to study this evening, when I want to listen to mother. I should think you would like to get your examples done; and anyhow, Jessie, you ought to comb your hair; it looks like a fright."

"I mean to, of course," said Jessie. "I dare say there is time enough. Father can't drive fast on such a warm afternoon; and besides, Mary said she wouldn't be at all surprised if he should have to wait for the evening train. Wouldn't that be just horrid! If it were not for the lovely story I am reading I couldn't endure this waiting another minute."

"It's easier to wait when you are at work doing what ought to be done," said Elsie, with the air of a philosopher.

"Oh! you are a regular Miss Prim," said Helen, laughing, as she stooped to pick little Joe out of another piece of carefully planned mischief; "for my part, I think it is horrid to have anything that ought to be done at such a time. Joe, you little nuisance, I do wish you would go to sleep, and give me a chance to watch for mother. I hope I shall get all the things picked up and put to rights that you have upset before mother comes; she will not be charmed with the looks of the room if I don't. However, there really must be oceans of time yet."

"Then why did you race down to the gate every few minutes to see if they were coming?" Jessie asked.

"Oh! because I did not know what else to do," said Helen; "I knew better, of course. Take care, Joe! There, I declare! he has done it now."

Sure enough he had! Jerked at the table spread where Helen herself had set the ink-stand, intending to put it away in a few minutes, and sent a black stream not only over his own white dress, but on the carpet as well. Mary, who still sat studying the letter, and thinking of the things which she meant to accomplish before her mother came, having by this time decided that it was entirely probable that they must wait for the evening train, heard the exclamations of dismay from the other room, and rose up to see what was the trouble; but at that instant an eager cry from Elsie: "There they come!" sounded on the ears of all. Helen gathered up the screaming Joe under one arm, and calling to Mary to look out for the ink on the carpet, ran out of one door, just as Jessie scurried out of another, eager to dash upstairs and brush her hair before her father saw her; for his last charge had been to her to see to it that she did not appear before her mother in that plight. Mary, burning with shame and disappointment over the little last things which she meant to have ready, waited to mop up the ink, while Elsie, closing the door on the disordered room, went forward to meet the beloved mother.   MYRA SPAFFORD.

"LET ME SEE!"

IN THE CABIN OF THE MAYFLOWER.

THIS is a company of Pilgrims in the cabin of the blessed ship *Mayflower*, on their way over a stormy sea from Plymouth, England, to find a place in America where they may worship God "according to the dictates of their own consciences."

This was two hundred and seventy years ago. Of course the people did not dress then

not complain, as they believed God held the waves in his hand, and he was guiding the *Mayflower* as much as he did the Israelites to Palestine — " a land flowing with milk and honey." So they patiently and cheerfully waited in the *Mayflower's* small cabin, often singing hymns and praying and encouraging each other.

At last on Monday, December 21, 1620, they landed on Plymouth Rock, Mass., happy as birds escaped from a cage.

They had much trouble with the Indians;

A COMPANY OF PILGRIMS.

just as they do now, as you can well see by noticing their broad collars and queer trousers. How queer our dress will look to our great-grandchildren.

The dear *Mayflower* was not such a grand ship as the Cunarder. It had to depend — not upon steam — but upon a favoring wind, and the wind does not always seem to favor, so it took her weeks to cross the stormy Atlantic, and the passengers (Puritans they were called) were very sick; but because they had suffered so much from cruel people in England they did

but after a time they began to build, with other Pilgrims, at other points, our great nation.

L.

THERE is a woman living in Manchester, England, who is said to have a Bible two feet long and nearly two feet wide. At the top of each page is printed in red ink : " This is a history."· The Bible is two hundred years old, and is the largest one in the world, it is supposed.

BABY'S CORNER.

BABY'S CLOCK.

NOBODY finks I can tell the time of day, but I can.

The first hour is five o'clock in the morning.

That's the time the birds begin to peep. I lie still and hear them sing:

Bimeby the sun gets up and it's six o'clock in the morning.

Then mamma opens one eye and I can hear her say:

"Where's my baby?"

N'en I keep still — jus' as still as a mouse, an' she keeps saying:

"Where's my baby?"

N'en all at once I go "Boo!" and she laughs and hugs me, and says "I'm a precious."

DABY TELLS THE TIME OF DAY.

"Tweet, tweet, tweet!
Chee, chee, chee!"

But mamma is fast asleep. Nobody awake in all the world but just me and the birds.

Mamma's nice, and I love her 'cept when she washes my face too hard and pulls my hair with the comb.

Seven o'clock!

That's when the bell goes jingle, jingle, and we have breakfast.

All the eight an' nine an' ten an' 'leven hours I play.

I run after butterflies and squirrels, and swing, and read my picture book, and sometimes I cry — jus' a little bit.

Twelve o'clock!

That's a ba'ful hour. The clock strikes a lot of times, and the big whistle goes, and the bell rings, and papa comes home, and dinner's ready!

The one and two hours are lost. Mamma always carries me off to take a nap. I don't like naps. They waste time.

When we wake up the clock strikes three. N'en I have on my pink dress, and we go walking or riding.

And so the three and four and five hours are gone.

At six o'clock Bossy comes home, and I have my drink of warm milk.

N'en I put on my white gown, and kiss everybody "good-night," and say "Now I lay me," and get into my bed.

Mamma says:

"Now the sun and the birdies and my little baby are all gone to bed, and to sleep, sleep, sleep."

So I shut my eyes tight, and next you know 'tis morning!

An' 'nat's all the time there is.

MRS. C. M. LIVINGSTON.

OCTOBER'S PARTY.

OCTOBER gave a party —
    The leaves by hundreds came —
The Chestnuts, Oaks and Maples,
    And leaves of every name;

The sunshine spread a carpet,
    And everything was grand;
Miss Weather led the dancing,
    Professor Wind the band.

The Chestnuts came in yellow,
    The Oaks in crimson dressed;
The lovely Misses Maple
    In scarlet looked their best.

All balanced to their partners,
    And gaily fluttered by;

The sight was like a rainbow
    New-fallen from the sky.

Then in the rustic hollows
    At hide-and-seek they played.
The party closed at sundown,
    And everybody staid.

Professor Wind played louder,
    They flew along the ground,
And then the party ended
    In "hands across, all round."
From "Song Stories for Little People."

FIVE-MINUTE ACQUAINTANCES.

(Character Studies.)

IT was a bright cool morning that we were riding down Delaware Avenue in a street car which had very few passengers. It gave me a chance to study human nature. I began the study with a very handsomely dressed boy. Jacket and collar and necktie and hair all showed that very careful people had planned for him, and that they had plenty of money to spend on him. They came into the car just after I was seated, the boy and his mother. She was tall and pale, and in deep mourning; I wondered if her husband were dead, and if this boy were the only one she had to think about or care for her. If so she was to be pitied, poor woman! for it soon became evident that the young man thought about and cared for himself. His first exhibition was to fling his heavy overcoat on his mother's lap as he said: "Here, mamma, hold that, and give me the tickets for the conductor."

"I haven't tickets, dear," she said; "I shall have to buy some."

"O, well! all right, give me your pocket-book and let me buy them."

"No, dear, there is a good deal of money in my pocket-book, and some valuable papers."

"What of that?" he said, in a tone loud enough for all the passengers to hear; "I ain't going to lose them; don't I know how to take care of things? Give me the purse." It was passed over without more words.

"Take a quarter from the silver money," the mother advised a moment later.

"O, no, mamma! I want to give him a bill, to see if he makes the right change. Here's a five; that will do; no, let me see." He jerked his arm suddenly away from the mother's hand, which reached after the pocket-book, and several pieces of silver flew out and rolled around on the floor.

"There!" he said, in a reproachful tone, "see what you have made me do; now you have lost some of your money."

"Pick it up, Harold, that's a good boy."

He stooped and picked up a twenty-five cent piece, then said:

"Never mind the rest. It has rolled round under the seat somewhere, and it is all dust; I can't get down on my knees and hunt; never mind, let it go. Say, mamma, give me that box of candy."

"Not now; I would rather you did not eat any more candy, Harold, until we get home."

"Why not? I don't want to wait; I haven't eaten much. Come, it's my candy, and I want it. You bought it for me, and I think you are mean not to let me have it."

"Hush, Harold! do not talk so loud. Hold your overcoat, dear; it is too heavy for mamma."

"Oh! I can't, it is too hot. I did not need that great big overcoat anyhow, and I told you so. I'm not going to hold it. Drop it on the floor if you don't want to keep it. But give me that box of candy. O, mamma! there's a procession coming down the street — soldiers, and everything. I'm going out on the platform to see them."

He made a dash forward, and the pale, anxious mother reached after him, trying to arrest his steps, dropping as she did so not only the overcoat, but the pocket-book again. The pennies and the ten-cent pieces rolled around freely, while Harold, looking behind him, gave a mocking laugh, and was out on the platform.

They had not been in the car over five minutes. And yet I was quite as well acquainted with Harold as I had any desire to be.

At the North Street corner the pale little mother left the car with the heavy overcoat over one arm, and the pocket-book, with what change she had been able to find, in her hand, while Harold, tugging at her sleeve, was heard to say, "Mamma, I want that candy this minute!"

At Reed Street came three passengers, a boy about the size of the one who had left us, and two little girls, one perhaps seven, and the other not over four. The boy was freckled-faced, and by no means so handsome as Harold. His clothes were very neat, but of the coarse,

A SHOCKING EXPERIENCE.

common sort worn by children of the moderately poor. The little girls beside him were as neat as wax — faces and hands and hair in perfect order; but their sacks and hats were of last year's fashion — perhaps older still than that — and I fancy Harold would have laughed outright at the little old overcoat which hung over the boy's arm.

They took their seats quietly, and made no disturbance of any sort. But there were so few in the car, and we were passing at that time through such a quiet street, that I could hear distinctly the words they spoke to one another.

"Better put on your sack, Janie," said the boy, with a thoughtful air, looking at the older sister, "the wind blows in pretty strong here." Janie immediately arose and began tugging at her sack. The boy, with the manners of a gentleman accustomed to the work, took hold of it at the shoulders and skillfully steered the little arms into place, pulling it down behind, and bestowing meanwhile side glances upon the little sister.

"Sit still, Bessie, that's a good girl. No, don't stand, dear; mamma wouldn't like you to stand, the cars shake so."

Down sat Bessie again, trying to put herself squarely on the seat. Failing in this her protector turned next to her, lifted her plump little form into place, then straightened her hat and returned a confiding smile which she gave him. Meantime the car was filling up, and in a few minutes every seat was taken. There came next a middle-aged woman, black of face, and very shabby as to toilet, with a market basket on her arm. Quick as thought the little gentleman arose, and touching her arm motioned her to his seat. Then Janie reached forward for his overcoat. "Let me hold your overcoat, Charlie," she said, "because you haven't any seat."

"O, no!" said Charlie, smiling back at her, "I can carry it as well as not. Bessie dear, don't climb up that way, you will fall."

Down sat Bessie, who had mounted on her fat little knees to look out of the window.

"Now, Janie," said the little man at last, when they were near the Dean Street crossing,

"we are to get out at this corner. I will take Bessie's hand and go ahead, and you keep close to me. We will stand still on the sidewalk until the car passes, then I will take you both across."

Away they went, and I watched them making their way carefully across the crowded street, the brother's arm thrown protectingly around Bessie, and his eyes on the watch for any possible danger to either of his charges. I had made his acquaintance in five minutes, too, and knew more about him than he would have imagined possible.

MYRA SPAFFORD.

THINGS WHICH SOME PEOPLE REGRET.

THE "Regret" which we give you this month comes from a very high source. Almost every scholar of ancient languages will recognize the name. It is a very pleasant thought that these great men out of their busy lives have stopped to give us a glimpse of their past, in order to help the young people of to-day, who will be the men and women of to-morrow, to avoid the mistakes which they did not. We hope and believe that the Pansies will receive great benefit from these glimpses from the youth of great people.

"I regret that I have not better acquired the art of pleasantly acknowledging the kindnesses shown me, and of showing my appreciation of people whom I really do appreciate. My influence with many would be greatly increased if I could but make them understand how warmly my heart goes out to them."

WILLIS J. BEECHER.

DR. W. J. BEECHER, *Professor of Hebrew in Auburn Theological Seminary.*

(*Luke* ix. 23; xiv. 27.)

AND didst thou hear the Master say
        He that would my disciple be,
Let him deny himself each day,
        Take up his cross, and follow me?
Oh! wondrous love, that did devise
        For us this "straight and narrow way,"
Beyond which, in the distance, lies
        The realms of pure and perfect day.

THE UPS AND DOWNS OF LIFE.

MAJOR'S AUTOBIOGRAPHY.

 I AM very fond of the little ones, and like to have them around me, and as the puppies are in the majority it will be their turn to have a short story this time.

If you do not have to go home too soon perhaps I will have time to tell you more than one; we will see. Oh! the children are to stay to tea, are they? All right. Now, attention!

All those who would like to hear a story about a chicken — "a real truly story," as the children say—wag your tails.

Those opposed, bark. Carried. The vote for the chicken story is about unanimous.

I suppose some of you have very poor opinions of chickens and hens; you think because they have but two legs, and are so easily frightened, they don't amount to much; but the master and mistress think quite differently when they eat the nice fresh eggs which the hens furnish. Why, some of those proud young crowers have hearts as well as we. I remember so well a little old white blind hen which my master once had, and how kindly she was treated. (She could see just a little with one eye, but we called her blind.)

The young man who worked upon the place took a fancy to "Old Whitey," as they called her, and when master wanted to send her to market this fellow pretended he couldn't find her, so she was kept till very old.

The gallant young crowers which roosted in the same shed with her would never fight this old "grandmother," but were just as kind to her as they knew how to be. Sometimes when one of them had found a nice lot of worms under something he had scratched over, "Whitey" would come along hungry, and he would leave the nice mess for her, and look further for himself.

Was not that gallant and kind? Would all of you do as well as that? Be as unselfish?

But this is not the chicken I was to tell you about. He was a poor orphan, his mother having died when he was but a little yellow ball upon two little pins of legs.

A HAPPY BOY.

HIS name is Willie Addis, and he lives in Plainfield, N. J. A few weeks ago his mother turned down the wicks of her kerosene stove, and leaned over it to blow out the flame, when the stove exploded, and in an instant she was in flames. With one bound Willie was in the kitchen, seizing the large woolen mat from the floor as he ran, and in less time than it takes me to tell it, he had wrapped the mat about his mother and extinguished the flames! The kitchen furniture was burned, but that was about all, and the dear mother was saved by her quick-witted ten-year-old son, who had heard somewhere that woolen wrapped closely about a burning object so as to exclude the air, will put out the fire. It is not every boy of his age who knows that fact; and there are many who, knowing it, would not have had presence of mind enough to have applied their knowledge promptly. Willie did, and he has his mother. Certainly I think he must be a happy boy, and I am sure she is a glad, proud mother.

How is one to help hoping and praying that he may never be other than a joy to her in the years to come?

AN ORIENTAL SHEPHERD.

I had not much to do with this pet, only as I visited his home occasionally, and saw and played with him a little.

It was my cousin Tip who had most to do with this bright feathered fellow, and to whom he was indebted for most of his education.

Tip was a great favorite; in fact, his mistress was fond of all sorts of pets; had a name for each of her cows, and for every one of her hens, so she had a name for this chicken.

Tip used to go about wherever he pleased, and so did the chicken. My cousin was in the habit of taking almost anything he could find, and dragging it to the spot where he wished to lie, then make a bed of it and go to sleep.

His little friend the chicken for awhile watched him with envious eyes — for I regret to say Cousin Tip was too selfish to provide a bed for any one besides himself.

But this chicken evidently thought "what had been done could be done," so he asserted his independence, and gathered up what he could carry or drag; put the articles — stockings, handkerchiefs or rags — in a heap near Tip's bed, and would then tread them down as he had seen Tip do, and squat upon them for a make-believe nap. Now wasn't that a pretty bright chicken, and was not Tip a pretty successful teacher for one so young?

No, that lesson wouldn't be much for a bright little dog to learn; but we do not expect much intelligence in a hen or rooster.

I suppose they cannot understand what people say to them as we do. And some people do not seem to think we understand what they tell us to do or not to do, even when they tell us we have done well.

I remember so well when I was young, though almost as large as I am now, how I astonished a lady by acting as though I understood what she said to me.

It was in the country, where the houses were quite a distance apart. I had been caring for this woman's little girl for more than a week, and had kept her out of lots of mischief, and prevented her from getting many an ugly fall, though I had never been asked to do it.

One day little Cynthia (that was her name) wanted to go over to see her grandmother, who lived in the next house, nearly a quarter of a mile away. The mother told her there was no one to go with her. She said she could go alone, and coaxed so hard that the mother said she might go. So Cynthia put her little hat on, and her mother kissed her good-by, and she started. Then her mother turned to me and said: "Major, you go with her and take good care of my darling; don't you let anything hurt her."

How proud I was! I went right by her side all the way, and never left her for one moment until she was safe at home.

Then the lady called me a "good, faithful fellow," and I was very happy. But when the men came in at night and she told them what I had done, I felt ashamed to hear her say, "He acted just as though he knew what I told him."

The idea! Why shouldn't I understand, I would like to know? They talk about things which I do not understand, but when they give me such a plain direction as that I guess I can hear it, and know what they mean, too.

There goes the whistle, and you must scamper. Good-by!   G. R. A.

A CAREFUL MOTHER.

A TRUSTWORTHY writer in one of our exchanges says that last summer near his room a humming-bird built her tiny nest and reared her family. One day when there was a heavy shower coming up, just as the first drops fell the mother came fluttering home, seized a large leaf which grew on the tree near her nest, drew it over the nest in a way to completely cover it, then went back to whatever work she had been about when the coming storm disturbed her. The amused watchers from the window wondered why the leaf did not blow away, and finally reached out and examined it; they found it hooked to a tiny stick which was just inside the nest, as if it had been built in for that purpose! The storm lasted but a few minutes, and after it was over home came the mother, unhooked the green curtain she had so carefully put up, and found her babies perfectly dry.

WHICH WILL GET IT?

CHRISTIAN ENDEAVOR SAINTS.

(Something for Mamma.)

NOT something to make, this time, but to buy. It is a lovely new book bound in blue and silver, and the title is "Christian Endeavor Saints."

It is written by Dr. F. E. Clark, the father of all the Christian Endeavor societies. If your mamma is not a member of that society it will make no difference, she will like the book very much; it has a great many short bright articles in it, not too long for a busy mother to read when she sits down for a minute or two of rest. The first part of the book has short letters addressed to different saints.

One, for instance, to "St. Neighborly," another to "St. Hopeful," another to "St. Speakwell," and so on.

Then there are many "Golden Rule Recipes" for the cure of all sorts of troubles, as well as what is perhaps better, for the prevention of many.

Let me give you one which is called:

A RECIPE FOR A HAPPY DAY.

"At the very beginning of the day take a large amount of good nature, and double the quantity of determination to make the best of things, a heaping measure of bodily vigor, and mix well in the mortar of gratitude with the pestle of the remembrance of past mercies. A season of prayer and praise is always necessary to the proper mixture of these ingredients. Then add to this a considerable, but not too large, portion of well-regulated tongue, a slice of charity that thinketh no evil and is not easily provoked, a portion of hopefulness for the future, and a large measure of faith in God and fellowmen. Season this with the salt of shrewdness and thrift, and sweeten with plenty of the sugar of love for all God's creatures. Put in a large handful of plums of parental or filial affection, and a number of pieces of neighborly friendliness; and somewhere in the day conceal one special service for the Lord's poor. Slide this good deed into the mixture quietly, without saying anything about it. Do not use any of the sour milk of disappointed hopes, or brooding cares, for this will spoil the whole; and while there should be a pinch of the pepper of fun, and considerable sweet oil of joviality, do not use any of the mustard of backbiting, or the table sauce of slander.

"Let the mixture boil gently, but do not let it boil over, for the delicate flavor of the ingredients is injured by too much heat.

"This recipe has been tried in a hundred thousand households, and has never been known to fail."

There are many more recipes quite as unique and as helpful as this.

Then follows a series of "Golden Rule Sermons" on all sorts of important topics, such as "Getting Muddled with the Unimportant," on "Living as we Sing," on "Poor Excuses," and the like. Finally there are letters addressed to "Grandmother Lois," "Mrs. Neataswax," "Miss Youngheart," "Mrs. Vitriol," and a host of other people whom we have met.

From one, addressed to "The Birds that can Sing, and won't Sing," I want to quote a little:

MY DEAR BIRDS:

"I watched you last Wednesday evening in the mid-week prayer meeting, and none of you moved your lips, even when we sang 'Rock of Ages' and 'Jesus, Lover of my Soul.' The singing was weak and languid and thin, when your voices might have put body and life and strength into it. I know that you can sing if you have a mind to, for do I not hear you every Sunday in the church choir? . . . Did I not hear you sing, too, at Miss Flora McFlimsey's birthday party the other evening? Yes, indeed; you gathered around the piano, and the way you warbled forth the glees and college songs did my heart good. But there you were at the church prayer meeting, members of the church, members of the Society of Christian Endeavor; you had promised more than once to do your duty faithfully, and yet you kept still, simply because the singing wasn't very artistic, or because somebody behind you 'screeched so,' as you inelegantly expressed it, or because the old deacon on the front seat dragged, and 'put you all out.' Now, my dear birds, pardon the plain words of an old man, and your pastor at that. The prayer meeting singing is just as important a part of worship, and just as acceptable in God's sight, as your choir or solo singing with all its frills and furbelows. The 'screecher' and the old deacon are both doing the best they can; and if you did the best you could their voices would not be so prominent, and the music would be far better. Then, too, do you not think it indicates a little touch of conceit to sing only when your voices will show off to advantage, and let the poor prayer meeting suffer for lack of them? I am sure, my dear birds, that you never thought of the matter in that light, for after all you mean to be conscientious as well as tuneful birds; and I am quite confident that when, next Wednesday evening, I give out 'Rock of Ages,' you will 'raise it' on your clear strong voices, and give the prayer meeting such a start and uplift as it has not had for many a day."

I did not mean to quote it all, but it was so good I could not find a place to stop. I think you will enjoy it, and so will mamma, or your older sister, or indeed any one who loves to read bright, pure, helpful thoughts.

The book has about two hundred and fifty pages. I really do not know how much it costs, but your bookseller can easily find out for you.

PANSY.

THE HARD TEXT.

(Matt. xviii. 2.)

NOW does this mean that all children are good Christians, and are surely in the Kingdom of Heaven? But you know many who are not good. They are profane; they break the Sabbath, and all the other holy commands of God. Some are so very bad that their parents send them to reformatories, which are a sort of prison.

Some years ago a boy by the name of Jesse Pomeroy, when he was quite young, began to torture children when he could get them into his power. As he grew a little older and stronger he would get children away from home and lead them out into some desolate place, and bind them to a tree and do dreadful things to them.

It is thought that this wicked boy caused the death of several children.

There are more Jesse Pomeroys. Jesus did not mean that all children are perfectly good. Indeed every one — children, too — must be born again — that is, converted — to get into the Kingdom of Heaven.

What, then, did Jesus mean in this verse? Why, simply that all must "humble" themselves; must repent and trust in him to be saved. Every true child is ready to do this, much more so than grown-up folks.

Grown-up people do not like to confess that they are sinners. They — most of them — refuse to humble themselves, as most very young folks do.

Now have you really humbled yourself?

L.

'Tis easy to be gentle when
  Death's silence shames our clamor,
And easy to discern the best
  Through memory's mystic glamour;
But wise it were for thee and me,
  Ere love is past forgiving,
To take the tender lesson home —
  Be patient with the living.

— Selected.

ABOUT ST. LOUIS.

BY THE PANSIES.

THE biggest thing in St. Louis is the bridge by which you get to it. It has three arches, each over five hundred feet long, and it makes a road over fifty feet wide. My uncle says it is a big thing, and he knows, for he is a bridge builder. There is a tunnel under it, and a railroad track. I rode into St. Louis once through this tunnel; it is a mile long. It is lighted with electricity, and they say it has ventilating shafts; but they don't give you much air to breathe, that I know. Father had to fan mother every minute, and we were afraid she would faint. I think I should have found it hard work to breathe myself, if I hadn't been so dreadfully worried about mother that I forgot all about it. But for all that it is a splendid thing — the tunnel is, I mean. The piers of the bridge are built on a rock, and they go down more than a hundred feet below the surface. This bridge cost over six millions of dollars. I could tell you more things, for I staid in St. Louis a whole week, but mother says my letter is long enough.

WILLARD J. MOONEY.

ALL the Pansies tell how the city they are writing about got its name. I cannot find out about St. Louis, but I know the first settlement there was made by Pierre Laclede Liguest. I was wondering if they did not put pieces of his queer name together, and make a word which in time came to be St. Louis? Anyhow, I am glad they did not name the place for him, it would have been so hard to pronounce. That is only about a hundred and thirty years ago. St. Louis did not grow very fast; for a long time nobody thought it was going to be a city, and fifty years ago there were only about sixteen thousand inhabitants; but it has grown fast enough since. There are more than five hundred thousand people there now, and large, beautiful buildings, and everything which helps to make a city handsome. It is hot there, though; at least my auntie thinks so. She used to have to wait three hours in a St. Louis depot for a train every time she came home for her summer vacation, and went back in September, and she says the warmest she has ever been in her life was during those hours; and she never in five years struck a cool day! So she says she cannot help thinking that St. Louis is always warm. But probably if she had been there in January, instead of June or September, she would have thought differently. Women

THE COURT HOUSE.

are apt to think that things stay always just as they happened to find them.

ROBERT CAMPBELL.

THE prettiest place to go to in St. Louis is "Shaw's Garden." It has other names, "The Missouri Botanical Gardens," and "Tower Grove Park," which is a piece of the gardens, but when I was there everybody said "Shaw's Garden." The land was presented by Mr. Henry Shaw, an Englishman, and he used to keep the lovely great park in order at his own expense; I don't know whether he does now or

not. There are more than two hundred and fifty acres just in Tower Grove Park. I have never been to Central Park, that some of the Pansies told about, but I do not see how it could be prettier than Tower Grove Park. There is a statue of Shakespeare, and another of Humboldt in the park, and they cost over a million of dollars. I don't see why; I didn't admire them very much; but that is what the gentleman said who went with us. There are a great many other parks in St. Louis — about twenty, I think — but none are so beautiful as this; and the Botanical Gardens are said to have the finest collection of plants of any city in the United States. My brother Roger says that cities always say such things about themselves, and that he doesn't suppose it is finer than can be found in New York and Chicago, but that is what they told us.

NELLIE SHERMANN.

I READ a description of the St. Louis Court House which was very interesting. It is built in the form of a Greek cross, and has a splendid dome whose lantern can be seen as much as twenty miles away. It cost a good deal over a million dollars — the building did, not the lantern. Aunt Kate told me to put that sentence in: I don't see why; of course you would know that a lantern did not cost all that! I like handsome buildings; I am going to be an architect.

I study all the different forms of buildings; I like the Greek cross style very well, but I don't know how it would look for a private house. Aunt Kate says all that has nothing to do with St. Louis, but I don't care. You don't mind my telling what interests me, do you?

ARTHUR BLAKEMAN

THERE is a building in St. Louis called "Four Courts," named after the "Four Courts" of Dublin. But I think it was queer to name it Four Courts, and then have only three courts held in it. It is a stone building, and cost a good deal of money. Stone buildings always do; I suppose that is because they last so long; things that last always cost a great deal. I have hunted and hunted to find something interesting about St. Louis that everybody else would not be likely to tell, and the only thing I could find was this about the Four Courts. I don't know as that is interesting, but it is the best I could do.

MARY BLAKEMAN.

THEY have a splendid Public-school Library in St. Louis. My father said when he was there ten years ago there were over fifty thousand volumes in it — books to help teachers and scholars. My father says he thinks other cities

THE CUSTOM HOUSE.

THEY have a splendid Custom House and Post-Office in St. Louis. Father says the building cost half a million. He was there when it was being built, and he says there is something grand-looking about it. And father says they have splendid schools there; not only public schools, but lots of private ones. The Washington University is there, and so, of course, is the St. Louis University; and they have the finest kindergartens there, I think, to be found outside of Germany. My uncle says I might as well leave that sentence out, for the kindergartens in the United States are better than those in Germany. But I am not going to leave it out; I don't like crossed-out lines in a letter, and I haven't time to copy this. Besides, lots of people think that things in other countries are nicer than our own, of course.

CHARLES J. PRESCOTT, Jr.

might copy after them in this. Colleges have libraries on purpose for their students, why should not public schools?

WILL VANDENBERG.

THE DENISON HOUSE.

RITA was riding on a road that went winding up hill and down dale, when she remarked, " Well, I never did saw such a curly road."

A SEED THAT BLOSSOMED.

ELISE was spending the afternoon with Miss Dora Turner. Miss Turner was several years older than Elise, but she had come to the country to live among strangers, and Elise had known her in her city home, and was lonely like herself, so they became intimate friends. Elise told all her sorrows and perplexities, as well as her joys, to this young lady. She was in Miss Turner's room now, waiting for her to rearrange her hair and make some additions to her toilet, then they were going for a walk.

"I don't know where we can go, I am sure," said Elise; "we have used up all the pretty walks near by. I wish it was early enough to go for a long tramp; I would like to do something different this afternoon. I feel tired of all the things I ever did."

"Poor little old lady!" said Miss Turner, laughing, "there will have to be a new world made for you, Elise." Then, as she turned, she caught the flash of the diamond at Elise's throat, and said: "How lovely your pin is! It seems too lovely and too costly for a young girl."

"It was mamma's," said Elise gravely, "and papa promised mamma he would give it to me on my fourteenth birthday. Didn't I tell you?"

"Why, no, indeed. That explains it. I wondered that your father should send you a diamond pin at your age; but it is beautiful for you to have your mother's pin to wear. Why didn't you tell me, Elise?"

"Because," said Elise, "there was a part to it that I did not understand, and I suppose I did not want to speak of it. Mamma sent me a message with it; at least papa said that the words inside were her message; she had them engraved on it before she died, so it seems like mamma's last words to me, and indeed it is; but I do not understand it, nor know how to do it, nor anything. I don't suppose you could show me?"

The question was asked with a half-laugh, and not at all as though Elise supposed that she could get any help from this quarter.

Miss Turner's fair face flushed. "I don't suppose I could," she answered gravely; "I don't know much about such things, Elise."

What she meant by "such things" perhaps would have been difficult for her to explain. But the thought in her mind was, that "last messages" from dying mothers would not be such as she could explain. Elise's mother had been dead for many years; at least they seemed many to Elise, though she could remember her beautiful mother distinctly; and when she thought it all over, as she often did in the twilight, could seem to feel her mother's kiss upon her lips, and the pressure of her mother's hand on the yellow curls which used to be hers in those days. She was not yet six years old when her mother went away, but there were times when it seemed to her that she had seen her only yesterday. And at other times the years which stretched between seemed very, very long. Her father was in India in the Government employ; had been there for five years. And Elise, who received long letters from him, and elegant presents, and talked a great deal about him, yet felt sometimes that she really knew him less than she did her beautiful pale mother, who used to love her so, and kiss her so tenderly. Elise lived with an aunt who was very fond of her, and did everything to supply her mother's place, and her uncle called her his adopted daughter; yet sometimes she cried when she was tucked up in bed for the night, because she longed so to have a mamma and papa and a home of her own, like other girls. It was perhaps because Miss Turner had no mother that she had felt drawn toward her in the first place.

"What is the message?" her friend asked. "May I see it, Elise? I am half-surprised that you do not understand it; you are such a thoughtful young person, and seem older than you are; I have a feeling that you can understand what most others do."

Elise made no reply save to unclasp the pin and pass it to her friend. Miss Turner moved toward the window, where the light would fall upon it. It was a lovely arch of gold, a tiny diamond flashing in its center, and on the reverse side was engraved, in small but distinct letters, the words: "Keep His covenant." "Why, Elise!" she said, "how beautiful this is. I should think you would like it very much."

"I do," said Elise, "of course; only it gives me a strange feeling, as though mamma had sent me word to do something that I could not do; and I have always thought that I would like to do things to please mamma, if I only knew just what she wanted done." .

"Well, but, dear," said Miss Turner hesitatingly, "surely you can find out what this means, in a general way."

Elise smiled sadly. "I remember mamma very well," she said, "and she always wanted me to do exactly as she said."

"Well," said Miss Turner again, after an embarrassed pause, "this is exact enough; she means you to live a good life, you know."

"I don't know what it means," said Elise, moving restlessly. "As for being good, I am not, and I don't know how to be; I cannot keep my temper a single day. You know I never get through a day without having a tiff of some sort with Cousin Annie; and there are ever so many people who vex me and worry me so that I cannot feel right toward them. That is not being good. Besides, the words seem to me to mean something more than that — something different. I would like to know exactly what they mean, but there is nobody that I can ask. Papa does not understand such things, and uncle and auntie do not. I don't seem to have any friends who could help in that way."

Miss Turner gave back the pin, looking very thoughtful indeed. She ought to know more about those things than Elise did, she told herself; her father was not a Christian, and her mother had died when her little girl was six years old, whereas Miss Turner had lived always in a home where the father and mother were earnest Christians, and she knew at this very moment that the greatest desire of their hearts was to see her doing this very thing — "keeping His covenant." Yet she knew as little about it practically as Elise Burton did; so little, that although she was at least six years older than Elise, she did not know in the least how to help her this afternoon. It was very humiliating. She could help her with

her music, and with her French lessons, and her drawing, and to have this most important of all lessons beyond her, seemed strange and wrong. She was still for several minutes, then she said, speaking very gently:

"Elise dear, I can imagine how you feel with this message from your mother; I wish I knew how to help you. But there is a way to learn what it means. There is a verse in the Bible somewhere that explains its meaning."

Elise looked up quickly. "Where?" she asked. "The Bible is such a big book, and I do not know much about it. I did try last Sunday to find something about covenants that would help me. I went away back to Noah and the rainbow, but I did not get any good out of it for me."

Miss Dora went to her table and took up an elegantly bound reference Bible, full of help which she did not understand, and turning in a half-bewildered, half-embarrassed manner to the Concordance, ran her eye down the list of words marked "covenant." Elise watched her curiously. She had no Concordance in her Bible, and did not know how to use one. At last Miss Dora turned to a verse.

"This explains a little of it," she said, and read aloud: "This shall be the covenant that I will make with the house of Israel in those days, saith the Lord; I will put my law in their inward parts, and write it in their hearts, and will be their God and they shall be my people." As she read a curious light came into her eyes.

"It is very strange," she said; "that is the verse that they are going to talk about this afternoon at the covenant meeting."

"What is a covenant meeting?" asked Elise eagerly.

"It is the young people's quarterly meeting at the church where I am attending. Every three months their Christian Endeavor Society have a gathering which they call a covenant meeting. I don't know much about it; I have not been; but they talk together about such things; the pastor comes and talks to them. They say the meetings are interesting. What if we should walk in that direction, Elise, and go in a little while? Mr. Westfield invited me to come, but I did not have an idea that I should do so. I do not attend such meetings much, you know. But if you would like to go, Elise, and find out about your pin, I will go with you."

"Well," said Elise, starting up with more energy than she had shown before for several days, "I will. I want to know about 'His covenant.' I do, truly. Mamma asked me to, you know; and perhaps if I understood it it would tell me just exactly what she wanted me to do all the time, and I should be so glad to do it."

"We will go and find out," said Miss Turner gravely.

Thus the little seed dropped by the loving mother's hand took root and blossomed in two lives, though the hand which sowed the seed had been dust for many years.   PANSY.

WHEN GRANDFATHER WAS YOUNG.

A SCARECROW.

ALEX HAINES and Eva were promised a piece of ground as their very own if they would cultivate (what is that?) it.

Each took a hoe and began. By night Alex and Eva had planted a rod square to corn. .

Then they watched the corn; that is, they watched for the corn. After a few days, sure enough, the spots where the corn was planted — that is, the hills — began to swell as though something wanted to get out. Then up came a bit of a green leaf. Higher it grew, and they came often to see it.

One day they came and found some of the hills pulled up, and while they wondered what thief had been about, they heard from the top of a tree, "Caw, caw, caw!"

The thief was a crow.

So they must scare the crows away, or the corn will be all pulled up, and their labor will be in vain.

Crows are afraid of men; but men cannot stay all the time in the field to scare the crows off. So something that looks like a man must be set up in the corn patch to scare the crows away.

With a pair of pants, a coat, a hat, and three old brooms, they are making a man! When it is all done it will not look much like a man. It has neither eyes, nose nor mouth. It can not walk nor talk. The scarecrow has no heart or soul, but it can scare crows away from the corn.

The gods of the heathen have eyes, but they can't see. They can't see or hear or feel or think.

They are made gods, and those who make such gods worship them. They think such things can scare away evil and do them good!

But such gods just scare the heathen, and of course cannot save them.

Ah! if the poor, deceived people knew of Him "who so loved the world that He gave his only begotten Son, that whosoever believeth in Him should not perish, but have everlasting life."

What Pansy among you will go and tell them, or help send a preacher to them?   L.

BUILDING THE SCARECROW.

THERE is a grand temperance organization in Sweden, which is trying to get rid of the saloon. Last year their Government appropriated twenty-five thousand crowns, a portion of which was set apart to be used as awards for the best essays on the different phases of the temperance question, with suggestions as to how soonest to rid the country of the curse of alcohol.

The tulip and the Butterfly
Appear in gayer coats than I.
Let me be dressed fine as I will,
Flies worms and flowers excell me
Then will I see my ♥ heart to find
Inward adornings of the mind!
Knowledge and Virtue, truth & grace
These are the robes of richest dress
Drusilla Dickinson is my name
America my nation,
Little Cheapside is my place
And ✝ Christ is my salvation

GREAT-GRANDMOTHER'S SAMPLER.

A DOUBLE LESSON.

"THERE!" said Davie Campbell, flinging as he spoke a large, sharp-pointed stick right where his brother stood, "take that; I don't care if it does hurt you. I hate you, George Campbell!"

The stick was aimed even more surely than Davie in his blind rage imagined. It struck his brother's side face, making an ugly wound, from which the blood flowed freely.

"Ah, ha!" said George, as he turned to the pump and began to bathe the wound, "look what you have done now. What will mother

SHE HELD UP A WARNING HAND.

say to you, young man? And as for me, that will make a scar, and I will wear it all my life to remember you by. You will like that, won't you? You will just enjoy having people ask me where I got that scar, and me having to tell that my beloved brother did it on purpose, because he hated me. Oh, ho! you are a jewel,

you are," and George Campbell laughed, and dodged just in time to escape a stone from his angry brother's hand; then went off down the street, leaving Davie in a perfect rage.

He was three years younger than his brother, and was said by the neighbors to have a great deal worse disposition than George, but I never felt sure of that. However, it is quite true that instead of being master of his temper he let it master him. He had, also, a wretched habit of throwing anything he might happen to have in his hand when the angry fit seized him, letting it strike wherever it might. In this way he had narrowly escaped doing serious mischief, and he had promised himself hundreds of times that he would never, never throw things again, and yet, as soon as he grew angry, so settled was that habit upon him, that the stick or stone was apt to fly through the air. As for George, I think he was quite as easily angered as his brother, but his habit was to laugh, or sneer, or say the most taunting words imaginable, with a sort of superior smile on his face the while. On the whole, I am not sure that George appeared any better in the sight of Him who can read hearts than did his brother Davie.

They were not the worst boys in the world, by any means; they did not quarrel all the time. For days together they would succeed in being very friendly, and in having good times, but it must be confessed that George had discovered certain directions in which his young brother could be easily teased, and that he delighted to tease him.

"Davie is such a little spitfire," he used to say to his Aunt Mary, when she argued with him about the sin of such a habit. "Why does he want to go off like a pop gun the first word that is said to him? I never do."

"No," said Aunt Mary; "you laugh — a laugh which makes him feel more angry than he did before, and you say something to increase his rage. Is that really being any better than he?" But these questions George did not like to answer.

On this particular morning, after having stopped the blood from his wound, he had sauntered away to see two of his friends who worked in the paper factory near at hand. There he mounted their work table and answered the questions which they eagerly put to him as to how he happened to get hurt.

"Oh! it is Davie's work; he's a great boy. If he had had an open jack-knife in his hand it would have been all the same; it would have been flung at me when he got mad. I hope when he grows up he will never take a notion to carry a pistol, for if he does he will shoot the first fellow who laughs at him, or who laughs when he is within hearing."

"Why, George," said one of the boys, "that will make an ugly scar."

"I dare say it will. I will carry it all my life to remember him by."

"It is a pity that he is such a little tiger; I wouldn't stand it if I were you," said the other boy. "You are a good deal older than he; why don't you make him behave himself?"

In this way poor Davie was discussed by the three, George telling story after story about his brother, led on by the sympathy which the two professed, into making Davie the one always to blame, and himself the injured, long-suffering elder brother. The boys did not know Davie very well, and George had always been good-natured with them, so of course they were on his side, and ready to sympathize with him for having such a wicked little brother. The longer George talked the more of a martyr he grew to considering himself; he racked his brain for illustrations of Davie's ill temper, and was in the midst of a very harrowing story when Joe Winters appeared, breathless with running, and panted out: "Is George Campbell here? I say, George Campbell, your folks want you to come home just as fast as you can. Davie has tumbled from the scaffolding of the big barn and killed himself! or—well, he ain't dead; but he lies there still; can't stir nor speak, and they have sent for two doctors, and everybody thinks he is going to die."

Poor George Campbell! To have seen the look on his face when he heard this dreadful piece of news you would not have imagined that he could have had so hard an opinion of his little brother as he had been trying to show for the last hour. He jumped from the table, and made a dash for the door before Joe had finished his panting sentences, but paused with the door in his hand to say: "O, boys! it isn't half of it true—what I have been telling you; I have been worse than Davie every time. If I hadn't laughed at him, and teased him, and made fun of him, he never would have got angry at me. O, boys! if he dies it will kill me." Then he ran.

What hours those were which followed, while the little brother lay on his bed, moaning steadily, but unconscious, so the doctors declared, and they shook their heads gravely in answer to questions, and would not give one ray of hope that he might by and by open his eyes and know them. Truth to tell, they thought he was going to die, and that very soon. But doctors are sometimes mistaken, and these were. Davie did not die; he lay day after day moaning with pain, not knowing any of the dear friends who bent over him; staring at George with wild, unnatural eyes, as if he were some comical object, instead of the brother who hovered about him, longing, oh! so eagerly for just one glance of recognition.

There came a day when the doctors said it was possible—just barely possible—that Davie might awaken from the long sleep into which he had fallen, and know his friends. How still they kept the house, and how silently the mother sat hour after hour by his bedside, relieved only by the little sister, who came on tiptoe to take her place, that she might go out and drink a cup of tea to help her bear the nervous strain. Even then she only went into the next room, separated from Davie's by a curtain, and came back when she had got half-way across the room because she thought she heard a sound behind those curtains. There was no sound; Jennie was sitting quietly at her post, a wise little nurse; she held up a warning hand, ready to motion anybody back into silence who might be tiptoeing toward them. She had imagined it was George, for he, poor fellow, hovered near, looking almost as pale and worn as the boy with his head on the pillow.

Terrible days these had been to George. He was not sure that he ever prayed in his life before, but during those days he prayed with terrible earnestness, that Davie might not go away with those last words of his ringing in his ears. "If he could only know me long enough for me to ask him to forgive me!" said poor George to himself, while the tears rolled down his cheeks. "Then I think I would be almost willing to have him die. O, God! let me just tell him that I am sorry, and that I will not remember him in any such way, but I will think

were quite as full of anxiety and care as those in which he had been unconscious.

But Davie steadily gained, and there came a bright morning in midsummer when George was permitted to take care of him alone, while his mother attended to some household duties, and Jennie swept the dining-room and set the table. It was George's opportunity. He had longed for it, but he did not know how to use it. How should he begin? While he considered, Davie began for him.

"It did leave a scar, didn't it?" he said

AT PONT NEUF.

of the thousands of good and loving things he has done for me."

I am sure you will be glad to know that his prayer was answered. Davie awoke from his long sleep with a look of quiet astonishment in his eyes, to think that he was lying in bed, and mother and Jennie were sitting beside him, and that George was standing over by the window. He did not remember any of the days that had passed between. He did not remember at first the fall from the scaffolding. He was by no means out of danger, the doctor said, yet there was a thread, just a thread of hope that he might rally. And so the days which followed

mournfully. "O, George! I remember all about it; it came to me just a few days ago. Wasn't it awful? George, the hardest part has been to think that maybe I should die and leave that scar for you to remember me by."

"Don't," said George, who had not the least idea that he should cry any more about this thing, yet who felt the tears starting in his eyes. "O, don't, Davie! forget those horrid hateful things I said to you. You can't think how many nice things I had to remember of you — hundreds and hundreds of them."

"No," said Davie mournfully; "I have always been throwing sticks and stones and hurting things. Don't you remember how I lamed the cat, and killed a bird once, and then made that scar on your face? That is the worst of all. O, George! if I had died what a way to be remembered. Think of the lots of things that people could have told of me like that."

George winced visibly, for these were some of the things he had told the boys in the paper factory that day.

"I tell you what it is," he said, swallowing hard to try and speak without a tremble in his voice, "you and I have both had a lesson, Davie. If you had died I could never have forgiven myself for having teased you for getting angry, and then having said that I would remember you by this little scar, which doesn't amount to anything, anyhow. It wasn't true, Davie; I wouldn't have remembered you that way."

"I don't see how you could have helped it," said Davie mournfully; "but I am truly and surely going to be different after this. If you see me getting angry and acting as if I was going to throw things, I wish you would tie up my hands, or hold them, or something."

"We will both be different," said George. "It won't do to plan such things as we had to remember. We will begin now and plan to have nice pleasant things, so that when — that when" — But his voice trembled and broke; he had been too near parting with Davie forever to put in words the thought that some time the parting would surely come.

But I fancy that they must have kept their words and begun over again, for this happened several years ago. George and Davie are young men now, and yesterday I heard them called "model brothers." They really seem to be planning to have only pleasant things to remember of each other when the time comes for one of them to go away.

PANSY.

MUSIC AND WAR.

GEORGE NOYES — that is not his real name — is now in Europe sightseeing. He spends one week in beautiful Paris, where the people talk French, and do not do everything quite as do Americans or Englishmen.

George is learning to speak French. He has got on so far that he can tell in French to the waiters just what he will have of the bill of fare.

Yesterday he and his Uncle Fred went to Pont Neuf, a bridge more than a thousand feet long, and three hundred years old. King Henry the Fourth had it built. Visitors of Paris must needs see this wonderful bridge, or

ON DRILL.

they have not seen Paris. That's what they say.

While George was looking this way and that from the bridge, and thinking of the war times of kings and princes, he heard sweet music, and turning to see whence it came, he saw a company of boys playing on drums and bugles, under the leadership of a soldier and one of their own companions.

There they drill every pleasant afternoon, and delight the multitudes who gather on Pont Neuf.

However, it is not all for fun they are playing charming French music, and among the rest the Marseillaise Hymn. They are getting ready for war times, for fierce battles and blood and death.

Most nations have had many wars, and millions of their people have been slain, and no words can tell the suffering. Some day I fear those nice French boys, grown to be men, will be playing the Marseillaise Hymn on some awful battle field, while thousands of French and Germans, or some other people, will be falling and dying!

All this because one nation wants some of the other nation's land, or for some other wicked cause.

"Blessed are the peace makers, for " —

L.

JEAN.

OME now, the good ship *City of Paris* sails in a few days, so let us away over the ocean to France.

Here we are in Paris, the most beautiful, though not the best city in the world, they say.

But after six days sightseeing we'll hurry to another place, and here we are in Domremy. Here we'll roam over the hills and think. See that cluster of trees? We must sit under them and upon that very stone. There on that grassy bank where the flowers are blooming, and at whose foot runs a gentle brook, we must spend an hour and think, think who sat upon that very spot nearly five hundred years ago and watched her father's flock of sheep or listened to the singing birds or talked with God through the sweet roses she holds. Now she looks up at the great sun, now at a passing cloud; now a soft wind fans her face; a shepherd dog lies at her feet; just yonder some lambs are nestled together.

She is but thirteen years old, but she loves to speak to God as though he were by her side — and is he not?

Late one evening she comes leading the sheep home. Sitting alone looking out into the moonlight, Jeanne's mother inquires: "My child, what keeps you so long in the field? You must

come home earlier, my darling, or something will happen to you."

"But, mamma, I've heard voices in the fields, and they seem to come from the roses and the rocks and the robins and in every wind, and they tell me of my native land and my home and God, that I must love *ma belle France*, and save it out of the hands of all its enemies, and this is what keeps me so late, my sweet, dear mamma."

"Voices, child?"

"Aye, mamma, voices from Heaven speaking in my heart. Your Jeanne hears them loud, in my heart, at least, and they say I must save my poor sad country."

Jeanne's mother could say nothing, but wonder if the child was out of her mind, or if she had really had a vision of angels, as in olden times they came to the shepherds while they watched their flocks.

So the years went by, Jeanne always saying that these heavenly voices were calling her to save her unhappy country, her friends and neighbors sometimes calling her crazy.

She was now seventeen, a lovely pure girl, sorrowing much over the wars and troubles of her own beloved France. Ah! they were dark days indeed; this one wanted to be king, and that one said he must rule; armies met and fought, and some of the young men who went from Domremy, and with whom Jeanne had played, were brought back from the battle fields wounded and dying.

Then came a great army over from England, and city after city of France fell before its awful march. The frightened King Charles the Seventh feared all was lost. He knew not whither to fly with his sad little army. But just when he was going to give up word came to him about the girl of Domremy, our sweet Jeanne. Quickly a messenger was dispatched to her plain little home, and out into the fields he hastened to find her feeding her flock. He urged her to come to her king with all speed. She knew what it meant; she knew her hour was now come to save her "*la belle France*."

Bidding her mother to pray for her, and covering her neck with kisses, she was soon galloping off with the messenger to the camp of the king. A smile of hope lit up his anxious face as she came into his presence. She told him about the "voices," and said she was sure she could lead his army to victory if he would give her soldiers.

So then and there he put upon her the strong armor of commander, and giving her a sword and a war horse she led her little band against the English. They had heard of her, and thought she was sent of God, and fear fell upon them, and they threw down their arms and fled away in dismay.

Meanwhile, though Jeanne waved her flashing sword she never struck a blow with it, but she was again and again wounded.

At last came complete victory, and Jeanne saw the enemies of her beloved France fleeing from Orleans before her rejoicing army. For this she was called "_La Pucelle d'Orleans_," or the Maid of Orleans. But she is usually called Joan of Arc.

After so much triumph she pleaded with her king to let her return to her dear Domremy home, but he would not consent. Meanwhile some of the great captains envied her all her victories, and managed to let her be taken prisoner. Now comes the sad, sad thing to tell. After this noble girl had saved her country, her king and the others let her be put into prison, tried, condemned, and burned to death as a witch! This is not the only case in which the best friend a country ever had was cruelly treated by that country. Jesus was crucified, crucified by his own people, whom he came to save. But scarcely had twenty years gone by before all the bitter persecutors of this dear brave Jeanne came to violent deaths, and the people, instead of calling her a witch, proclaimed her innocent, and a statue was erected to her memory on the very spot where she was burned, and her family was promoted by the king.   L.

HEATHEN WOMEN.

ONE of the two is smoking. She likes it, too. Men say it is nice to smoke and chew tobacco; why should not the women have as good a time as the men? Or why is it any worse for a woman than a man? And yet

TYPES OF HEATHEN WOMEN.

if the girls and women of America should begin to smoke and race horses, and do similar things they would be called heathenish.

So it is, women in heathen lands all have bad times and fall into bad ways. If they ever dress themselves, and behave themselves as they ought, and have good, lovely homes, and care tenderly for their children, it will be when they learn about Jesus, who came and died to save a lost world. How can they learn without a preacher?   L.

STATUE AT COPAN, GUATEMALA.

TYPES OF UNCIVILIZED CHINESE WOMEN.

"FAX AND FIGGERS."

WE clip from the Union Signal a remarkable "queer story," joined to an arithmetical problem. The story has a moral well worth considering, and a " sum " worth doing.

" I hav of lait got at sum stubbun fax and figgers. 2 siggars a day, costing oanly a nikkle eech, for 20 yeers at 1st Site appeers to Bee a smol matter. Let us figger the cost. 10 sents daly for 365 daze reeches the sum ov $36.50. We will not rekkon interrist the first yeer, but the interrist on $36.50 for 19 yeers at 6 purr sent is $73.92, and the Totle ov prinsipple and interrist at 6 Purr sent, kompoundid yeerly, at the end ov 20 yeers maiks the neet little Sum ov $1,338.54. That izzn't a grate eel, but it wood Bi 200 barrils ov good flower, and in Sum sekshuns ov the kuntry wood maik wun the oaner ov a good farm, with houce, barn, wel, sisstern, froot treeze and wood-lot on it, possibly a jurzy cow and sum Uther niknax throne into the bargin. But my expeeryunce has tot me that fax and figgers prodoose but a Slite impresshun on wun who has fully dessidid to maik bacon ov his Branes bi turning his mouth into a smoakhouce. He communly prefurs the hi and eggzaltid privvylige ov bloin smoak thru hiz noze to having enny uther erthly pozeshun."

A PUZZLE.

IF an S and an I and an O and a U,
　With an X at the end spell Su;
And an E and a Y and an E spell I,
　Pray what is a speller to do?

Then, if also an S and an I and a G
　And an H, E, D spell cide,
There's nothing much left for a speller to do
　But to go and commit siouxeyesighed.
　　　　　　　　　　— Selected.

CELIA'S share of the flowers was lovely. She buried her face in the blooms again and again, and seemed unable to get enough of their sweetness.

They had spent the entire morning in the woods hunting for treasures, she and her particular friend, Helen Beardsley. Helen attended another Sunday-school, so they had carefully divided the flowers, for they were to be used in decorating the church for the Easter service.

" You will smell all the sweetness out of those things, child," said Miss Agatha Foster, look-

HESTER THOUGHT ABOUT IT.

ing up from the bit of satin she was carefully embroidering. Miss Agatha was Celia's oldest sister.

"O, no, I won't!" said Celia, laughing;

"they have all the sweetness of the woods in them. You can't think how the woods smelled this morning! It seemed just like heaven."

Agatha and the middle sister, Lorene, looked at each other and laughed.

"What an idea!" said Lorene; "it is the first time I ever heard the woods compared to heaven."

Mrs. Foster came into the room at that moment, and stopped by the table near the door to arrange the books; there was a tired, somewhat troubled look on her face. "Poor Hester has had to be disappointed again about going home," she said.

"Why, mother," said Agatha, "that is really too bad. It is the third Saturday she has missed, and their baby is sick, you know."

"I know it," said Mrs. Foster, looking more troubled still; "but what can I do? There will be company to tea, and cook cannot leave the kitchen to answer the bell; she can not even attend to the downstairs bell; it rings every few minutes on Saturdays; besides, there is extra work for her to do, and somebody must set the table for her. I don't suppose either of you could give her a lift, could you, and let Hester go?"

There was inquiry in the mother's tone, but no expectation. Agatha lifted her eyebrows,

but there was a difficult spot in her embroidery just then, so she made no reply; but Lorene turned quite away from the piano to answer:

"Why, mother, how could we? I have my practicing to do; I have to sing twice to-morrow, you know. Of course that would not take me long, but we couldn't run to the door every time the bell rang, could we, and receive callers at the same time?"

"And as for setting the table," said Agatha, who had righted her embroidery and was taking neat stitches, "I never could get all the things on a table. It wouldn't be possible for me to set it for company."

"I suppose it cannot be arranged," said Mrs. Foster. "I must finish Grandma's cap so she can wear it this evening; her other is really unfit, and I have several stitches to take for Celia, as well. Hester must wait another week. I told her so; but she seemed so disappointed that I wondered if there were not some way to plan it."

"Perhaps she can run down there after tea to see how the baby is," Lorene said, but Mrs. Foster shook her head. "Cook will need her to look after things in the kitchen while she waits on table, and it will be quite dark before we shall be through; she could not go alone after dark."

It was Agatha's turn to sigh. "We need a second girl," she said; "it is ridiculous for a family of our size to try to get along with only cook, and that little bit of a Hester."

"We shall certainly have to get along," was her mother's answer, spoken with quiet positiveness; "you know as well as I that we can not afford more help this season."

Meantime Celia, her fingers still busy with the masses of flowers she was trying to arrange in a basket for carrying, had listened, her face growing more and more gravely thoughtful.

It was Sabbath evening in her thoughts, and she was in the Christian Endeavor meeting, listening to Agatha's voice while she quoted from some grand old writer a thought like this: "We plan our Easter offerings, and beautify His temple for the glad day, and that is well; but we are to remember that as there would have been no Easter had He not given Himself, so the highest and best offering we can bring to Him is our unselfish consecrated selves." Celia remembered the thrill with which she had listened. Agatha's voice was like music, and the thoughts had seemed to fit her voice and make a poem of them, which had thrilled the beauty-loving heart of her young sister.

That was a week ago. Why should the words come back to her this afternoon, and ring in her heart like soft bells, calling her?

What had they to do with Hester, and the door-bells to answer, and the table to set for company, and a sick baby at home? "The highest and best offering we can bring to Him is our unselfish consecrated selves," rang the bells in her heart, and her lips spoke: "Mother, may I take Hester's place this afternoon, and let her go home? I can set the table; cook said I did it beautifully the last time."

"You!" said her mother, in surprise, and both the sisters exclaimed. "Why, I thought, dear, your class was to meet at Marion's to help arrange the flowers for the Easter service?"

"And I thought you were all invited to stay to tea at Marion's?" added Agatha.

"So we are," said Celia, answering them both in one; "but the girls can get along well enough without me. There are eight of them, and Marion's Aunt Laura is going to show them how to arrange everything; and as for staying to tea, why, I can do that another time; and the baby is sick, and Hester is worried about him, I know. I should like to stay, mother, truly, if you will let me."

"Let you, child! I shall be thankful for your help. To tell the truth, it seemed really selfish to keep Hester this afternoon, only I did not know how to plan; I was sure cook could not get along without help, though she was willing to try, because she felt sorry for Hester."

"May I tell Hester about it, mother?" Celia asked, her eyes shining; "and she can carry my flowers and leave them at Marion's."

The flowers and their owner went away together, followed by Mrs. Foster. As for the young ladies, Agatha took pretty pink silk stitches on the lovely white satin and said not a word, while Lorene, turning to the piano, played a few bars, and sang softly:

"Low in the grave he lay,
Jesus my Saviour,"

breaking off to say: "Celia is a strange little girl, isn't she?"

"Very strange," answered Agatha, and she finished a pink bud as she spoke. She was making an Easter offering.

Nobody, it is safe to say, was more surprised at the turn of affairs than was Hester. She thought about it while she hurriedly combed the tangle of hair before her bit of broken glass, and made ready for going home. She was worried about the baby, but she divided her thoughts with this strange offering from Celia. She knew all about the Easter flowers, and the plans for the afternoon, and the high tea together at Marion's lovely home. Celia's talk had been full of it for the past two days. "I'd just like to know what made her do it, anyhow," was Hester's concluding question, offered aloud to the tin basin, in which she energetically washed her hands when the hair was done.

Easter morning was beautiful with sunshine and the song of birds, when Celia, looking from her window, saw Hester tripping around to the back door. She had been allowed to stay at home all night.

"O, Hester!" called Celia. "how is the baby?"

Hester looked up with a glad smile. "He is better," she said, "ever so much better. Mother would have sent me word, only she expected me. He laughed and crowed as soon as he saw me, and you can't think what a lovely time I had with him. Say, Celia, I want to know what made you do it?"

Celia's sensitive face flushed, and she hesitated. How was she to tell Hester why she did it? From the next room came the notes of Lorene's voice, as clear as any bird's, rising high and pure:

"Low in the grave he lay,
Jesus my Saviour."

"It was that," she said simply.

"What?" asked Hester; "I don't know what you mean."

"That that Lorene is singing. He 'lay in the grave,' you know, for us. That is why it

is Easter. I wanted to do something for somebody, and I hadn't any big thing."

"It was a big thing to me," Hester said, and
went inside the back door. Celia's face was
just a trifle shadowed. Despite every effort to
put it away, the thought would come: "After
all, I needn't have given it up. The baby is
better, and her mother would have sent her
word, and another Saturday would have done
just as well; and I missed all the beauty and
the fun. I know how to arrange flowers."

The shadow staid just a little during the
Sunday-school hour. The girls were eager
over the delights of the day before — eager to
know how she could possibly have staid away.
The lovely cross made largely of her own flowers, and bearing on their green background in
pure white blossoms the words, "He is risen,"
was the most beautiful floral decoration in the
church. "Aunt Laura made it," Marion said.
"You did not deserve to have it arranged so
beautifully; we thought you ought to have had
interest enough to have come and seen it, anyhow. Why didn't you?"

"Never mind now," said Celia; "I cannot

explain, only I thought I could not go." Her
offering seemed to her small and uncalled-for;
she could not talk about it. Yet, before the
morning prayer in church was over, the shadow
had lifted. "I did it truly for Him," said
Celia softly, to herself; "He knows I did, and
whether it was of use or not, it is all right."
And when Lorene sang, in a voice like an
angel's:

"Low in the grave he lay,
Jesus my Saviour,"

she could not help being glad that she did it.

That evening, when they were coming out of
the Christian Endeavor meeting, the minister,
who was shaking hands with the young people
on every side, held in his left hand a single calla
lily of rare beauty. As he held out his hand
to Celia he laid the lily against her cheek and
said: "That is for you, little girl. A token
from the Master, I think, since he made it.
Let me tell you something which will make it
bloom for you forever. Hester came to me
this evening to say that she wanted to belong
to Jesus, and learn how to grow like him, just
as you had."   PANSY.

BURSTING INTO LIFE.

A STORMY MORNING.

CROSSING THE ATLANTIC. (See "The Old World Too.")

WHITE AS WOOL.

WOOL is not always white. Its owner sometimes is black — was born black. It can't help it, you see. Sometimes, however, it gets into the dirt, and the snowy wool becomes dirty.

Sometimes it creeps among the burned stumps and logs, and soon looks as black as the stump itself.

Now what happens? The shearer does not want to clip off such stuff, and the merchant can't sell dirty wool, nor can the weaver weave a nice shawl from it; and, if he did, no clean Pansy would want to put it on week days or Sundays.

What then? It must be washed. The dirty black sheep must be put into the water, and washed and washed and washed.

Then let him go up from the water and give himself a good shaking and stand in the green grass and let the warm, shining sun dry its hair — I mean wool.

Now it is white and soft and beautiful, and if Mr. Sheep could see himself in the looking-glass he might be proud of his beauty.

The blood of Jesus Christ cleanses from all sin. Sin is a dirty thing — worse than mud. Heathenism is a dreadfully dirty, filthy thing. The Gospel we send them is like water for the dirty wool.

The Bible says to the worst sinner there is in the world:

"Though your sins be as scarlet, they shall be as white as snow; though they be red like crimson they shall be as wool." (Is. i. 18.)

L.

EASTER GREETING.

BE thy risen Lord, to-day,
All thy help and all thy stay;
All thy comfort in the night;
All thy gladness in the light;
Filling, with his love divine,
Every hungering of thine !

ALICE F. DUNLAP.

MISS LOUISE JOHNSON'S LETTER.

SHE wrote it from Lien Chow, China. It was published in "Woman's Work for Woman." Here it is:

"We expect to be packed into smaller boats this P. M. to go the last ten miles up the Sam Kong River. People are looking at the windows. Women are expressing astonishment that I can write. . . .

"We have had a charming trip. The beauty of the country grows upon me. Many of the clear crystal waterfalls were several hundred feet in descent. The river winds around the bases of mountains, and so seems to be a suc-

"WE TRAVELED IN THE DAYTIME."

cession of beautiful lakes. It reminds one of Delaware Water Gap.

"We traveled in the daytime, stopping an hour or two. Then came the sick to our Dr. Machle. We gave tracts to the people. At one place the women came in little boats. I stood at the window and read to them. They listened, and thanked me for 'teaching' them.

"I want to write more letters, though I now write many. It takes three months for a letter and its reply from New York to Canton; four months to Sam Kong. I like to write, and am delighted to get letters. Some of the best have been from strangers. So all my dear young friends may continue to write me; I will answer as soon as I can get time."

BABY'S CORNER.

A MAY MORNING.

IN a green yard stands a gray old house. In the house live six happy children. They have many things to make them glad and happy.

All around are green fields and hills and tall trees. Every day they see the pretty pictures which the sun makes in the sky when he gets up and goes to bed. There are no big houses in the way to hide the red and pink clouds.

A little brook goes dancing by at the foot of the hill. You can see the little white stones through the water.

They have a great many pets — colts and calves and chickens and rabbits and cats.

And there are ever so many nice things for them to do. They fish in the brook or take off their shoes and stockings and wade in the water. They hunt in the grass for red berries. They swing in the big swing under the maple-tree. They go after the cows and hunt butter-flies, and tumble on the hay in the barn.

Such good times!

This bright May morning mamma and all six of them are out in the orchard. The apple-trees are full of pink and white flowers, and the cherry-trees are all white, like pop corn.

What a pretty sight!

The air is sweet with the breath of the blos-soms. Everything is gay and happy. The brook is tinkling, the bees are humming, the birds are singing.

Little children must sing, too. Hark! hear them.

It is a little song which begins:

"Blooming May
Makes all gay."

And this little song ends like this — the children all like to sing it:

"Tra la la la la la la. Tra la la la la."
MRS. C. M. LIVINGSTON.

KITTY KNEW ABOUT SHEEP.

"SEVEN sheep were standing
By the pasture wall.
Tell me," said the teacher,
To her scholars small.
"One poor sheep was frightened,
Jumped and ran away.
One from seven — how many
Woolly sheep would stay?"

Up went Kitty's fingers —
A farmer's daughter she,
Not so bright at figures
As she ought to be.
"Please, ma'am" — "Well, then, Kitty.
Tell us, if you know."
"Please, if one jumped over
All the rest would go."

SAID Willie: "The Man in the Moon
In Mother Goose came down too soon,
For I've read it over and over;
But he'd done a sillier thing to-day,
When Flossie and I went out to play
And roll in the field of clover.
For up in the sky, right overhead,
When every star had gone to bed,
And the sun was shining bright,
We saw his moon, looking pale and thin,
Because he'd forgotten to take it in,
After hanging there all night!"
— *Selected.*

BURNS's HIGHLAND MARY.

THE HARD TEXT.

(Matt. xii. 34.)

"O GENERATION of vipers."

Thus Jesus called the Jews or their leaders. Put this with other names he gave them—"hypocrites," "fools and blind," "serpents" (read the twenty-third chapter of Matthew)—and maybe you will wonder how he, so gentle and forgiving, could do it.

"Yes," you say, "they did provoke Him; they treated Him most outrageously, calling Him all sorts of bad names, and finally putting Him to death in the most cruel manner. But it does not seem quite right for Him to call them vile names back again. It looks as though He lost his temper and became awfully angry with his enemies."

Indeed it does say He once looked around upon them with anger. So you are right with that word, but its real meaning is indignation, the righteous feeling every one should have against wrong. Thus you ought to feel against swearing, stealing, the liquor business and all such things. It would be wicked for you to smile at such things. So much for anger—the anger of Jesus. Now about "calling names."

You must remember Jesus knew the hearts of these Pharisee Jews—how black, how vile they were, while they thought themselves quite good and beautiful. Gentle talk to them did no good. To have them see themselves as they really were, he must be plain; he must speak out. What he did was not "calling names" as one boy does to another, when he is "mad" with him and hates him. Jesus did not hate them, bad as they were. He would save them if they would repent and come to him. So he must warn them by telling them the awful truth.

So it was; Jesus could draw some by gentle, loving words and ways; others, if saved at all, must be driven. Jesus acted according to the kind of people he was speaking to.

May we sometimes deal this terrible way with sinners? May ministers do it? Some years ago Rev. C. G. Finney did often speak to many who came out to oppose him and make fun of religion—he did speak very plainly and severely. It is said Mr. Moody once rebuked a wicked

THE BEE'S WISDOM.

SAID a wandering little maiden
　To a bee with honey laden,
"Bee, at all the flowers you work,
Yet in some does poison lurk."

"That I know, my pretty maiden,"
Said the bee with honey laden,
"But the poison I forsake,
And the honey only take."

"Cunning bee, with honey laden,
That is right," replied the maiden;
"So will I, from all I meet,
Only draw the good and sweet."

—Selected.

man this very way. But not every one can wisely do it. It must be done with great sorrow. No doubt it almost broke Jesus' heart to say such plain things. A parent sometimes must punish a naughty child; it hurts him to do it, however. He often weeps more than the punished child. L.

SOMETHING FOR PAPA.

BY this time you are feeling that papa is being neglected, and that mamma and sister are having all the gifts; though I believe papa would like the nice writing-case with pockets which we planned in November quite as well, perhaps, as any member of the family. However, I am sure of one thing he will like, and it is something which you, my girl, can make, with some industry and very little expense.

I do hope you know how to knit, the nice old-fashioned knitting which our dear grandmothers understood so well? If you do not, my first advice to you is to master that fine art which has of late years gone so nearly out of fashion; it is coming to the front again, and there is no end to the neat little comforts which you can make with the aid of a ball of tidy cotton and two large knitting needles. I will not attempt to teach you the stitch on paper, though if you sat by my side I could show it to you with very little trouble. If there is not a dear white-haired grandmother in your home, as I hope there is, borrow one of some friend, and beg her to teach you how to knit. Of course it is just possible that mamma herself understands the stitch; you might try her.

Having learned it — which I am sure you can do in an hour — get two large-size needles of steel, or ivory, or wood — I like to use wood — and a ball of the very coarsest tidy cotton you can find, and set to work. Cast on as many stitches as the needle will conveniently carry, and knit back and forth, back and forth industriously, until you have a strip a yard long. Oh! it will require patience and industry; I told you that in the beginning, you know.

Having finished the strip begin again, and make another precisely like it; then a third, and perhaps, if your needles are not very long, a fourth — you might consult with mamma or Auntie as to that. When the four are finished — in order to be sure to have the article large enough we will say four — fold the side edges of two neatly together, and knit them together with a crochet hook, or sew them with a needle and some of the tidy cotton, as you will; add the third and fourth in the same manner, and when all is complete if you do not have a bath towel which will please papa better than any Turkish towel he ever bought, I shall be astonished and disappointed. For fear of discouraging you at the outset, I mentioned a yard as the length, but let me whisper to you, entirely in confidence, that if you should make it a yard and a half long, or even a trifle longer, papa would like it better still. You see I have heard the gentlemen groan over short bathing towels, and I know all about it.

You see with how very little expense such an article could be made, and I really do not know of any one thing which will add more to the comfort of the toilet. Some gentlemen like very coarse and rough bathing towels, in which case macremé cord is sometimes used instead of tidy cotton; probably mamma could advise you wisely in this direction, also.

If you undertake such a gift, I hope you will have the kindness to write and tell me how you succeeded, when and how the gift was presented, what was said, and all about it.

Your friend, PANSY.

If anything unkind you hear
About some one you know, my dear,
Do not, I pray you, it repeat
When you that some one chance to meet;
For such news has a leaden way
Of clouding o'er a sunny day.
But if you something pleasant hear
About some one you know, my dear,
Make haste — to make great haste 'twere well,
To her or him the same to tell;
For such news has a golden way
Of lighting up a cloudy day. — *Selected.*